THE UNEXPECTED INSTINCT

THE UNEXPECTED INSTINCT

JOHN DICKSON CARR

Introduction and Notes
by DAN NAPOLITANO

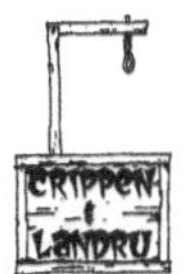

Crippen & Landru Publishers
Cincinnati, Ohio
2026

For information contact:

Crippen & Landru, Publishers
P. O. Box 532057
Cincinnati, OH 45253 USA

Web: www.crippenlandru.com
E-mail: Info@crippenlandru.com

ISBN (softcover): 978-1-971489-02-5
ISBN (clothbound): 978-1-971489-03-2

First Edition: April 2026

10 9 8 7 6 5 4 3 2 1

Table of Contents

Notes on the Text

This collection is a companion volume to 2022's *The Kindling Spark: Early Tales of Mystery, Horror, and Adventure by John Dickson Carr.* Nearly all the selections in this book are likewise from Carr's apprenticeship period, written between the ages of fourteen and twenty-one. The exceptions are "The Other Hangman" (1935), Carr's first short period tale since those appearing in this collection, and *The Adventure of the Last Bustard*, written in 1950.

Carr's school-years fiction had predictable editorial issues, as minor as misspellings and punctuation errors and as significant as layout and continuity issues. In response to these, the present editor has performed minimally necessary line editing, generally correcting the text only in cases of clear errors, and modernizing spelling and punctuation conventions (or not) where appropriate.

Given that even Carr's tales of the "present" take place more than a century ago and those of the past occur during periods ranging between the thirteenth century and the French Revolution, as in *The Kindling Spark*, footnotes appear directly below the text, explaining points of history or obscure references, as well as defining uncommon/antiquated words.

Also as in *The Kindling Spark*, wherever passages and their page numbers are quoted from Carr's novels, these are uniformly drawn from the U.S. first editions, first printings (generally Harper or Morrow). All quotations from Douglas Greene's biography of Carr, *John Dickson Carr: The Man Who Explained Miracles*, are from its first edition, first printing (Otto Penzler Books, 1995). Quotations attributed to Greene, unless otherwise specified, are from the biography. Any excerpts from other sources, including letters written by Carr, cite those sources in context.

Note that the editor, for some of those other sources referenced, has relied upon electronic editions. For these, the number of total pages as well as the specific page numbers are determined by screen and font size. Given this, please note that page numbers may not match for some readers curious enough to follow cited passages to their sources.

While a single story ("The Other Hangman") is reprinted from Carr's professional period, collected more than half a dozen times during his lifetime and at least once posthumously, and while none of the stories composed between 1921–1927 was ever professionally published until now, the provenances of two other stories deserve the reader's special attention.

"Héloïse" is a newly discovered work. The reader will find no prior references to it elsewhere, even in Douglas Greene's esteemed biography. The "Notes for the Curious" commentary accompanying "Héloïse" explains further, but Carr published the historical vignette in 1927 anonymously under another writer's initials (as he often did at Haverford). The present editor, who rediscovered it, and Greene agree that it is clearly Carr's work.

The Adventure of the Last Bustard, a formerly lost Carr manuscript, is a playlet (a very short play), Carr's third and final Sherlock Holmes parody written for performance at the Mystery Writers of America's awards banquet in 1950. Its two predecessors were initially published in *The Unicorn Mystery Book Club News* after being performed at the preceding two years' banquets. Douglas Greene preserved and collected the earlier two in 1980's The *Door to Doom and Other Detections*. Because it was never performed, *The Adventure of the Last Bustard* was not commonly known to exist, let alone ever published. Two editorial hands, Carr's own and a would-be editor's, appear on the original typescript. The present editor, mindful of Carr's admonition (in correspondence with an editor of his) that, "Any copy I write, be its quality good, bad, or indifferent, needs no editing for spelling, punctuation, or any technical cause," has rejected all the prior editor's changes and preserved only Carr's original text and Carr's own handwritten corrections.

As with the introduction and commentaries of *The Kindling Spark,* it is the editor's disposition in this companion volume, even when a given observation occurred independently to him, cautiously to credit others who made similar observations in earlier publications. Whether any given point in discussion is fully the editor's own original insight, coincidentally similar to another writer's, or first encountered in another's work, then properly borrowed and attributed to its originator, each of the points made about Carr here has value, if it does, because it is presented in useful context for the reader as part of the discussion. The editor is gratefully obliged to others who have thoughtfully enriched his reading of Carr and would prefer wherever possible to refer the attention of interested readers to those other worthwhile commentaries. One goal of this book is to foster fresh, twenty-first-century, critically appreciative discussions of Carr. So the editor is glad of other engaged writing about Carr, and glad to point attention to it.

Additionally, the reader of both volumes by this editor will likely note that *The Unexpected Instinct,* in the introduction and the commentaries following the selections, sometimes revisits points the editor raised in the introductory essay to *The Kindling Spark*—even at times citing the same documentary sources or re-presenting a given point in nearly identical language. This is not for lack of any new insights! Rather, the editor wished to apply those arguments proposed in the earlier book to reading the selections in this one—to bring that higher-level discussion down to the specific texts of these stories—and without obliging the reader either to recall or to reread *The Kindling Spark*'s long opening essay to consider the application of some of its contentions.

The introduction to *The Unexpected Instinct* continues the project begun in *The Kindling Spark* by tracing a continuing set of general observations about Carr, his techniques, his literary influences, and concerning the relationships between the selections here—even and especially those very unlike detective fiction—and Carr's other early work, as well as with the classic mystery novels that have attracted readers to Carr for five generations.

Also of note: like its predecessor, the introduction to this book omits any unwelcome revelations...no delicious secrets, no plot twists, let alone identities of murderers from any Carr novel will be spoiled. It is safe to read the introduction first; the editor hopes it will better prepare the reader to enjoy the stories. It is also perfectly reasonable to be impatient with the editor's literary peregrinations, hastening right past them to the good stuff!

As to the post-story commentaries, as in *The Kindling Spark*, each is written with the understanding that the reader has already read the selection(s) preceding it. The commentaries openly discuss plot points and revelations, even in rare cases (where unavoidable) discussing the particulars of some of Carr's novels. In instances where key details of those novels are mentioned, the reader is warned, explicitly, and advised to pass over the commentary until having first enjoyed whatever works of Carr's are in discussion.

What Is the Unexpected Instinct?

Sanders's ideas were in some confusion. A practical instinct said: What the devil am I getting into? A conservative instinct said: I have never done anything like this before. An unexpected instinct said: I want to keep on as long as possible in the company of Marcia Blystone. (*Death in Five Boxes*, 1938, p. 6)

The unexpected instinct is romance. Dr. John Sanders, unmarried, a toxicologist and consultant to the Home Office, who works in his laboratory until one in the morning, is in the moment when he will exchange the staid predictability that has shaped all his life for Adventure in the Grand Manner.[1] Ahead of him are excitement, chaos, terror...love. Dr. Sanders feels the pull of an adventurous life he has never experienced, nor even realized he desired, but with which suddenly, Sanders instinctively yearns to replace his commonplace lot.

John Dickson Carr is a romanticist. He is chiefly remembered as the Head Hoodwinker (an endearment tracing back to at least 1968),[2] and "the supreme conjurer, the King of the Art of Misdirection" (praise from Agatha Christie),[3] in short, the all-time greatest perpetrator of the impossible crime. Carr is these and more: he is a romanticist. For Carr's detective novels, however baffling their plots, are also literary romances.

The genre of literary romance is different and more than a love story, and not mainly sentimental; not every literary romance features a love story, in fact, and certainly not every cloying story of a love affair is a

---

1 A coinage by Carr in *The Red Widow Murders* (1935), used again in "Strictly Diplomatic" (1939) and *The Nine Wrong Answers* (1952), without the capitalization; Douglas Greene added the title case in his biography of Carr, and the phrase has been specially associated with John Dickson Carr ever since.

2 While the editor can uncover no explicit, first publicly published use of this sobriquet and suspects it was in use earlier, Carr's family has generously disclosed a hand-drawn season's greetings poster sent to Carr in 1968. Above a list of his characters, it depicts Carr, Poe, Chesterton, and Conan Doyle and pays tribute to our author by naming him the Head Hoodwinker.

3 In "Detective Writers in England," originally written in 1945, reprinted as the preface to *Ask a Policeman*, Harper Collins (2013), p. xvi.

literary romance. The literary romance is a tradition dating back to the medieval period. It is a tale of adventure, often involving the magical, a tale of chivalry, and usually, including a subplot of love. The literary romance is a descendant of the epic poem, a long narrative celebrating heroic deeds and the most cherished ideals of the epic's culture. Epics' principal subjects are legendary figures, whose adventures reveal the metaphysical order of the universe. Well-known examples include Homer's *Iliad* and *Odyssey*, *Beowulf*, Dante's *Divine Comedy*, and Milton's *Paradise Lost*. The epic provides all the high-level building blocks for the literary romance, which, while it may include some characters of legend, is less sweeping, recounting its events on a mortal scale, and including characters possessed of commonplace qualities. The literary romance is not theodicy; it details not overarching myth, but human experience; it is a quasi-mythical narrative brought down into human terms, and concerning people. Because of this, readers recognize traits, sympathies, and life experiences they share with the romance's characters. Nearly always, a literary romance ends happily—such an ending satisfies readers' anticipations and preferences—but as with all broad categories, there are exceptions. The most famous literary romance in the English-language tradition, and the most enduring, is that of King Arthur, which does not end happily; in the same tradition, the chivalric romance of *Sir Gawain and the Green Knight* ends well, but it includes no love story.[4]

The association of detective fiction with literary romance is not merely some hindsight invention of the editor's, either. No less eminent a critic than G.K. Chesterton, who of course was also the single most significant influence upon Carr, wrote in his essay, "A Defence of Detective Stories":

> There is, however, another good work that is done by detective stories...[D]ealing with the unsleeping sentinels who guard the outposts of society...tends to remind us that we live in an armed camp, making war with a chaotic world...When the detective in a police romance stands alone...it does certainly serve to make us remember that it is the agent of social justice who is the original and poetic figure...The romance

---

4 Readers familiar with the fourteenth-century poem might object, suggesting that Bertilak's wife, the Lady of Castle Hautdesert, is Gawain's love interest. Not so; she is a temptress. There is no love story between her and Gawain, nor could there be one consistent with the chivalric ideals the poem espouses.

> of the police force is thus the whole romance of man. It is
> based on the fact that morality is the most dark and daring
> of conspiracies. It reminds us that the whole noiseless and
> unnoticeable police management by which we are ruled and
> protected is only a successful knight-errantry.[5]

Carr himself was mindful enough of the tradition of literary romance to formulate his own working definition of it in *Deadly Hall* (1971), a lens on the tradition through which his readers can view Carr's modern versions: "Romance, by definition, is a narrative in prose or sometimes verse with scenes, incidents, and love affair remote from everyday life" (p. 192). Earlier in that novel (p. 180), Carr also explains the relationship between his historical romances and his more conventional detective fiction:

> ..."You yourself, Mr. Caldwell, have made some reputation
> as a romancer in the grand tradition. You *are* Mr. Caldwell?"
> "I am."
> "And each of your historical novels contains some small
> element of mystery which is cleared up at the end?"
> "Yes, that's so."

Caldwell is, naturally, the novel's reflection of Carr himself. Carr's readers will recognize all the elements of literary romance in his works, despite his modern narratives being absent the times-gone trappings of castles, jousts, and the like. Literary romance remains to Carr "the grand tradition."

Readers of Crippen & Landru's 2022 collection from Carr's apprenticeship period, *The Kindling Spark*, have already seen that the young Carr delighted enough in the medieval romance to try the form on for size, set in its proper period, as part of the story cycle, "The New Canterbury Tales." They also understand that one of Carr's favorite authors, and one of the few most influential upon him, James Branch Cabell, was likely the last English-language modern practitioner of the medieval romance, at least until the emergence of the genre of modern fantasy, which arose after Carr's formative years.

No matter the era in which a John Dickson Carr narrative is set, it

---

5 In *The Defendant*, R. Brimley Johnson, 1901, pp. 122-123.

participates in the tradition of literary romance with its core components of adventure and gallantry...and frequently, a subplot of romantic love.

How did this tradition descend to Carr? In late eighteenth-century English literature, literary romances transformed into Gothic romances, atmospheric novels rich in suspense, in twilight collisions between the present and the past, frequently between the mundane and the supernatural. These are narratives charged with dark imagination and troubling obstacles to love: anger, jealousy, doubt, deceit. Like medieval romances, Gothic romances are tales of personal adventure, of conflicts between propriety and transgression, but because they are modern, their emphasis is not on courtly traditions, but on the intimately felt struggles of their central characters. They are iteratively more personal versions of medieval romances, substituting as their preternatural element, where it occurs, modern manifestations of the supernatural: instead of medieval magic or (as in epics) the intercession of deities, the Gothic romance conjures witchcraft and demonology, hauntings and correlative haunted lives. The reader will recognize some writers in this tradition who are favorites of and influences upon John Dickson Carr: Horace Walpole, Ann Radcliffe, Matthew "Monk" Lewis, Mary Shelley, Edgar Allan Poe, Charles Reade, Bram Stoker, and Robert Louis Stevenson.

Another descendent of the literary romance, closely related, is the historical adventure novel; the family tree of this popular form also includes well-remembered (and a few less-well-remembered) authors branching directly to Carr: Stevenson here, too, and Sir Walter Scott (indeed, Scott was also an influence upon Stevenson), Conan Doyle, Rudyard Kipling, Alexandre Dumas (*père*), Anthony Hope, George Barr McCutcheon, E. Phillips Oppenheim, John Buchan, Baroness Orczy, and Katherine Cecil Thurston. As with Gothic romances, historical romances are works concerned with personal experience written from a modern perspective. Readers can trace Carr's literary descent beginning at the highest and broadest level with epics, narratives about legendary persons explaining universal myths, then transforming in the fourteenth century into England's first medieval romances (most of these translations of earlier French chivalric romances), tales of human experience often speaking to distinctions in rank or social order, and finally, taking the form of modern incarnations primarily concerned with individual human lives. This is a progression along a spectrum, in which the subject matter, if remaining intriguingly outside everyday experience, is more and more relevant to it. In epics, characters exist to explain why the world is the way it is: miracles are the subject matter. By the time the literary romance assumes its modern forms—Gothic and historical romances, and Carrian detective fiction—miracles are dramatic elements lending interest to tales about characters, their human imperfections, and their struggles.

Both of the modern romance genres and Carr's works descended from them are wrapped in the conventions of Romanticism, the creative movement across artistic media (poetry, fiction, visual arts, music) that depicts the world not as it is, but as it should be, and which Samuel Taylor Coleridge, one of its founders in Anglo-American literature, purported to have "the power of giving the interest of novelty by the modifying colours of imagination" including only "a semblance of truth sufficient to procure for these shadows of imagination that willing suspension of disbelief" in order to "give the charm of novelty to things of every day."[6] Carr knew this tradition well; among early Romantic figures, he appreciated and embraced Coleridge particularly. In *The Mad Hatter Mystery* (1933), Dr. Fell asks whether a stolen manuscript is Coleridge's "Kubla Khan" (it is not, it is a lost Poe story); Carr alludes to Coleridge's "The Rime of the Ancient Mariner" in this collection's "The God of the Gloves," in 1940's *And So to Murder* (p. 254), in 1946's *My Late Wives* (p. 141), and in the 1948 radio drama *The Island of Coffins*, in which Carr serves up, directly and evocatively, a full stanza he loves from the poem:

> Like one that on a lonesome road
> Doth walk in fear and dread;
> And having once turned round walks on,
> And turns no more his head:
> Because he knows, a frightful fiend
> Doth slow behind him tread.[7]

Of note, this may have been a *double* tribute: Carr also enjoyed M.R. James, who in his ghost story, "Casting the Runes" quotes the same stanza as vivid explanation of how one character (quite literally) fears that he is being stalked by a demon. "Casting the Runes" appeared in James's *More Ghost Stories* (1911), a favorite collection of Carr's.

Carr also borrowed from another story in the same collection, "The

---

6 *Biographia Literaria*, Leavitt, Lord & Co., 1834, p. 174. All subsequent excerpts are drawn from the same edition.

7 Carr quotes Part the Sixth, ll. 37–42. The drama appears in Crippen & Landru's *The Island of Coffins and Other Mysteries from the Casebook of Cabin B-13*, editors Tony Medawar and Douglas Greene (2020). All subsequent excerpts are drawn from the same edition.

Rose Garden," the character name George Anstruther, who became a modern baronet in Carr's 1933 novel *The Bowstring Murders*, the author's first appearance in print pseudonymously as Carr (typically Carter) Dickson.[8] Anstruther appears again in *The Red Widow Murders* (1935). For both novels, too, Carr likewise borrows from one of his own early stories (included in the present collection), "The Harp of Tairlaine." He names a second character appearing in both books after that story's protagonist, Michael Tairlaine.

Romanticism is very much about the power and importance of the imagination; Carr recognized imagination as one of his most effective tools, whether his own or the reader's. "Never apologize for imaginative boldness; there is all too little of it in this world" insists Senator Judah Philip Benjamin in 1968's *Papa Là-bas* (p. 117). This may as well be Carr's literary war cry. While he was occasionally explicit, offering descriptions of the grotesque or the horrifying, more often, Carr unloosed each reader's imagination to achieve the strongest effect. A stand-in for Carr, a ghost-story writer named James Colton in the radio drama *The Devil's Manuscript* (1944, an adaptation of the Ambrose Bierce horror story, "The Suitable Surroundings"), explains why he feels he will win his bet with Willard Marsh to write a story so frightening that it will scare Marsh to death:

> I have studied fear for twenty years. I have experimented with
> fear....I have done that, Marsh, for one purpose. To capture
> on paper those subtle forces that mend the soul or destroy it.
> The slow, fine toil of getting the words just right.[9]

In *The Skeleton in the Clock* (1948), Carr alerts the reader to the power of the imagination, exercised upon oneself through Dr. Laurier's observation of the relative vulnerability of Martin Drake, an artist, WWII veteran, and former Captain of the Gloucesters, as compared with John Stannard, a pompous and unimaginative King's Counsel:

> "My friend Drake has a disadvantage that will always beat
> him...Your imagination, my dear fellow. You will see nothing,

---

8 Readers of *The Kindling Spark* will also recall that Carr first borrowed the surname Anstruther from James for his 1926 horror story, "The Devil-Gun."

9 Published in the collection *The Dead Sleep Lightly*, (Doubleday & Company, 1983), p. 140. All subsequent excerpts are drawn from the same edition.

hear nothing; but you will feel. It is only when you *imagine* you see them crawling up from the gallows trap—man-eating tigers like Hessler and Bourke-Smith and pretty Mrs. Langton—that the brain will crack like a china jug." (p. 113)

Beyond Romanticism, the literary romance, and the epic, there is another closely related tradition important to Carr, and which consciously underlies his work: fables and fairy tales, which are in essence literary romances for children. Carr recognizes the form's importance, even equating it with detective fiction. How he positions fairy tales aligns Carr with accordant sentiments of Coleridge (and Stevenson, and Chesterton, and others among Carr's key influences):

> The children know it. The children love ghost stories, and pirate stories, and tales of the goblin who lives under the stairs. And detective stories are only fairy-stories for those who have grown up. There comes a time, in our electric-lit world, when we want to step out of our familiar door—out into a mysterious street, where a mail-box becomes a dragon, and men wear the monstrous shapes of a masquerade. If the mystery story gives us this, it is startling to reflect that the mystery story is not so strange or so incredible as these real streets of our familiar world. In marvelling at fiction, we shall be taught a secret which in this age of sophistication we have nearly forgotten—I mean that we shall be taught the old secret, the great secret: to marvel at the truth.[10]

We see, then, that Carr's oeuvre largely begins with, and is encompassed within, literary romances. Carr admitted that his historical novels, which dominated nearly the last quarter century of his career, were "really detective stories in disguise,"[11] but it is evident that his detective-fiction novels are, in turn, literary romances in disguise. Of course, neither is really disguised; to the degree that Carr's 1950s historical novels seem different than his 1930s Gothic detective fiction, this is merely accord-

---

10 Uniontown *Daily News Standard*, in a guest appearance by Carr in the paper's recurring column "Current Comment", February 24, 1930, p. 4. Eagle-eyed readers will recognize that this essay later appeared in its better-known form as *The Detective in Fiction*. The 1930 column is the true first appearance in print of Carr's seminal essay.

11 Letter to Oscar Baron, April 3, 1972.

ing to the particulars Carr's literary model, G.K. Chesterton, cataloged within...

> ...what may be called the historical detective story. The play of masks and faces in the mysterious heart of man [are] just the same, but...use a hundred variations, and some emancipations, touching the externals of the action...[12]

While Carr disdained the "egghead eyes"[13] of academia, considering popularity, more so than elitist approval, to be one virtue of good fiction, and while this reminds both editor and reader not to retrofit a critical framework too forcibly (or falsely) upon Carr's work, all the same, Carr was quite conscious of his literary influences, their precepts, and his participation in their traditions, particularly Romanticism. This is most evident during Carr's apprenticeship period, before he became, let alone acquired his reputation as, a detective-fiction writer. Carr's December 1926 poem "The Old Romance," written at Haverford, included the refrain:

> "Are you living, are you living?" sang the ages,
> "Is your touch upon our France, ancient France?
> Are you with us in the glory of her legend and her story?"
> "I am here, I am here," said Romance.[14]

It is well to remember, too, that Carr's first attempt at a novel-length work was not detective fiction, it was a historical romance, which had "lots of gadzookses and swordplay,"[15] begun in Paris in 1927 but abandoned. (There is reason to suspect that Carr later revised this project as 1934's *Devil Kinsmere*, so while abandoned, it wasn't actually lost.) In any event, one cannot fully understand even Carr's most characteristic detective fiction without recognizing the contributions by John Dickson Carr the romanticist. When we puzzle over Carr's detective fiction, we wrestle with the genius that sets him apart as a craftsman; but when we read John Dickson Carr the romanticist, we perceive the author's spirit, his heart. We become acquainted with Carr more intimately through

---

12 "The Historical Detective Story," *Strand Magazine*, September 2024, p. 6.

13 Letter to Nelson Bond, March 8, 1967.

14 *The Haverfordian*, Volume XLVI (No. 5), December 1926, p. 106.

15 Quoted by Greene, p. 63.

the revelation of his passions and sympathies. Carr the romanticist, after all, wrote every word of every narrative that Carr the King of the Art of Misdirection did not. Carr's commitment to the tradition of what he termed novels of sensation, descended from the literary romantic tradition, explains why only one of Carr's most important declared literary ancestors—Chesterton—wrote detective fiction, but three of the other five—Cabell, Donn Byrne, and Stevenson—and sometimes, O. Henry, as well, wrote literary romances.

Consider the case of Carr's seventeenth Dr. Fell adventure, *The Sleeping Sphinx* (1949). It has as its central puzzle a seemingly impossible circumstance as enticing as in any of Carr's detective-fiction novels: inside a family vault, coffins weighing hundreds of pounds each have been lifted and flung about, and a bottle of poison that may have killed a woman entombed there has somehow been left inside *after* the crypt was sealed—all without the trace of even a single footprint in the sand that was scattered across the floor at the time the chamber was locked. Simultaneously, the novel exhibits all the traits of its ancestral traditions. Its dramatic premise is one common in romance literature, really; it originated in *The Odyssey*: the return home of a protagonist, presumed dead, after a great war. He contends with circumstances and opponents to reclaim his place, his honor, and his love. Carr also likely had in mind Sir Walter Scott's *Ivanhoe*, which is a variation on this same plot. In *The Sleeping Sphinx*, the returning hero is Don Holden, come back following the Second World War. Holden, by virtue of being a new baronet is even, like Scott's eponymous hero, a knight. Carr explicitly compares Don to Enoch Arden, the titular character in a long narrative poem by Tennyson who is shipwrecked, presumed dead, and whose wife, like Homer's Penelope, is reluctantly courted for a new marriage a decade after her husband's disappearance. Carr also doubtless relished James Branch Cabell's version of this dramatic premise when he read it in "The Story of the Tenson," appearing in *Chivalry*, a favorite book of Carr's since boyhood. In sum, we can explicitly trace the structure and elements of Carr's novel back through fiction we know him to have read and adulated, beginning with one of the earliest recorded epics and down through its successor traditions and specific works reusing the poem's archetypal premise. Nor is this interpretation an imposed reading: in addition to the "Enoch Arden" allusion, Carr teases the reader early in *The Sleeping Sphinx* with his conscious participation in the longer literary-romantic tradition. Holden despairs dismissively that his former love, Celia, will not likely have waited for him after his alleged death:

> But how could she be expected to? Changes, new faces, the passing of years—! This grand passion is a notion out of the *Roman de la Rose*; it died with the Middle Ages, if it ever existed. When one man's gone, a woman eventually finds she can be just as comfortable with another; and that's—well, it's only sensible. (p. 12)

What varies consequentially in Carr's detective fiction from its antecedent traditions is circumstantial explanations, a tension that came to a crux in Gothic fiction of which Carr was not merely aware, but which he exploits in his own eerier works. Muriel Seagrave, a character in Carr's final novel, *The Hungry Goblin* (1972), pithily identifies this divergence in Gothic literature:

> Mrs. Radcliffe let her imagination soar but explained everything on natural grounds. Monk Lewis went one better and introduced the devil himself for a fitting fiery end. (p. 77)

Carr of course preys repeatedly upon the reader's doubt: is the explanation of the seemingly impossible the devil himself, or is it only the devilishly clever acts of persons? Carr always wishes the reader to believe infernal powers *might* be at work, because this is more tantalizing—and even that routine debunker of the supernatural, Dr. Fell, confesses in *He Who Whispers* (1946) that he believes in the otherworldly:

> 'I do not deny,' said Dr. Fell, sweeping out one arm in a gesture which gravely endangered a bronze statuette on the bookshelves, 'I do not deny that supernatural forces may exist in this world. In fact, I firmly believe they do exist.'
>
> 'Vampires!' said Miles Hammond.
>
> 'Yes,' agreed Dr. Fell, with a seriousness which made Miles's heart sink. 'Perhaps even vampires.' (p. 100)

The editor's introduction and commentaries for *The Kindling Spark* dealt with some themes and techniques that emerged during Carr's apprenticeship period and which can be traced into his professional works; in demonstrating these, those essays considered predominantly the novels Carr wrote during the first ten to fifteen years of his career, with some attention to his 1950s historical romances. Similarly, the present volume's discussion, including both its introduction and the commentaries following each selection, brings the stories it collects into conversation both with those included in *The Kindling Spark* and, likewise, with Carr's professional works, observing affinities in themes, techniques, and literary influences. The conversation in this volume, though, extends to perhaps-unexpected titles, not very many of them discussed in *The Kindling Spark*—not very many of them, in fact, generally points of focus for most discussion of Carr. While the editor has not artificially set boundaries, a notable number of Carr's novels newly under consideration in *The Unexpected Instinct* were published between the late 1940s and 1972.

Why is this? If the mission of *The Kindling Spark* was to remind readers that the author John Dickson Carr with whom they were familiar—an awarded Grand Master of mystery—did not yet exist at the time he wrote his apprenticeship stories, and to prepare readers to understand Carr throughout his career as a romanticist, the mission of this companion volume is to invite readers to consider John Dickson Carr *more wholly as an author*. This is to say, even readers who count Carr among their favorites, as explanation, commonly cite their most-loved titles, e.g., *It Walks By Night* (1930), *The Eight of Swords* (1934), *The Three Coffins* (1935), *The Arabian Nights Murder* (1936), *The Crooked Hinge* (1938), *The Judas Window* (1938), *The Problem of the Green Capsule* (1939), *Till Death Do Us Part* (1944), *He Who Whispers*, etc.

In other words, *to many readers, Carr is less a favorite author than he is a collection of favorite detective-fiction novels*. Readers appreciate Carr's individual works more so than they appreciate Carr as a writer.

Most readers' preferred novels share two traits: first, readers love them because of the brilliance of the novels' seemingly impossible situations and solutions; second, all of them were written before 1950.

In fact, the commonly received wisdom, which the editor disputes, is that Carr's first, highly prolific fifteen years (in which he published an average of three books a year), include not only all his *best* work, but virtually all Carr's *worthwhile* work. The editorial ambition of this book then, beyond delivering readers some highly enjoyable short fiction by Carr, is to offer stylistic and thematic observations about him that apply consistently, beginning with these earliest, short pieces and manifesting themselves all the way through Carr's final novel. The editor hopes that readers, with the advantages of such broad, unifying insights, might venture into some of Carr's less celebrated works, especially those published between 1945 and 1972—the remaining third of Carr's output—and perhaps find heretofore unexpected enjoyment in them, given the gratifications of style, language, of their vivid recreation of historical periods, of his humor, and of all the other graces one discovers in Carr. Perhaps readers will even find a new favorite title or two.

That Carr is more celebrated for his earlier works is true for reasons beyond the skillfulness of their execution. Consider that when he first began publishing detective fiction, detective fiction itself was a relatively new subgenre of crime fiction. This made detective-fiction novels themselves, given their novelty, implicitly more exciting to readers. So there was more cultural excitement around a new Carr novel, and more receptivity to it, during the first decade and a half of his career. Add to this that Carr was an experimentalist within the detective-fiction genre, beginning with his fusion of detective fiction with Gothic horror in the Bencolin novels and others; but as well, by his success in improbably pairing detective fiction with humor, sometimes again with horror; because, of course, of his nonpareil mastery of the impossible crime; Carr's creation of the historical mystery novel with *Devil Kinsmere*, followed in later years by another baker's dozen; his shocking subversion of the detective-fiction genre, *The Burning Court*; Carr's inception of the true-crime novel with *The Murder of Sir Edmund Godfrey*; and his experiments in narrative, such as breaking the fourth wall and the use of multiple perspective. All this helped to germinate Carr's well-earned reputation.

In the postwar period, Carr changed less than the world around him did. Crime novels became grittier, with the emergence of hard-boiled and more naturalistic thrillers that explored violent crime in everyday life. Spies stole the glamor role from detectives, their thrillers ascendant on best-seller lists. Carr railed against this, particularly against hardboiled fiction, in a 1950 *New York Times* review, "With Colt and Luger." In it, he focused on Raymond Chandler, characterizing Chandler's views on crime fiction as "naïveté" with taunts such as, "it would brighten my declining years to hear this" were Chandler to debate Dorothy Sayers about the craft of crime fiction.[16] Carr defended "cool-headed constructionists" of detective fiction, whom Chandler claimed lack lively characters, sharp dialog, pace, and well-observed detail, by placing himself and other detective-story constructionists into the company of such writers as:

> Edgar Allan Poe, Nathaniel Hawthorne, Mark Twain, Charles Dickens, Wilkie Collins, Robert Louis Stevenson, Thomas Hardy, Joseph Conrad, John Galsworthy, Hugh Walpole, G.K.

---

16 John Dickson Carr, "With Colt and Luger," *The New York Times*, September 24, 1950, Section BR, p. 19. All subsequent excerpts are drawn from the same article and page.

Chesterton—all of whom joyously wrote bloods as well as detective stories.

In any event, Carr remained the same and watched as his reputation transitioned from "the finest contemporary writer of detective stories"[17] to an "old and professional hand at murder and suspense chillers"[18] to "that respected veteran of the mystery novel,"[19] "an old-fashioned champion of gentility, taste, standards and romance."[20] Carr, as so many before him had in so many contexts, went from being revolutionary to being conventional, even quaint. Carr's novels simply seemed more *expected* at the times of their issue in the 1960s and 1970s than those he wrote in the 1930s and 1940s did when they premiered.

It would be disingenuous to deny that Carr's later works are sometimes a little more bloodless, that some feature less exciting atmospheres and less page-turning suspense than his best work from earlier decades— but it is nonetheless probably true that after two or three decades, no matter how reliably well he wrote them, Carr's mysteries came, somewhat fairly, simply to lack novelty for both critics and longtime readers. By this point in his career, nobody—except perhaps Carr himself—was looking for greatness in his latest efforts. The most difficult thing, ironically, for any great practitioner in any art to have recognized may be late-career greatness. Especially in literature, greatness is usually acknowledged in writing for which the author will be remembered to have taken a place among the best writers, and particularly for work breaking new ground. Readers and critics almost always watch for this in authors' earlier works, perhaps the more so from those so prolific and consistently good as Carr. From 1950 onward, the closest Carr came to innovating was his historical detective fiction, which has since emerged as its own subgenre of crime fiction, but Carr's historical romances were received more as curiosities and throwbacks than innovation. Had Carr written 1951's *The Devil in Velvet* in 1935, its reputation and influence would likely be greater...but nobody was looking past noir, hard-boiled crime fiction, psychological thrillers, or spy thrillers newly to find unexpected

---

17 Anthony Boucher, "Report on Criminals at Large," *The New York Times*, August 14, 1949, Section BR, p. 21.

18 Alden Whitman, "Debonair Destroyer; CAPTAIN CUT-THROAT," *The New York Times*, April 3, 1955 Section BR, p. 28.

19 Newgate Callendar, "Criminals at Large," *The New York Times*, March 14, 1971 Section BR, p. 22.

20 W. Murchison Jr., "Books in Brief," *National Review*, October 8, 1971, p. 1127.

greatness in the latest book by John Dickson Carr. If warmly, he was long since taken for granted. This is generally the expected career course for successful artists, but that Carr was so productive at such a high level of quality, and for so long, is also part of his greatness.

This recognition offers the consolatory possibility that a modern reader whose early exposure to Carr includes some of the better novels from the last third of his output, such as *The Devil in Velvet*, *The Nine Wrong Answers* (1952), *The Witch of the Low-Tide* (1961), and *The Ghost's High Noon* (1969) might well enjoy them, finding as much spice and thrill in them as Carr's contemporary readers did in his novels of the 1930s and 1940s.

The editor hopes that, with this understanding and prompted by this book's discussion of Carr, readers will more roundly perceive the characteristics and consistencies in his fiction and style, those beyond Carr's already well-known, appropriately appreciated genius for creating impossible crimes, perturbing atmospheres, and dramatic suspense. Ideally, readers will come to enjoy Carr's works during any period of his career, not merely because they are good mysteries—most, nearly all, are—but because readers recognize and appreciate that Carr is a very good writer, that his skills bring pleasures and rewards whether newly reading or rereading nearly any of the seventy-nine titles Carr published during his lifetime.

After all, if all the satisfaction of a detective novel is in its surprising conclusion, why reread it? Hasn't its pleasure been spoiled? Tony Medawar, in his excellent introduction to *Speak of the Devil* (1994), makes an adroit observation concerning Carr's late work: "only one of his contemporary detective stories written after 1953—*Dark of the Moon* (1967)—featured a solution that he had not already used in a radio play or a short story."[21] While Carr was so expert at disguising a reused solution such that even his experienced readers were unlikely to discover the ploy before he revealed it, is the surprise all there is to a John Dickson Carr work?

The admired critic Torquemada (a pseudonym of E. Powys Mathers) answered no. In his review of *The Arabian Nights Murder*, he summarized his endorsement of Carr by proclaiming, "You borrow detective stories; you invest in a Carr."[22] Why *do* readers of mystery continually reinvest their attention (and their shelf space) in Carr, for five genera-

---

21 *Speak of the Devil*, Crippen & Landru (1994), p. 21. All subsequent excerpts are drawn from the same edition.

22 *The Observer*, February 23, 1936, p. 7.

tions now? For the surprise? Certainly, but not solely. The remainder of the answer lies in Carr's writing. It is not only that, as Dorothy L. Sayers famously complimented him, "he can write—not merely in the negative sense of observing the rules of syntax, but in the sense that every sentence gives a thrill of positive pleasure,"[23] but that the techniques and elements of Carr's writing—which form in his earliest efforts, most of which are *not* mysteries, and which readers have the opportunity to see in illuminating and unexpected ways in these early stories—draw in readers with an allure that well complements Carr's gratifying capacity for misdirection. Compositionally, Carr's fiction in all genres, mystery or otherwise, is built upon those reliable, timeless elements of the literary romance—and very well executed.

Readers will discover in this collection that Carr's tales of the past and Carr's contemporary ("literary") stories feel like genuine siblings to his detective tales—not because they are detective stories in disguise, they are not—but because Carr delivers them with the same well-crafted language; the same engaging detail, effortlessly presented; the same evocation of mood and atmosphere; the same capacity to generate suspense; and in the end, with the same ability to surprise pleasingly.

Beyond writing technique, if there are thematic affinities between Carr's detective and non-detective fiction, they are: first, as Greene explained, all are "stories emphasizing the continuing values of the past—romance, fair play, and honor";[24] second, all Carr's fiction shares a common view concerning human experience, which it reveals to readers. Dorothy L. Sayers shivered at Carr's ability to "lead us away...into the menace of outer darkness,"[25] and Greene agrees, pointing to Carr's use in his detective fiction of "setting and mood to make the reader expect the supernatural and thus misdirect him from the clues that eventually lead to a rational solution."[26] While not always *outer* darkness—and the shivers these two identify are only boundaries along Carr's true destination—his narratives lead us consistently away into *human* darkness. This is the true cause of evil, and it is the subject of both Carr's detective fiction and the stories collected in this volume. In Carr's world, evil usually comes from unexpected directions—including, sometimes, well-intentioned characters, who do not understand their precipitant roles

---

23 "Mystery Out of the Ordinary," *Sunday Times*, Sep 24, 1933, p. 7.

24 Introduction to *The Dead Sleep Lightly*, p. 2.

25 "Mystery Out of the Ordinary," *Sunday Times*, Sep 24, 1933, p. 7.

26 Introduction to *The Dead Sleep Lightly*, p. 3.

in disaster until it has overtaken them. As Carr commented regarding his radio dramas, not all of which, either, concerned the supernatural, "all deal in *diablerie* in one form or another."[27]

Because in most of the stories collected here there is no murder to solve, no fair-play competition of wits between author and reader, readers can more easily recognize how seductive Carr's writing technique is, what a good storyteller he is. Then, once we have recognized why, even in his juvenilia, Carr can draw us in through humor, through compelling contrasts and tensions, we rediscover these same strengths in his detective-fiction novels when we reread them.

Upon the first reading of a Carr detective novel, the mystery is everything, and the surprise, as Chesterton would say, "in the form of lightning,"[28] often blinds readers to the narrative's other strengths. In the same manner that, sometimes, a second reading affords us the pleasure of understanding Carr's concinnity—how he fools us, appreciating how deftly and smoothly he delivers each clue in plain sight and reassembles them all in the explanatory denouement—repeat readings also allow us to recognize how Carr, as a writer of characters, situation, and dialog makes us despise one character, love another, suspect them both, and keep turning the pages to discover how his storylines converge with a satisfaction that, at its best, rivals even Dickens.

The reader may perhaps, upon reflection, agree with the editor to excuse Carr, upon justification by the literary-romantic tradition, in matters concerning which reviewers occasionally have not. One repeatedly unforgiving—not unfriendly, but nonetheless unforgiving—critic of Carr's was Harold Schonberg, writing as Newgate Callendar for *The New York Times*. He more than once alleged that Carr's characters do not speak as ordinary people do: in his review of *Deadly Hall*, Schonberg asserted, "Dialog is not as people speak in real life";[29] against *The Hungry Goblin*, he complained, "as a writer he is one of the clumsiest ever to try a parsed sentence or a bit of dialogue."[30]

Schonberg missed the point. Carr is of course a capable and effective writer. Sayers, Powys Mathers, Anthony Boucher, Ellery Queen, Agatha Christie, Greene, and others all recognize this—as do we. Our own reading experience attests to Carr's skill. It is simply that Carr does

---

27 "It's a Dare!" *Radio Times*, September 3, 1943, p. 4.

28 "Errors about Detective Stories," *Illustrated London News,* August 28, 1920.

29 "Criminals at Large," March 14, 1971, Section BR, p. 22.

30 "Criminals at Large," July 16, 1972, Section BR, p. 32.

not aspire to *realism*—if anything, he shuns it. Carr's dialog has the same deliberate theatricality about it as his novels' tenebrous settings do. Schonberg, who also commented on the unreality of *The Hungry Goblin*'s plot, may as well complain that the New York City in Carr's novels seems nothing like the odiferous, trash-strewn metropolis Schonberg perambulated on his way through Times Square. Carr's New York is not Schonberg's; it is, rather, Baghdad-on-the-Hudson, an evocation of Arabian Nights-style romance and mystery. *The Hungry Goblin* is not realism, it is a celebration of some of the novels and authors, Gothic "novels of sensation," which inspired Carr as a young reader and, later, as a writer.

In it, in fact, the novel's characters discuss some of their favorite Gothic authors and works—Carr's favorites—including *The Mysteries of Udolpho* (Ann Radcliffe), *Ambrosio, or The Monk* (Matthew Lewis), *Bleak House* (Dickens), and *The Woman in White* (Collins). These mentions are not superfluous, either: *The Hungry Goblin* draws important elements from its Gothic romance predecessors. Perhaps most easily overlooked, since the characters do not mention the novel, is that the title of *The Hungry Goblin*'s fourth part, "The Other Dear Charmer," is a direct allusion, to Helen Mathers' 1892 romance *T'Other Dear Charmer*, in which the main character, Hugh Valentine, is conflicted by his attraction to two different women. This plot is not only echoed within *The Hungry Goblin* itself, but a recurring theme of Carr's tracing back almost thirty years to his first use of it in *Till Death Do Us Part*.

In Mathers' novel, a character comments, "If you were an author... and put what I am going to tell you into a book, no one would believe you."[31] Neither Mathers' book nor Carr's is intended to be believed. They are literary romances, intended to be enjoyed. One may as well criticize the unreality of *Jane Eyre*, or of a Dumas historical adventure.

So yes, even Carr's dialog is "unrealistic," but this is no failing or accident. A reader should no more expect it to cling to the tedium of everyday discourse than the reader would expect a chivalric knight's boast of arms in some medieval romance to resemble the prattle of a plumber come to unstop a homeowner's pipes. Carr's characters speak with affectation and drama because it is more entertaining than the language we hear around us every day. Bill Dawson, the protagonist of *The Nine Wrong Answers*, mutters to himself (p. 74), "Satan's teeth!... Have I been cherishing lecherous thoughts about the wench without even knowing it?" Who speaks like that? Practically nobody—and that

---

31 Helen Mathers, *T'Other Dear Charmer*, John W. Lovell Company (1892), p. 113.

is the sheer fun of it. There is nothing realistic and everything entertaining in Bill's flaring diction. The language of Carr's characters is not clumsy; it is, rather, one further coruscation of the unexpected instinct.

Each "Notes for the Curious" following the tales in this collection will lend itself to the project of more fully appreciating Carr by examining somewhat deeply the points of interest in the selection and their presence in Carr's subsequent works, identifying and closely discussing recurring techniques, sources, themes, and influences. The reader is warned particularly that these post-selection essays intend to extend the general understanding of influences expected and unexpected upon Carr, including commonly less recognized ones such as Cabell, Dumas, O. Henry, Dickens, and others. Surprises await!

Let us begin, then, to catalog, at a high level, some of the influences and recurring considerations that can help inform enjoyment of Carr's narratives in this volume and generally. The first section of this collection is titled *Tales of the Past*. Douglas Greene, in the biography, writes:

> In many ways, John Dickson Carr was a historian manqué.[32] "To write good history," he said in 1936, "is the noblest work of man." But he did not think that all types of historical writing produced "good history." Not for him the analysis of economic and social trends, or how geography and demography affect a people. He preferred narrative history, the sort of thing that Thomas Babington Macaulay had written some eighty years earlier and that Winston Churchill continued to write. History to Carr, as it was to his father, was a mighty, romantic collection of adventures, a sweeping panorama of swordplay, and kings, and battles, and fair damsels, and mystery. (p. 183)

Greene, as always, is on target, but in the biography he does not have the luxury of elucidating in detail Macaulay's influence upon Carr.

Who was Macaulay? Thomas Babington Macaulay, made Baron (Lord) Macaulay in 1857, was a nineteenth-century politician, a Whig who served as Britain's Secretary of War between 1839–1841 and as Paymaster General between 1846–1848. In his political career, for its own sake, he would otherwise matter little to Carr and less to his writing, but Macaulay's lasting fame is as the author of his five-volume *History of England*, written between 1849 and 1861, as well as of essays upon

---

32 A potential historian who never was.

history and even some poetry. To Carr, he is always *the* historian. In his eyes, Macaulay eclipses and predominates the whole of his profession. While Macaulay had precursors on the continent and even some in England who prepared the path, as Conan Doyle did for detective fiction, Macaulay became the seminal figure of English Romantic historiography. Although history is non-fiction, Romantic history, because it embraces literature and other arts as elements proper to chronicling the past, and because it is narrative in style and focuses on key figures, is a descendent of the literary romance, even to depending upon its writers as source material. Carr loved history—and had he become a professional historian, Macaulay would have been his idol.

While Carr of course did not, as many readers will know, Carr's fiction brims with history—and Macaulay is Carr's model. Macaulay was, in fact, to Carr's understanding and explanation of history what Chesterton was to how Carr fooled readers. Both were indispensable influences upon him, and without either, Carr would not be the same distinct writer of detective fiction generations of readers have come to enjoy. Much of the richness of Carr's narratives, in their observation of cultural detail, in their incorporation of verse, even in their spirit of satire, owes a direct debt to Lord Macaulay.

And it is virtually certain that, without Macaulay, Carr would never have become the first historical detective novelist. Readers more broadly familiar with Carr know that although history was a distinguishing element of his detective fiction from the first, and that he wrote the first English-language historical mystery novel, *Devil Kinsmere*, in 1934, Carr's career changed direction strongly in 1950, when he released, to very warm reception, *The Bride of Newgate*. Historical detective novels were a rejuvenation for him; Carr would go on to write another dozen between then and 1972, while only releasing another ten conventional detective novels. This is, in essence, a third of Carr's career, in both time and output, without even accounting for the dimension of richness history adds to all Carr's work before 1950. It is difficult to imagine the writer Carr would have been without Macaulay, but clearly, he would have been a less interesting and versatile one.

Carr evidences Macaulay's importance to him throughout his career, beginning with his earliest writing. As a fifteen-year-old, in his column "As We See It" for the Uniontown *Daily News Standard*, Carr pointedly defends Macaulay against a rather off-hand and superficial dismissal by another newspaper's columnist:

> The other night Heywood Brown, in the New York World, says:
>
> "...Nobody reads Macaulay, except schoolboys under compulsion."
>
> Really, we shouldn't have written this article. The name of Macaulay is "far above our poor power to add or to detract." Of the nineteenth century essayists the most brilliant, the most polished, the most versatile was Macaulay. His style has a smooth, singing quality that makes the reading of his works a delight.
>
> And he is read, despite the assertion of the aforementioned Mr. Brown. If the latter would spend less time harping on South Sea Island tales and take the trouble to glance about him, he would discover that Macaulay is the most widely read of all the classicay [sic] essayists.[33]

That Carr invokes the language of Lincoln's hallowed, neo-religious Gettysburg address, implicitly equating Macaulay's efforts with the last full measure, their lives, by which the "brave men, living and dead... consecrated" the battlefield at Gettysburg, is a bit stunning—it is fully revealing of the young author's deeply felt veneration for the historian. In fact, that one sentence Greene cites, "To write good history is the noblest work of man," is consciously imbued by Carr with Macaulay's ideology and written in language reminiscent of the historian's own: "To write history respectably...is perhaps the rarest of intellectual distinctions."[34]

Carr's proposition appears in the introduction to *The Murder of Sir Edmund Godfrey*, his first-of-its-kind true-crime novel. In *Godfrey*, Carr endeavors to solve an unexplained death during the reign of Charles II, in 1678 when all London was aflame with fear of the Popish Plot. Was Godfrey murdered, and if so, how and by whom? Carr writes his history not as a dry recitation of fact and argument in the idioms of history or journalism, but, rather, in the style of a mystery novel. This, too, is an act faithful to Macaulay, who argues:

> Let us suppose that Lord Clarendon, instead of filling hundreds of folio pages with copies of state papers...had made his Cavaliers and Roundheads talk in their own style; that

---

33 "As We See It," Uniontown *Daily News Standard*, March 20, 1922 (p. 4).

34 *Thomas Babington Macaulay, Complete Works*, Delphi Classics (2016), p. 6488. All subsequent excerpts are drawn from the same edition.

he had reported some of the ribaldry of Rupert's pages, and some of the cant of Harrison and Fleetwood. Would not his work in that case have been more interesting? Would it not have been more accurate?....A history in which every particular incident may be true may on the whole be false." (p. 6531)

What is instead inevitable, Macaulay contends, is that every history is of necessity an abridgement, and that no history "can present us with the whole truth: but those are...the best histories which exhibit such parts of the truth as most nearly produce the effect of the whole" (p. 6498). This assessment is a faithful description of every Carr historical romance, whether his earliest ones, as collected in this volume, or his later masterpieces.

Of course, Macaulay is vigilant against the danger of distortion through too much or indiscriminate attention to trivialities, the exploitation of which he prescribes in a nuanced manner:

> That a historian should not record trifles, that he should confine himself to what is important, is perfectly true. But many writers seem never to have considered on what the historical importance of an event depends. They seem not to be aware that the importance of a fact, when that fact is considered with reference to its immediate effects, and the importance of the same fact, when the fact is considered as part of the materials for the construction of a science, are two very different things...The poisoning of an emperor is in one sense a far more serious matter than the poisoning of a rat. But the poisoning of a rat may be an era in chemistry; and an emperor may be poisoned by such ordinary means, and with such ordinary symptoms, that no scientific journal would notice the occurrence...A cause...in which a small sum is at stake, may establish some great principle...The case is exactly the same with that class of subjects of which historians treat...What general truth do we learn...? This is the really precious part of history, the corn on which some threshers carefully sever the corn from the chaff.... (pp. 828–829)

Through these arguments, we begin to understand Macaulay's tenets and how they are mined in Carr's twentieth-century fiction—but the vein of the historian's influence upon Carr is a deep, full, and subtle, not a shallow, one. It takes time and effort to tap. For instance, to Macaulay, fiction and history employ the same key technique, narrative, and pursue the same goal, truth, but they converge upon it from opposite directions:

> In fiction, the principles are given, to find the facts: in history, the facts are given, to find the principles; and the writer who does not explain the phenomena as well as state them, performs only one half of his office. Facts are the mere dross of history. (p. 6500)

In fact, Macaulay considered history itself to be a:

> province of literature...a debatable land. It lies on the confines of two distinct territories. It is under the jurisdiction of two hostile powers...Instead of being equally shared between its two rulers, the Reason and the Imagination, it falls alternately under the sole and absolute dominion of each. It is sometimes fiction. It is sometimes theory. (p. 6488)

To Macaulay, history's being in the family of literature accords it a sibling relationship to fiction: "He who can invent a story, and tell it well, will also be able to tell, in an interesting manner, a story which he has not invented" (p. 6496).

Carr agrees, mouthing his own conflation of the two through Dr. Fell; the doctor's statement in *The Case of the Constant Suicides* (1941) likely amounts to a bit of surreptitious Carrian autobiography: "The talent for deduction developed by judicious historical research can just as well be applied to detective work...*I* learned it at an early age" (p. 154). *Constant Suicides*, notably, centers upon dueling he-and-she historians who, throughout the course of the novel, cannot decide whether they prefer lovemaking or bickering over the seventeenth-century Duchess of Cleveland.

Although the two are closely related, Macaulay still readily, and importantly, distinguishes between history and fiction. Writing about two greats of these respective genres, he observes:

> The talent which is required to write history thus bears a considerable affinity to the talent of a great dramatist. There is one obvious distinction. The dramatist creates; the historian only disposes. The difference is not in the mode of execution, but in the mode of conception. Shakspeare [sic] is guided by

a model which exists in his imagination; Tacitus, by a model furnished from without. (p. 6516)

Given Macaulay's phylogenic classing of history and fiction, it is unsurprising that, to him, the two share so much genetic material. This is a key distinction between Romantic history and preceding schools: Romantic history is not simply the aggregation of received historical circumstances and judgments concerning them, but rather a revivification of some period of interest through its surviving primary records and works. While Macaulay does record and weigh events, in order to understand a particular time and place better and contextualize its historical incidents, he looks to what that culture created: its social chronicles, memoirs, its other first-hand accounts, and (even and especially) the culture's artistry. Macaulay summarizes his approach this way:

> It will be my endeavour to relate the history of the people as well as the history of the government, to trace the progress of useful and ornamental arts, to describe the rise of religious sects and the changes of literary taste, to portray the manners of successive generations and not to pass by with neglect even the revolutions which have taken place in dress, furniture, repasts, and public amusements. (p. 3041)

All this is readily appealing to Carr, especially during his formative period, when he is as keen a reader of history as of literature—and, like Macaulay, particularly of works in which the sibling genres converge, the historical romance...but more on that later.

As a historian, Macaulay is a pragmatist, no armchair historian: whenever and wherever he could, Macaulay traveled to see the places about which he wrote, attempting to gather the local sense of history and to understand the area's traditions. He sought to trace whatever pulse of the past still thrummed perceptibly in the present. Macaulay traveled to Scotland, Ireland, and regularly abroad to continental Europe to see battlefields and battlements, architectural remnants, cities, and more. According to his sister Margaret, Macaulay told her on March 30, 1831, "My accuracy as to facts...I owe to a cause which many men would not confess. It is due to my love of castle-building. The past is in my mind soon constructed into a romance."[35]

---

35 *The Life and Letters of Lord Macaulay*, Volume I, ed. George Trevelyan, Longman, Green, and Co (1876), p. 183.

Macaulay's method is reflected not only by Carr's similarly intense research into the periods about which he wrote in his historical fiction, or by the fact that Carr, too, liked to set his own writings in places where he had traveled (e.g., Paris, Tangier, Cairo, etc.), in order to lend his fiction verisimilitude—but also rather lightheartedly, by Carr's "research" into contemporary police work, trying, as Macaulay did, to capture the living sense of his subject matter so as to write more convincingly about it:

> He would pick out a cop and follow him around on the beat, carrying on an impertinent monologue that fell just short of being actionable. Sometimes, he'd ask the officer to help him across the street or salute him pompously when they passed each other. Then he'd search lawns with a magnifying glass, looking for clues, and take notes in a little black book. The police in the area knew him and treated him with heavy patience. "Why don't you go on home, Mr. Carr?" they'd say. "Write some more mysteries. Show us how a real detective works."[36]

Macaulay's innovative approach to history is the stronger because of his rejection of political or scholastic frameworks dictating preemptively how to record and interpret bygone events. He consciously discards theory to the extent he is capable. This is a departure from the dominant practices preceding his, in particular, those of the Enlightenment's philosophical historians. Although Macaulay agrees with Enlightenment historians that the relevance of the past is its utility to consideration of the present, and while he (and Carr, for that matter) is, like them, secular, Macaulay dissents from Enlightenment historians most importantly in his abstaining from the selective abstraction of lessons from recorded events to support (however worthy) predetermined conclusions and goals such as the assertion of natural rights, freedom, and governmental separation of powers. Macaulay criticizes non-Romantic history (including both his predecessors and contemporaries) for being distracted by ideology, even at the expense of first-hand testimony:

> While our historians are practising all the arts of controversy, they miserably neglect the art of narration, the art of interesting the affections and presenting pictures to the imagination.

---

36 Robert Lewis Taylor, "Two Authors in an Attic" (Part I), *The New Yorker*, September 8, 1951, p. 47.

> That a writer may produce these effects without violating
> truth is sufficiently proved by many excellent biographical
> works…. [W]riters of history seem to entertain an aristo-
> cratical contempt for the writers of memoirs. They think it
> beneath the dignity of men who describe the revolutions of
> nations to dwell on the details which constitute the charm
> of biography. (pp. 6529-6530)

Macaulay endeavors instead, in his Romantic-narrative approach drawing upon source material that earlier historians dismissed, to distinguish
the pertinent differences between past and present as a basis for gaug-
ing a given period's relevance to the present. This search for lost times
is not in the least philosophical or artistic. Macaulay does not practice
history, as his Enlightenment predecessors did, " to champion preferred
political views. Nor is a goal of his, as it was of the artists he studied to
understand their ages, the perfection of an aesthetic. Rather, for Macaulay, the writing of history attempts to establish as perfect a balance as
possible between reason and imagination, those hostile powers that dispute for control over historical narrative.

For Macaulay, this balance, if properly achieved, serves a substantive,
measurable goal, one shared with Enlightenment historians: progress.
Even in this, though, Macaulay differs from his predecessors by regarding
progress as increasing general prosperity, not, as they did, the advancement of predetermined ideals.

Indeed, Macaulay disliked fixed ideals, and in this, Carr was sympathetic. As Greene notes (p. 185), Carr "never could sympathize with
views based on idealism. He had long thought that people who commit
themselves to a theoretical view of human behavior end up dehuman-
izing all of us." Macaulay especially disliked (as did Carr) radicalism.
Readers of Carr will understand this statement, broad as it is, because
Carr broadly demonstrates it in his fiction, in his correspondence, and
in his life, well recorded in this respect by Greene's biography. As to
Macaulay, he pointedly makes his own distaste for radicalism clear, for
instance, in his final major essay (1844) prior to undertaking the *History of England*. That essay's subject is the Jacobin Bertrand Barère, a
pivotal figure of the French Revolution, whom the historian condemns
as a habitual liar and political renegade.

Macaulay's and Carr's common commitment to the use of primary
sources to construct their narratives, and to their shared view of history as literary-romantic, neutralized any political antipathy Carr might
otherwise have felt for Macaulay. After all, Macaulay was a Whig, and

despite his politically agnostic intentions, was nonetheless prone some-times to interpreting progress according to Whig principles. Carr was a Tory. Because the two shared a disposition toward the Romantic view of history and an admiration of great men (although differing on which men were!), Carr admired Macaulay, was influenced by him, and shared some literary ancestors with him.

Regarding these common ancestors, as we have seen, Macaulay turns consciously and especially in his history to literary-romantic narratives. He asserts, "History commenced among the modern nations of Europe, as it had commenced among the Greeks, in romance" (p. 6517). Macaulay grooms his approach and sources accordingly; this also means, for him, measuring the historian's accomplishment in a new and different manner. Following upon his assertion, "to be a really great historian is perhaps the rarest of intellectual distinctions" (p. 6488), Macaulay continues:

> Many scientific works are, in their kind, absolutely perfect. There are poems which we should be inclined to designate as faultless...There are...some speeches of Demosthenes...in which it would be impossible to alter a word without alter-ing it for the worse. But we are acquainted with no history which approaches our notion of what a history ought to be.... History, it has been said, is philosophy teaching by examples. Unhappily, what the philosophy gains in soundness and depth the examples generally lose in vividness. A perfect historian must possess an imagination sufficiently powerful to make his narrative affecting and picturesque. Yet he must control it so absolutely as to content himself with the materials which he finds, and to refrain from supplying deficiencies by additions of his own. He must be a profound and ingenious reasoner. Yet he must possess sufficient self-command to abstain from casting his facts in the mould of his hypothesis....It may be laid down as a general rule...that history begins in novel and ends in essay....The perfect historian is he in whose work the character and spirit of an age is exhibited in miniature. He relates no fact, he attributes no expression to his characters, which is not authenticated by sufficient testimony. But, by judicious selection, rejection, and arrangement, he gives to truth those attractions which have been usurped by fiction.... The instruction derived from history thus written would be of a vivid and practical character. It would be received by the imagination as well as the reason...Many truths would be

learned, which can be learned in no other manner....A historian, such as we have been attempting to describe, would indeed be an intellectual prodigy. In his mind, powers scarcely compatible with each other must be tempered into an exquisite harmony. (pp. 6488–6489, 6533, and 6537)

Given this, although Macaulay is thoroughly read in major historians dating back to antiquity, he does not rely upon them and make bland appeals to their authority. His history, as established, aims instead to be a living reconstruction of a place and a period based upon how it understood and depicted itself. Macaulay describes his idealized practice of history this way:

> ...a truly great historian would reclaim those materials which the novelist has appropriated....The early part of our imaginary history would be rich with colouring from romance, ballad, and chronicle. We should find ourselves in the company of knights such as those of Froissart, and of pilgrims such as those who rode with Chaucer from the Tabard. Society would be shown from the highest to the lowest,—from the royal cloth of state to the den of the outlaw; from the throne of the legate to the chimney-corner where the begging friar regaled himself. Palmers, minstrels, crusaders,—the stately monastery, with the good cheer in its refectory and the high-mass in its chapel,—the manor-house, with its hunting and hawking,—the tournament, with the heralds and ladies, the trumpets and the cloth of gold,—would give truth and life to the representation. We should perceive, in a thousand slight touches, the importance of the privileged burgher, and the fierce and haughty spirit which swelled under the collar of the degraded villain. (pp. 6533–6534)

Consider how faithfully Carr, describing his own ideal narrative in the preface to his *The Murder of Sir Edmund Godfrey*, echoes Macaulay's spirit and tone:

> Let there be drums behind a great stage—of a nation caught with panic, of kings playing at chess, of fiddles in the drawing-room, and of ladies more fair than any this side of the grave. (p. 13)

Carr also reveres the same medieval authors as Macaulay. Readers of the collection *The Kindling Spark* have already read Carr's tribute to Chaucer, "The New Canterbury Tales." As to Froissart, a fourteenth-century author and court historian in France, his Chronicles was a prose history of the Hundred Years' War, and his creative masterpiece was *Méliador,* an extended Arthurian romance. Carr pays tribute to Froissart in *The Nine Wrong Answers* when Bill Dawson, quotes him from memory:

> "Remember your Froissart? The fifth volume, I think? It's about Bertrand du Guesclin, the great champion of the fourteenth century."
>
> Now Bill could not help himself.
>
> *"'Then he saith, yet speaking but to his squire: Upon this day, by God's grace and my lady's favour, will I do a deed of arms shall ring in Christendom; not for my poor name, but for love of my lady and for honour of my friend, in the high court of all chivalry.'"*
>
> He closed the silver lighter, and dropped it into his pocket.
>
> "Don't!" whispered Marjorie. "Please don't! You can tear me in pieces when you say things like that! Because I know you mean it." (p. 127)

Of interest, Dawson confesses himself a "would-be historian" (p. 72).

The poetry of a community is as revelatory of it to Macaulay as its fiction, if not more so, because in his view, beginning with ballads, poetry (again, including the epic, which scholars generally agree began as an oral ballad tradition) is necessary for an early culture to understand and preserve its own identity:

> All human beings, not utterly savage, long for some information about past times, and are delighted by narratives which present pictures to the eye of the mind. But it is only in very enlightened communities that books are readily accessible. Metrical composition, therefore, which, in a highly civilized nation, is merely a luxury, is, in nations imperfectly civilized, almost a necessary of life, and is valued less on account of the pleasure which it gives to the ear, than on account of the help which it gives to the memory...Such is the origin of ballad-poetry, a species of composition which scarcely ever fails to

spring up and flourish in every society, at a certain point in the progress toward refinement. (pp. 7716–7717)

Macaulay even traces just such a progression, documenting how two early Roman romances found their way into a modern history of Hume's:

> Such is the way in which these two well-known tales have been handed down. They originally appeared in a poetical form. They found their way from ballads into an old chronicle. The ballads perished; the chronicle remained. A great historian, some centuries after the ballads had been altogether forgotten, consulted the chronicle. (p. 7725)

In advocating an association between history and ballad, Macaulay is following B.G. Niebuhr (1776–1831), a leading German authority on ancient Rome, who argued for the interrelation of Roman ballads and Roman history. Macaulay's interest in ballad poetry not only informs how he writes history (as it did Niebuhr), but upon visiting Italy and seeing the ruins of ancient Rome personally, Macaulay was inspired to compose, based upon four heroic tales from Roman history, his *Lays of Ancient Rome* (1842). These are long narrative poems Macaulay believed were faithful approximations of those the poets in ancient times might have sung.

Carr, in turn, read, admired, and remembered *Lays of Ancient Rome*—not only by allusion, for instance quoting Macaulay's "Ivry" in his short story "The Deficiency Expert" (a selection in this collection) and his *Horatius* in both *The Judas Window* and *The House at Satan's Elbow* (1965), but by emulating Macaulay's subject matter, and even sometimes Macaulay's rhythms, in his own verse. It is apparent that both Macaulay and Carr considered the virtues of ballad poetry to include strong rhythms giving pleasure to the ear and bold meters and rhyme schemes that lend help to the memory. Much of Carr's poetry is incantatory.

Of the fifteen poems attributed to Carr (some were published anonymously at Haverford), nine, like Macaulay's, "are praises of heroes and lost causes" (Greene, p. 31), or at least, strongly incorporate such imagery. Greene cites as influences upon Carr's poetry Kipling, Browning, and Swinburne, and these poets are (and Tennyson!), but so, too, is Macaulay. Consider as a representative instance Stanza XLV from Macaulay's *Horatius* as compared to the opening stanza of Carr's earliest poem "Valley Forge, 1777":

> He reeled, and on Herminius
> He leaned one breathing-space;
> Then, like a wild cat mad with wounds,
> Sprang right at Astur's face.
> Through teeth, and skull, and helmet
> So fierce a thrust he sped,
> The good sword stood a hand-breadth out
> Behind the Tuscan's head.[37]

—

> We have eaten the crusts of a nation's despair,
> We have drunk the black water of woe,
> In the light of our fires there is naught that inspires—
> No voice in the dumbness of snow.[38]

Note the similarly alternating use of lines in tetrameter (having four stressed syllables) and trimeter (having three stressed syllables). Like Macaulay, Carr generally favors lines of these lengths, sometimes composing stanzas consistently in one line length or the other, occasionally mingling them. Both poets, too, to mitigate the "sing-song" character that might otherwise result from hewing too closely to rhymed trimeter or tetrameter, sometimes mix different metrical feet within lines of the same metrical length. A metrical foot is a consistent pattern of stressed and unstressed syllables that, in traditional prosody, is the basic unit, or building block, of a poetic line. In English, perhaps the most frequently used metrical foot is the iamb, which is two syllables: an unstressed syllable followed by a stressed one. Every student who read poetry in English class, whether in secondary school or college, will recall references to iambic pentameter, the five-foot-long line of poetry having ten syllables. An excellent example of metrical substitution in Carr's case is the opening stanza of his "The Passing of the Leader," written in trimeter, but which strategically uses iambs, trochees (a stressed followed by an unstressed symbol, the inversion of an iamb), anapests (two unstressed syllables followed by one stressed, that metrical foot of limerick fame), pyrrhics (two unstressed syllables) and amphibrachs (three unstressed, stressed, and unstressed syllables in that order):

---

37 *Thomas Babington Macaulay, Complete Works*, pp. 7746-7747.

38 *A Book of Hill School Verse*, The Macmillan Company, 1927, p. 73. All subsequent excerpts are drawn from the same edition.

No word for a dream that is shattered,
No tear for a light that is fled,
While the heart-weary armies are battered,
And half of the nations are dead?
Does he pass, and yet think but of gladness,
Does his spirit go out with the breath?
How mute are the black plumes of sadness?
How cold the dim hallways of death?[39]

The substitution of other feet in the stanza for the base iamb varies the rhythm of the trimeter line enough to prevent it from being too "jingly," a criticism Greene offers against Carr's less varied lines in "The Voice and the Harp."[40] Here is a comparable example of substitutions by Macaulay, in Stanza XLIX from *Horatius*:

But all Etruria's noblest
  Felt their hearts sink to see
On the earth the bloody corpses,
In the path the dauntless Three:
  And, from the ghastly entrance
    Where those bold Romans stood,
    All shrank, like boys who unaware,
    Ranging the woods to start a hare,
    Come to the mouth of the dark lair
    Where, growling low, a fierce old bear
Lies amidst bones and blood.[41]

Note that because classical poetry based its feet on syllable *length*— long versus short, not as English does upon stressed versus unstressed syllables—the use in English of pyrrhics and amphibrachs is much less common than by poems composed in Greek and Latin—but suitable to the classical verse they emulate, the poems of Macaulay and Carr sometimes exploit these classical feet. Naturally, Carr would also have learned lessons in foot substitutions and line length from other poets

---

39 *A Book of Hill School Verse*, p. 26.

40 In the introduction to *Helmsman of Atlantis and other poems*, a limited-edition 2004 holiday chapbook privately published by Per Olaisen Förlag, which reprinted eight of Carr's poems. The pamphlet has no page numbers, but Greene's criticism appears at the bottom of the third page.

41 *Thomas Babington Macaulay, Complete Works*, pp. 7748-7749.

he admired—these practices are universal, and Carr was (as Greene observes) particularly fond of Browning, Kipling, and Swinburne, imitating aspects of their poetry, too—but especially in the election of classical feet, and in his selection of martial subject matter, Carr reveals a particular affinity for Macaulay.

Both these poets participate in the ballad tradition because of its strong relationship to cultural identity, and because both follow deliberately in the tradition of a common literary ancestor, Sir Walter Scott. Macaulay, as a historian, was peculiarly grateful for Scott's preservation of the Border Ballads. The Border Ballads were traditional Anglo-Scottish songs, rich in lore of battles and border raids, of romance, and even of the supernatural. He wrote, "Sir Walter Scott, who united to the fire of a great poet the minute curiosity and patient diligence of a great antiquary, was but just in time to save the precious relics of the Minstrelsy of the Border." (p. 7719).

Carr, too, remembered Scott gratefully, in *Speak of the Devil*, putting him in attendance at a nineteenth-century party given at Carlton House, the Prince Regent's Westminster mansion (pp. 116–117): "the only literary man present is a Scotchman named Walter Scott, suspected of being the author of *Waverly*, who is reciting Border Ballads on the staircase. Astonishing."

Scott, fascinated by ballads since he began collecting them on broadsheets at only ten years old, published his first edition of *Minstrelsy of the Scottish Border* in 1802. This book gathered ballads dating back centuries, many existing until Scott's time only in oral traditions and in danger of disappearing with those who knew and sung them. Scott continued collecting ballads for successive editions through 1830, two years before his death. Of course, as a lover of ballads, Scott also composed some himself. He collected his "The Gray Brother" and other later imitations of ancient ballads (by other poets) in *Minstrelsy*. He planned for his famous "The Lay of the Last Minstrel" to appear in the 1805 edition of *Minstrelsy*, but instead, published it separately. Scott nonetheless connected this new ballad back to the other, larger project in its preface, explaining, "The Poem...is intended to illustrate the customs and manners which anciently prevailed on the Borders of England and Scotland."[42]

Macaulay revered Scott, admitting that for his *Lays of Ancient Rome*, "Something has been borrowed...from our own old ballads, and

---

42 Sir Walter Scott, *The Lay of the Last Minstrel*, Longman, Hurst, Rees, and Orme (1805). The brief preface is on an unnumbered page, but which is the fifth page of the text.

more from Sir Walter Scott, the great restorer of our ballad-poetry" (p. 7728). Macaulay also praised Scott's fiction with what was, for him, an acknowledgment of highest regard:

> Sir Walter Scott...has used those fragments of truth which historians have scornfully thrown behind them in a manner which may well excite their envy. He has constructed out of their gleanings works which, even considered as histories, are scarcely less valuable than theirs. (p. 6534)

Macaulay even set Scott apart from other poets who wrote about history with observations such as, "No man can possibly think that the Romans of Addison resemble the real Romans so closely as the moss-troopers of Scott resemble the real moss-troopers" (p. 2260).

Among the group of literary romantics, Macaulay singles out Scott and Lord Byron as being most useful and instructive stylists for historians, the latter through his journals and correspondence, which...

> are in the highest degree valuable, not merely on account of the information which they contain respecting the distinguished man by whom they were written, but on account also of their rare merit as compositions. The letters, at least those which were sent from Italy, are among the best in our language. They are less affected than those of Pope and Walpole; they have more matter in them than those of Cowper. Knowing that many of them were not written merely for the person to whom they were directed, but were general epistles, meant to be read by a large circle, we expected to find them clever and spirited, but deficient in ease. We looked with vigilance for instances of stiffness in the language and awkwardness in the transitions. We have been agreeably disappointed; and we must confess that, if the epistolary style of Lord Byron was artificial, it was a rare and admirable instance of that highest art which cannot be distinguished from nature. (pp. 2247–2248)

There was much Macaulay actually disliked about Byron, his poetry, and his ethics, but all the same, he credits Byron for helping complete the Romantic revolution in English poetry, acknowledging of the poet, perhaps remarkably given those reservations, that:

> None of the writers of this period, not even Sir Walter Scott, contributed so much to the consummation as Lord Byron.... Lord Byron founded what may be called an exoteric[43] Lake school; and all the readers of verse in England, we might say in Europe, hastened to sit at his feet." (pp. 2271–2275).

Carr, too, draws on these two icons of Romanticism; in Scott's case, not only in the radio drama previously cited, but of course, in his novels as well. The most interesting instance occurs late in *Papa Là-bas*. Carr silently disagrees with Mark Twain about Scott by having Aunt Isabelle relate an 1858 conversation between her and Twain, in that year still a river-pilot and not yet an author:

> My husband, as you may be aware, is fond of meeting and taking up with extraordinary characters, whom he brings home for my delectation or the reverse. The latest acquisition, some days ago, was a young river-pilot named Clemens or Clements: Sam Clements. Young Clements, though a little too brash, was most amusing. He spent a whole evening arguing that the novels of Sir Walter Scott have been the curse of the South, infecting us with grandiose notions of a chivalric code no society could possibly carry out in practice. (p. 239)

The reader understands that, apart from Isabelle de Sancerre's bemusement at Twain, reinforced by her mistaking his surname, Carr himself reveres the chivalry that Clemens criticizes. Carr defends Sir Walter Scott without so much as an explicit objection.

Carr in his works calls with some frequency on Scott's poetry, and occasionally, on Byron's. Scott's *Marmion*, an extended historical romance concerning sixteenth-century warfare between the English and Scottish, is summoned in Carr's novels *The Case of the Constant Suicides* (which also alludes to *The Lady of the Lake*, another long Scots historical romance of the sixteenth century), 1939's *The Problem of the Wire Cage* (in which Dr. Fell also quotes "The Chase," Scott's first published work, a translation from German), *The Bride of Newgate*, and *Deadly Hall*. A character, William Harvey, quotes from Scott's "Lochinvar" in *The Cavalier's Cup* (1953), the final novel featuring Carr's series detective, Sir Henry Merrivale (H.M.).

In that same novel Carr quotes Byron's "She Walks in Beauty"; as

---

43 Exoteric means, "readily accessible to be understood by the general public."

well, he cites Byron's *Childe Harold's Pilgrimage* in both the novel *Castle Skull* and the stage drama *Thirteen to the Gallows* (1944).

While the difference in their disciplines meant that Carr could not draw upon Macaulay as generously or directly as he could upon G.K. Chesterton, Robert Louis Stevenson, James Branch Cabell, and other authors of literature of sensation, the reader will witness in this collection's first section, *Tales of the Past*, how Carr's historical romances consciously emulate Macaulay's technique. As appropriate to the scope of each, the stories are redolent in both consideration of the histories of peoples and governments for the periods in which they are set. The tales do indeed...

> ...trace the progress of useful and ornamental arts...describe the rise of religious sects and the changes of literary taste...portray the manners of successive generations and...even the revolutions...in dress, furniture, repasts, and public amusements.

As does Macaulay's history, Carr's narratives also measure the impact of "great men" on their circumstances and outcomes—and naturally, these early tales also anticipate Carr's novel-length historical romances, themselves rich in their Macaulay-inspired approach to the periods in which they are set. Carr was clearly fascinated with Macaulay's Romanticism: the historian's glorification of past eras and their ethoses; his interpretation of the best in the present as a progressive consequence of an idealized past; his historical narrative's reliance upon recapturing the color, atmosphere, and culture of a period; and Macaulay's formulation of historic figures, particularly "great men," in the literary style of Romantic characters, which simultaneously heightened these figures and flattened them. All these characteristics seem consistent stylistically with Carr's historical romances, even influentially so.

Could Macaulay have read Carr's historical romances, it is the editor's opinion that he would have approved of them for the same reasons he did Sir Walter Scott's fiction: for their utilization of those fragments of truth historians neglected, presented in a narrative writing style that might well excite those historians' envy, tempered as Carr's tales are into an exquisite harmony. Carr's histories, as the reader will see, do indeed, as Macaulay aspired to do in his history, "exhibit such parts of the truth as most nearly produce the effect of the whole." Macaulay would have considered Carr's romances, as he did Scott's, works that, even considered as histories, are hardly less valuable than many actual histories—because, as Macaulay demanded history should, Carr's narratives probe—as closely as fiction can, in Macaulay's estimation—the truths of times past and the people who lived in them. Doubtless, the vigilant reader will perceive in the stories collected here, and in Carr's historical romance novels, Macaulay's influence in numerous other, inexplicit manifestations and moments that cannot otherwise be neatly generalized. Once one grasps Macaulay's Romantic approach to history and recognizes Carr's emulation of him, it is a pleasure to trace within Carr's historical works the dialog between the two.

Finally in consideration of Macaulay, Carr found moments in his detective fiction to pay tribute to the historian through direct mentions, just as he sometimes did for other authors he admired. Bill Dawson and Uncle Gaylord Hurst snipe over Macaulay's anglicization of Louis Quatorze's name in *The Nine Wrong Answers*; a bit more substantively, in *The White Priory Murders* (1934), a breakfast-table discussion transpires concerning reading history—in which Maurice Bohun apparently shares sentiments with his author:

> Masters nodded his big head, with a show of deep interest.
>
> "Ah," he agreed wisely. "Reading history, sir. Quite. Very instructive. I'm fond of it myself."
>
> "Surely," said Maurice Bohun, "that is—ah—not quite what you mean, sir?" A faint crease ruffled his forehead. "Let me see. You mean that you once read a chapter of Macaulay or Froude, and were pleased with it and yourself when you discovered it to be a little less dull than you had anticipated. You were not inclined to read further, but at least you felt that your interest in history had been permanently aroused... But I really meant something deeper than that. I referred to the process that is nowadays—slurringly termed 'living in the past.' I frankly live in the past. It is the only mode of existence in which I find it possible to skip the dull days." (p. 127)

Carr's most prominent—and absurd—use of Macaulay, though, occurs in *The House at Satan's Elbow*. In that novel, the main character, Garrett Anderson, has become improbably wealthy through the adaptation of his Macaulay biography into, of all things, a Broadway musical:

> The famous team of Halpin & Peters, commissioned to do the show, had their own sweet will. Thomas Babington Macaulay, Sydney Smith's "book in breeches," became a romantic hero whose passionate affair with a (fictitious) earl's daughter

> inspired him to write both his *History of England* and *Lays of Ancient Rome*. Lady Holland, the formidable hostess of early Victorian days, capered as a figure of broad farce; one of her songs, "Read Any Good Books Lately?" almost every night afterwards would stop the show. Macaulay's own lyric, "Little Bird from a Bough," sung to his lady-love on the terrace at the House of Commons, made sentimental hearts palpitate. And so, against an alleged background of literary and political London in the eighteen-thirties and -forties, was born *Uncle Tom's Mansion*. (p. 4)

(You read the rumor here first that Lin-Manuel Miranda imitated Carr's novel by turning Ron Chernow's biography of Alexander Hamilton into an unlikely 2015 Broadway musical and Pulitzer Prize winner, because your editor has entirely fabricated this rumor. Do not let this stop you from spreading it.)

While additional direct influences upon Carr are discussed in each "Notes for the Curious" following the selections, with respect to perceiving Carr more holistically as an author, the reader may also consider some of Carr's recurring major themes and techniques—elements that unify his early stories, regardless of genre, with the rest of the works in his career, inclusive of his novels, short stories, and even his stage and radio dramas.

The first and most important among these is the theme of *gallantry*. It binds virtually all Carr's fiction and, indeed, evinces itself in Carr's personality and life, too. Greene capsulizes this:

> John Dickson Carr's legacy was his books; through them he gave, and continues to give, matchless pleasure to both puzzle fanciers and to those who agree with him that the world would be better if it reflected the standards of romance. (p. 453)

While chivalric principles are understandably a dated concept for twenty-first century readers, and old-fashioned notions of gentility often problematic in their reliance upon gender inequities (certainly, at least, in Carr's works), this tradition of courtesy is nonetheless central to Carr's worldview, literary and otherwise. Carr held it sincerely and personally as a virtue. For instance, Greene reports that Carr "was unfailingly generous about helping his friends" (p. 306) and offers demonstrative anecdotes throughout the biography.

In Carr's narratives, gallantry arises relentlessly, occasionally from surprising angles. Consider Dr. Fell, arsonist, as one illustration. In a novel the editor will not name (in order to preserve the surprise for any readers as yet unfamiliar with it), at one point, Dr. Fell burns down a house to protect an innocent party from being successfully framed by the actual criminal for murder. This exists within an occasional pattern of Carr's detective fiction in which the detective, practicing principles he holds higher than criminal law, puts the law aside and permits a malefactor, for humane reasons, to escape punishment—or in darker but equally high-minded evasions of the law, permits one to commit suicide honorably and quietly, rather than be publicly abased by arrest and trial.

Most gallantry in Carr's works, though, is plain to see, and it begins with his earliest stories. Readers of *The Kindling Spark* will have noted it in "The Blindfold Quest," "The New Canterbury Tales," and "The Cloak of D'Artagnan." In the present collection, gallantry is an important theme in all the first section's stories (*Tales of the Past*), as well as in "The Kindling Spark," "Candlelight: A Ghost Story of Christmas," and "The Haunting of Tarnboys"—more than half the selections. If among Carr's early fiction there is one best, most concise, and passionate expression of its importance, it is likely one appearing in "The Red Heels," when Napoleon Bonaparte eulogizes a deceased Girondin:[44]

> "The last of the gallants! The last of the old regime, Monsieur Ansmith, who put a higher price on a dream than on a kingdom, who died for a love they could never win. Foolish—and splendid, monsieur!"

Carr's tales of the past can, opportunistically, present gallantry, unadulterated, in its original forms: knightly chivalry and conspicuously honorable combat according to forms and traditions. To Carr, gallant courtesy was the contemporary form of chivalry; he all but confesses his personal devotion to it through nearly countless, thinly veiled declarations by characters all throughout his fiction. Many of these characters, of course, are clearly Carr's surrogates in the works within which they appear. Consider Martin Drake, one such proxy, that imaginative professional artist of *The Skeleton in the Clock*, who issues an old-fashioned challenge to a romantic rival:

---

44 The Girondins were a loosely affiliated political group during the French Revolution that, allied with the Mountainists, were initially part of the Jacobin movement. The Girondins favored ending the monarchy, but were idealists who resisted political violence. They were purged in 1793 at the start of the Reign of Terror. See the footnotes accompanying "The Red Heels" for further details.

"Is Mr. Richard Fleet there?"

"Yes, sir. Whom shall I say is calling?"

Martin spoke deliberately. "This," he said, "is an enemy. Tell Mr. Fleet that an enemy is waiting for him at the Dragon's Rest to give him a message of great importance."

If young Fleet had an ounce of sporting blood in his body, Martin thought, that ought to fetch him. He expected further questions. But the unruffled voice merely said, "One moment, please." And then, after a long minute, "Mr. Fleet will be with you immediately." (p. 41)

Subsequently, Ruth Callice exposes Martin to his half-recognizing self:

"Darling, your fair-play-and-no-advantages attitude was ridiculous. If Ricky Fleet hadn't been up to his ears with Susan Harwood, there'd have been trouble. You insisted on keeping your word about the vigil here, though I was a cat and tried to make Jenny even more jealous than she is.

"Look at your best, or rather your most popular, work! Look at your fencing! Look at Stevenson! You're an old-fashioned romanticist, that's what you are, only temperamental and a bit crazy." (p. 121)

As in Carr's historical tales, Drake's modern chivalry is at times equally foolish and splendid. Readers familiar with Carr will recognize how resonantly so many iterations of gallantry he utilizes in one work or another are bound together here: fair play; keeping one's word; the honorable contest of fencing; Robert Louis Stevenson, for whom nobility of spirit was also a significant and recurrent theme; all these and more are part of the romanticist's temperament, in which Carr wraps them. And slyly, Carr hints to the reader, asking how "ridiculous" or "crazy" Martin Drake actually is: after all, Ricky Fleet's blood rises, and he responds to Drake's challenge.

The importance of traditional courtesy only increased to Carr as it receded from the contemporary world, especially after the Second World War and the disillusionment sparked by its atrocities. Whether through Carr's composition of historical romances beginning in 1950, which were narratives in which he could more naturally assert the importance of courtliness, or whether in his contemporary mysteries, in which Carr would feature protagonists clinging proudly to anachronistic principles,

Carr never retreated from his views or accepted their diminishing relevance. Crystal Manning's confrontation with Cy Norton in *A Graveyard to Let* (1949) signals Carr's personal unhappiness with a world he felt was changing for the worse:

> "You want Europe, and especially England, as England was before the war. But those old days have gone forever. You know that, you hate it, and it's poisoning your life."
>
> Crystal spoke steadily, breathing quickly, yet in a passion of words.
>
> "You want a life of graciousness, and dignity, and a 'decent reserve.' Oh, don't deny it! I heard what you said to Jean awhile ago. That's why you've liked Dad, ever since you've known him. And you hate him now, because he's broken the pattern. As for your wife..."
>
> "Crystal, for God's sake!"
>
> "You're trying to cherish her memory, in the Browningesque way. And you can't do it; nobody can. But you hate Dad because—he couldn't." (p. 103)

Indeed, Professor Riguad, in *He Who Whispers*, rather succinctly expresses Carr's frustration with the unstraightforward character of the twentieth century:

> 'My friends, you are no doubt familiar with the great Musketeer romances of the elder Dumas. You will recall how the Musketeers went to England. You will recall that the only two words of English known to D'Artagnan were "Come" and "God damn". He shook a thick arm in the air. 'Would that my knowledge of the English language were confined to the same harmless and uncomplicated terms!' (p. 200)

Exactly how did Carr, as a modern writer, perceive chivalry as something personally viable in his own century? In its definition, Carr agreed with G.P.R. James, who attained to the office of British Historiographer Royal during the last years of William IV's reign. James (a devoted admirer of Sir Walter Scott, whose approval he sought and received) authored more than sixty historical romances and (among other academic works) a study, *The History of Chivalry*. Carr makes brief tributary reference to James in *Papa Là-bas*:

> "...Don't underestimate man's appetite for the sensational.
> I believe that in fairly recent years a countryman of yours, the
> novelist G. P. R. James, was British Consul at Norfolk, and
> married an American lady before leaving us. Is he still in the
> government's service?"
> "Yes. He is now consul general at Venice."
> "Mr. James's works used to delight me. Little mystery,
> unfortunately, but roaring sensationalism in plenty. More than
> a decade ago, when my mother was still alive, I used to read
> aloud from those books to my mother and my sisters." (p. 121)

James explained chivalry this way, separating its trappings from its essence:

> Before proceeding to inquire into the origin of Chivalry, I
> must be permitted to make one more observation in regard to
> my definition; namely, that there was a great and individual
> character in that order, which no definition can fully con-
> vey. I mean the Spirit of Chivalry; for, indeed, it was more a
> spirit than an institution; and the outward forms with which
> it soon became invested, were only, in truth, the signs by
> which it was conventionally agreed that those persons who
> had proved in their initiate they possessed the spirit, should
> be distinguished from the other classes of society. The ceremo-
> nial was merely the public declaration, that he on whom the
> order was conferred was worthy to exercise the powers with
> which it invested him; but still, *the spirit was the Chivalry*.[45]

This indeed is Carr's concept of gallantry: the accoutrements and the
era may change, but its spirit traces back, unchanged, to the chivalry of
the earliest medieval romances.

The reader can easily perceive that gracious integrity was also a central
theme for virtually all Carr's significant influences—G.K. Chesterton,
Robert Louis Stevenson, Brian Oswald Donn Byrne, Sir Walter Scott,
Lord Macaulay, Sir Arthur Conan Doyle, James Branch Cabell, Alexandre Dumas, Charles Dickens, Anthony Hope, George Barr McCutcheon
(most of these discussed and explained in *The Kindling Spark*, others
here)—but Carr, receptive to nobility of spirit wherever he could find,
consume, and internalize it, had it reinforced by less obvious influences,
too, such as O. Henry. Readers recognize Henry's direct influence on

---

45 G.P.R. James, *The History of Chivalry*, Harper & Brothers, 1840, p. 19.

Carr through his twist endings and the Arabian Nights-style overtones of his stories, comic though these may be. As we will see in commentaries following selections in this collection, Henry was also a strong influence on Carr's construction and delineation of character. Less well recognized, though, is that gallantry, too, underlies Henry's fiction, both as an authorial perspective and as motivation of his characters. Consider, for instance, the story "Between Rounds," appearing in O. Henry's first collection of short fiction, *The Four Million*:

> "Woman! " said Mr. McCaskey, dashing his coat and hat upon a chair, "the noise of ye is an insult to me appetite. When ye run down politeness ye take the mortar from between the bricks of the foundations of society. 'Tis no more than exercisin' the acrimony of a gentleman when ye ask the dissent of ladies blockin' the way for steppin' between them."[46]

Carr was sensitive to it. Nobody would confuse Henry's writing style or his diction with Carr's, but that spirit of courtesy was indeed, to both of them, the mortar between the bricks of the foundations of society.

Closely intertwined with the theme of gallantry in Carr's fiction is the honorable quarrel of fencing, which Carr finds every conceivable excuse to incorporate into his narratives, whether literally or metaphorically. Whenever he does, entertainment results. In one example of merely metaphorical dueling, note the romantic rivalry in *The Nine Wrong Answers* between Bill Dawson and Eric Cheever, with its undercurrent of violence:

> "I see," observed Bill, with a loving kindness of bile rising in his soul. "Where are you doing the show?"
>
> "Here at Broadcasting House: studio 8-A, top-floor. If you could be there twenty minutes before transmission at ten-thirty, you could vet that one part of the script. I shall be in the listening room to hear the program. Afterward, if you are willing, we can go down to my office and discuss a problem concerning our mutual friend. Of course, if you can't be there...?"
>
> "Don't worry. I can be there."

---

46 O. Henry, *The Four Million*, Doubleday, Page & Company, 1920, p. 37. All subsequent excerpts are drawn from the same edition.

"It is possible," said Cheever, "that I may be able to convince you I am right. In any case, I promise you something you don't expect."

"And I promise you," snapped Bill, unconsciously loosening his shoulders under his coat, "you'll get something you don't expect."

"Agreed, then?"

"Agreed!"

Both phones slammed down at once, with a suggestion of fencers crossing swords. (p. 109)

Readers of *The Kindling Spark* will recall that Carr, an amateur fencer himself, began incorporating swordplay into his fiction with "The Will-o'-the-Wisp," featuring it again soon in "The Cloak of D'Artagnan," and "The Blindfold Quest." More crossed blades await in several of this collection's tales. Literal swordplay breaks out in a number of Carr's subsequent works, including *Devil Kinsmere*, *The Case of the Constant Suicides*, and a number of Carr's historical romances. Worth noting, Carr also considered pugilism to be an honorable confrontation. For a discussion in detail of boxing throughout Carr's works, please see the "Notes for the Curious" commentary following "The God of the Gloves."

Another theme in Carr's work that aligns with gallantry is grand passion. This is a dramatic element more easily incorporated into tales of the past, or at least tales in that spirit, and Carr does so in his early works. "The Blindfold Quest," "The New Canterbury Tales," "Héloïse," "The Dim Queen," "The Blue Garden," "The Harp of Tairlaine," and "The Kindling Spark" all wrestle with the concept of idealized love. So do the modern leading men in Carr's detective fiction who hold antiquated notions of honor and chivalry. They cannot woo women only with mere modern tawdriness.

Admittedly, it is paradoxical that in Carr's contemporary novels, both the author and his male protagonists can simultaneously put women on the clichéd pedestal and yet, the men frequently approach them with brusque libidinousness—nearly as often reciprocated by the women. It is sometimes difficult to discern whether Carr's world is one of old-world courtesy or modern coarseness. Paradox though this is (and it is fair to construe the women's reciprocal concupiscence as simplistic wish fulfillment), Carr is, nonetheless, a heartfelt champion of the grand romance. If the reader is willing, as Coleridge would recommend, to suspend disbelief and remain mindful that Carr is thoroughly uninterested in realism, to recognize that he is only dressing up homespun literary romances in the flashier garb of modern detective novels, then these grand passions, playing out side by side with the pursuit of murderers, can be as entertaining as the impossible crimes driving the main action, and which endanger their happy consummation.

Men and women alike in Carr's fiction, whether believably or not, surrender to outsized conceptions, and declarations, of love; the editor offers a single example of each, but encourages the reader to watch as Carr revisits it, regularly, beginning in the 1940s.

One of Carr's earliest male romantics is Don Holden, in *The Sleeping Sphinx*. His avowal of love to Celia Devereux is about as striking an admixture of the archaic and the modern as any in Carr's works:

> "I love you, Celia. I always have."
> "Are we in love?"
> Don Holden felt lightheaded with happiness.
> "My dear Celia," he began oracularly, "consider indisputable proof in this matter. Did you hear what the driver of that car said when he roared past?"
> She looked puzzled. "He—he swore at us."
> "Yes. To be exact, he said 'god-damnedest thing I ever saw.' The remark, though inelegantly phrased, contains a deep philosophical truth. Shall we search the story of famous lovers...of Daphnis and Chloe, of Hero and Leander, of Pyramus and Thisbe, of (to be more prosaic about it) Victoria and Albert...for many instances of two persons standing locked in each other's arms in the middle of a main motor road?"
> "I love you when you talk like that," Celia said seriously. "It's not exactly romantic; but it seems to make everything so much more fun..." (p. 40)

In a Carr novel, though, women can be just as extravagant in their feelings and the expression of them—right down to his last novel, *The Hungry Goblin*, in which one such woman professes her elevated passion:

> "...But I can't help myself, can I?
> "I had read of what's called a grand passion, and up to then had decided it must be a beautiful dream like so many other dreams. Could I, believing as I did, really feel in my heart and body the storm that would sweep me away?

"This is an explanation...it's not a defence. But the dream
was true, you know; the dream had become reality even before
I opened my arms in surrender..." (p. 196)

Many of Carr's romance-seeking protagonists operate in their novels as surrogates for Carr himself. Doubling, whether of characters within a work (e.g., lookalikes, imposters) or as resonant stand-ins for the author, are common in his fiction. Readers of *The Kindling Spark* encountered several echoes of their young author. These stand-ins, as is appropriate and even expected for a teenaged author, are generally tied to wish fulfillment, especially to the desire for Adventure in the Grand Manner. Selections in *The Kindling Spark* that narrate the imaginative aspirations of their young author, fulfilled through the tales' leading characters, include "The Blindfold Quest," "The Cloak of D'Artagnan," and *Grand Guignol*.

In *The Unexpected Instinct*, the reader will again meet characters echoing their young author, but not always happily, including "The Blue Garden," "The Harp of Tairlaine," "The Red Heels," "The Kindling Spark," "Candlelight: A Ghost Story of Christmas," "Pygmalion," "The Deficiency Expert," and "The Gordon Djinn." The protagonists of these tales share not only their author's desires, but some of his characteristics, sympathies, and his viewpoints. They are incrementally more sophisticated in their relationship to Carr than those in the wish-fulfillment group of stories.

Their different relationship to Carr is significant. Instead of imagining himself as an adventuring perspective character, in each of the tales collected in this volume, Carr instead imagines, effectively, that *the surrogate character is he*: Carr's reflection character not only assumes some of the author's personal aspects, he also faces problems of some intimate interest to Carr. None of these surrogates is a student; they include a poet, a bard, an orator, a journalist, a novelist, and even a painter. All have stepped into the intimidating and complicated world. Each reflects Carr's artistic aspirations and young doubts.

One recurring theme with which they are associated, predictably, is the pursuit of love (still in one sense wish fulfillment); another, of more distinctive interest, is the difficulty the artist has in influencing others as hoped, even of reconciling his idealized artistic ideas with the commonplace world. Without divulging the storylines of these tales, the editor nonetheless assures the reader that the commentaries following each selection explore this question, which was so important to "a boy in Pennsylvania, toying with the notion of adopting the profession

I did adopt."[47] As one hint, though: Carr puts the objection that most worries him generally into the mouth of a character, Monsieur de ma Belle Dame, in "The Red Heels." Monsieur is disparaging Danton, who at the time is politically on the rise among French revolutionaries—but who, as history informs us, would ultimately be beheaded. Another character, Vandaliers, an advisor to Danton, believes that through his oratory, Danton can control the mob and guide the French Revolution. Monsieur, a cynic—or perhaps insightful—slaps his hand on the table and dismissively remonstrates: "Oratory!...Does oratory tame beasts, I would know?" That is the question, in its varied fictional guises, Carr explores through his reflection characters in the stories collected here.

There is one variation on this dilemma, too, of which the reader is warned: in "Pygmalion" and "The Deficiency Expert," Carr examines his anxiety concerning influence from a different angle, the *perversion* of the artist and artistry. In the latter story, a journalist becomes a propagandist, with the result that circulation, profit, and notoriety all increase; in the former, the artist is pressured to secure fame and affluence by pandering to the commercially popular. In both tales, the abuse of artistic and rhetorical skills promises the kind of success and influence every artist desires—but bending to those commercial considerations also threatens unanticipated consequences. While Carr does not use a Faustian metaphor in either story, in artistic terms, these two stories are; both examine the Biblical question (Mark 8:36), "For what shall it profit a man, if he shall gain the whole world, and lose his own soul?"

Carr further represents his anxiety concerning the artist's social place metaphorically: a number of the tales in this collection present the artist grotesquely: a disfigured poet in "The Blue Garden"; a sexless musician in "That Ye Be Not Judged"; the slightness and perceived femininity, and resultant sexual frustration of, the eponymous protagonist Michael in "The Harp of Tairlaine"; the conjuration of the historical figure Danton in "The Red Heels," who was disfigured from youth, and who is contrasted with a fictional counterpart, Ansmith, "the young man with the twisted beauty"—the latter's oratory, similarly twisted, contributes to the story's crisis; and the painter Luke Ferguson, in "Pygmalion," who is in his disposition socially twisted, and therefore emotionally isolated.

These anxious concerns about the artist's potential for finding happiness are timely questions to the young Carr as he weighs his hopes of establishing his career—and his life—through writing fiction. The productive manner in which Carr transforms his apprehensions into lit-

---

47 Letter to Oscar Baron, April 3, 1972.

erary devices and plot complications is gratifying, and it indicates Carr's rapidly maturing gifts as a writer.

Carr continues employing reflections of himself throughout his career, each likewise a mirror to himself who works dramatically within the given narrative's context while also enabling the reader to see the author as Carr sees himself at that age, in that moment. Occasionally, Carr even splits himself between characters, because he feels different sides of himself that respond differently to the story's premise. Typically, in these instances, one of the characters will represent that still-persistent aspiration to Adventure in the Grand Manner, while the other can look on the first tolerantly, but more world-wisely, and offer the reader a different perspective.

In the novels from Carr's early professional years, the young adventurer group is well represented. Jeff Marle, a carryover from Jack Carr's college novella *Grand Guignol*, appears in Carr's first four novels, all set in Europe and featuring Bencolin: *It Walks By Night*, *The Lost Gallows* and *Castle Skull* (both 1931), and *The Corpse in the Waxworks* (1932). Jeff also narrates *Poison In Jest* (1932), set back home in Carr's native Pennsylvania. Ken Blake, perhaps the same Ken Blake in this collection's "The Gordon Djinn," adventures his way through the early H.M. novels *The Plague Court Murders* (1934), *The Unicorn Murders* (1935), and *The Punch and Judy Murders* (1937). He also narrates *The Judas Window*. Ken's final appearance is a brief one in *And So To Murder*.

As to split representations of Carr, *The Eight of Swords* offers both its perspective character, Hugh Donovan, a former student and amateur middleweight pugilist, and Henry Morgan, a successful mystery writer whose views on the art are clearly Carr's own.[48] In *Night at the Mocking Widow* (1950), Carr again divides himself into two juxtaposed personalities: the passionate naïf, the Reverend James Cadman Hunter, and the mature and settled, successful thirty-something adventure novelist and writer of radio dramas for the BBC, Gordon West. West summarizes his two-decade career, which of course, is Carr's own:

> "It was...scrimp and save, scrimp and save, to the meanest little farthing that'll get you steerage passage through the Malay Straits or a bug-filled room in San Francisco! But that's not the way to do it. If you can't afford the best orchestra stalls,

---

48 The first Carr reader to publish this observation was Douglas Greene, in pp. 142-144 of the biography; he echoed and expanded upon it in his 2021 introduction to the Penzler Publishers edition.

then don't go to the theater. If you can't afford to travel first-class, with special tips for special favors, then don't travel at all.

"That means work. And rightly! At my job it means work, work, work; grind, grind, grind: eighteen hours a day or twenty if you can stand it. Never look away; never look up. No other activities except books; no holidays; who wants a silly trip to St. Ives when you're headed for the Mountains of the Moon? Hit 'em with book after book; force 'em to recognize you; make 'em know you've got quality; grind, grind, grind, for five years, ten years, even fifteen years...

"Well, it doesn't take quite as long as that. About halfway through—you don't know why; nothing seems to have made a dent—all of a sudden it changes. Streams of cash begin to come running in from all directions. Suddenly you realize you're nearly at the top. But you must make sure...You must make sure." (p. 56)

We earlier mentioned those middle-aged adventurers Sir George Anstruther and Michael Tairlaine, who appear in *The Bowstring Murders* and *The Red Widow Murders*. Anstruther is the Director of the British Museum and a lecturer at Cambridge. Tairlaine is, like Carr, an American abroad, but a professor at Harvard. Both have obvious intellectual affinities with Carr, and neither in his manner or appearance seems a typical academic (which, to Carr, recommends them). That they are torn between their professional identities and the unexpected instinct, the pull toward a life of romance, accurately reflects their author's mindset in those years. Carr in the 1930s more than once celebrated writing his novels by traveling in between the completion of one and the start of the next.

While middle-aged avatars of Carr appear more numerously throughout his works than it is practical to document here, a few of interest merit mention. There are, for instance, the Stuart historian Nicholas Fenton, of *The Devil in Velvet*, and in *Deadly Hall*, Jeff Caldwell, a writer of romances, at least one of whose very titles are borrowed from Carr's own fiction. Fenton wishes to recapture his youth; Caldwell, although financially successful, looks back at his novels and questions whether they had much value. Both are good representatives of how Carr's avatars matured with him, and how Carr continued using the questions of emotional moment in his life to lend his characters believability and sympathy.

Bill Dawson, of *The Nine Wrong Answers*, is like his creator and

Gordon West, an American who wrote propaganda broadcasts for the BBC during World War II. The episodes of the novel involving the BBC borrow, barely disguised, details from the years of Carr's own life spent doing the same work. Bill is also, like his author, a historian manqué.

As to doubles functioning as a plot mechanism, Carr was formatively exposed to this expedient in Thomas and Mary Hanshew's adventures of Cleek, the Man of Forty Faces, as well as in the Ruritanian adventures and historical romances that the young Carr devoured written by George Barr McCutcheon (*Graustark*), Anthony Hope (*The Prisoner of Zenda*), Alexandre Dumas (*Les Misérables*, *The Man in the Iron Mask*, *The Vicomte de Bragelonne*), and more such by the same authors and different ones.

The Hanshews published a dozen Cleek collections and novels between 1910 and 1922. Cleek could, through unspecified natural gifts, assume the appearance of any other person at will. These stories were among the young Carr's favorites. He later wrote to Fred Dannay (aka Ellery Queen):

> If you told me a new Cleek story had been discovered, I would rather read that story than any discovery except a new story about Father Brown....Almost every Cleek story contains a new—and usually spectacular or apparently supernatural—method of committing murder."[49]

Carr praised the Hanshews in tandem with the likes of Doyle and Chesterton, noting, "All of them loved an impossible situation, and gave me the push in that direction."[50]

As he does other favorites and influences, Carr remembers Cleek through direct references in his own works. Dr. Fell praises the Hanshews in his famous locked-room lecture (*The Three Coffins*, pp. 228-229) for the creative use of an icicle as a murder weapon: "Well, it has been fired, thrown, or shot from a crossbow as in one adventure of Hamilton Cleek (that magnificent character of the *Forty Faces*)." In *Seeing Is Believing* (1941), H.M. admiringly laments an "ingenious feller, who knows the names of Sergeant Cuff and Hamilton Cleek in a day when most people have unhappily forgotten 'em" (p. 254). Carr never did.

Carr imitates McCutcheon and Hope for the first time in his 1923 Ruritanian story "The Blindfold Quest." That tale borrows inspiration

---

49 Quoted by Greene, p. 18.

50 Letter to Nelson Bond, March 3, 1968.

from the title and action of the first chapter in McCutcheon's *Graustark*, "Mr. Grenville Lorry Seeks Adventure," for the title and theme of its own opening section, "Adventure Boards the Train." In turn, near the end of Carr's career, Part One of *The Ghosts' High Noon* is, in coy recollection of his earliest adventure narrative, titled "Blindfold Quest"—and the novel's action does indeed begin on a train and provide the theme for the section. Carr of course pays tribute to the pair later in the novel as Jim Blake, another echo of Carr, and Leo Shepley, a friend of Blake's, debate the likelihood of war in the Balkans. Jim says:

> There's always war in the Balkans. That means nothing by itself. I can't visualize Ruritania or Graustark as a real trouble-spot, though it just may happen sooner or later if the Prussian warlords decide on *der Tag*.[51] (p. 50)

Doubles, frequently in the form of imposters, appear as early in Carr's fiction as "Ashes of Clues," in 1923. While without spoiling them, the editor can only mention a few of Carr's detective novels in which a mysterious double is central to the problem—*It Walks By Night*, *The Crooked Hinge*, *My Late Wives*, and *The Ghosts' High Noon*—there are others among his novels, as well as the dramas and short stories, which exploit this same device. Given the unlikelihood of close resemblance, Carr recognizes the challenge in relying on this particular ruse, which he sets out overtly in *The Nine Wrong Answers*, when Larry Hurst proposes paying Bill Dawson to impersonate him:

> "That ought to please you!" said Larry. "*That's* out of books!" He uttered his rusty, disused laugh; but very briefly. "*The Prisoner of Zenda. The Masquerader. The Great Impersonation.* Read 'em all when I was a boy. Must be dozens more. Only, d'ye see, it all depended on two men looking exactly alike: same face, same height, same voice, same everything. Rot! Wouldn't happen once in a hundred years." (p. 20)

Nonetheless, the imposter is a juicy plot element in any novel of sensation, and Carr always manages to get a good squeeze out of it.

Larry Hurst, attempting to convince Bill Dawson to go, in his place, to England to meet Larry's long-estranged uncle, Gaylord Hurst, admits

---

51 German for, "the day."

and proposes, "You and I don't look very much alike. Don't even think alike. Eh? No. This'll be a new kind of impersonation."

The mechanism of imposture is adjacent to another salient Carr motif, masks—which appear frequently in Carr's fiction, nearly always with subtext—and both generally, in the category of disguise. Disguise in Carr's novels is as common and important a contrivance as the solutions to his impossible crimes are—and it comes, as those do, in imaginative variety: at various times, persons in Carr's fiction are adequately disguised by as little as a pair of black spectacles, or by speaking in a whispered voice. In Carr's work, disguise, whatever its form, is not merely the concealment of *appearance*, but of the disguised person's *nature*. As Greene notes:

> The charming rogue who seems to be included...merely for
> comic relief, the fussy lawyer whose role appears to be to
> supply evidence, the young policeman who is a friend of the
> narrator—each of these might turn out to be a murderer in
> John Dickson Carr's books. (p. 278)

A mask in particular, for Carr, is transformative of both perceptions— other characters do not recognize the mask-wearer, to whom they respond differently, based upon newly perceived verbal and physical cues—and of behavior: a mask wearer is anonymous, less inhibited, in effect a different person. The wearer can act outside normal constraints, whether social, sexual—or even by committing murder.

Carr invokes the power of masks beginning with his earliest fiction. Among the apprenticeship tales, a mask hides a criminal's identity in both of his first stories, "The Ruby of Rameses" and "The House of Terror." In "Ashes of Clues," an inverted detective tale, we meet the murderer and know his name, Saunders, immediately. What we do not know until the story's climax, because of his sufficient resemblance to the victim and the proficient application of stage makeup, is whom Saunders kills and impersonates. Saunders taunts his victim that, "not even your wife could tell us apart...or your friends." To Carr, disguise is powerful.

In Carr's final amateur work, *Grand Guignol*, and in his first professional novel that it became, *It Walks By Night*, the killer's identity, Laurent, is similarly already known—but like Saunders, his face is not. Before the action commences, Laurent has already put himself under the care of Vienna's finest plastic surgeon (for whose services he pays by killing him) and remade himself, down to his fingerprints, into an unknown stalker, close at hand and with jealous designs on the life of his ex-wife's fiancé.

In *The Corpse in the Waxworks*, everybody wears a mask to the notorious Club of Coloured Masks:

> A social gathering of men and women. Women unhappy in marriage, women who are old, women looking for a thrill; men whose wives are a bore or a terror, men in search of adventure—these meet and mingle, the woman to find a man who pleases her, the man to seek out a woman who does not remind him of his wife. They cross in [the] great hall, which is dimly lighted and muffled with thick hangings—and they all wear masks. One may not know that the masked lady he sees, and who appeals to him, and who leads him for private speech into the corridors...that this seductive charmer is the very dignified woman whose sedate dinner he attended the night before. They sit and drink, they listen to [the] hidden orchestra, then they vanish into the depths of their amours.... Those who have no lover, but are merely looking at random for someone who pleases them, wear black masks. Those who are seeking out a definite person wear green. Finally, those who are there by assignation with some definite person, and will speak to no other, wear—as a hands-off signal—scarlet. (pp. 63–67)

The connection between mask and ritual is implicit; it is an association Carr explores late into his career. In some of Carr's earliest work, he suggests that a mask can convince others that the one wearing it is another person. Carr quickly recognizes the impracticality of this and begins focusing instead on the *effect* a mask has on others and the *reasons* one might don a mask. To obscure identity? Yes, sometimes, but for Carr, simple disguise hardly taps the potential of masks. A mask, in its unexpectedness or grotesqueness, might promote fear; it might in hiding the wearer's identity be emotionally liberating; it might entertain, of course, or serve a ceremonial purpose.

The Sleeping Sphinx features a party in which a rich country squire's guests play the parlor game Murder wearing:

> all of them painted and lifelike...a small collection of murderers' masks, as they looked after they'd been executed....three or four...had been taken direct—first in wet paper, then in papier-mâché—from real death masks preserved in the museums at Scotland Yard and Centre Street and the Sûreté in

Paris. Afterward, they'd been colored to the likeness of these people after death, after the pain of death; with real hair or beard attached; and in some cases, with the mark of the rope still..." (pp. 57–58).

The masks are so frightening that Celia Devereux shudderingly admits:

> My Maria Manning mask was swollen, one eye open and the other partly shut, though it was the face of a woman who had been pretty. And all of the sudden I thought to myself: Suppose this thing against my face is one of the *real* masks, and I'm looking out through the eyes of a woman standing on a scaffold? (p. 59)

Later, Celia dreams she *is* Maria Manning, standing on the scaffold as the crowd jeers and mocks her shortly before her execution.

The squire, Danvers Locke, is just the sort of character Carr clearly relishes creating:

> He's got a big place down in the country near Caswall. Fellow collects masks; all sorts of masks; even got a metal one worn by a German executioner hundreds of years ago; crazy hobby. But filthy with money—absolutely filthy—and of course, in with all the right people in the business world. (p. 22)

As to the game itself:

> "The idea, Sir Danvers said, was that we were to play an old-fashioned game of Murder. Only this time, we were each to wear the mask of a famous murderer in real life. Afterward, when the 'murder' had been committed, we were each to answer questions as much as possible in the manner of the original.["] (p. 58)

Carr's delicious parade of murderers includes "Landru, the French Bluebeard, with a thin bald skull and a ginger beard" and "George Joseph Smith, the brides-in-the-bath murderer," among others less famous, but whose crimes were uniformly gruesome. Of course, because this is a John Dickson Carr novel, the history of one of the true-life murderers ultimately provides a clue to Dr. Fell as to the identity of the criminal.

Below Suspicion (1949) demonstrates a mask's capacity to change not just others' perceptions of the wearer and their behavior toward the wearer, but the wearer's behavior, too. Whereas everything in the Club of Coloured Masks is arranged and consensual—expected—*Below Suspicion* intimates that masks have their own, unexpected power, even to provoke involuntary responses:

> *"Mademoiselle,"* he intoned, *"Je vous ai remarque. Votre beauté, c'est comme un fleur dans un puisard. Vous permettez?"*[52]
>
> Without further ceremony he took her hand, yanked her to her feet, and whirled the startled woman out into the throng of dancers.
>
> ....Patrick Butler could not be unconscious, in any sense whatever, of the woman he held in his arms.
>
> "Your beauty," he continued in the same fluent French, "intoxicates and maddens me. Your breasts burn. Your body is a..."
>
> "Patrick," murmured the hesitant voice of Lucia Renshaw, "I don't think that's very nice."
>
> Butler's step stumbled on the music-beat, so that he almost fell over her feet.
>
> "Good God! You're not—"
>
> "Of course!" The blue eyes regarded him strangely through the eyeholes of the mask. "Didn't you know who I was?"
>
> "Good God, no!" said Butler, hastily relaxing his tight hold. "I apologize! I thought..."
>
> "Oh!" Lucia was silent for a moment, while the music throbbed and the blank mask-faces leered in changing lights. "Is that how you treat any woman," she asked sharply, "when you think she isn't—quite nice?"
>
> "Frankly, yes."
>
> For a moment, if he had noticed it, the blue eyes were furious. But their expression changed.
>
> "It's all right, isn't it," asked Lucia in an indifferent voice, "if you tell me those things in French? That's not the same as in English, is it? And, even if you wanted to tell me those things in..." (pp. 126–127)

---

[52] "Miss, you caught my eye. Your beauty is like a flower in a cesspool. With your permission?"

One clever aspect of this exchange is Carr's implication that language, too, becomes a mask; it likewise can change what people believe is acceptable, even change what they are willing to do.

Later in the same novel, this is chillingly reinforced, as masks serve a more sinister role: Satanism. Dr. Fell and his companions explore an unholy chapel in which they discover...

> "Confessional boxes," said Dr. Fell.
>
> "You mean they confess their..." Lucia stopped.
>
> "They creep in, masked, not to confess their sins. To confess their desires for sins. They speak to the head of the cult, Satan's representative, who can grant all.
>
> "On the ordinary, or even extraordinary, sins we need not dwell. They are easily provided. But suppose a woman wishes her husband dead? Or a husband would be rid of his wife? Or an old dotard with money lingers on and refuses to die....Satanism gives all the answers. Its members are outwardly respectable because, to join at all, they must be at least faintly well-to-do. They wear masks, of course. But masks may slip, in a moment of frenzy—"
>
> "Masks!" Butler interrupted with bitterness. "Masks again! Always masks!"
>
> "And so it will be," Dr. Fell retorted, "until we snatch the mask from the present head of the witch-cult." (p. 173)

An additional interesting variant on the ritual use of masks demonstrates that they can even transgress the social hierarchy. In *Papa Là-bas*, masks and a quadroon ball, used to secret purposes, throw circumstances into chaos. Carr draws the ball and its reliance on masks from real life. A quadroon ball was a "society ball" of sorts, which all the ladies attend masked. In the novel, Dick Macrae, the British Consul to New Orleans, explains this institution peculiar to the antebellum city:

> "In New Orleans...there are many mulatto or quadroon girls: half white or three-quarters white, sired by white fathers who may not acknowledge them publicly. They form a special class of their own, superior to black but still below the level of white. Most of them are pretty; they have good figures and wear clothes with *chic*. Some are well-educated and accomplished, the unavowed father having paid for it. Not

a few are beauties, in appearance as white as any of us; they may even have fair hair and blue eyes.

"Now what may such a girl expect in life? To become a maid or a hairdresser? Sometimes, yes. As a rule, however, she is carefully brought up by her mulatto or quadroon mother for one particular purpose: that she may be chosen as paramour, less mistress than a kind of unofficial wife, by some well-to-do young man of the ruling caste, Creole or American." (p. 47)

What results when masks conceal who is really at the ball, and why? Read *Papa Là-bas* to find out.

In one final example, *The Nine Wrong Answers* inverts how masks usually work, Uncle Gaylord dons a mask to *reveal* his true, malicious nature, which, the rest of the time, he carefully conceals. His denial to Marjorie of an episode in his nephew's boyhood when he cruelly terrorized the boy is, of course, a transparent admission:

"And so, my dear," he concluded, "there was the sorry chap, blubbering on the floor. Naturally his parents could not believe that I—I, of all people had put on a papier mâché mask, representing the face of a victim of the Great Plague in 1666, covered with blue pustules and mouth open. Or that I—gentlest of men—should have come running and dodging toward him, making what he called mewing noises, in an ill-lighted passage on Christmas Eve. I cannot wonder, my dear, if you find it incredible. Sometimes I doubted his sanity." (p. 136)

This reinforces the insinuation, both in this novel and numerous others works by Carr that often, a person's real face is a mask, its carefully controlled expression hiding unsuspected malice (or some equally revelatory attitude, guarded carefully). This idea is explicitly in play in *Papa Là-bas*: Carr builds a quiet dialog between actual masks and metaphorical ones, the express concern at several points that what is in a character's face contradicts what is in the character's mind.

There are nearly countless other instances of masks, actual and metaphorical, in Carr's fiction. Carr loves the evocative power and metaphorical utility of masks, and so the alert reader may quickly be intrigued when an ancestral house is unofficially called, "Masque House" (*The Gilded Man*, 1942), or a theater named, with seeming appropriateness but deeper undertones, "The Mask Theatre" (*Panic in Box C*). In Carr's fiction, a mask is never "merely" a mask. It disguises identities and intentions. It frightens, arouses, confuses. It comes with situational implications and authorial subtext. While hiding one thing, a mask reveals another... so it is often a clue. No matter where or when used, the mask always signals the unordinary—and so in Carr's work, it is always a point of special attention.

Before inviting the reader to move onto the reading selections, the editor offers two final benedictory considerations concerning Carr's detective fiction, written during whatever period of his career. The first is encouragement to observe and enjoy what Carr learned from his literary idol, G.K. Chesterton, in its indispensability to Carr's grand game of trickery: the Chestertonian art of misdirection. This includes, frequently and prominently, a trope Chesterton himself borrowed from Sir Arthur Conan Doyle: the enigmatic utterance. Carr explains that this "is the trick by which the detective—while giving you perfectly fair opportunity to guess—nevertheless makes you wonder what in sanity's name he is talking about" (*The Life of Sir Arthur Conan Doyle*, 1949, p. 234). Carr relishes it; in his use of it, he may actually surpass both his literary ancestors.

Carr's detectives relish it, too. While they deny staunchly trading deliberately in obscure utterances, these denials sometimes seem (amusingly) insincere. For instance, Sir Henry Merrivale doth protest too much when he answers a charge of deliberate obfuscation with, "Obscure? Why, burn me, I'm the purest rill of limpidity that ever tinkled on a rock! Just listen carefully!" (*Night at the Mocking Widow*, p. 131). It is only a short time later when, in all his limpidity, H.M. explains:

> Poison pen...Easy to deduce; hard to prove if The Widow
> shuts up now. Locked room. Hard to deduce; easy to prove—
> I thought. It'd be taken away, yes, but the traces! I thought
> I'd solved the right problem by solvin' the wrong problem. I
> thought I'd opened the right door with the wrong key. Maybe
> I still have. (p. 169)

The reader is not missing context; rather, the reader is experiencing that Chestertonian mystification which verges on paradox.

Dr. Fell, modeled directly on Chesterton and who, at his most Chestertonian declares, "But I have—harruumph—a certain Christian confidence" (*The Sleeping Sphinx*, p. 104) is likewise often—and entertainingly—accused of such obscurity (here, in the mind of his exasperated companion, Superintendent Hadley):

> Dr. Fell is, possibly, too much concerned with proving that the right thing is always the wrong thing, or at least the unexpected thing; and waving flags with both hands above the ruin of logic. (*The Crooked Hinge*, p. 134)

But the Chestertonian paradox is more than entertaining wool-gathering by amateur detectives. It is also the author's art of rotating what is plainly in front of the reader's eyes to an angle at which the information, plainly stated, confuses rather than illuminates. Carr offers a wonderful simile for it in *The Gilded Man*:

> Here, however, the evidence was less like a series of trails than like a circle of burrs. You turned it in your hands without being able to decide what was start, middle or finish. (p. 183)

And of course Carr misdirects the reader proudly, boasting, "Your craftsman knows…that it is not necessary to mislead the reader. Merely state your evidence, and the reader will mislead himself."[53] It is this Chestertonian misdirection, so well executed by Carr, which makes him special among detective-fiction novelists, and which is even more essential to his mastery of impossible crimes than the mechanical explanation clarifying how some seemingly miraculous event was always humanly possible.

The second savory theme (or, the final one in this introduction) the editor recommends to the reader's attention is Carr's flair for interjecting the discussion of detective fiction into his narrative, without authorial smirking or any loss of cogency. The reader remains engaged with the story. In Carr's most famous instance, Chapter XVII of *The Three Coffins*, "The Locked-Room Lecture," he even breaks the fourth wall:

> "I will now lecture," said Dr. Fell, inexorably, "on the general mechanics and development of the situation which is known in detective fiction as the 'hermetically sealed chamber.' Harrumph. All those opposing can skip this chapter. Harrumph. To begin with, gentlemen! Having been improving my mind with sensational fiction for the last forty years, I can say—"
>
> "But if you're going to analyze impossible situations," interrupted Pettis, "why discuss detective fiction?"

---

53 John Dickson Carr, *The Grandest Game in the World*, limited edition publication by Ellery Queen (1963), p. 10. All subsequent excerpts are drawn from the same edition.

> "Because," said the doctor, frankly, "we're in a detective
> story, and we don't fool the reader by pretending we're not.
> Let's not invent elaborate excuses to drag in a discussion of
> detective stories. Let's candidly glory in the noblest pursuits
> possible to characters in a book." (pp. 220–221)

Here is another, excellent example, from *Papa Là-bas*, in which Carr's characters mislead themselves, and consequently, the reader:

> "Any sensational romance," argued Tom, "would provide
> an unexpected development to turn the whole affair upside
> down. We've been thinking of three potential victims: Judge
> Rutherford, George Stoneman, Barnaby Jeffers. One of those
> is a victim; he's dead. But what of the other two? What if ...?"
> "What if one of the prospective victims, standing by in
> apparent innocence, should actually be the murderer him-
> self? Last night, it seemed to me," Macrae told him, "Senator
> Benjamin suggested something very like the same possibil-
> ity." (p. 196)

Carr inserts such discussions into multiple novels, without ever again breaking the fourth wall as he had in *The Three Coffins*, but, as well, without making it seem he is concocting elaborate excuses for his characters to compare their own situations to detective fiction. He even uses this technique in his dramas: in *Inspector Silence Takes the Air* (1942, co-written with Val Gielgud), a character suggests, "How about the least likely person? It always works in fiction."[54]

Carr's strategy is not superfluous: if anything, it is a clever enhancement of his Chestertonian misdirection, albeit in a manner Chesterton himself did not so frequently practice it. By citing the conventions of detective fiction and having his characters apply them to how their own "real-life" mysteries should be unraveled, Carr distracts readers from the actual insights that would uncover the truth. Carr considers this fair play (as does the editor), according to his principle, *"Once the evidence has been fairly presented, there are very few things which are not permissible"* (*The Grandest Game in the World*, p. 20).

Nor does Carr bother to hide his strategy from readers any more than Dr. Fell disguised his self-recognition as a character in a book. In *The*

---

54 Collected in *13 to the Gallows*, p. 77.

Hungry Goblin, Wilkie Collins himself (serving as the novel's detective) explains how to fool the reader, and then, Carr fools the reader, anyway:

> If you would really take the audience by surprise...follow one basic plan. Be fair with your readers; tell 'em everything. But don't tell 'em everything in a simple-minded way. First decide what the average reader will suspect—anticipate it, and fool him. Then decide what the clever reader will suspect—anticipate it, and fool *him*. Thus, all openly, you prepare your thunderbolt for the end. (p. 123)

Even Carr's first-person narrators participate in this framing of detective fiction within detective fiction. Carr uses this rhetorical strategy from the very first; it is not part of an increasing self-consciousness on his part, and if anything, these professions by the narrators make the given novels more emotionally convincing. Here is Jeff Marle's direct address to the reader, from *It Walks By Night*:

> I do not know whether the reader has ever been entangled in any such gruesome mess as this, or even peeped into the events surrounding any mysterious and violent death, not seeing them through the medium of the newspapers—where the worst tragedy seems unreal, incomprehensive, and often absurd—but terribly close in the company of the people who produced them...Crime, in written outline, is as far off and unconvincing as the account of a battle in a history book, full of unreal sound and fury...so that you find difficulty in imagining that it ever happened at all. If, then, you who read this have never experienced the hopeless and caged uncertainty, the bewilderment and black suspicion of everybody, that comes with such things in your own life, I cannot make it clear...Yet here it is. It is like looking in a mirror and seeing hideous things reflected in one's own face. (pp. 252–253)

For comparison, here is old Dr. Luke Croxley's, from *She Died a Lady*, thirteen years later:

> Now, you who read this record have been expecting it. You have been waiting for that word "murder," and perhaps wondering when it would first occur. To you it is only the preparation for a battle of wits. But to me—having the thing flung in my

face like this—every word Craft said came with a cold shock better left to your imagination. (p. 67)

The alert reader will also find disguised advice from Carr on other considerations when writing novels of sensation, often with a tip of the hat to one of his inspirations:

> Reflect on it yourselves. Villainy or mere slander, it has every artistic element Mr. De Quincey calls indispensable to the best work in crime. 'Design, grouping, light and shade, poetry, sentiment!' They are all there. (*Papa Là-bas*, pp. 22–23)

The editor thanks the reader kindly for reading and encourages the reader, now, to turn the page and experience that unexpected instinct, romance, in all the unexpected shapes John Dickson Carr delivered it, and which until now, few readers have had the privilege of enjoying. In recommending these tales to the reader, most of them something other than mysteries, the editor confidently joins Carr (as a gift inscription in his latest novel to friends once expressed it) "in the hope that when they read this, only the gargoyles will yawn."

Friend reader, enjoy!

Tales of the Past

Héloïse (1927)

"Say that name again! Just once again, if you please!"

"The name, monsieur, is Héloïse. As I was telling these gentlemen when you interrupted me, her eyes..."

"Never mind her eyes. Do you refer to Mlle. Héloïse de Roget? Come now, be careful! It may mean your life!"

"Yes, monsieur, I refer to Mlle. Héloïse de Roget."

And so, they had fought. It had been an odd fight—for the honor of living to murder the woman they had both loved. But it had been so agreed. One of them was to die for her, but she was to die for him also. There had been no other way. Honor extended beyond love, certainly beyond deceitful love.

And now one half of the ghastly business was over. It remained but for Héloïse to be removed, and all would be well. Irony, that—all would be well—with the splendid young Comte Valois and the most beautiful woman in Marseilles both dead! Yes, and there might be a third...

* * *

As he walked fiercely through the rainy night, the entire procedure whirled through his mind in fantastic review. He saw the little group of officers in the dusk. They were discussing women—perfect women—as little groups of officers will. Lips that were glorious, and forms that were divine, and eyes that were lovelier than the dawn. Yes, that was it—eyes. And this unfortunate youth who had said, *"But the eyes of Héloïse are symphonies in gray..."* Certainly, "symphonies in gray"—what else could they be? Héloïse's eyes. And then he remembered them as they had followed him down the hall, at his departing eighteen months ago. They had seemed so faithful...Lord! At least they had seemed faithful enough to belong only to him. And now he knew that they had said goodbye to two in exactly that manner. Well, they would never say goodbye to another that way! No, by God!—that much was certain!

* * *

"So," she had said (how he wished her voice hadn't had that same low beauty!) "So, you have come back to me at last?"

They sat down, and talked, as they had before. Her eyes. She was at least as charming as she had ever been, he thought. And she was still the same Héloïse who had made him believe that he was her only thought in all the world. There was no use denying it—he had loved her.

All night they were there together. No one would have suspected that they were other than two reunited lovers. Neither did she suspect it. And there was no use denying it—he still loved her.

"For the thousandth time, Héloïse, do you love me as you did? Was there never another...?"

"Never."

"Then," he had said (and his change of tone had startled her)—"Then the Comte Valois paid dearly for a lie!"

She had turned a deathly pale. And she was still a deathly pale when they found her, there, next morning...with a small dagger, like a slender angel, through her heart.

Notes for the Curious: "Héloïse"

Like the magnum opus of Carr's juvenilia, *Grand Guignol*, this vignette appeared in *The Haverfordian* after Carr's departure from Haverford College. As Greene reports in the biography (p. 59), "Jack [as Carr was known there] ended his sophomore year with a combined grade of 52.6. For promotion to the junior class, he needed an average of 65.0." Despite Carr's best efforts, he scored only 35 on his plane geometry exam. Haverford was willing to keep Carr around: "...the administration offered him a deal: 'If you will take what we consider the hardest course in college and pass it, we'll forgive you the math.' They assigned him Greek..." Carr, refusing this offer, departed Haverford having learned little geometry and less Greek.

"Héloïse," published in the June 1927 issue (two months after Carr's withdrawal), identified its author as "J.R." Presumably, in keeping with Jack's mischievous practice of publishing his work under the names of others, and as a kind of welcome gesture, the attribution implied that the tale was by John Roedelheim, Carr's successor as editor of *The Haverfordian*. On May 23, 1927, the *Haverford News* reported:

ROEDELHEIM IS ELECTED HAVERFORDIAN EDITOR
Succeeds Bramwell Linn, '29, as Head of Undergraduate Publication

Succeeding Bramwell Linn. '29, who has acted in the capacity of editor since the resignation of J. D. Carr, '29, in April, John Roedelheim, '29, was elected editor of the Haverfordian at a joint meeting of the business and editorial boards of that publication last Friday. Linn will remain on the editorial staff of the magazine.

Roedelheim was elected to the editorial board of the Haverfordian on April 25. He is on the J.V. tennis squad and served for over a year on the editorial board of the News.

At the same meeting Roedelheim announced that the recently inaugurated policy of using a greater variety of material in The Haverfordian than in the past would be continued throughout the coming year. He also stated that members of the editorial board could devote a part of the summer to writing and assembling material for the issues of next year. D. H. Hedley, '29, business manager of the publication, outlined plans for an extensive advertising and circulation campaign to be held next fall.

Regarding "Héloïse" itself: it is the present editor's supposition, given the story's length, subject matter, and the date of its composition, that Carr probably drafted the vignette as a candidate "legend" for "The New Canterbury Tales." Although Carr did not use it in that story cycle, having the finished tale on hand, liking it, and wishing to help his successors complete *The Haverfordian*'s final issue prior to the summer hiatus, Carr offered it to Roedelheim and Linn. The attribution under Roedelheim's initials may even have seemed more appropriate, so soon after Jack's resignation and exit.

That the unnamed protagonist's unfortunate antagonist is named Valois, Carr's habit of borrowing character names from works he admired is one clue that this brief narrative is his. The Valois family were a collateral French royal line who succeeded the Capets, and upon the Valois line's own end with Henry III (who died childless in 1589), they were in turn succeeded by the collateral Bourbon line. Two of Carr's favorite authors, James Branch Cabell and Alexandre Dumas (*père*) chronicled the Valois family; he almost surely had both in mind when borrowing the surname for his tale.

Cabell chronicled the Valois and Plantagenet families in his story collection, *Chivalry* (1909), which Cabell explained is "a little book wherein I treat of divers queens and of their love-business."[1] The collection intertwines fictional acts by both fictitious and historical persons in a series of ten romances, culminating in the final tale's account of the union of the two families through the marriage of Henry V to Catherine of Valois in 1420. We know not merely that Carr read *Chivalry*, but that it was among his lifelong sentimental favorites. (For additional discussion of Cabell's influence on Carr, please see the introduction to *The Kindling Spark*, beginning on page 37.) In 1972, Carr inquired with a book proprietor, Oscar Baron, while searching for a copy of *Chivalry* and three other favorite Cabell titles (plus books by additional authors fondly remembered from Carr's youth). Carr explained that he had lived abroad in England for more than thirty years, but upon his now-permanent return to the U.S.:

> Some six years ago, settling down here in the South, I began
> gathering such titles as could be found of books—novels or
> short-story collections—I remember reading with pleasure
> when I was a boy in Pennsylvania, toying with the notion of

---

1 James Branch Cabell, *Chivalry*, Harper & Brothers Publishers, 1909, p. 3. All subsequent excerpts are drawn from the same edition.

adopting the profession I did adopt. There are many more of which I am still in search, and for which I ask your help, both mysteries and non-mysteries.[2]

The subject matter of Cabell's book was the Valois family's ascent to the French throne in the fourteenth century; Dumas' series of seven historical romance novels concerned the end of that family's reign in the sixteenth. Like Cabell's, Dumas' novels liberally intermixed fiction with history. As Dumas was a favorite of Carr's, Carr doubtless read his Valois novels.

In another possible nod by Carr to the French novelist, Héloïse is the name of a scheming character—manipulative in romance and a poisoner—in Dumas's *The Count of Monte Cristo*. She would have been memorable to the young reader, and perhaps even an inspiration for some of the problematic women in Carr's own stories and detective novels. Carr did, after all, very much admire poisoning as a means of murder, declaring it "the best method because the evilest and the most subtle."[3]

Carr seemingly meant for "Héloïse" obliquely to complement the Valois tales he enjoyed by two of his favorite authors. Like those romances, Carr's deliberately does not too-closely embrace historical fact. It is not even possible to identify the dispatched romantic rival as an actual, historical person. There were four Counts of Valois. The earliest, Charles (1284–1325), was the progenitor of the Valois dynasty, so it could not have been he who died on the blade of Héloïse's jealous lover. The next Count of Valois, Philip, ascended to the throne in 1328 as Philip VI. His son, also named Philip, became the first Duke of Orléans in 1344, living another thirty-one years. The fourth and final Count, Louis, was assassinated in 1407 by fifteen brigands given the order to slay him by John the Fearless, regent to Louis' brother, King Charles the Mad (Charles VI). This murder, for which John openly claimed credit, sparked the twenty-eight-year Armagnac–Burgundian civil war, which ended with the Treaty of Arras in 1435.

So Carr's Valois, whatever his relation to the French dynasty, is a figment. Given this, the story almost certainly takes place in the thirteenth century, before Charles became the first Count of Valois in 1290. Carr's Valois was intended, perhaps (if Carr really had any intention to fit his character into history, which is doubtful, as opposed to paying homage

---

2 Letter from John Dickson Carr to Oscar Baron, April 3, 1972.

3 "Blackmail, Antimony and Sometimes Old Lace," *The New York Times Book Review*, June 24, 1951, p. 5.

to Dumas and Cabell) to be a forgotten ancestor occupying an extinct branch on the family tree.

The anonymous vignette, too, as so many of Carr's apprentice-ship-period stories do, anticipates some of the author's most distinctive professional work. As a novelist, Carr first openly emulated Dumas in another work that was similarly, generally unattributed, for four decades, before being rediscovered by Douglas Greene: *Devil Kinsmere*, published under the pseudonym Roger Fairbairn. As Greene reports:

> In a junk shop in Missoula, Montana, around 1970-1971 I noticed this book on a shelf. The title on the spine intrigued me, and in flipping thru it I recognized that it was by Carr. I wrote to him and he acknowledged his authorship but told me to forget all about it.[4]

Greene honored Carr's instruction, keeping the novel's authorship secret until after Carr's death; he announced its rediscovery in an article, "John Dickson Carr, Alias Roger Fairbairn, and the Historical Novel," published October 1978 in *The Armchair Detective*. Pointedly, in fact, the American first-edition dust jacket of *Devil Kinsmere* (Greene posits, on p. 186, its language perhaps composed by Carr), woos prospective readers, "IF YOU LIKED The Three Musketeers, READ—DEVIL KINSMERE." The novel, like the inspirations by Dumas and Cabell for "Héloïse," seamlessly interweaves its titular character's adventures with both actual and fictive historical events and persons.

Nor would Carr's cavalier spirit soon diminish: *The Bride of Newgate*, *The Devil in Velvet*, *Captain Cut-Throat* (1955), *Fear Is the Same* (1956), and *Most Secret* (1965, a rewritten version under Carr's own name of *Devil Kinsmere*) are all swordsman's tales set in the periods between the Stuart reign of Charles I and Napoleonic France.

Even H.M. had an adventure related to the days of swordsmen: in his final novelistic adventure, *The Cavalier's Cup*, the creation of the eponymous relic begins with the legend of a Cavalier, Sir Byng Royden, one of two Royalist survivors of the battle of Naseby. Royden rides wounded many miles for a last farewell with a Lady, Marian, who has been his chaste chivalric inspiration. What is the significance of the last, incomplete phrase Royden scratches into a leaded window, "God bless King Charles and"? Is it Royden's ancient rapier that hangs centuries later in Telford Old Hall? And what is the secret of the Cavalier's Cup created in Sir Byng's memory? If you liked "Héloïse," read *The Cavalier's Cup*.

---

4 Greene in a personal note, December 16, 2018.

The Blue Garden (1926)

Rome! In that name the trumpets blare, in that name a million ghosts rise from their graves. For in the year of grace 1492 Rome had not yet crouched down among her ruins, and wept beside the inscrutable Tiber. Lorenzo the Magnificent[1] was dead with the curse of Savonarola[2] upon him, dead and white under the seven tall candles.[3] And now from the Porta del Popolo[4] to the Coliseum the mob thronged, tossing red caps.[5] It hung in black clusters from the windows, it moved in dense-packed streets as you may see a wind move over grain. Shouting and buffeting; jingle of the jester's bells and rattle of armor...Now they roar! Now the clouds over Rome open with thunder and rain as good Cardinal Sforza[6] announces from his balcony at the Vatican that Rodrigo Borgia, Archbishop of Valencia, has been chosen pope.

Behold the might of Rome. Rodrigo Borgia, gray and wolfish, has assumed the name of Alexander—a shrunken figure in his mail, but likely to be more powerful an Alexander than the Macedonian. A clever

---

1 Lorenzo de' Medici was a powerful Renaissance arts patron who had great influence in banking and politics, and who effectively ruled Florence, indirectly and corruptly.

2 Girolamo Savonarola (1452-1498) was a Dominican friar noted for his reformist views, especially his criticisms of corrupt clergy, and for despising secular art and culture.

3 The origin of the seven candles is the menorah dictated by the Lord in Exodus 25:33; the menorah lights the tabernacle. The Catholic Church adopted the seven-candle candelabrum (seven being a sacred Christian number); seven golden candlesticks feature prominently in the symbolic imagery of Revelation (1:12, 1:13, 1:20, 2:1, 11:4). Here, of course, Carr uses the seven candles synecdochally to represent the funeral mass.

4 The Porta del Popolo had only recently been built, in 1475, by Pope Sixtus IV to celebrate his proclamation of the Jubilee Year (in the Catholic Church, a holy year marked by solemn, holy acts). Sixtus IV named it the Porta Flaminia. Pius IV renamed the gate to Porta del Popolo after its reconstruction in 1562, for which he commissioned Michelangelo. The architect Nanni di Baccio Bigio executed Michelangelo's design.

5 The red Phrygian cap, in Rome called the pileus, was worn by freedmen (including manumitted slaves). The French Revolution adopted it as an emblem, the red cap of liberty. Dickens features it in *A Tale of Two Cities*; in "The Red Heels," Carr does not, although he might otherwise have made it a counterpoint to those titular red heels.

6 An Italian cardinal known for his diplomatic skills, Ascanio Sforza was influential in the election of Rodrigo Borgia as Pope. He hoped to become Pope himself, but did not have sufficient support. In trade, Sforza endorsed Borgia, who appointed him Vice-Chancellor of the Holy Roman Empire. Sforza served in that role until his death in 1505.

man, peering about him for enemies to be crushed. Everywhere the steel fighting-men ride to do homage; north and south and east and west they come sweeping in with uplifted lances and hurtling pennons. Now the trumpets volley, blast after blast! Ceaseless trampling of hoofs, ring of steel...By night fireworks make a blaze of the city, green-clad mountebanks dance in the flare to horn and zither, and there is hand-clapping and rollicking song. Immortal Rome...

...But on the far hills, where the olive trees shine gray by the moon, lived the young Francesco. In his wild shepherd's way he was of almost unearthly beauty. For Francesco was not yet sixteen, and he was a lad of dreams and tears, whom the thought of jewels and velvet had made mad. By day he would recite verses to the sheep—swinging verses of his own composition, and presently as his voice rang to a climax he would shout, "Bravo!" and fling his hat into the air. The pale cheeks would be flushed...

By night he would steal again to the hills from his home, where, up against a lonely slope and the stars, a girl would meet him. On that slope was a tree, an old tangled tree that was laden with white blossoms. Just that, among the winds and the stars. Seated on a carpet of fallen blossoms under the tree, Joanna waited for him. He was scarcely older than she, but her quiet, tender smile was the smile of a woman, and in her eyes was a dark mirror of God. Tonight she saw him approach, brooding. And Joanna said:

"You are fevered, Francesco."

He stood there looking upon the moon, so that presently she joined him, taking his hand.

"I have seen her, Joanna," he answered. "Last night I wandered upon her by a blue pool in which a white temple was reflected, very near to here. I have seen my goddess."

She was crying, just a little. But the deep steady eyes smiled on him.

"Then you must go to her, my Francesco. You must go, because you are a poet, and know those things in which I am stupid. It means that we must part; I have known it many days. But oh, heart of my heart," she cried, "you will not forget?"

Thus she spoke to the vain foolish boy, patting his cheek and trying to keep back the tears.

"I will remember you when I am a rich and famous poet, yes, Joanna..."

"You—you are kind, Francesco..."

He kissed her quietly, and then he went away, up over the hill of the tree, whence he took with him a white rose. And when he had gone she stared out steadily, with her lips twitching. Finally she sank down under the tree—motionless, with her black hair against the white blossoms, and her black lashes against her white cheeks. But more petals drifted down...

* * *

Madonna Lucrezia Borgia,[7] with her yellow hair and her half-shut eyes, would wander among the flowers in the blue garden.

The old gods had not yet fled from Rome. The popes might humble Zeus, but they could not find Pan. He was off in the woods, piping, and you might see his brown sly face peering from bushes. Ever as dusk came the groves whispered with ghosts, and the moon upon the stone walks made you think of those you had loved before they died. For the hills are lonely, but pressing up and crying to you are the dead. It is one thing that man may not express—the deep longing, the doubt and ache and wonder—and moving through it all black Dante, with his lantern-lit face and eyes of pain...Dark mother Italy....

Here was Madonna Lucrezia's villa, away from the acclamation in Rome when her father was elected pope. Here lay the blue garden, and between lines of cypresses was the pool which mirrored the Greek temple at its end, and through white columns of the temple shone the stars. This night Madonna Lucrezia stood by the pool, the yellow hair in braids over the white of her cloak. Affairs of state had not yet concerned her; she was young, with soft shining life. Her eyes were clearest blue.

Francesco the shepherd boy appeared from the cypresses. He moved toward her, and he knelt by the pool against the blue-lit temple.

"Oh, Madonna," he said breathlessly, "I am here, for that night we met you bade me return. That was when I first loved you, madonna mia. And yet I am but a peasant lad, though soon—"

They spoke in whispers, brokenly, and sometimes the vain boy laughed. While she murmured, she gave him a rose in the way of lovers, which seeks to preserve memory in tokens. She gave him a rose from the red cluster she wore at her girdle. It had grown beside the water. And she told him how love had come from the dim waters, an ancient tale of a blind man, but she said that until the waters were all dried away love

---

7 Carr's fictional episode in Lucrezia Borgia's life remains uncomfortably close to the truth in some respects. While Lucrezia would only have been 11 or 12 at this time, she had already been engaged twice (for the sake of political alliances), and in the following year, was married for the first of three times. Carr's inspiration for her love affair with the fictive poet Francesco may be inspired by Lucrezia's real-life adultery with the poet Pietro Bembo, which transpired during her third marriage.

could not die. To the sophistry of smiling, moving lips he bent, and the white rose that he had taken from the hill fell all tattered at his feet...[8]

* * *

Now history spoke with a voice of bugles. Weeks passed, and the armies of Rome were never still. How the gallant, crafty-eyed Cesare Borgia, brother of Lucrezia, had battered into cities and left them afire—how the French king trembled for his Italian possessions—how Cesare went striking straight at Naples—these are matters for the chronicler. Fire, sword, and poison, ever the din of cannon while the pope watched greedily. Men shut their ears as all the devils of Lucifer went hallooing across Europe. The rolling of drums had announced a new empire. There had come a cruel set to Lucrezia's mouth when she contemplated her power. She laughed more often, and she planned more often; with her father and brother, she ruled Rome.

All this time Madonna Lucrezia's young favorite had been taken over by tutors, who flattered his verses because Lucrezia ordered it. There were tailors to clothe him in black velvet, cut with ermine, and jaunty caps. Rome loved him; he was so haughty and handsome, with his spoiled mouth. They cheered as he rode through the streets among the spears, lifting his eyebrows to toss gold to beggars. From Nicolo Machiavelli he learned statecraft;[9] there he would stand, murmuring with lowered eyelids to the falcon on his wrist, while the tutors smirked about him, or he would engage in splendid swordplay to shouts of applause. But none ever heard of his poems.

One evening a troop of horsemen came to Lucrezia's villa, jingling in armor, with Cesare Borgia riding at their head like a centaur. Under the torchlight he stood before the gates, with his narrow pale face pointed into a brown beard, and the half-shut, sardonic eyes like his sister's. Then he smiled in a way that kindled the eyes—the suspicious and cunning smile of his family. When the gates were opened he strode in to Lucrezia.

She sat in a white room that was lit with candles tall as pillars, a round chaplet of fire. Shadows fell flat below them. In the carven chair

---

8 Carr's perhaps awkwardly overt white rose-red rose symbolism (innocent love versus lust) here is the mark of an apprentice writer, but also redeems itself a bit through its evocation of the English War of the Roses, which comes into resonance with this tale. The editor encourages the reader to note how Carr exploits the War of the Roses trope and how he ties it to an unexpected outcome in a manner consistent with the dramatic irony of Carr's detective fiction.

9 Francesco's tutelage by Machiavelli is a subtle joke on Carr's part, since that figure's enduring work, *The Prince*, was in large part modeled on Cesare Borgia's machinations toward power.

she was hard and lovely, the bare shoulders and the rippling bright hair and the smiling mouth. Ugly, that smile was reflected between them, like a mirror...

Presently they walked in the garden, where the guard's torches glimmered red among the cypress trees. He spoke to her of battles and plans. Then he kissed her roughly, heavily, so that she breathed fast...A watcher might have shuddered....

"And so," he went on, "so, my sister, it is necessary that you take a husband. When nations do not know how else to arrange a quarrel, they marry about it. Here am I returned, after hanging all manner of people, and find that such exercise is to be set at naught unless we can make some swinish Spaniard your husband[10]—Ah, mother of Christ, but you are beautiful!"

There was a silence.

"Then as to another matter," continued Cesare, suddenly brutal, as though his head had whirled about like a figure of Janus and revealed another face; "this Francesco of yours must be done away with, you understand? Our Spanish friend does not approve, nor does our father—"

"Our father!"

"Well, then, nor do I!"

"You are bruising my wrist," she said sweetly. And then she laughed. "Why, he shall be done away with; not because it is your will, but because it is mine. These self-confessed poets—bah, Cesare! He is a vain pompous nobody; it will do me good to see him humbled. Look you: the boy has a quick tongue; we will make him our jester. He shall wear bells and motley. Will it not be amusing to see that face which prates of greatness draped in a green hood—bells and motley—"

They were very near a marble seat by the end of the pool. A person had been sitting there quietly, fumbling with a bush of white roses. Now it emerged from shadow.

"I have worn them long, madonna!" cried Francesco.

He came slowly out into the moonlight, and the pale face was torn with puzzled sick wrath. He stared at them, the mouth struggling in hate. Now there was no jauntiness in his cap; his fingers plucked at the rose.

---

10 Carr is departing only minimally from the historical timeline. Despite her being 11 years old, Lucrezia's first two engagements were in 1491; both were annulled, but they were to Spanish noblemen: Don Cherubino Joan de Centelles, and then Don Gaspare Aversa, count of Procida. Her father Rodrigo's ascension as Pope Alexander VI made Lucrezia more valuable to him to secure the new pope's Italian alliances, and so he gave her in marriage in 1493 to Giovanni Sforza, the Lord of Pesaro and Gradaro and a distant cousin to Cardinal Ascanio Sforza.

"You baby!" said Cesare.

Lucrezia saw that the whole pretense had fallen away with abrupt and ghastly revelation; she did not attempt to restore it. Instead she began to bait him, as she had often longed to do. She leaned and smiled.

"Why, yes; bells—and a bauble for a shepherd's crook. You ought to thank us, Francesco—"

He knew that he was being goaded, writhing like a fly on a pin with these faces and soft voices before him. The horrible fury of it mounted...

"But was not his father a swineherd—" began Cesare in a tone of surprise; then with a smash Francesco had come out with the truth about Cesare's own parentage.[11]

Lucrezia had no time to finish her sentence, "He is fit to lead sheep into a shambles!—" when a rush of cloaks darkened an instant on the moon. It merged into a scream. Francesco had flung up an arm as though in a gesture of farewell, after which sword and dagger were flashing in the moonlight. Francesco had drawn just as Cesare lunged.

A surge of halberds, a crackling of bushes! The soldiers were crowding in with uplifted torches, a glare that lit the whirling blades. And in the midst of it there was Cesare laughing, and Francesco fighting by the pool, head erect and the white rose in his teeth....

"Stand back!" Cesare shouted, gurgling with laughter; "let no man move—"

It became a distorted thing—Francesco's staring eyes over the rose, and Cesare's giggling. They shifted and stamped—*ring—ring*—monotonously terrible. Over and under—snick! that thrust grazed the cheek! A shuddering sound as a dagger-arm fell on a shoulder. Hands growing red. *Clack—ring—*

Silence; the men in armor stood motionless, holding up their torches, and Lucrezia was watching calmly, with a faint smile...*Would it never cease?* Wilder and faster!...Cesare had stopped laughing, and breathed in great wheezing gasps, exposing his teeth. The dirty swineherd's son— humiliation before his soldiers—brace! The boy's sword is out of line now; he knows he's done for...why, he's a coward; his eyes are growing wide!... The double riposte—and then, flash! straight in with the rapier. *Now!*...

"Joanna!"

It was a single wild cry, when the rose dropped from Francesco's teeth. They heard him cursing them in an unearthly voice even as Cesare

---

11   Cesare was the illegitimate half-brother to Lucrezia, conceived by Rodrigo in 1475 with Giovanna "Vannozza" dei Cattanei, mistress to the then-Cardinal.

withdrew his blade; struggling, Francesco tumbled backwards into the pool. His face was only a moment in sight.

Cesare stood leaning on his sword, staring at the red-lit agitated water. And upon it now floated only the white rose.

***

That was a long time ago. It is strange how fierce overpowering people seem so small—and inconsequential—when they are riddled through with crossbow bolts, as Cesare was seventeen years afterwards. People began to smile at him then; was he not dead? Tiny and helpless on a petty battlefield like a mean dog. With him the might of the Borgia name was apt to be forgotten in knowing looks and quirks. Already before him his father the pope had been poisoned by young Garcini della Trebbia, another of Lucrezia's lovers.[12] And presently Lucrezia's beauty, which had driven men (inexplicably) to crime, was leaving her. She was Duchess of Ferrara now, honored and a bit pitied.

There she sat, nodding far into the sixteenth century. Why, the great man now was bluff Harry, king of England, a handsome young blade, and one who could never be old and perhaps gouty like Lucrezia. The world was full of tournaments. Silks and fine words, lighted barges on the Thames, roystering ballads and plumed hats. Why was it so dark in Italy?

Brave with painted cheeks and dyed hair, though shrunken of face, Lucrezia would haunt Rome. To all who would listen she told of her lovers, laughing roguishly.[13] She was carried about the streets in her chair, that she might peer out and ogle ever so slightly. To her maids she confessed that she had conceived a new passion, the last love of her life, but

---

12 Garcini della Trebbia appeared in a 1926 Carr detective story, "As Drink the Dead" (published in the 1980 Carr collection, edited by Douglas Greene, *The Door to Doom*), the detective-hero of which is Ludwig von Arnheim, whom readers of 2022's *The Kindling Spark* will have met in "The New Canterbury Tales." In "As Drink the Dead," Carr credits della Trebbia with the invention of a mysterious chalice, the Trebbia cup, which by an act of divine punishment poisoned Alexander VI and Cesare for their sinfulness, but spared della Trebbia. Likely, the Pope actually died of food poisoning. He and Cesare both fell ill after dining with Cardinal Adriano Castellesi on August 6, 1503. While his father did not, Cesare recovered.

13 Readers of *The Kindling Spark* will doubtless note the resemblance between Lucrezia Borgia and Carr's Duquesa Lucrezia, the eponymous bella duquesa of the final legend in "The New Canterbury Tales." The historical Lucrezia was an inspiration for Carr's *femme fatale*.

the only one—the only one! She yearned for this new leader in Rome, whom men called Il Duce.[14]

Once she had met him, at a banquet to which her name entitled her an invitation. All about him bustled rumors of strife; they said that he schemed to be dictator. The papal party would oppose him, and, of course, the worn people would sigh and rise again to fight...A tall, heavy man was Il Duce, with a powerful face, repulsively ugly because it was scarred half-blind with sword cuts like an old door. One eye perpetually bloodshot, a misshapen nose, and a mouth not quite true to fine, all brown with battle. He used to bluster about in full armor, a gusty figure that flayed and cursed. And yet somehow he did not seem so imposing, except to Lucrezia. She dreamed of new power at his side.

Uneasiness crept about Rome that summer day. Faint like an echo came a stir of what the city had once known—the Genoese twanging their crossbows and singing, big men gulping down wine in the saddle and then clattering away hell-for-leather to some unknown place, striped fools doing their contortions before a crowd. But the old thrill was not there. A broken, blind pope sat in the Vatican and tried to be brave though the English king had laughed at him. Sometimes there were Caesars. This was unconvincing....

Lucrezia did not understand; with the pulse-beat of war all about her, she felt tired, and the bracelets weighed her arms. Her thousand courtiers—were that many people in Rome itself? she pondered. With the coming of dusk she left the city, bidding her escort carry her into the hills lest Il Duce should march in and cause any half-hearted bloodshed. That was how she came to the blue garden.

The blue garden...she had not seen it for many years. The old tenderness was in the air, more achingly beautiful because it too was about to go. Down the vista of cypresses she wandered, where the rank grass grew by a dried pool and by the naked columns. Her skinny face glistened in the moonlight, wistful. She was in half a trance. Il Duce had not seemed pleased with her coquettish ways, and the fashion in which she had tapped his arm with her fan....

Was that a noise? With the vague haze of a sleep she realized that a

---

14 While of course the sixteenth-century figure using this title is fictional, note that at the time Carr wrote this story, Mussolini had already been named prime minister in Italy (1922). Mussolini's cognomen, Il Duce, goes back, ironically, to his installation in 1912 as editor-in-chief of *Avanti* (the Italian socialist daily newspaper). Carr was probably aware of this. Before Mussolini, Garibaldi, the great uniter of Italy, was informally celebrated as Il Duce, and in 1915, Victor Emmanuel III even proclaimed himself *Duce Supremo.*

troop of horsemen had come pounding up to the gates, where she had left her own retainers. The newcomers carried torches, moving among the trees. This could not be real. Now, if it should be Cesare, riding up to greet her after he had been dead so many years, all stuck through with crossbow bolts—A blaze of torches in the temple, the pressing of many curious faces in steel caps. There was Il Duce, in rusty armor, standing out from them while he grinned with his hacked face. His thin beard waggled when he grinned.

"Duchess," roared Il Duce, "duchess, you are keeping a last tryst..."

She was bewildered. But she advanced coquettishly, swinging her skirts and greeting him with coy welcome. He came toward her, very pompous.

"Listen!" he said, "listen, and you will hear my cavalry go down to Rome. I have five-score men, duchess! There, you hear it? Soon they will sound the chimes of St. Peter's—and that will be a signal, madonna! It will be a signal for slaughter."

Suddenly she realized that it roused no emotion in her. He was thundering out the words with such boasting that it seemed a travesty.

"Once you told me," went on Il Duce fiercely, "that I was fit only to lead sheep to a shambles. Behold me now, madonna, and see what years as a soldier have done. Now, by the living God, you shall have your shambles in a city where you once ruled. Your slaughter, and I caused it!"

The sound of the army was faint. Here only a strutting, posing boy, with hacked face. Madonna Lucrezia looked at him, hysterical.

"You know me, then?" he said, and he leered. The beard was still waggling.

She shut her eyes.

"Francesco!" she murmured; then, faintly: "Oh, blood of saints—Francesco!" After a long silence she spoke with petulance:

"You could have spared me this, Francesco; seeing you cut in the face—"

"I will be supreme dictator!" proclaimed the man in rusty armor.

"No, Francesco...No! You are crying..."

The face seemed absurd, with tears upon it, especially with the tears of self-pity which had sprung up from some time that was nearly forgotten. These two were simply an old man and an old woman.

Francesco turned with a snarl.

"I have hated you, Lucrezia! But I have won now," he said. "Here am I famous, a ruler, and what are you? Old! Pah, and how ugly! The night your brother knocked me in the pool and left me for dead, you did not suspect that I should return—like this—and laugh..."

"Yes! You are crying!"

But though she tried to be dignified, she knew that he had succeeded. It was merely his presence; it was merely that he saw an old woman...But there was peace in the garden, and calmness. It had never been so quiet there as when he moved over and took her hand. Old lost things were coming back like a melody. They were close enough to the ghosts to hear them whisper...Presently these two were side by side on the marble bench, very subdued. It was not complete bitterness. It was that thing which man may not express—the deep longing, the doubt and ache and wonder, and moving through it all black Dante,[15] with his lantern-lit face and eyes of pain...

"We have loved each other, Francesco—"

From far over the hills drifted the chime of St. Peter's that was the signal. Francesco raised his head. Even here Francesco postured, blinking his bleary eyes.

"The jester's bells!" he said.

---

15 Carr is invoking comparison with Paolo and Francesa da Rimini, the doomed, sinful lovers who capture the pilgrim's sympathy in the second circle of Dante's *Inferno*.

Notes for the Curious: "The Blue Garden"

Despite this story's being historical in genre, its central character, Lucrezia Borgia, is of a type common across all Carr's fiction, very much including his detective fiction. This makes "The Blue Garden" a useful jumping-off point for observing some of Carr's representative approaches to character.

> I saw pale kings and princes too,
>   Pale warriors, death-pale were they all;
>   They cried—"La Belle Dame sans Merci
>   Hath thee in thrall!"

In the biography, Douglas Greene, drawing upon the title and climactic stanza of Keats' ballad, "La Belle Dame Sans Merci," groups the problematic women in several of Carr's 1926 tales as "women who bait and betray men" (p. 49). Greene specifically cites Lucrezia Borgia, an important background character in Carr's impossible-crime mystery, "As Drink the Dead";[1] Denise Aubley, of "The Red Heels"; and the Señorita Dolores (the derivation of whose name, a bit unsubtly, promises sorrow and pain), the titular "Dim Queen" of Carr's historical story.

In creating this last character, Carr had in mind Swinburne's poem, "Dolores (Notre-Dame des Sept Douleurs)." Swinburne was a favorite poet of Carr's, and Swinburne's *belle dame* an effective description of Carr's own Dolores. Consider the first stanza of Swinburne's poem:

> Cold eyelids that hide like a jewel
>   Hard eyes that grow soft for an hour;
> The heavy white limbs, and the cruel
>   Red mouth like a venomous flower;
> When these are gone by with their glories,
>   What shall rest of thee then, what remain,
> O mystic and sombre Dolores,
>   Our Lady of Pain?

The poem remained a Carr favorite. He returned to it in three times

---

1 Readers interested to read these two very good early Carr tales can find them in Douglas Greene's collection of short fiction by Carr, *Fell and Foul Play* (published by International Polygonics).

in his detective novels: Jeff Marle cites it to himself dreamily, knocked mentally off balance by Gina Prévost's charms in *The Corpse in the Waxworks*: "O mystical rose of the mire—!" (p. 161); in *The Crooked Hinge* (p. 230), after ironically reciting several lines of Wordsworth's "She Was a Phantom of Delight" ("A perfect woman, nobly planned...") Dr. Fell combines them sardonically with the first two lines from "Dolores," assigning that lady's "charms" to the novel's creepy automaton, the *Golden Hag*; and in *She Died a Lady* (1943), Rita Wainright, seemingly without realizing the implications, confesses her husband Alec's nickname for her: "He used to call me Dolores. After Swinburne's Dolores, you know" (p. 22). Carr also has his radio detective Dr. Fabian recite the poem's first stanza in 1948's *The Count of Monte Carlo* when he learns that Bart Stevens' troubling *amoureuse* is called Dolores. Stevens confesses:

> She attracted me; it burned up everything like a forest. I couldn't think; I couldn't see; I couldn't reason! I wasn't in love with Dolores. I'm not even sure I liked her. But she hypnotized me with an attractiveness that—now do you understand?[2]

Greene traces this motif of the siren throughout Carr's professional works, summarizing his observation this way:

> With only a few exceptions—especially Eve Neill in *The Emperor's Snuff-Box*—his women are described from the viewpoint of men, and much more obviously than the male protagonists they are types rather than individuals. Carr's stories written at Haverford show him attracted to but afraid of women. Over and over he had used the image of the seductive woman who lures men to their destruction...He objected to anyone...who seemed to take the romance and mystery out of sex. (p. 278)

There certainly are numerous *femmes fatales* throughout Carr's works, beginning early and often. Considering only Carr's juvenilia, in addition to the three cited by Greene, Carr's apprenticeship stories also include: Jeanne Darin, who appears in "The Ruby of Rameses"; Marcia Gallivan of "The Will-o'-the-Wisp"; Lady Joan Gardline, in "The Harp of Tairlaine"; Lucrezia Borgia, here in "The Blue Garden"; Hildegarde, the old lord's daughter in "The Legend of the Black Monk"; the unnamed

---

2 Collected in *The Island of Coffins*, p. 97.

German temptress, she of the softest lips in "The Legend of the Softest Lips"; the Lady Joyaunce, center of the unhappy love triangle in "The Legend of the Neckband of Carnelians"; the Duquesa Lucrezia, the eponymous sexual predator in "The Legend of the Bella Duquesa"; and *Grand Guignol*'s duchess, Louise de Saligny. Arguably others.

While the *belle dame sans merci* designation fits well enough a too-long list in Carr's works of this problematic staple character, the present editor finds it useful to parse this category in the context of Carr's key influences. What Greene labels the *belle dame sans merci* closely correlates to the "black" variety in James Branch Cabell's categorization of women into several sorts of witches. (Cabell was one of the five authors Carr cited as being most influential upon him.) Cabell wrote of:

> "white witches" who could help, but not hurt; "black witches," who could hurt, but not help; and "gray witches", who could do either at will....in dreams man has shown no aversion to the witch-woman...but, to the contrary, man has always clung, with curious tenacity, to the notion of some day attaining the good graces of that fair-haired and delicate-voiced witch who is a bane to men, and yet sometimes takes mortal lovers.[3]

Carr's diction aligned with Cabell's; the number of instances in his fiction in which a woman is described (affectionately or otherwise) as a witch is, effectively, too many to count.

As limited in variety and usually unrealistic as Carr's depictions of women are, Cabell's catalog reminds us that Carr modeled his leading women, if almost always according to unoriginal types (and for that matter, his men, too), on a number of familiar categories. Scattered throughout the early tales readers can also find a considerable company of Cabell's "white" and "gray" witches: Julia Mansfield ("The Marked Bullet," and she a little closer to being a genuine female protagonist); Peggy Lynn ("The Kindling Spark"); the Lady Katherine Ness and the Princess Jeanne ("The Blindfold Quest"); albeit *in absentia*, Jane Wainwright ("Candlelight: A Ghost Story of Christmas"); Virginia Bower ("The Gordon Djinn"); the Lady Ippolita ("The Legend of the Hand of Ippolita"); and Marguérite, in *Grand Guignol*.

Cabell's witches are not the sole recognizable category among Carr's women. Equally consequential among Carr's female protagonists are ingé-

---

3 *Beyond Life*, Robert M. McBride and Company, 1924, pp. 61-69. All subsequent excerpts are drawn from the same edition.

nues. In the early works, readers meet Milly Langwith (in "The Cloak of D'Artagnan") and Lady Elizabeth Howard ("That Ye Be Not Judged"), who are ingénues, not Cabellian witch-types at all. While the ingénue is an often-unflattering female cliché, Carr readers encounter ingénues plentifully, even more plentifully than *belles dames sans merci,* in his detective novels. They are important; even more important, in Carr's view, is the reader's initial inability to discern whether a woman is one or the other:

> In fact, you can seldom have a good case without a fascinating woman....Was she guilty? Was she not guilty? Did she think about murder—but refrain? Or was she only a dimpled innocent lurking amid the curtains?[4]

Carr's insistence on the romance and mystery of sex relies upon these two types in particular, seductresses and ingénues, the latter often unaware or only partially conscious of (even conflicted over) their raw sexual appeal. Occasionally, Carr lets the reader understand that he knows better; consider Stella Lacey's complaint in *Night at the Mocking Widow*:

> "...I've flirted a little, yes. But on one side they say I'm a kind of—of a Messalina. On the other side they say I haven't blood enough to be interested. Will, I'm neither! I'm an ordinary human being, with feelings and temptations like anyone else." (p. 197)

Despite knowing better, Carr only occasionally creates his women characters with corresponding layers of sophistication. More typically, he treats them in a manner consistent with that a character of his, Patrick Butler, professes in Below Suspicion:

> "You exalt the sex," Butler told him dryly. "Now I love 'em, mind you! I love their ways and their eyes and their lips." He mentioned other charms as well. "But I keep 'em in their place..." (p. 2)

While Butler, like his author, is possessed of a "very real streak of eighteenth-century gallantry, which underlay all his bombast" (p. 65), we

---

4 From the forward to John Williams' *Suddenly at The Priory*, Heinemann, 1957, p. ix.

nonetheless perceive that chivalry, in Carr's works and in his person, unfortunately does not always rise above sexism.

Women's existing in Carr's works so much from the male perspective and for the male gaze, in the frequency and flagrancy with which they do, can test the modern reader's patience. It is difficult, without groaning in disappointment, to read lines (typical of Carr's handling of women) such as Miles Hammond's admission to Dr. Fell in *He Who Whispers* (p. 139): "We don't fall in love with a woman because of her good character."

As ugly as that sentiment is, Carr could occasionally be even uglier. Perhaps the most troublesome demonstration of this is the narrator's explanation for the female of the species in *She Died a Lady*, which is as toxic (and more) an assessment of women than any uttered (for a pertinent comparison) by the misogynistic Sherlock Holmes, whose failing both his author and readers recognize and deplore. Occasionally, Conan Doyle even mocks Holmes' contempt for women. In *She Died a Lady*, while the misogynistic thoughts expressed are explicitly those of the narrator, old Doctor Luke Croxley—and without spoiling any plot details, they prove to be heavily, dramatically ironic—Carr's reader is nonetheless never fully confident that there exists that same distance between the views of his characters and their author's as does between Conan Doyle and Holmes. This is Dr. Luke's assessment of women:

> Though it is dangerous to make generalities, this was far from being the first time in my life when I have observed the absolute incapacity of any woman for telling the truth when truth becomes unsuitable. There is no intent to do wrong in this. To the female sex, it simply does not matter. Truth is relative; truth is fluid; truth is something to be measured according to the emotional needs, like Adolf Hitler's. (pp. 200–201)

It is difficult to salvage any benefit of the doubt for Carr from that passage.

But are women in Carr's works nothing more than reflections of a parochial, twentieth-century sexism? (Carr, if no worse than his times in this respect, was unfortunately no better.) His women characters are that, but not solely. There is a more purposeful catalyst of Carr's sexist approach to women: in his mind, none of his characters exist, whether male or female, as they might in literary novels. In literary novels, characters exist for their own interest, for exploration of them believably as people, often in support of observations concerning social structures or the human experience—but *the single authorial purpose of Carr's characters is to be mechanisms driving storylines.* Even that relatively shocking sexist statement from *She Died a Lady* reveals that Carr only cares about feminine stereotypes to the degree these facilitate plot possibilities (and again, that passage turns out to be much more revelatory of Dr. Luke than of the novel's women). To Carr, such generalized, "recognizable" feminine characteristics are conveniences, bases he exploits for (as Greene puts it, p. 267) "explaining the *how* rather than the *why* of human behavior." Carr's is a utilitarian, populist psychology expedient to the writer of detective fiction—not a deliberate aspersion (although, again, a lack of malice does not annul the sexism).

Still—and this is what explains Carr's handling of them, whether through sexism or other clichéd approaches—as depictions of people, Carr's characters, male and female both, are only as interesting, on the rare occasion only as layered, as Carr needs each to be. The different character types in which Carr trades, while hardly innumerable in variety, all exist to precipitate the various dramatic conflicts and situations in his works—right down to minor types such as "the funny landlady, the doddering lord, the silly-ass young man, the peppery Colonel Blimp who says, 'Gad, Sir!',"[5] etc. True, the character types Greene identifies in the biography are among Carr's more frequently used ones, employed to pervasive effect, but none of Carr's character types are statements or social arguments; they are nothing more than instruments in the service of his foremost narrative priority (*The Devil In Velvet*, p. 333): "The first duty of any novelist, a duty so often forgotten nowadays, is to tell a story."

Greene raises two excellent points in explanation of Carr's practical-minded approach to drawing characters (p. 278):

> Another point must be kept in mind. In a detective story, the reader cannot know everything about a character or there is no mystery. In understanding the works of John Dickson Carr and in fact almost all masters of detective fiction, the point is not so much comprehending a character as believing in him or her and in the role he or she plays in the story.
>
> Moreover, Carr sometimes uses the reader's expectations that he is dealing merely in character types as a tool to misdirect suspicion. He knew that people are complicated, that their

---

5 This is Carr's own list of overused British character types, taken from *The Cavalier's Cup*, p. 10. The walrus-mustached, Colonel Blimp was a famous, stereotypical cartoon character created in 1934 who, wrapped in a towel, satirically pontificated his reactionary views while luxuriating in a Turkish bath. Carr's Colonel George Bailey (*Night at the Mocking Widow*), as one example, seems to have a hint of Colonel Blimp in his character.

motives are ambiguous. He used human ambiguities—and the fact that masks may not be the same as what they hide… people whom he describes as "good natured" or "kindly"… under the right (or wrong) circumstances…might also be killers. The charming rogue who seems to be included…merely for comic relief, the fussy lawyer whose role appears to be to supply evidence, the young policeman who is a friend of the narrator—each of these might turn out to be a murderer in John Dickson Carr's books.

Carr's dependence upon types does not indicate an inability to draw sophisticated or convincing characters, but rather, it reflects his conscious and intentional, literary familial descent as an author within the traditions of historical and Gothic romances, as he updates these traditions within the detective novel. The literary ancestors Carr acknowledges (allusions to them occur throughout his works), most of them romanticists, are all great storytellers, none among the drier figures of the canon— some of course not dignified with places in the academic canon at all. One particularly amusing demonstration of Carr's fealty to them, and his rejection of the "literary" canon, takes place in *Night at the Mocking Widow*:

> "…And, speakin' of windows, here are these three Russian crutch-walkers on the table by the bed. We'd better get rid of 'em now."
>
> There was a whirr of leaves and then three separate thuds as Dostoevski, Tolstoy, and Checkov flew out of the open window and struck the bole of an oak tree.
>
> "The idea is," explained H.M., "I want you to read some fellers named Dumas and Mark Twain and Stevenson and Chesterton and Conan Doyle. They're dead, yes; but they can still whack the britches off anybody at tellin' a story…" (p. 187)

If Carr only rarely supersedes genre, he reliably, even expertly, fulfills it for his modern audience. One of the core characteristics of a literary romance being a happy conclusion, while one might distinguish narrowly between Carr's "merely" historical tales ("The Blue Garden," for instance) and his fully-to-type historical romances, all of them draw upon the same compositional elements and techniques. There is no practical distinction between his "happy ending" literary romances and his others when enumerating the kinds of characters Carr creates. Given this, what we observe about characters in Carr's juvenilia we can reliably apply to assessing characters across all Carr's works, across all the decades of his career.

Yes, in certain respects, Carr continues with time to grow as a writer, to handle some characterizations better, and to experiment with how he draws characters. In the end, though, Carr's characterizations remain driven primarily by his inheritance from Romanticism and from literary and Gothic romances, traced not only from Cabell, but from Sir Walter Scott, Robert Louis Stevenson, Alexandre Dumas, Horace Walpole, Ann Radcliffe, and other Carr favorites.

In this spirit, consider the *New York Times*'s review of *Devil Kinsmere*, when (upon publication) all that was known of the novel's author was that Roger Fairbairn was "the pseudonym of an American author whose previous writing has been along different lines."[6] Acknowledging that the book had already been acclaimed in England as "the work of a new Stanley Weyman,"[7] the reviewer writes admiringly of Carr's characters, identifying them as one of the book's strengths:

> The historical portraits, though obviously intended only as background, are dashed onto the canvas with strength and color. They are in no sense caricatures but the author has laid the same emphasis on idiosyncrasy as does the caricaturist. The King's careless jollity masking uncommon shrewdness, Lady Castlemaine's uneasy insolence, the Duke of York's goggling stupidity and the self-effacingness of the neglected Queen are indelibly impressed upon us, however brief may be the appearance of the individual in question.
>
> It is in its imaginary characters, however, that the book scores most noticeably. Besides the two devil-may-care Kinsmeres there are the glum villain, Ratty Harker; Pirate Souter, a likable rascal; Bygones Abraham, a hard-drinking old plotter; and, for love interest, Dolly Landis, an actress; every one of them as large as life and quite as real.

Similarly, consider the praise masked as a "defense" of the young Carr, in a review of *The Lost Gallows* published in his hometown newspa-

---

6 *The New York Times Book Review*, February 10, 1935, p. 7. All subsequent excerpts are from the same article and page.

7 An English historical novelist popular and admired in his time, who published between 1890-1928.

per the Uniontown *Daily News Standard*. Doubtless penned by his close friend O'Neil Kennedy, the review responds to notices acknowledging Carr's strength of writing, but which criticize him for stooping to detective fiction:

> Critics have accused Carr of too fine writing for detective thrillers and some have even bemoaned the fact that he has harnessed such splendid literary gifts to the mystery vehicle... But we do not hold that he is at fault in bestowing fine writing to his mystery stories. We rather believe he will confound his critics by creating classics to endure for future generations to stand side-by-side on bookshelves with Conan Doyle and other great ones.[8]

To weigh Carr as a "modern" novelist, deficient in characterization as compared to Sinclair Lewis, Edith Wharton, D.H. Lawrence, E.M. Forster, and others is a mistake of misunderstanding. Carr's characters represent not what he *could* do with them, but what he *would* do with them. In the afterword to *The Devil in Velvet*, Carr explains the best of entertaining interchanges between characters as being "fireworks displays of wit...a combination of the adolescent and the sophisticated" (p. 333). In other words, Carr's are staple, traditional romance characters, plus accompanying types, developed only to a certain level of sophistication, the level at which each serves Carr's narrative purposes.

This same inheritance comes equally from Carr's detective-fiction influences, including Arthur Conan Doyle, G.K. Chesterton, Wilkie Collins, Thomas and Mary Hanshew, Gaston Leroux, and other crime-fiction writers even less familiar to most readers today. Carr worked not so much within limitations of skill as he did consciously within the traditions he cherished.

What's more, character typing was the usual practice among GAD (Golden Age of Detection) authors; the limited degree of character development in Carr's novels is consistent with the detective fiction of that period generally, especially of the more successful authors, attesting not only to the differentiation of detective fiction as a genre, but broadly, to audience expectations for it, as measured by commercial success. Character expectations during the Golden Age of Detection were, in fact, consciously universal between not only authors and readers, but publishers, too. Consider as one example Dodd, Mead's editorial guide-

---

8 "Current Comment", Uniontown *Daily News Standard*, March 4, 1931, p. 4.

lines, published in its prospectus detailing the rules of the publisher's (semi-) annual Red Badge contest for the best mystery-detective novel:

> The *detective* is the most important figure in the story and must be the intellectual hero of the case. Characterization of the other persons in the novel (except the detective and the villain) should be plausible and interesting without intruding on the plot or distracting from the puzzle.[9]

This contest to discover and publish new talent, which featured a $1,000 prize and publication, launched careers as notable as those of Hugh Pentecost, Christianna Brand, and Clifford Knight.

Consistent with this, in a contemporary study of thrillers and detective novels, Basil Hogarth advised would-be writers of detective fiction:

> Your function is not that of a biographer, but of a novelist. Accordingly you do not aim at painting full-length portraits in your novel; you are content to seize the salient characteristics, so that they impress the reader and enable him to identify each character by his mannerisms and traits. [10]

Carr agreed, himself writing:

> To set his mind at work on a problem, the reader must have every character vivid and distinct in his mind; he must be able to watch the turn of their eyes and hands; he must be close enough, in short, to see blood on their cuffs. Hence we must concentrate attention on a leading group of characters, and leave others as names or voices in the shadow.[11]

---

9 Dodd, Mead returned this prospectus by post to inquirers, who generally learned of the contest from the dustjacket flaps of the publisher's current titles. The prospectus detailed an acrostic eight-point test for entries, the initial letters of which spelled out R-E-D B-A-D-G-E. Dodd, Mead's contest began in 1937 as an annual one, but the publisher did so well with it that in 1941 its contest became semi-annual. Carr wrote for Dodd, Mead once, teaming up as Carter Dickson with Cecil Street (using his John Rhode pseudonym) to write *Fatal Descent*, published in 1939.

10 *Writing Thrillers for Profit: A Practical Guide*, A. & C. Black Ltd, 1936, p. 80. All subsequent excerpts are drawn from the same edition.

11 From the introduction to *The Murder of Sir Edmund Godfrey*, p. 18.

Hogarth understands that this is easier said than done:

> The great "snag" of the detective novel resides undoubtedly in its characterizations. In the ordinary novel, characterization is of supreme importance, indeed it usually constitutes its sole *raison d'être*. Thus J. D. Beresford writing of the orthodox novel form says: "It is the people who count, not the idea, or the plot. The people only do certain things because they are a certain kind of people. The plot comes out of them—comes from being within them. Ideally you should invent your incidents to illustrate your characters."
>
> Now this counsel of perfection is difficult to apply to the detective novel, concerned as it is with plot in which the centre of interest is the crime puzzle around which the novel is woven....in a detective novel...the characters have not a free hand to indulge in all those pleasant excursions and side issues that make the ordinary "straight" novel so comparatively easy to write. These additional suspects...must be created, less for their own intrinsic importance than for their purpose in confusing and side-tracking the reader. They serve to deflect attention from the real criminal. If, however, they are obviously puppets, then the reader will quickly penetrate their real purpose....It is up to the writer to make these suspects real and alive. (pp. 65–78)

Carr would agree with Hogarth concerning the function of secondary characters in a detective novel, but in his essay "The Grandest Game in the World," Carr takes issue with whether characters' words and actions originate merely from plot exigencies:

> No speech in the book is included just because it sounds mysterious, or because it makes a given character look guilty, or because the author doesn't know what the devil his character does mean and simply throws in the words to fill up space. Not at all. In turning over the pages afterwards, the reader can see for himself—how rare it is!—just what each character was *thinking* at any moment....the author has described voice-inflections, shades of feeling...He has not forgotten to study his characters merely because he is writing about them in reverse. That turn of the eyes—of course! That momentary

> hesitation when Betty puts her hand on the window-ledge as though to steady herself—naturally![12]

Carr puts his principle into practical demonstration in *The Crooked Hinge*:

> "When I heard about the claimant to the estate and his lawyer, I knew what John had been thinking. You know now what was in his mind all along. You can follow every step of his thoughts and every word he said. You now know why he smiled, and why the relief was almost too much, when he heard the claimant's story about the seaman's mallet and the blows on the head in the wreck of the *Titanic*..." (p. 192)

All the same, Carr trades deliberately in character types, however organic their motivations. Shorthand, type-based characterizations were prevalent in Carr's work, indeed in all detective fiction of the period. This fact, while surface-evident to any reader of classic detective fiction, is confirmed, too, in academic studies. One such attestation is LeRoy Panek's. In his essay concerning Carr, Panek distills the author's supporting players into "the usual collection...the same crowd that one meets in most of the detective books of the period."[13]

Does any of this deliberateness make Carr a "better" author, in the literary sense, in his handling of characters? Naturally not, but it does properly contextualize Carr's authorial perspective on characters and what made them and the stories in which they were featured viable, both stylistically and commercially.

Even one of Carr's most well-regarded literary ancestors, Charles Dickens (whose Victorian novels may include the requisite literary attention to social issues, but which are in their structure romances), trades in types. The literary romance, as a form, simply demands them—but nobody would derogate Dickens' characters, combinations of the adolescent and the sophisticated, even if one would not equate Dickens' characterizations with those of his more realist contemporaries such as

---

12 This is Carr's longest and best-known literary critical essay, which champions the fair-play mystery. He wrote it as the introduction to an abortive 1947 anthology Carr was to select and introduce for the publisher Crown: *The Ten Best Detective Novels*. The quotation here is from page 10 of Ellery Queen's 1963 issue of Carr's essay in a limited edition that commemorated the eponymous magazine's 22nd anniversary. All subsequent excerpts are drawn from the same edition.

13 *Watteau's Shepherds*, Bowling Green University Popular Press, 1979, p. 168.

Henry James. An almost countless number of Dickens' young, romantic protagonists, male and female alike, are, apart from their names, as otherwise unmemorable and interchangeable with one another as Carr's are. This is a demand of form and an authorial prerogative, not a shortcoming. It is the same for both authors—indeed, in part, Carr learned this approach from Dickens.

Still, Carr recognized the limited range of personalities peopling his works: he wrote, "I wish I could enlarge my range of character types, since I find myself writing about the same old people under different names."[14] This problem became especially acute in the novels written during the final decade of Carr's career. Carr recognized the same risk in his work as Hogarth recognized for the genre:

> In detective fiction, as elsewhere, the principle of the survival
> of the fittest will apply; and only those writers will survive
> who can hold a fairly equal balance between the ingenious
> mechanics of plot-construction and the human interest of
> their characters. (p. 68)

Clearly, Carr has endured, in part because his detective-fiction novels maintain that balance.

There is also in Carr's narratives the occasional convincing and reasonably rounded character, but it is not his rare, more literary characters (for instance, Jimmy O'Brien, the protagonist of "The Kindling Spark") who dependably vitalize Carr's works. Such characters are too infrequently present, even unsuitable for accomplishing what the young Carr defined, in the concluding section of his "New Canterbury Tales," as the author's most important measure:

> If their random talk, scattered through all the pages, has
> entertained one person who reads; if the dash and fire of fly
> ing hoofs has struck one responsive spark; if, when the dim
> window falls, it causes one person excitement or laughter,
> our experiment in pure romanticism will have been a success.

Greene (pp. 277–278) offers helpful insight into why Carr's finite character types do not fail him (which explanation, indeed, applies similarly well to Dickens):

---

14 Letter to Francis Wilford-Smith, September 10, 1967. Also cited by Greene, p. 277.

...When we read a Carr book, we are struck by the lively characterizations; the actors in his detective dramas are anything but cardboard. When we look at his work as a whole, however, we recall the larger-than-life sleuths, but many of the other figures fade in our memories.

The problem with characterizations in Carr's books is not that they are unrealistic but rather that Carr does not vary them enough. The same people appear and reappear with their names but not their natures changed. For example, all of his young visitors to the Continent or England seem alike, and the naïve but passionate female lead is repeated in book after book.

As a counterbalancing technique, Carr, again like Dickens, often lends characters vigor and seeming individuality through their personalized diction, their dialects and accents, their other verbal traits, and the characters' salient, defining physical attributes or behavioral mannerisms. The writerly tools with which Carr constructs these are exposition, description, (character) action, and (character) voice. With respect to voice, Greene argues interestingly (p. 178) that Carr could "differentiate characters by giving each of them different rhythms of speech." Carr focuses the reader's attention on all these constructed attributes such that the underlying, generic emotional complexion of any given character is less noticeable, or in any event, unbothersome. All Carr's supporting characters, as Greene fairly asserts, while they "fade in our memories" over the longer term among such a nearly endless parade of similar denizens in his novels, remain in their moments arresting, sufficiently serving Carr's goals. Carr has a talent for making a stock character's voice and outward characteristics seem cogently, instead, like an individual's. Each character's first purpose is dramatic necessity, but secondarily, in its vivacity, each is an enticement to the reader's interest.

Particular attention to these characters' voices reveals that while Carr's skill for dialog was already emerging during his apprenticeship period, the capable construction of dialog became for him an indispensable skill, one demonstrated purely, for instance, during the more than fifteen years Carr wrote radio dramas—in which he could rely upon very little other than a character's idiomatic voice to capture his audience's attention and sympathetic imagination.

Even Carr's *femmes fatales*, as clichéd as they may be, do not fail to move us: in "The Blue Garden," Lucrezia Borgia is thoroughly unlikable, but unlike the virginal ingénue Joanna with whom Carr contrasts her, Lucrezia fascinates. S.T. Joshi notes, "if Carr had a single strength as a portrayer of character, it is his ability to depict loathsome and hateful figures."[15] "The Blue Garden" helps us understand how Carr (and his successful Romantic predecessors) leveraged this: Francesco's final utterance imparts precisely the small and neat, ironic shock its author intended. In the moments of recall and reflection following the story's closing line, the reader recognizes how efficient Lucrezia's personality, so accessible and affecting, is, precisely because it is a recognized type, not in spite of its being so. Carr balances her destructive malice as one element within the story's admittedly melodramatic, but successful, execution. If Lucrezia had been more realistic, more rounded, if she had been deserving of any redemption, "The Blue Garden" would have been less effective.

---

15 *John Dickson Carr: A Critical Study*, Popular Press, 1990, p. 58. All subsequent excerpts are drawn from the same edition.

That Ye Be Not Judged (1926)

Elizabeth pulled open the lid of the big, rectangular box and peered in at the mass of different-length strings. She touched a short one and a high, sweet sound came out of the box.

The swarthy little music teacher laughed. "No, we do it thus. You see, I press what we call a key. Do you hear that sound? Now I press more and we have music. Soon you will play music as I do."

Elizabeth put the lid down and fingered about the keys for a minute. "You must play more for me, Rosso. I am carried up in the clouds when you press the keys as you did then. Take care that you do not abuse the magic power you have over me, for I am helpless under your spell of music." Then, looking at him laughingly, "My little maid, Ellen, whispered that it was a tool of the devil when the men brought it in this morning. She was afraid to look at it—can that be true?"

"In Florence our great churches have instruments much like this one. Where I played the priest told me I had saved more souls by my playing than he by his praying. 'The wicked men I cannot reach with my entreaties, you bully them into reverence with your solemn organ music' he told me. 'They leave the church when I plead with them, but when you play, they stay 'til you are done. Could I gather here a band of angels with their golden harps, there would be no more wickedness in Florence—the people could not keep a wicked thought in their heads when such sweet music touched their ears.'

"Ah, no, it is a holy instrument—the virginal[1]—in our language 'virginalis'—'proper for a girl'; my lord, your father, chose well when

---

[1] The virginal was an early member of the harpsichord family; it emerged in fifteenth-century Europe. Henry VIII popularized it in England by the purchase of five for use at court. The virginal was contained within its portable, rectangular case and sat easily on a flat surface to be played. Until the seventeenth century, the term "virginal" was used generally to describe any plucked keyboard instrument, but a virginal proper had a single set of strings running parallel to the keyboard, which is clearly the sort Carr evokes here. The virginal's popularity was eclipsed in England during the late seventeenth century by the spinet, a small harpsichord that stood on its own legs and had strings running diagonally to the keyboard. The larger spinet had five octaves, as opposed to the virginal's four, and a beautifully crafted spinet could serve as an elegant point of home décor, just as a piano does in the present day.

he had me bring it to you from Mersenne. The fine ladies of Florence would envy such a beautiful instrument." He flicked a speck of dust from the handsome case of tooled leather and polished wood.

"And you will teach me to save souls with my virginal, Rosso. That will be poor reward indeed for my hours of practice. Tell me, do you think I can get me a lover when I have learned to play as you do?"

Rosso sighed. "I have never had but one love," he said, "that has been my music. I have no room for any other. But your heart is large, my lady. You may love many things—that they will all find room in your heart I am certain."

"You speak prettily to me, Rosso. However, I will do well to be safe and not practice too often or too long."

Seated before the box, the music teacher ran his fingers caressingly over the keys. He chose first a few bars of an old Italian melody that took Elizabeth out on a leafy, silent lakeshore with the silver beams of an Italian moon rippling the blue-black water. The notes gave her an odd feeling of pain—there were so many of them—and so sweet. She untwisted a blue ribbon from her hair and wound it about her fingers; then she unwound it and tied it in an impossible tangle. The music made her feel so queer, like—she blushed red as it came to her—like being kissed by a handsome fellow with dark hair and ruddy cheeks. It was such unbearably sweet music she half buried her curls in a lacy cushion to escape from it and then strained her ears to hear better and drew up out of the cushion as far as she dared. Then, as she surrendered and sat boldly upright to listen, Rosso swung into a stirring march and the spell was broken; she was watching a scarlet and gold parade in flashing sunlight and when the handsome fellow came riding past on a white horse, she didn't blush and feel like being kissed—only a little.

"Yes, it is my only love. You think it is not enough, my lady. Ah, but she will always be true to me! I can never be jealous of her, for it is my delight to share her with others. When I am sad I spend an hour with her and am glad again. I am satisfied to love her alone. Are you not envious of me?"

"I cannot believe you, Rosso. You must have loved someone once to be able to play as you did just then. But come, we must not sit here talking of love when I should be learning about your ugly black notes and rest marks. What does this jumble of printing mean and how can I ever tell which keys to press by looking at these dots and lines? Quick, Rosso, show me how I may do it."

The little Italian gently drew away the paper that Elizabeth was holding and laid it carefully in his case. "That is the sweetest song in

Europe," he said. "I must see no harm comes to it even from such gentle fingers as yours."

"You do not trust me, Rosso, but I cannot be grieved. Father says no one is to be trusted in these times of treason and strife. I must not say a word about the king or the government, even to you, for the walls have ears and the judges call it treason to ask your neighbor of the king's health. A week ago the old farmer, Peter Orton, older than my grandfather, Rosso, was coming home from the inn a little tipsy. You remember how dry the weather has been? Well, old Peter said to his companion, 'It has not rained, I believe, since King Herod began to rule.' They said it was a treasonable inference and now he is to be hanged like a traitor."

Rosso darted a glance at her. "The wine played him a cruel trick," he said, and deftly shifting the conversation—"a man addles his wits when he gives himself to an evening of drinking—if it happens that he cannot afford to be without them he must pay the price, often a cruel one."

"In this country, yes. There are cruel men in England."

"A man must be cruel to be great."

"But father is not cruel, and he is a great man in the neighborhood."

Rosso thrummed a few bars of melody. "My lord, your father, is very interested in music," he said at length. "He knows many great masters in Europe. Virtung, who designed this wonderful instrument, is his close friend. You English are not as given to music as we continentals, though your poetry is often as musical as our sweetest songs."

"Will you play for father and me tomorrow, Rosso? I will find some English tunes and we will listen to them together, father and I." A gong sounded and a servant appeared in the arched doorway of the room. "You must excuse me now while I find father and take him to dinner. He has a guest tonight whom I have not met—an old acquaintance whose son I know well."

Elizabeth slipped between two heavy draperies of silk into the long hall. The music that still ran through her head made her gayer than usual. Donald's father was going to be at dinner with them tonight! "What a charming young girl," he was going to think. She would blush when they met. No doubt Donald had spoken of her to him and he might be very observant. "How embarrassing that will be," thought Elizabeth. She knew she would look flustered and maybe spill some wine. When Donald had come to their house once for some legal advice from her father, Elizabeth had showed him about the garden. It was springtime and when the walk was over, Donald was busy inventing excuses to come back to the house again. Thereafter each successive visit needed less and less excusing until now he used no excuse at all except the very obvious one that he was in love with Elizabeth.

In the big room at the end of the hall, Elizabeth's father, Sir Giles Howard, was playing a game of chess with his guest. They were deep in the game and pushed the ivory men about the board for some time without speaking. The guest was an iron-gray man, strikingly sad and determined looking. An atmosphere of high-strung nerves, so keyed up that he seemed almost ready to weep.[2] He gave the impression of being a man who hated life thoroughly but was determined not to be beaten by it. However, he smiled pleasantly enough as Sir Giles deftly made off with a pawn, and pulled smoke through a clumsy pipe with evident enjoyment.

"My pipe has saved me until now," he laughed. "I marvel how our fathers played chess without them. A poor player with a good pipe may be a match for a master who has only the pure air of nature to help him win. However, I intend you shall pay for that pawn before long."

Sir Giles arose. "I'm afraid you will have to wait until after we have dined, if you will forgive me," he said. "We are about to go to dinner... Elizabeth," she had just entered, "allow me to present an old acquaintance, Sir Richard Bohun. Sir Richard, my daughter, Lady Elizabeth Howard. You know Sir Richard's son, Donald, who has called on me often, do you not, Elizabeth?"

Sir Richard rose hurriedly and bowed courteously. He saw a young girl, almost a woman. Dark lashes that curved out over pink and white cheeks and a pure, white throat. He instinctively straightened himself and offered her his arm.

All three chatted pleasantly at dinner. Even Elizabeth, who was little more than a girl, had acquired the faculty, universal among the upper classes of three hundred years ago, of carefully veiling her ulterior motives with a mask of inconsequential conversation that often brought out what would have been evaded were direct questions asked. To be sure, Elizabeth had nothing on her mind more delicate or unmentionable than Donald, but she preferred to dally about with the subject and satisfy her curiosity with hints and allusions as a lady should and does. It gave her a pleasant, warm feeling to find out what she already knew—

---

2 Carr, with a bit more subtlety than in "The Blue Garden," is inviting the reader to compare the guest, Sir Richard, to the virginal, both depicted (Sir Richard metaphorically) as instruments that can be played. As well, music mediates the climax and resolution of this story. Carr's technique here is tighter and more unified than in the earlier tale. As readers witnessed in *The Kindling Spark*, Carr's improvement from one story to the next is perceptible.

that he was in love with her, and she never tired of reassuring herself by making Sir Richard tell her so, though scarcely in so many words. If Sir Giles or his guest dropped anything of importance in their dinner conversation, it was not obtrusively apparent. They chatted about the new fad,[3] the toothbrush, which was unsuccessfully struggling for popularity in the ranks of the more radical English exponents of sanitation. A queer twist of the conversation brought up the subject of the new plays that were showing in London, though indeed the censorship of the Puritans was not discussed.

After the meal was over, the two men went back to the living room and wine was brought. They were jovial after a good dinner and very ready to talk over the affairs of the county with each other. Both being men of the greatest importance in their locality, it was their custom to get together now and again to touch on local business and policies; what went on in the boroughs and how the constable's power was constantly increasing.

Sir Richard was relaxing more in his chair and puffing his pipe less nervously. He was slowly dropping off the strained nervousness that seemed usually to permeate his personality. The wine pleased him. Sir Giles was his friend, his pipe was lighted and he was seated comfortably, ready to have a pleasant talk. He was dangerously near himself. His mask of sophistication was slowly slipping off under the warm glow of the fire and the sweet coolness of the wine.

"Magnificent wine," remarked Sir Richard. "If you will forgive my using the new court term. I speak of it as magnificent because when I was last at court, the wine steward brought out some much like this in flavor and strength—he used the same word as I to describe it. A man who may drink this wine and retain a cross temper is not a natural man. I, for one, often am tempted to sing."

"I often sang, too, as a young blade with a singing heart and a swift horse beneath me. But we cannot sing with a heart full of trouble."

"Your wine steward would have you sing again, however, my lord. Take care that he is a man of sober judgment and loyal principles and let him not be a crafty or meddlesome fellow. We will never know how many a poor man up before the king's council has had his life and goods taken or spared by the wine steward's judgment on what that august body should drink."

"I see you like to philosophize. I should say that if a judgment were

____

3 This is arguably an anachronism. The word "fad," which may be the narrator's word choice or may be meant as indirect discourse, and therefore attributed to the characters, arose in the late 19th century.

so balanced that a bowl of wine more or less might swing it to and fro, it would be of little consequence which way it swung."

"Except to the judged, my lord."

"To the judged, you are right. I have always been the judge, never the judged. For me a decision is merely a matter of logic, of justice, of expediency. For another it may be a matter of life and death." Sir Giles spoke lightly but his evident sincerity made his guest wince. These hard, iron men! How he envied their ease and skill of decision! A man, a family, a nation, what was it to them if these were in the path of justice—and ambition? Stern men, that trampled ruthlessly on everything in their path.

Sir Richard became strained and taut again. He could be stern, he could be hard and ruthless, he could be great and powerful—he *would* be great and powerful and it would cost him his happiness and his conscience. He laughed but the laugh was mirthless.

"And our finer feelings, our sympathies, why did our Lord give them to us who have so little use for them. They mock us in our work of justice, they torture us in the evil we do. They would drag us down where there are none lower for our pity to fall on, and those are greatest who—" Sir Richard stopped abruptly. "Those who are greatest—he who is greatest—dangerous to talk about—"...he did not dare finish the sentence.

"They who are greatest have least use for them," finished Sir Giles for him. That was all right. He would have said "little of them" which might not be all right. You could never tell.

Sir Giles thought his guest's evident seriousness quite funny. Sir Richard was a man grown up. Surely he could play the part of a man without having a woman's feeling about it. Englishmen learned that to take care of themselves was the first principle of any code. "Oh, we could never be without our sympathy, our friendship, our pity in times of peace and ease. It is only in war and strife that we must make ourselves hard without mercy."

Sir Richard was thinking. "Only in war and strife." That was a big exception in England. A noble, even a lesser noble, lived by his ability to bully, fight, quarrel, wrangle, struggle. With the men under him, with the men over him, with the parliament, with the church, with the—yes, he might admit it to himself—with the king. Intrigue, plot, flattery, lies, force of arms—they were the weapons. How despicable they all were—and how necessary. The king—of course, he was the worst of the lot. Smooth, sly, deceitful, the king had done more to render Sir Richard's life miserable than any other ten men.

Had made his life miserable; and why should he be miserable with a manor house and land and wealth? Miserable when his wine steward and head gardener went about their work with light hearts. Or were their hearts heavy sometimes like his? Now there was religion. He shuddered at the thought. His grandfather had been a devout Catholic and worshipped as one, he had been a devout Catholic too, but he worshipped as a Protestant, as a member of a church that he could never believe in. For beneath the crushing hand of the king he must hide behind an all-concealing cloak of hypocrisy or be smothered in the persecution that fell on all who defied the king's edict, and as much from a silly feeling that he should be loyal than from any fear. For Sir Richard was not really a coward. Right or wrong, his family had always stood steadfastly by and for the king. Here was a time when the king was wrong. Until a month ago he had sided with the king against his own conscience. Such thoughts were unpleasant.

"Shall we finish our game of chess?" he asked. "You have me in a corner, but I might easily squirm out and make it uncomfortable for you."

"We will go back to it later and I will take up our five minutes before bed-time with finishing off your knights and attacking your king." At the word "king" both men started ever so slightly.

"Attacking your king." The words burned into Sir Richard's brain. Who was there dared to attack a king? Not he nor the twenty or more other country nobles and gentry in that part of England, who had felt the monarch's iron hand ever crushing them from above and the people clamoring and clamoring beneath for greater liberties. Taxes, religion, benevolence, forced loans slowly and certainly eating into their diminishing wealth. They all bore the same burden. How might Sir Giles feel under the burden of royalty? He would have just cause for grievance. The grandson of an earl—a younger son, to be sure—but still the king had sliced out enough in fines and tolls to make this land a mere shadow of the great estate it once had been. He would like to know just how much Sir Giles loved his sovereign lord. Sir Giles had no son and a beautiful daughter. He had a handsome son. Sir Giles was a widower, he had only himself and his daughter to live for.

Swish, patter, patter! A drumming rain beat on the small lead and glass windows. The red firelight flickered up across the faces of the two men. Sir Giles' fine blond hair—he did not wear a wig[4]—tumbled over

---

4 This is a surer anachronism on the part of the young Carr. In this period, if a man's own hair would not do, he was more likely to wear postiche—extensions—than to wear a wig. Charles II brought the wearing of wigs by men into English fashion in 1660. In the days of Charles I, the royalist/cavalier fashion was to wear one's hair shoulder length, cut asymmetrically, perhaps also curled or dyed. Some style references survive into modern times: one side tied with a ribbon was known as the "love-lock"; another, hanging away

the dark wood of his chair and glinted in the ever-changing light beams from the fireplace. A youthful looking man, thin-cheeked but pink and smooth; nose and eyes clear cut and fine like a woman's, fine and hard, too, like a delicate marble statue. "A man as handsome as you, Sir Giles, may enjoy the court and city more than the lonely green fields and forests of our country. Have you ever considered living at court?"

"I am too busy with my fields and forests to worry, and the court ladies bore me."

"A lady should never bore a handsome man."

"The court is for men who live by gifts and favors or who delight in plot and intrigue to get the wealth of another. I like better our simple country folk who can be trusted not to deal in lies and flattery."

How much did Sir Giles love his king, Sir Richard wondered. It would be well to find out. "No, we go about our own business here. Maybe that is why our estates grow smaller every year."

Sir Giles did not move an eyelash.

"And," went on Sir Richard looking keenly at his host, "I hate to think that the lands my ancestors spilled their blood for are taken from me without a struggle to be given to—to an oily lawyer, to a flattering, cozening informer whose forefathers were afraid to use a sword or ride a horse for the old England our forefathers knew."

Sir Giles still sat motionless. Inwardly he was laughing. His guest seemed to wish to lead him on to talk about the king. Well, he would see what Sir Richard thought himself.

"Much that you say is true," he said slowly, "but they are favorites of the king, it is all done at the king's order"—and he waited for Sir Richard's answer.

Sir Richard's nerves jumped taut. He had stepped in. He drained the last of a huge wine flagon and his thoughts wandered for a moment to where the sparks snapped up out of the dying fire. Things he had thought before flitted before his mind and half-formed plans and ideas that he had always kept half formed—pushed back.

Twenty or more nobles—*No, we go about our own business here. It is all done at the king's order.* He *would* be great and powerful. His family—his uncles—one of the most powerful in England. Sir Giles' family, powerful, too. Twenty or more nobles, they felt the iron hand crushing. How much did Sir Giles love his king? Twenty or more nobles, how much did they love their king?

Sir Giles must be handled carefully. He would be evasive.

---

from the face and over the ears was the "heart-breaker." Curls on the cheek were called "confidents," and on the forehead, "favourites."

"Ah yes, it is all done at the king's command."

"And the king can do no wrong," pursued Sir Giles but his half mocking tone belied the words.

"You say the king can do no wrong?"

"I have been so told." They were silent a minute more.

"The king is to pass through this part of the country soon. He may do one of us the honor of paying a visit," Sir Richard spoke.

"An honor indeed, though sometimes a costly one. Once, many years ago, the king stopped at the castle of one of my relatives—by marriage—the Earl of Oxford. It appears there were more soldiers about the castle than was allowed by law but the king said nothing. At the end of the visit, after being royally entertained, he bade the Earl good-bye with much ceremony and added as an afterthought that his attorney wished to speak to him. That speech cost the Earl ten thousand pounds."

"No man, however great, is safe from the king's displeasure."

"The king is never hard to displease." So Sir Giles felt the king's hand, too. They were treading on ground that earlier in the evening they would have scrupulously avoided. Both of the same mind, why did they not bring forth their ideas more frankly? Sir Richard was beginning to form ideas that he was afraid to think of. Surely Sir Giles was his friend. He would not lead his guest on to say anything treasonable and then turn informer. In fact, he was as ready as Sir Richard himself to speak on the unpopular policies of the king. But policies—no, they must condemn more than policies to carry out all the wild schemes and half-laid plans that Sir Richard felt fermenting in the back of his head.

"But it is hard to be displeased with the king."

"There are some who find it easy."

"It goes hard with them, nevertheless, if they are open in their displeasure"—a pause. "Therefore," went on Sir Richard, "let us not be open in our displeasure."

"You are very kind to speak for us both."

"Do I not speak for us both?"

Sir Giles thought a moment.

"We have long been friends, Sir Richard. I see you would like to speak your mind. You have my promise as a friend and a gentleman to keep whatever you say in confidence. I am interested because I may—ah—sympathize with your views." The firelight played on his fine mouth and cold, clear eyes as he was speaking. A delicate marble statue!

"There are many men in this part of England who feel as we do."

"But they are not here. Are we interested in what other men think?"

"We may do well to have them on our side."

"And what do you speak of as our side, pray?"

"Our side against the king."

"Ah!"

"The king is making a journey through this way soon."

"Ah!"

"There are many nobles in this part of the country who are on our side."

"Ah! You speak wildly, Sir Richard. Time was when men plotted to take the king's life—long ago, men who might become kings themselves. We do not use murder today—unless it be legal murder. And you, I hope, have no illusions about becoming king."

"We do not use murder today. No, we do not use any weapons at all. That is why our lands grow smaller every year and our taxes more. The king's son is a boy; in this part of England are two great earls, distant relatives of ours. Think, Sir Giles Howard! If the king died while riding through the forest, who knows who might rule England? We do not use murder today, that is true, unless it be the legalized murder of the royal criminals. We do not use murder today. We use intrigue and the king has proved himself more than a match for us at that." Sir Richard spoke as in a trance. He had committed himself. Could he persuade Sir Giles to join him in some wild plot?

"Your speech takes me suddenly, Sir Richard. I cannot speak with you without much thought. I confess what you suggest has never come into my mind 'til you mentioned it just now."

"He lies," thought Sir Richard, "and though I am not as displeased as surprised, I think the idea a bit impracticable and foolish."

"However, it is getting late. Let us retire and think about what you have suggested. Our sober judgment in the morning may be very different from what our wine-heated brain gives us to think tonight. I will talk more with you tomorrow evening. For the present, let us get to bed and sleep out foolish thoughts."

The rain was still beating and whirring outside the window and the fire was a mass of glowing embers—a time for bed and sleep. The men bade each other good-night and Sir Richard was shown to his room.

It was some minutes, however, before Sir Giles left the chair in front of the fire. He was thinking over what had passed between him and his guest. A wild scheme—still there was a chance, a chance it would work and then—then he would be an earl, or what? And if they failed—it was more likely to fail, too—why then he would be a corpse, his daughter penniless. He had no moral scruples, of course. But he could not afford to mix in any scatter-brained plot that would ruin him and his family with him. No—his thoughts were interrupted by a servant who stepped in from the hall. A messenger, it seemed, had just arrived with a letter. A messenger—what a queer hour. He had been fed and his horse taken care of? Very good, and the message? A letter. Very well, he would see him immediately before bed-time. Send him in. He has no message but a letter. Bring the letter and a light.

Beneath the flickering candlelight Sir Giles opened the wooden box that contained the letter. He started and bent nearer to view it more closely. The Seal of the Wardrobe! That meant one thing—it was from the king. And in English. Yes, it was from the king.

"The king to Sir Giles Howard, Greeting.

"Whereas by the laws and customs of our realm, which we are bound, by the oath made at our coronation to observe, all our Lieges within the same realm, as well poor as rich, ought freely to sue..." unimportant, what was it he wanted? Sir Giles was halfway through *"...of the great and outrageous oppressions and maintenances made to the damage of us and our people, in divers parts of the same realm, with divers maintainors[5], instigators, barators, purveyors and embraceors of quarrels and..."* There was trouble somewhere. The purport was beginning to flash through Sir Giles' mind *"to discover and inform us of those who, of late, by subtle imagination and by art, and device may plot treason or harm, or quarrel, or rebellion, against us and our state..."* He had guessed right. And more *"...wherefore we command and charge you...to be executed in all points...to your own great reward and advancement and to our peace and order in the realm."* It ended. *"...Given under our seal of the wardrobe at Westminster, the twelfth day of May. By the king himself."*

Sir Giles carefully laid the box and the letter on the red embers. And he smiled as he watched the flames devour greedily what a mes-

---

5 The king's letter demonstrates Carr's penchant for incorporating period language and spelling. Although the dominant spelling of this word in the seventeenth century was, "maintainers," preceded in earlier centuries by "maintainours," " mayntenours," and "meintenours,"—the spelling "maintainor" emerged in the nineteenth century—Carr standardizes on the suffix "-or" for the list of nouns conjoined here. "Instigators" and "embraceors" are accurate mid-seventeenth century spellings; "purveyors" has always been spelled as such; "barator" had numerous variations over time. So Carr balances his period scholarship with the readability of his prose.

senger had brought him all the way from London—and from the hand of the king.

He smiled and the firelight playing in his fine golden hair added a satanic redness to the graceful head. His eyes gazed steadily at the fire while he thought, still and motionless. A delicate, marble statue. Then he turned and went to his chamber.

* * *

The next afternoon was bright and cheerful. Elizabeth, Sir Giles, and his guest were seated in the newly created music room and Rosso had just seated himself before the virginal.

Elizabeth handed him a sheet of music and he struck the first chord— a resounding major. Sir Giles listened to him unconsciously. He was thinking about the letter he had received from the king. Should he warn Sir Richard that the king was suspicious of the nobles in that part of England, or should he let events take their course and gain the king's reward by disclosing the plot before it became ripe?

One way, he thought was the duty of a friend and a gentleman who did not betray a confidence. But who was a gentleman when he would lose an earldom by it? The other way was the path to advancement and greater riches. That was a path that any Englishman would like to follow. Was not Sir Richard willing to sacrifice his king to advance himself?[6]... What was that tune?...

Rosso pounded out the solemn chords of a hymn. Slow and rhythmical the great major cadences rose and fell. Sir Giles was entranced. "Come, come, come to the Lord!" the music rolled, solemn and slow. "The Almighty glory of God, the Father, the judge, the judge of all men!" The thought smote Sir Giles like a hammer. The judge, was not *he* the judge of men? He, the great Sir Giles Howard, was never judged. And the music said he lied. Eternity, power, majesty were in the music, the notes seemed every one symbols of the Heavenly Power that would sometime fall on every man who would betray his promise to a friend— that he might be greater in this world below.

Suddenly the fear of the Lord, with all the primitive passion that it inspired in the medieval man, swept over the listener. Sir Giles was trembling like a child, fascinated, awed by something more than human. He felt his resolution dissolve within him in the solemn harmony from the instrument. And never did he once think of stopping the music or leaving the room to escape from it. He was under a holy spell that it

---

6 Note the chess pun, picking up on the men's game the prior evening, and Carr's implication: in chess, to sacrifice one's king is to lose the game.

would be eternal damnation to break. Rosso was playing with the fervor that had sent the wicked men of Florence from the church in tears.

Boom, boom, every chord seemed a blow. Judged, you will someday be the judged. Doom, doom, doom, there is a doom, doom, a solemn doom. Fear the Lord, the Lord Almighty...

The music softened to a whisper. Now it was pleading, soft, gentle. It flowed along even and slow. Fragments of thought flashed through Sir Giles' heated brain. He relaxed a moment from the stone-still spell that Rosso's passionate music had cast upon him. ''The merciful, the merciful, for they shall obtain mercy,'' it was saying to him now and the slow solemn rhythm of the bass told him of the power behind the pleading sweetness of the melody. And now, with a crash, it swung into the grand chorus. Oh, the power! How could a mere man defy the power that music expressed.

He let out a restrained breath; at last, Rosso had finished. Sir Richard was speaking to him, but he did not hear. He would wait 'til he was himself again, he was mad now. He had laughed at Sir Richard. Who was the man now? Who cringed like a dog and trembled like a leaf?

Elizabeth was sorting over the music. "What shall you play now, Rosso? I have an old Saxon war song, thrilling—it will make a coward fight like a demon. It was put to music in London a few years ago. Shall we play it?" She paused a moment. "Or, no, here is a love song. If I had the words I would sing with you. Play it for us."

Rosso had not touched the keys thrice before a new pang had touched Sir Giles' hard heart. His daughter—that tune—his dead wife. His daughter, the thing on earth he loved most. And who on earth did she love most? Was it he—or was it the son of the man he would betray...the son of the man he would have hanged as a traitor? But then—he might marry her to the son of a duke; she would like that better. Again the music told him he lied. How sweet it was. He had loved to sing that song as a young blade with a singing heart and a swift horse beneath him, sung it to—to the lady who was dead. She had met her Maker face to face, could he? Would she wait for him in heaven 'til eternity because he wanted gold and power? No, no, no! Never! The old love in his heart seemed to swell with the music 'til it was about to burst—burst for joy, and off in the dim clouds he saw—he saw the vision of her face looking down at him from heaven. He laughed—not the cold hard laugh that he had laughed since *she* died but a laugh of joy, of gladness. The world was a world for love and joy and—friendship. Happiness, that was what he wanted—happiness and love and some day he might meet her there in the clouds. Happiness—not power.

The music stopped. His eye turned to Elizabeth, who was strangely blushing—blushing red. He wondered why. Then their eyes met—and he knew.

He rose and turned to Sir Richard. "If we may be excused, I will ask you to come with me to the next room for a moment. Sir Giles Howard, who will be some day the judged, has something to say to you."

Notes for the Curious: "That Ye Be Not Judged"

The reader is warned: While this commentary does not reveal the solution, it explicitly identifies two suspects and excerpts discussions concerning them in Carr's *Death Turns the Tables* (1941). If you have not read that novel yet, you may wish to do so before reading the following commentary.

—

The other historical stories in this collection are, except perhaps in their conspicuously unhappy endings, literary romances, and their characters are the expected literary types who populate such traditional romances. With respect to its characters, "That Ye Be Not Judged," written relatively late in Carr's apprenticeship period (December 1926), has more in common with his contemporary tales than with his historical narratives, or with his other genre work. Carr's characters in all the other tales are generally flat, often well-recognized types, however vibrantly drawn through his technical combination of exposition, description, action, and diction. This is likewise true for most of the characters in Carr's professional stories and novels.

Occasionally, though, whether in the young Carr's contemporary tales, which are literary efforts, or here in "That Ye Be Not Judged"—or in a minority of Carr's later novels—the central characters are more rounded, realized through moments depicting their inner lives, moments with which the reader can empathize. These characters stretch beyond types and their externalized presentation, achieving some degree of internalization. Nonetheless, even in presenting these rounder characters, typically, Carr's goal is *only* to heighten sympathy in the service of intensifying the narrative drama. The author remains focused on the effectiveness of his story, rather than on character development; Carr simply utilizes one of his less commonly employed tools to accomplish this.

Carr's plot-driven motivations differentiate his work generally from literary fiction, which deliberates upon human nature, and in doing so, tells the story of a central character's insights into the self or the world, as well as observing the changes this prompts. The literary author's perspective, in this respect, is more panoramic, concerned with broader questions about culture and life. Such a narrative often becomes a vehicle for the reader's own life reflections. While Carr's work, as genre fiction, only occasionally delves into a character's introspection for the sake of the plot, the opposite is true of literary fiction: it much less frequently deals in drama for the sake of resolving tensions related to its characters' inner lives and associated conflicts. The plot services the introspection.

Its atypical approach in this respect is what makes "That Ye Be Not Judged" such an exceptional tale for the young John Dickson Carr—exceptional both in its comparative quality to his other short fiction and in its departing from the aims, strategies, and techniques typical to him—really, exceptional with respect to any point in Carr's career. S.T. Joshi, evaluating Carr's relative strengths and weaknesses, asserts:

> The simple fact is that Carr is not a good short story writer. To say this need not, paradoxically, imply a criticism—not entirely, at any rate. It is precisely because Carr had certain definite strengths as a writer that he failed at the short story. We have suggested these strengths in our previous discussions... all these qualities are antithetical to short story technique.
>
> It is also the case that Carr had certain weaknesses that prevented him from being a consistently good short story writer. Carr cannot draw characters with a few bold strokes... when he tries to do so, his characters become mere caricatures... (p. 75)

While Joshi can sometimes be an unperceptive reader of Carr, his distinctions between the effectiveness of Carr's technique in the short versus the long format are generally arguable. During Carr's professional career, he published only about three dozen short stories (a half dozen of which were Sherlockian pastiches created in collaboration with Adrian Conan Doyle). Fewer than half of Carr's professional short mysteries are of outstanding quality. Carr was uniquely, even masterfully, suited to long-form detective fiction, in which he really did have few peers—but if Carr's reputation as a mystery writer depended upon his short stories, Carr would not enjoy the same high regard and recognition that he does more than fifty years after publishing his final novel.

G.K. Chesterton saw this dichotomy not only more charitably than Joshi, but more organically—not as a shortcoming in Carr, but as a general distinction applying to all crime-story writers, which he entertainingly summarized in this manner:

> ...I say that we writers are really divided into two types; which exactly correspond to cut-throats and poisoners. The cut-throats among us are those who, realizing that the murder story must cut short the life, decide also to cut the story short.

It is their pride as artists to deal in daggers; and startle the unfortunate reader with the stab of the short story. Those... who prefer to live the more learned and laborious life of a poisoner, are those authors who prolong the agony of anticipation or bewilderment in the reader through a long series of chapters...These authors justly pride themselves on the delicate gradation, the scientific calm, and the slow but subtle progress...This second method, of a detailed and developed science, both of crime and of detection, can only be worked out in the wider limits of a full-length novel, and demands many of the qualities of a serious novelist.[1]

By coincidence, Chesterton's assessment appeared in the introduction to an anthology in which Carr's "The Other Hangman," a short masterwork (and which appears later in this collection), first appeared. Although Joshi was focused on Carr's mystery fiction, the skills his critique addresses are not genre-specific, applying generally to short-form writing.

This makes the inapplicability of Joshi's comments, in the case of "That Ye Be Not Judged," the more interesting. In this story, Carr successfully draws the three major characters with the bold and economical strokes often lacking in his professional mystery tales. None is remotely a caricature, either. Quite the opposite: Carr demonstrates in "That Ye Be Not Judged" his capacity to peer into a character's mind, whether directly or suggestively, as well as he does in any of his fiction, including his later professional work. Further, Carr does so with some technical virtuosity: "That Ye Be Not Judged" is neatly buttressed by subtle parallels and images, putting it among the best writing in the young author's career to that point.

Consider as one example the contrapuntal responses of daughter and father to Rosso's music. In the girl awakening to womanhood, the virginal's notes stimulate her as the presence of a lover would. Elizabeth experiences sexual arousal:

She untwisted a blue ribbon from her hair and wound it about her fingers; then she unwound it and tied it in an impossible tangle. The music made her feel so queer, like—she blushed red as it came to her—like being kissed by a handsome fellow with dark hair and ruddy cheeks. It was such unbearably sweet music she half buried her curls in a lacy cushion to

---

1 *A Century of Detective Stories,* Hutchinson & Co. (1935), p. 9.

> escape from it and then strained her ears to hear better and drew up out of the cushion as far as she dared. Then, as she surrendered and sat boldly upright to listen…

In Sir Giles, distracted by questions of politics and conflicting loyalties, attempting to resolve these as a cost-benefit calculation to himself and decide whether to answer Sir Richard's recruitment or the king's, Rosso's music summons a different sort of profundity: conscience. His conscience calls Sir Giles back to his love for and obligation to his daughter, and to the importance on some occasions of substituting mercy for judgment. It recalls to him what he un-self-interestedly believes to be morally absolute.

Carr traces Sir Giles' transformed consciousness through some clever imagery. As Sir Richard tries to assess his host's mindset, he perceives Sir Giles to be "fine and hard…like a delicate marble statue." Sir Richard cannot see past Sir Giles' carefully sculpted, opaque demeanor, one appropriately guarded given the sensitive subject matter of their discussion. Carr relied on marmoreal similes more than once, for the same purpose, during his career. For instance, in "The Black Cabinet" (1951, a period piece set in Paris during the reign of Napoleon III),[2] of the protagonist Nina, Carr writes, "her intense composure gave Nina's beauty a chilly quality like marble" (p. 107). Even Sir Giles, after reading the king's letter, attempting to peer into himself and decide what to do, cannot: "His eyes gazed steadily at the fire while he thought, still and motionless. A delicate, marble statue."

It is only, finally when Rosso's powerful hymn plays that the thoughts it awakens "smote Sir Giles like a hammer." The obfuscatory marble is shattered, and Sir Giles' fragmented thoughts, now clear, flow through his mind buoyed upon the stream of even, slow music. Sir Giles feels "his resolution dissolve within him in the solemn harmony from the instrument." It is, in playfully ironic imagery, a "stone-still spell that Rosso's passionate music had cast upon him" which brings Sir Giles sufficient self-awareness and guides his conscience toward mercy: understanding how he will be judged for his potential actions, by himself; as his dead wife might have judged him; by his daughter, living with the consequences of Sir Giles' choices; and most importantly to Sir Giles, by his God.

This titular judgment itself is another well-managed theme in Carr's

---

2 The story originally appeared in *Twenty Great Tales of Murder* (a Mystery Writers of America anthology, published by Random House). It was later collected into Carr's *The Men Who Explained Miracles* (Harper & Row, 1963). The excerpt here is drawn from the latter.

story. Avoiding the temptation to be blatant or over-emphatic, Carr invites readers to consider judgment from multiple perspectives and what it means to each character, both practically and ethically. Sir Giles' own contemplation of this, in which he recognizes that he, too, will be judged, leads to an experience relatively few of Carr's characters undergo: change and growth between the story's start and its conclusion. Sir Giles has an epiphany.

While Carr was typically no fan of "literary" novels, even as a youth, he was very well read in them, as he was in classics and history, mythology, genre fiction, and other subjects. (Readers of *The Kindling Spark* will recall, as an example, that Joseph Conrad's *Heart of Darkness* was a key precursor to Carr's horror story, "The Devil-Gun.") While it is almost certainly a coincidence that the main character's surname in this story is Howard, the editor wonders whether the young author didn't borrow the inspiration for Sir Giles' sudden insight from E.M. Forster's *Howards End* (1910). In that novel, Helen Schlegel, a principal character, experiences her own existential awakening while listening to the scherzo and allegro of Beethoven's Fifth Symphony:

> ...the music started with a goblin walking quietly over the universe, from end to end. Others followed him. They were not aggressive creatures; it was that that made them so terrible to Helen. They merely observed in passing that there was no such thing as splendour or heroism in the world. After the interlude of elephants dancing, they returned and made the observation for the second time. Helen could not contradict them, for, once at all events, she had felt the same, and had seen the reliable walls of youth collapse. Panic and emptiness! Panic and emptiness! The goblins were right. Her brother raised his finger; it was the transitional passage on the drum.
>
> For, as if things were going too far, Beethoven took hold of the goblins and made them do what he wanted. He appeared in person. He gave them a little push, and they began to walk in a major key instead of in a minor, and then—he blew with his mouth and they were scattered! Gusts of splendour, gods and demigods contending with vast swords, colour and fragrance broadcast on the field of battle, magnificent victory, magnificent death! Oh, it all burst before the girl, and she even stretched out her gloved hands as if it was tangible. Any fate was titanic; any contest desirable; conqueror and conquered would alike be applauded by the angels of the utmost stars.

And the goblins—they had not really been there at all? They were only the phantoms of cowardice and unbelief? One healthy human impulse would dispel them? Men like the Wilcoxes, or ex-President Roosevelt, would say yes. Beethoven knew better. The goblins really had been there. They might return—and they did. It was as if the splendour of life might boil over and waste to steam and froth. In its dissolution one heard the terrible, ominous note, and a goblin, with increased malignity, walked quietly over the universe from end to end. Panic and emptiness! Panic and emptiness! Even the flaming ramparts of the world might fall. Beethoven chose to make all right in the end. He built the ramparts up. He blew with his mouth for the second time, and again the goblins were scattered. He brought back the gusts of splendour, the heroism, the youth, the magnificence of life and of death, and, amid vast roarings of a superhuman joy, he led his Fifth Symphony to its conclusion. But the goblins were there. They could return. He had said so bravely, and that is why one can trust Beethoven when he says other things.[3]

Whether or not Carr had Forster in mind, it almost certainly occurred to him to devise Sir Giles' musical transport because, nearly five years earlier, the fifteen-year-old had described a similar reverie of his own in his Uniontown *Daily News Standard* column "As We See It." In it, Carr recounts his own exaltation, like Forster's highly metaphorical, and drawing upon visions of epic warfare, while attending a piano concert in Pittsburgh:

The moment the first bars of that song thundered from the piano under the player's master touch, audience—lights—stage—all faded away. We found ourselves swept backward into the dusty, remote past—borne, as it were, on the wings of harmony—and saw before us the pageant of history unfold itself. And though past us trooped in a glittering array monarchs in their imperial robes—generals whose awe-inspiring names had rung down through the dim ages—still there loomed in the background a majestic figure under whose magic hands a piano spoke. We saw mighty Rome rise and fall—

---

3 *Howards End, Duke Classics* (2012), pp. 66-68.

Rome, with whose walls crumbled the civilization of the ancient world. We saw through the dark days of the middle ages a heaving sea of shining helmets and glittering swords sweeping over blood-soaked Europe—a sea that never rested. We saw that sea engulf nations and dash them to pieces on its rocks. We saw never-ending battles with savages in the wilds of a newly discovered country—savages who moved like menacing shadows through the forest, and who walked with a patient, deadly watchfulness for a chance to swoop down on a quiet settlement when an attack was least expected. We saw through the battle smoke during the bloody days of the American revolution the erect figure of George Washington, and above the roar of the cannon in the war which brother cut down brother throughout four black years we heard the gentle, kindly voice of Abraham Lincoln. Again long lines of soldiers and statesman poured before us until we shrank appalled from the bloodiest conflict the world has ever known—the Great War. We saw the fury-crazed fighting men of the Allied armies trample the vaunted German war machine underfoot; saw the awful toll taken by the aeroplane—poison gas—liquid fire—the hand grenade; saw—

The music stopped. Like a picture on a magic-lantern slide taking form as the focus is slowly effected, the interior of the brilliantly illuminated theater thrust itself across our vision. But we heard no more selections tendered by the master. Our thoughts were taken up by the pageant we had just witnessed—the march of the world. It was stamped on our memory in letters of blood. Always blood! Progress, steeped in it throughout the ages, is dyed crimson. The history of the earth might be written in it. It stains the hands of monarch and murderer alike.

....And they call the history of men's follies the march of the world![4]

This reverie, if anything, is even more evocative of *Howards End* than Sir Giles' musical rapture in "That Ye Be Not Judged." If neither of

---

4 "As We See It," Uniontown *Daily News Standard,* February 27, 1922, p. 3.

Carr's musical visions was inspired by Forster, this seems enormously coincidental, but either way, the rewarding comparison between them remains, and it enriches our reading of "That Ye Be Not Judged."

There is, further, an interesting (and more certain) connection between "That Ye Be Not Judged" and one of Carr's detective novels, a telling contrast between Sir Giles and Justice Horace Ireton, a chief suspect in Carr's *Death Turns the Tables*. These two comparisons (the short story to Forster's novel, and to Carr's own) highlight the difference between Carr's handling of a more literary character, Sir Giles Howard, and of a typically static one, Mr. Justice Ireton, when confronted with the same, previously unfamiliar situation: becoming the judged instead of the judge. In the detective novel, as Sir Giles has, Mr. Justice Ireton views judgment, according to his long-accustomed position, as a cold-eyed process. Justice, according to his privileged status (not through merit), is his to determine and dispense. In a scene demonstrative of Carr's penchant for echoing the metaphorical chess match between characters by having them meet over an actual chessboard,[5] as Sir Giles and Sir Richard do, Dr. Fell and Mr. Justice Ireton parley about judgment and conscience while playing chess.

> "Your move," said Mr. Justice Ireton patiently.
>
> "Eh? Oh, ah!" said Dr. Fell, enlightened. He moved a piece rather wildly, for he was engrossed with some silence in the argument. "What I wish to know, sir, is this. Why? Why do you take such pleasure in these cat-and-mouse tactics? You intimate to me, softly, that young Lypiatt won't hang after all—"
>
> "Check," said Mr. Justice Ireton, moving a piece.
>
> ...."You see," explained Dr. Fell..."You're rather a gimlet eye, you know. Or at least you have that reputation."
>
> "So I understand."
>
> ..."If you will pardon my own candor," he replied, "what interests me is this rigid Roman spirit of yours. It is admirable. No doubt! But (just between ourselves) don't you have any qualms? Can't you ever see yourself in the position of the man on the dock? Don't you ever have the Christian humil-

---

5 Carr consciously employs this common metaphor at various points in his career. A third example is the detective Melis's description in the 1948 radio drama *The Man with the Iron Chest* of his stalking his suspect as "a game of criminal chess." (Collected in *The Island of Coffins*, p. 159.)

ity to shiver and say to yourself, 'There, but for the grace of God—'?"

The other's sleepy eyes opened.

"No. Why should I? That is no concern of mine....I am a realist....Doctor," he went on, "hear me out. I have been accused of many things in my time, but never of being a hypocrite or a stuffed shirt...Now, why should I murmur any such pious catchword as you suggest? *I* am not likely to rob my neighbor's till, or murder my neighbor in order to get his wife....Unfortunately, the criminals of this world...have no more right to behave as they like than I have...But they do. And then they beg for mercy. They will not get it from me." (pp. 16–21)

Ireton's becoming a leading suspect in a murder does not change his inflexible views, nor (in contrast to Sir Giles) does consideration of any personal loyalties or relationships sway the judge—pointedly so, regarding how his daughter's life might be emotionally destroyed by the justice's evasion of prosecution on a technicality, shifting suspicion and prosecution onto her suitor, Fred Barlow.

"I refer," said Doctor Fell, moving in reply, "to the supposition that this day cannot have been very pleasant for your daughter. She is fond of Frederick Barlow. Yet in the interests of justice she will be forced to go into the witness box and send him to death. Still, there is the philosophical side. As you said yourself, nothing in this world is of less importance than human relationships."

Again they were silent, studying the board.

"Then there is young Barlow himself," pursued Dr. Fell. "A decent lad, when all is said and done. He had a great future before him. Not any longer. Even if he is acquitted of this charge (which I consider unlikely), he will be ruined. He stood by you at a difficult time. You must feel rather friendly toward him yourself. But, as you say, nothing in this world is less important than human relationships."....

Mr. Justice Ireton glanced up briefly, behind his big spectacles, before he resumed his scrutiny of the board.

"What sort of chess are you playing?" he complained, displeased with the position he saw there.

> "It is a little development of my own....You would prob-
> ably call it the cat-and-mouse gambit....What do you think
> of Graham's case against Barlow?"
> The judge frowned.
> "A strong case," he conceded, with his eyes on the board.
> "Not a perfect case. But a satisfying one." (pp. 241–243)

Unlike Sir Giles, Horace Ireton experiences no epiphany, never reconciling his calculated and unmerciful view of justice to a more self-reflective, modest standard. The potential consequences to his daughter move Sir Giles, but those to his own daughter do not sway Mr. Justice Ireton. He is not even especially concerned whether *justice* and *truth* actually coincide: asked by Dr. Fell whether he has ever tried an innocent man, the justice replies, "Frequently. And I flatter myself that he was always acquitted" (p. 22).

One final point worth noting about "That Ye Be Not Judged" is its effective use of concrete detail. Detail, of course, is one of the half-dozen basic tools of the writer; only through its use can an author create a plausible sense of the place, time, and atmosphere in which a narrative occurs. Carr was invariably vigilant about this, even to the point of putting his standard into the mouth of H.M. as instructions to a witness:

> I want you to give me an account as complete and minute
> as a surveyor's plan, without a detail left out. In the words of
> Joseph Conrad, I want you to make me see it[6]

One of the qualities that sets Carr apart from many of his contemporaries is how masterfully he handles detail to striking effect. In his detective novels, Carr's manipulation of detail is noted and praised for generating an atmosphere of dark menace that can suddenly, urgently evoke a sense of dread. Reviewing *The Mad Hatter Mystery*, Dorothy L. Sayers attested to this:

> Mr. Carr can lead us away from the small, artificial, brightly-
> lit stage of the ordinary detective plot into the menace of
> outer darkness. He can create atmosphere with an adjective,
> and make a picture from a wet iron railing, a dusty table, a
> gas-lamp blurred by the fog. He can alarm with an illusion,
> or delight with a rollicking absurdity.[7]

---

6 *The Cavalier's Cup*, p. 47.

7 "Mystery Out of the Ordinary," *Sunday Times*, Sep 24, 1933, p. 7.

What is notable about the detail in "That Ye Be Not Judged" is its anticipation of Carr's historical romance novels, which all rely upon the use of period detail to convince and seduce the reader. In each of these, Carr converted a researched, detailed understanding of the historical backdrop into fascinating, period-accurate details. Even as sometimes-grudging a critic of Carr's as S.T. Joshi praised Carr's accomplishment in this:

> Carr's historical mysteries are noble experiments, and many of them are highly successful...the historical novels...can be recommended for their narrative drive, lively characters, [and] precise recreation of their historical periods...Carr's "Notes for the Curious" at the end of each novel...supply the historical sources for the work, and they reveal Carr to be a sound and careful historian: he went back to primary documentation of each period (diaries, letters, contemporary treatises) and augmented them with the best modern scholarship available to him. It is true that he parades historical erudition a little too self-consciously at times, but on the whole his synthesis is seamless and seemingly effortless. (pp. 73–74)

The young Carr, in fact, scores some victories with respect to historical details in "That Ye Be Not Judged," such as his understanding of the seventeenth-century London stage, the virginal (so central to the tale), and (as noted in the footnotes) his utilization of period-faithful spelling. Of most interest, perhaps, is his attention to the everyday life of a young country noblewoman in the time of Charles I, which Macaulay would have commended:

> To us surely it is as useful to know how the young ladies of England employed themselves a hundred and eighty years ago, how far their minds were cultivated, what were their favorite studies, what degree of liberty was allowed to them, what use they made of that liberty, what accomplishments they most valued in men, and what proofs of tenderness delicacy permitted them to give to favoured suitors, as to know all about the seizure of Franche Comté and the treaty of Nimeguen. (pp. 827–830)

One mark of Carr's meticulousness in the mature historical novels serves as a contrasting touchpoint with this novice tale. This story's mention of the toothbrush as a controversy just before the English Civil War is all but certainly erroneous. The toothbrush would not come to general attention in England until the next century, when William Addis would "invent" it in 1780. (It already existed elsewhere, but Addis seems to have stumbled onto the idea independently and was the first to mass-market toothbrushes in England.)

What would two country gentlemen have known of the toothbrush around 1640? The earliest confirmed English reference to this implement in writing is in 1651, in the memoirs of M.M. Verney, a member of the upper gentry. Verney records that he received a toothbrush as a luxury gift from Paris. There is not another surviving mention of the toothbrush in English writing for thirty years: it next appears in the 1680s memoirs of Anthony Wood, an antiquary. Given the available record, the chances are doubtful that Sir Giles and Sir Richard, at least a decade before Verney, would have been well acquainted with the tooth-brush, or that the implement would have been a topic of much public discussion, a "controversy."

Now consider *The Devil in Velvet*, in which Carr notes:

> Big Tom constructed a toothbrush for him [Fenton, the main character, transported mysteriously back in time to 1675], and another for Lydia, after a design which Fenton drew on paper and carefully explained six times. (p. 142)

As an older, more careful researcher who understands that the tooth-brush will not be "invented" in England for more than a century after Fenton desires to brush his teeth, Carr contrives in his professional novel an entertaining and historically accurate episode based upon the lack of that everyday instrument.

While the young Carr imperfectly manages a historical touch here or there in "That Ye Be Not Judged," the story nonetheless presages the emergence of Carr the historian manqué, who as a professional novelist enhances the verisimilitude of his period mysteries by swathing them in period-accurate particulars. Douglas Greene was fair in reminding read-ers, "His early stories are as completely researched as his later historical novels."[8] In this early youthful effort, the historical details result from the same close engagement with period-specific, primary texts as each of Carr's later, times-past novels would.

---

8 *The Door to Doom and Other Detections*, Harper and Row (1980), p. 10. All subsequent excerpts are drawn from the same edition.

The Harp of Tairlaine (1925)

I

Poet and Swordsman

The wheels of the coach rattled and jolted in the inn yard, and there was a blurred white flicker past the windows, which the man in the bar parlor saw. He got up, a towering shadow, and went to the window with a jingle of spurs and a thump of riding boots. Beyond the sheet of rain he could see only a vague mass of men moving in a dance of lights that glistened on the horses' coats. The postilions were hurrying to the tap-room for a drink; the man at the window could hear the banging of doors which swung to in a leap of blown candle flames. At the window the man's big shape turned—rather starkly grim, for he wore a mud-spattered doublet and a rapier swinging at his hip. But it was his face which held the ominous look—a harsh face, rugged as a cliff, and with a sort of fierce charm in the beast-like eyes. The man resembled a gnarled oak-tree with a wildcat in its branches. For some minutes he had been impatient, and now as he strode back to the fire his anger burst out.

"Ale!" he roared, with a sudden lift of his voice like a bellow. "God's word! Are you all deaf? Ale!"

The door to the hall opened, and he swung toward it.

"I pray you, friend," said a soft voice, "not so loudly, if it please you. 'Tis the loud shout betokens the empty head."

"So you're here!" snapped the other. "Why, come in. You arrive, friend Michael. And you arrive late."

Slowly the newcomer closed the door behind him, unslinging the great swathed case on his shoulder and setting it down. A small, pale fig-ure in the gloom, with the firelight dull on the sodden cloak that clung to him, he stood pulling off his gloves.

"My coach, Gareth," he answered, "was as lifeless as my tidings shall be. These devilish roads—the king's highway—"

Gareth struck the table, making the candlelight jump and quiver.

"God in heaven! Will you always dally? What has happened?"

"—the king's highway," repeated the man called Michael; "soon to be Cromwell's highway, Gareth. What has happened? Why, the inevi-table; they have sentenced Charles to die as a traitor."

His companion stared back with his unwinking, tawny eyes. He showed no gust of anger at hearing the message, but only a rather deadly silence. Then slowly he drew his rapier from its sheath and flung it on

133

the table, where it rang and rolled over and caught the light like a flash of ragged teeth.

"By that blade," he said calmly, "I swear the sentence shall never be executed. Kill Cromwell? Aye, if it can save Charles!"

Michael tossed aside his cloak and went toward the fire, kneading his wet hands above it. He was small and slim, with the delicate beauty of a girl, and eyes that were dreamy above the blaze.

"You are a fool, Gareth," he remarked to the fire. "You are my friend, but you are a fool. You have the strength of an ox—and the other attributes of an ox, I fear...Soft! I meant no harm. But, I pray you, what can all your strength do against the Ironsides? Dumb as dogs they follow Cromwell—they rule England—"

"So a Stuart shall be done to death without a finger lifted to save him!"

"Come, you are forgetting. What think you, Gareth? That I love not Charles as well as you? Yet we cannot meet them with their own weapons."

"And we stand aside while they kill him! Aye!" said Gareth.

Michael laughed in a quiet, inoffensive way. He sat down with his boots thrust out to the blaze.

"Sit down, Gareth. You speak treason, mark you; tread gently, my friend. I have ordered my dinner here; there were few people down from London, and we shall have the room to ourselves. Light you a pipe. Let us discuss this matter less heatedly."

"No!" Gareth banged the table again. "This be no time for idling with your pretty words! You are a poet, and the poet's sword-arm ever winces. Play the damned coward if you care to, but we act instantly, else I saddle me a horse and ride for London tonight—to seek Cromwell!"

"A care!" said Michael, and his voice clashed suddenly. "Yours is the cunningest blade in England, but, ah, Gareth, take care when you trespass in the poet's field of words! Faith, would you have me a coward, then? Recall you yon roaring stream by Londonderry—and you with a great hole in your side, and the water washing your blood away—and I scarce able to swim? Your armor-plates were heavy; I thought never to reach shore with you—"

"Enough," cut in Gareth, making a little twitch with his knotted hands. "I had forgot, Michael; I ask your pardon. We were discussing Charles."

"Why, truly. And since you are so impatient, let us continue, in the devil's name! Think you I care naught for action? Mark me, Gareth; the judges have decreed that he die. It will cause more sympathy than any act of Charles' own. Sympathy breeds loyalty. We may rouse the country for him yet; we could do so if he were free. Imagine you Charles escaping; imagine someone daring enough to effect his escape while the counties of the north are roused to arms—to take up his cause. Aye, and the drums beating a march all over England, and a Stuart riding at the head of Rupert's old matchless cavalry—ah, Gareth, the very dead from Naseby[1] would fall into line!"

"Mean you that we—"

"You guess well. To escape from the Tower is all but impossible, yet it has been done. The impossible must happen, late or soon. Why, you have spoken it yourself. Who, pray, is more qualified than you—than Sir Gareth Ardell, the defender of England when the Scotch king dallied with Somerset and Buckingham[2]—to be the savior of Charles?"

Gareth was pacing the room with heavy, exultant strides.

"I perceive it...Michael, Michael, empires are swayed by poets. The fighting-man controls, but the singer influences. They call you the Irish nightingale—"

"Peace, I beg of you. The sword may fashion as deft a compliment as the quill, but we need no compliments. There"—he pointed to the case by the door—"stands the harp of Michael Tairlaine. With it I may speak to the people who are ripe to revolt. Do you effect the escape of Charles; I will ride from York to Cornwall and weave a song to set their hearts afire. We shall be playing a dangerous game with a dangerous foe, but the Puritan must fall, for he has forgotten how to laugh. It is fatal to scorn laughter; it is fatal to scorn song. Charles is a fool, but he is a great man, and all great hearts are fools. Oh, I hate your Puritan smugness, and the religion that defies God because it hurts man! We strike to avenge Wentworth—"[3]

"And to free Charles," said Gareth, sheathing his blade with a snap. "If I be not mistaken, there is the landlord's step and your supper. Come, Michael; your harp, and sing me a song...sing me a song of your Irish countryside, which breeds men..."

---

1 Fought on June 14, 1645, the Battle of Naseby was the decisive battle of the (first) English Civil War, in which Cromwell's Parliamentarian forces defeated Charles' Royalist forces, effectively destroying his army.

2 James, Charles I's father, was James VI King of Scotland before becoming James I of England upon the unification of the English and Scottish crowns in 1603. Carr here refers to the rumor, extant since James's reign and with some historical evidence, that Robert Carr (Earl of Somerset) and George Villiers (the Duke of Buckingham) were James's homosexual lovers. There were similar rumors concerning James and Esmé Stewart, the Duke of Lennox. So Tairlaine is tracing Gareth's royalist loyalty back easily three decades.

3 Thomas Wentworth, 1st Earl of Strafford, who served Charles loyally for more than a decade, but whom the king sacrificed in 1641 as a political pawn in his struggles against the Long Parliament. Charles signed Wentworth's death warrant despite assuring the Earl that he "should not suffer in his person, honour or fortune."

And Michael Tairlaine, with his head sunk between his hands, plucked at the harp-strings of his fancy as he stared into the blazing heart of the fire and the blazing heart of the future.

II

Of Hoof-Beats in the Dawn

The hush of the dawn-stars was on the inn. It had gone three by the clock upstairs, and the strokes were dying away in the ghostly silence as Tairlaine raised his head. In its embers the fire was winking red—drowsy, like the brushing of the rain against the windows. The Irish poet still sat by the hearth long after Ardell had clumped up to bed, his pipe black and dead on the table, his glass empty, but his fingers caressing the strings of the harp or moving along the bright curve of its side. Mute the harp stood there, mute in the wistful rapture of vanished song—mute in the love of the man whose touch could bring to the white lips of silence the blood-red of romance.

Slowly now his hands moved to the strings. In a soft breath he began to play—so softly that the sound penetrated scarce beyond the confines of the room. And as he played his voice crooned a dim song to the walls.

> *"If this could be!*
> *From out the sea to raise the crystal spires*
> *Of cities dimly known to me,*
> *Where move the shapes of fantasy*
> *And bards of dreams in fancy free awake their sleeping*
> *lyres—*
> *If this could be!"*

He was a symbol as he sat outlined against the dying light. He did not hear the door open, nor hear it close. But he heard the voice which called to him.

"Michael!"

The music died away. Tairlaine started up, blinking, and stared through the twilight. It was a woman he saw at the door—a woman in a long wrapper, with her hair tumbling about her shoulders and her shadowed face the whiter by contrast. Noiselessly she moved toward him.

"Lady Joan!" he said dully. "Lady Joan! How came you here?"

"I thought I heard you playing," the woman replied. "Hush, Michael! I could not sleep..."

Tairlaine put more wood on the fire and watched the blue flame curl around it. He lighted another candle.

"I had not thought to see you. How—"

"I am a fugitive," she told him, coming into the circle of the fire.

Her pallid beauty was that of a ghost, and when she smiled it was like a shadow across her lips. "Had you not heard? Sheltered here tonight; tomorrow..." She shrugged and sat down, resting her chin on her palms. The logs began to quiver in the sheet of flame.

Tairlaine stood as though dazed, and she went on:

"My brother was caught in the dragnet; treason, they called it, and he dies tomorrow. They have used the rack on the servants and implicated me. It is only a question of time before I am caught. Then, of course, I shall die."

"Joan!"

"It is true. Gardline Castle has been sacked by Cromwell's order—"

"Cromwell!" The word shot between Tairlaine's lips. "Had he but served his fellow man as faithfully as he has served his God, he would not now be a murderer for a doctrine!"

"Hush, Michael!" She laid a hand on his, and he tingled to its warmth. The leaping fire was deep in her smoldering eyes.

"You must escape—in some fashion. I may effect it—"

"You would help me? Honored as the bard of Ireland, you would risk—"

He laughed.

"You imagine me not in the habit of taking risks? Why, perhaps you are right. But it is no risk, because..."

"You pause. Because..."

"I have told you before. Because I love you."

"I am sorry." Her eyes were soft now, and her slim arms moved slowly. "I am very sorry. You *have* told me before, when the moon was in the garden at Gardline, and the eyes of the night were heavy with dew. Yea, I remember it well...But, Michael, you are kind, and yet I love you not. You are but a spinner of golden phrases. You should have been a woman. None can love you, for you are not a man. A woman loves one who can sway empires, with a brain to plan and a heart to dare— who would plunge into a boiling sea to rescue a friend—who stops at nothing...You are not that, Michael. You are frail. You do not plan great enterprises...But oh, Michael, I know such a man, and it is he whom I love. His sword is as mighty as himself..."

"And his name?" he asked quietly.

"His name is—Sir Gareth Ardell!" Her voice rang now.

"You are right, Joan—as you always are." His eyes were dead as ashes, but he smiled eagerly. "He is a great swordsman, and a gallant gentleman...But I think you had better go to your room...I think you had better go to your room...Tomorrow we shall see..."

"What? Why do you turn away?"

"It is nothing. I was but laughing, Joan—laughing as though my heart would break. It may break sometime—with laughter."

"I do not understand you, Michael," she announced, and looked at him with her dusky eyes.

"That is true. Aye! You do not understand me...and I cannot explain, for if I did I should kiss those lips of yours, Joan, that are red—with the sullen red of a city swept in flames. I should bruise their softness—"

"Joan!" It was half a cry, half a gasp from the doorway. Blinking in the light, with his doublet unlaced and his hair like a mane, Sir Gareth Ardell stood there. An instant the tableau held—Joan Gardline staring at the apparition, like a vision of power, and Tairlaine with his dark handsome head flung back and one arm extended along the mantel shelf. Then the deep tides swept Joan to the center of the room, where Gareth caught her. Tairlaine had a sudden curious sensation that he had been stabbed and he groped vaguely for a dagger with his slim, white, woman's hands. He became aware that he was very tired; then he sat down, and looked stupidly at the fire. Behind him the firelight glistened on the curve of Joan's arm as it tightened...

"Why," Tairlaine heard a voice say, "he is laughing again! What a queer person you are, in truth, Michael!" and a sort of forced and breathless laugh.

"But you must tell me!" boomed Gareth. "By the rood![4] To see you here—to blunder on you when I sought but Michael—"

"Explanations," interrupted Tairlaine, rising and slapping his knees, "must tarry. There is much to be done. In brief, my friend, Joan is homeless; she hath need of you. The plans we made ere you went upstairs must be altered slightly. Yet it merely means another person—"

"Stay!" said the girl; "he shall know!"

Her beautiful, vacuous face upturned, she poured out the story, and her hand trembled on Gareth's arm.

"To you I look for protection," she said. "You can take me safely from England. Once out of this country—"

Gareth gave a heave of his mighty shoulders, like a mountain shaken by dynamite.[5]

"Do you hear, Michael?" he demanded, seizing Tairlaine's arm. "Do you hear?"

"You would forget Charles?" asked the other gently.

---

4 By the cross. "Rood" is the Old English word for cross.

5 While not put into the mouth of a character, this simile is anachronistic. Dynamite was invented in 1867. The use of casual anachronisms is a weakness in the younger Carr's historical tales, which the professional Carr eliminated.

"I would forget—God!"[6]

"Be not so hasty. You need forget neither. We have made our plans—carefully. There are but three days. Bradshaw has pronounced the sentence; there remains but the warrant. Follow you the plans. On the eve of the twenty-ninth, we meet at the Crowns. If the ruse I have shown you be successful, Charles shall be with us. And then—"

"What mean you?" She was breathing heavily, and her wide eyes sought Tairlaine s face.

"That you will be safe at the Crowns while—friend Gareth strikes for England! Ah, you were right, Joan; I am but a woman! I can but play on my harp and blow the breath of the whirlwind after your knight has rescued the king from check—I am a mere rook, who would only in straight line—"[7]

"Nay!" Unmindful of the hour, Gareth thundered out his protest. "Nay! Think you I throw love of country against love of woman? If you be the man I think, dare St. James' palace and rescue Charles—sing your songs and ye care! Let any man question my courage who will meet my steel, but I ride with Joan for France and her freedom. I wash my hands of the plan! A man loves but once."

For a moment the dove-like eyes of the poet were frightening. Blind fire swept up from inside, consuming reason and scorching his body so that it quivered. Then the fire died out; his hands dropped, and he bowed.

"You are right, Gareth," he responded, so low that they hardly heard him. "A man loves but once. And sometimes—it hurts."

"Hurts?" Gareth laughed. "And truly! The poet speaks the truth in his fancy—the poet, who knows naught of hurt—who never felt the steel of battle or the steel of life!"

Tairlaine sat down again. They did not see his face.

"In God's name," he said, "Go!—go now. I will help you, but—go."

"But mark me, Michael," asserted Gareth, clinching his rugged hands as he looked down at Joan, whose eyes were fixed on him; "I fear no man; I fear naught upon earth! My sword hath tamed mighty men. Were I but allowed to strike at these Puritan cowards and turncoats... Michael! Why look you so?"

---

6 This is a bit of literary subtlety here on Carr's part. Ardell's declared willingness, for his passion, to forget God echoes Tairlaine's criticism of Puritans, whose religion "defies God because it hurts man." In his deviation from principle, Ardell even becomes complicit, by Tairlaine's standard, in Cromwell's execution of Charles: "Had he but served his fellow man as faithfully as he has served his God, he would not now be a murderer for a doctrine!"

7 Take note of Carr's use here of the chess metaphor, leveraged more strongly in "That Ye Be Not Judged" (written two years after this story) and (as the "Notes for the Curious" commentary following documented) characteristically reused by Carr for decades.

Tairlaine was upon his feet with the quick, lithe grace of the swordsman or the dancer. He went to the window; when he turned he was silhouetted against the graying dawn like a figure of prophecy.

"Why," he returned, "I but thought that soon your words might be tested, Gareth. I have lived too long not to know the sound of Fairfax's horsemen!"

And in the stillness of the new-born day they heard in the inn-yard the rattle and clash of hoofs.

III

Bradshaw Asks a Question

In the big, gloomy room a former king of England sat at the long table with a pen dragging from his hand. The flames of the candles waved like battle-pennons[8] in the wind that blew from the river, sending streaks of fog through the iron-grated window. There was a gurgling and dripping of rain. Unseeingly the man at the table stared across the dark stains crawling down the darker stone under the window. His face was drawn and pale, as though it had been seared by fire long ago; his moustache and imperial were like a caricature of Satan. Yet there was nothing Satanic in that countenance—only the mockery of a proud, spoiled child who has lost its mother and is now only hauntingly wistful. Charles I, a strange mixture of the Scotch and the French, was like a tired groping child now. He rose with a gesture of weariness.

"I cannot write, Sydney, " he said, and flung down the pen. "This false hand hath wrought too much evil already of which the heart was guiltless. Ah, Sydney, Cranmer[9] held in the washing fire the hand that had offended...Would God I could!..."

In the shadows a face moved and a man stirred in his seat among the rushes. The faint weird glow showed the doglike devotion and earnest eyes of a servant who knew no praise or blame save its master's.

"Grieve not, sire," he rippled softly. "The iron Puritan may not for-

---

8 A battle-pennon is a long, triangular flag, especially of the sort that might be attached to a helmet or lance, perhaps the favor of a lady exhibited by a tournament knight. Carr is again conflating the imagery of love and war, the central tension of this story.

9 Thomas Cranmer was a key architect of the Reformation and Church of England. He helped arrange the annulment of Henry VIII's marriage to Catherine of Aragon. Henry later appointed Cranmer Archbishop of Canterbury in the Church of England. When Henry's daughter Mary ("Bloody Mary"), a Catholic, ascended to the throne in 1553, Cranmer was arrested and tried for heresy and treason. (He had also supported the ascension of Lady Jane Grey over Mary; Jane was queen for only nine days.) Cranmer recanted his heresy and reconciled himself with the Catholic Church, but in 1556, Mary executed him anyway.

give because he has no nobility. You are above all such. You are yet the king of England—"

"No!" the cry was wrung from Charles. He went to the window, and the clammy breath of the river stirred his hair. "Stop, in the name of heaven! You—paid as—all their judges did not; nay, not even when the wand was broken and the Stuart blood disgraced! Think ye I fear death? It is but a narrow chasm over which we fear to step because we may not turn back from its farther shore. Nay, but dishonor—and I did only those things entrusted to me as my right. Had I to live again—yet I am troubled. Sydney; here, in this very Tower. There are ghosts, Sydney, I see Wentworth's face, Wentworth, whom I had not the courage to save. There is blood upon him, and he cries, 'Put not your trust in princes!'[10]—ah, prophet is—"

"Stop!" Sydney cried, and his voice held an agonized ring. "Stop, sire! It be ghosts and not men which drive us mad! These gloomy imaginings will stifle you an you take not care!"

"And what matters it?" asked the tired tones, dreary as the drip of water from the ancient stones. "I die soon, and the crooked hands of hate write my memorial."

"Nay, sire! Think not so! Even yet from the north may come the avenging blast—"

"I am already upon the scaffold. The help from France failed—would God I had not writ those letters of Naseby[11]—ah, but Sydney, I fear no kingly end. Yet the knife in the dark, even as the second Richard must have felt within these walls. I fear them all; Cromwell least, for he is a soldier; Bradshaw most, for he is not a soldier."

"You need not, Charles Stuart."

The voice was harsh, but it was arresting, and Charles swung round, sensing for the first time the presence of a third person in the room. The heavy door was open now, and a lantern burned yellow on the threshold. A figure, booted and cloaked, had appeared like a specter—a figure to whom the lieutenant of the Tower in the passage behind, was respectfully silent. Charles did not move. His eyes were full of somber fire.

---

10 Psalm 146:3, a reminder that worldly power is limited while God's is eternal, so hope and salvation can come only from God.

11 At the Battle of Naseby, Cromwell's forces captured Charles' personal baggage; among it were letters revealing his plan to seek support from Confederate (Catholic) Ireland and the Catholic nations in Europe. The publication of Charles' correspondence gave Parliament the political support it needed to fight the Civil War to its end, victoriously.

"I know not why you have come, John Bradshaw," he said. "Perhaps to scoff, or wrest secrets from your quarry ere you kill him."

"Leave us," Bradshaw ordered to the men behind him, "but be within call."

He stood slapping his gloves against his side while the door creaked shut. Then he advanced to the table and spread out his hands upon it. His bearded face was a mask.

"Mark me well, Charles Stuart, for time leaps on apace. I have been your enemy. I have fought you in parliament and on the field. I was the judge who condemned you. Yet you profess that your desire is to save England. Do I speak truly?"

"Why bait you the trap?" Charles questioned impatiently. "I am content to die; what other pitfalls would you dig? To crawl on my knees before Cromwell—"

"You dally. What would you—save England?"

"Aye! From the fire and the sword—"

"Recall you, Charles Stuart, that no longer do you rule your knavish and drunken cavaliers with that lying tongue. You have blasted England, Charles Stuart, and your treachery has been thwarted only by Cromwell and God! Why, the very dogs despise you!" His words cut like a lash across Charles' pale cheeks. He tottered and pressed his hand to his temple.

"You are no better than the thief who cheats at cards," continued Bradshaw, smiling with the tight-lipped and calm deadliness of a Torquemada;[12] "you have brought dishonor forever upon your ancestors and your descendants. If there be a hell, assuredly you must be in it when your forfeit is paid."

"Are you here to torture me?" cried the other. "You know that I am helpless—"

"If there be a spark of manhood in you," interposed Bradshaw, "then I charge you, tell me—what do you know of Michael Tairlaine?"

For a moment Charles' hands fluttered before his face.

"What know you," Bradshaw went on inexorably, "of Michael Tairlaine? Where makes he his home? Who are his friends? What influence does he exert—and to what end?"

"You ask me these things!" Charles had lowered his hands now. He stood superb and defiant with his white fingers stroking his neckcloth, and his voice scornful with the proud scorn of despair. "You, the conqueror, dare come and ask information from him you have condemned? Ask your men at arms before you crawl to me! Ask your model spies— Aye, and ask all England for the identity of Michael Tairlaine! Ask the

---

12 The first Grand Inquisitor of the Spanish Inquisition.

stars that hear his song at midnight! Ask the winds that are wine to his harp-strings! Ask the moon that nods at his back when he rides—but, Bradshaw, *ask not me!*"

"He is a traitor!" snapped Bradshaw, and jingled his sword-belt with his long, dagger-shaped hands. "He was at the Eagles Brood on the edge of London; a dangerous foe, Charles Stuart, for he appeals to the passions rather than the judgment. He was shielding a runaway baggage from Gardline when Hacker himself arrived. There were three—with your own Sir Gareth Ardell, whom we are watching. God in heaven!" He picked up the pen and hurled it down again. "Sir Gareth saw the hopelessness of it, and he submitted. But what does your Irish cutthroat do? He knocks over the candles and drives a chair through the window. I lunged, be sure, but the wind roared in, and I heard him shout, 'God for King Charles!' and he was gone!"

"And well? What became of your three refugees?"

Bradshaw caught himself up. He looked narrowly at Charles and laughed.

"Why, it occurs to me that you have been told enough. I am not here to play the buffoon—" He flung his cloak over his shoulders.

"Perhaps," said Charles, bowing as the door closed on Bradshaw's retreating figure, "you had not originally that intent, my friend..."

In the gloomy hallway outside, with a forest of murmuring tapestries moving in the wind, a man in light armor was pacing up and down.

"Well, Colonel Pride?" demanded Bradshaw.

"Quite successful," rumbled the other's heavy voice. The determined jaw of this man who had cleared Parliament of its royalist sympathizers was in evidence now. In the wan light he was almost the counterpart of Sir Gareth Ardell.

"Good!" Bradshaw paused a moment; then very slowly he spoke: "Put the Lady Joan Gardline in the room next to this. We shall have the others before morning!"

IV

A Blood-Red Sky

It was late afternoon of the twenty-eighth day of January, 1649, the same day as that upon which the events of the previous paragraphs fell. Dirty, squalid London, with its crooked streets and stifling air—the London of the days before fire had purged it of its deformities—was bawling its wares outside. Michael Tairlaine watched it from the second story of the inn, jutting out over the tangle of passers-by below. The bitter wind cut into thin, scrawny flesh; there were huddled heaps on doorsteps and skeleton hands outstretched...

Moodily the poet sipped his wine. Ardell, on the hearth-rug, was watching him with anguished eyes.

"Can I ever ask your forgiveness, Michael?" he burst out wretchedly. "I have played the coward—the coward when my life hath been as free from fear as the Black Prince's! Could I but atone—"

"Nay, Gareth," Tairlaine said wearily, "you have naught to be ashamed of. 'Twas my own foolish move—though I did but imagine you would spirit her away in the dark."

"As I had done were my wits not those of a child! I must have been mad that night, Michael; I played not only the coward but the fool. When I saw the great number of them with their pikes, I could think only of escape. Yet—" He swung round from pacing. "Yet there is time. You have done that much, my friend. I will show you that my blood be not all water. I will test my courage before your very eyes...What is your plan for saving Charles?"

Tairlaine showed no surprise at the question; only a little flicker of relief went over his lips.

"My thanks, Gareth," he asserted. "I knew you must see the situation. I knew you must push onward in spite of the devil and his Ironsides[13]...Ah, but it is difficult now Gareth, for we are marked men. The city is on the watch; we dare not stir from here by day, and trusted I not mine host—"

"But the plan?"

"In the Thames lies a sloop of my own procuring. Once Charles has escaped to France, the French king will lend every assistance. I will rouse the north counties—"

"But how to rescue Charles?" interposed Gareth impatiently. "Always you have been silent—you insist that I am the one man to help you. But why? Other blades are as stout as mine. How am I to pluck him out of a hundred guards?"

Tairlaine drained his wine and stood up. The shadows were already creeping in the room, but a red slit of sky like an eye peered over the roofs. It threw a wild glow on Ardell's face. He looked like a figure in a mediaeval manuscript.

"You shall do it," Tairlaine replied, "because you look exactly like Colonel Pride...Listen, Gareth; listen..."

V

Telleth How the Harp Was Stilled Forever

Booted and spurred, with his cloak drawn about him and his hat beaten around his eyes by the drizzle, Tairlaine paced the yard. The fog

---

13 The troopers of the Parliamentarian Cavalry, so by extension, Tairlaine refers to Cromwell as the devil.

swirled like choking gray smoke, touching him clammily. Rain danced on the stones. The lantern that hung in the archway looked through like a pale, tired face. Faintly the watcher could hear the rustle of horses.

"Twelve—and far after," he muttered. "Had aught gone wrong, I should have heard of it—"

"Michael!" a voice thrilled across the inn-yard, husky and quivering. Dark blots moved on the gray like ghosts.

"Michael!" the voice called again—low, but with a note that was portentous.

"Hither!" Tairlaine responded cautiously. "The horses—"

Gareth's bulk towered over him. Another figure with draggling hat and tight-wrapped cloak loomed through the fog. Tairlaine's heart leaped; joy surged inside him like the sweep of a dazzling wave. His lips moved in a smile that only the fog saw—in the next moment he had slid to his knees on the stones before the newcomer.

"Your majesty," he said with a kind of fierce intensity, "this night hath England been delivered from the Puritan. This night Sir Gareth Ardell hath accomplished a deed—"

"Peace, Michael!" Gareth's hoarse voice cut him short. "No time for demonstration! They must have discovered it by now. The watchers also must be close."

Michael felt a hand brush his head; in the next instant he was on his feet, and his deft fingers were at the horses' reins.

"There—do you hear?" snapped Gareth. His hand darted out; in the dripping silence they discerned the thump of staves and the shuffle of feet that denoted the watch. A sword-belt jingled. Along the wall the flicker of a lantern shot like an accusing finger.

"We must not be questioned!" Tairlaine's tense orders gripped the situation. "To horse, and ride—where I have indicated!"

In the next instant the clatter of hoofs tore the stillness to bits; there was a champing and snorting, and through the archway swept the black mass. Under overhanging roofs the sharp staccato beat rang, like blows on an anvil. Tairlaine, a little in advance, guided them almost by instinct through the black emptiness and the roaring tunnel of the wind. Across their path shot the sudden wild gleam of a lantern and was swallowed up. The fog pressed down...

"Behind us!" shouted Gareth against the wind. "'Tis—pursuit..."

Through the creak and groan of the old houses that bent their necks over them they could hear the pounding of hoofs somewhere behind. The streets reeled like a nightmare. *Clap-clap* rang the iron; *clap-clap*...

A weird elfin glow danced behind. Lights were fluttering up. There was a flash of armor and a shout from another of the watch patrols. Men were tumbling out of houses. All over the city a great mad cry went winging, seeming to tell of a sad-eyed king and a dim ideal riding like a whirlwind through the tortuous streets of London.

Ahead the bobbing flare of torches spattered a trail of blood on the night and made the shine of armor ugly and deadly. Lights were fluttering up. Bearded faces whisked up; Tairlaine could see a whirl of cloaks… and he could see the dull gleam of Sir Gareth's darting blade…

Horses reared and plunged. A pistol roared deafeningly, and then another. The three fugitives bent lower. Ahead they could see only a black whispering gulf, but they knew that they were nearing the river.

"The skiff is—ahead," Tairlaine gasped. "moored by—where—"

He turned in his saddle as the wild crimson eyes of the torches leered around the corner, far behind. Against it horsemen were silhouetted black and gigantic. A ragged streak crashed from their ranks—and Michael Tairlaine gave a little shuddering moan, clutched at the case that hung from his saddle-bow, and toppled into darkness…

By the wharf-side Sir Gareth Ardell was already sweeping his companion into the boat. Silently the skiff glided into the dark water.

"Gone!" said Sir Gareth, and laughed oddly. "Gone!" He turned to the figure in the stern. "And did he imagine I would save Charles when *you* were in the next room, Joan? He provided the faculties for us—to escape to France. Idealism! The damned little fool!"

"You are a brave man, Gareth," she murmured, "to risk so much."

And twisted in the street with his face white against the black stone, the smile was fading from Tairlaine's face—the smile of a great ideal realized, of a king escaping in safe hands. He did not feel the throb in his temples or the wet blindness in his eyes. He thought he was crying. Then he stretched out his hand. The great harp lay shattered beside him. Through the coverings he touched the twisted strings. They murmured and died out. The harp of Tairlaine was still.

Notes for the Curious: "The Harp of Tairlaine"

The Hill Record, Carr's prep-school student publication, printed "The Harp of Tairlaine" in April 1925. Carr modestly revised the story, retitling it "The Inn of the Seven Swords" and reissuing it that same month two years later in *The Haverfordian*, his college literary journal. On the whole, the editor finds the earlier version to be better—but some of Carr's 1927 changes (including a few textual corrections) were good choices, and so the editor has brought them into the present text. This version is therefore technically a combination of both those Carr wrote—but all the words are Carr's own.

With its approximation of period dialect and awakening eye to period detail, "The Harp of Tairlaine" is an incremental step forward in sophistication for Carr's historical narratives. In his first tale of times past, "The Will-o'-the-Wisp," set in 1825 Uniontown, Pennsylvania, the reader glimpses the nineteenth century blurrily, as it slips out of a darkness between fevered transitions of consciousness. The circumstances "The Will-o'-the-Wisp" describes may only be a reverie; Carr reinforces this possibility in the story's lack of detail about its people and setting. There is no distinct, careful inventory of any distinguishing nineteenth-century appointments. Rather, Carr confines the action to "a long, low-roofed room whose oak-paneled walls glistened dully in the blaze of a hundred candles." There is also a crystal chandelier, mirrors, windows covered in crimson velvet, and a waxed floor; so nothing in "The Will-o'-the-Wisp" cogently conjures a nineteenth-century ballroom. It might as easily be a ballroom in the year 1922 (when Carr wrote the story).

Similarly, the denizens of "The Will-o'-the-Wisp" are "gayly attired....a richly clad thong." Carr passes over sartorial particulars entirely. The lack of detail, while almost unnoticeably indistinct, is more befitting of a dream than it is a recreation of history.

Chronologically, "The Harp of Tairlaine," is Carr's next historical tale, second in a string of well more than a dozen spirited stories and novels featuring "swashbuckling stuff, not altogether free of gadzookses or the like, but at least historically accurate"[1] that Carr would write over the coming half century. The reader can witness Carr moving from strength to strength in this genre: "The Red Heels," "The Blue Garden," and "That Ye Be Not Judged" followed this story in that order, each

---

1 Jeff Caldwell's confession of the sorts of books he wishes to write in Carr's *Deadly Hall*, pp. 4-5.

demonstrating how the young student of history fashioned the facts he learned capably into the trimmings of fiction.

"The Harp of Tairlaine" coalesces some of the apprentice author's emerging idiosyncrasies, some of which he carried over into his professional career. Most notably, Michael Tairlaine is another lovelorn Irish proxy of his youthful Irish author; Tairlaine is a successor to Jimmy O'Brien (1923's "The Kindling Spark") and Terence O'Riordan (1924's "The Cloak of D'Artagnan"). Carr would populate his fiction with such surrogates throughout his career, and, as noted in the introduction, sometimes even mirror himself in the shards of a single narrative. For instance, in *The Eight of Swords* (1934), both the young aspirant to adventure, Hugh Donovan, and the mystery writer Henry Morgan are partial reflections of Carr.[2] Carr pulls off a similar personality split in *Night at the Mocking Widow*, contrasting the adventure-seeking naïf, the Reverend James Cadman Hunter, with Carr's more obvious avatar, a successful thirty-something adventure novelist and writer of radio plays for the BBC named Gordon West. Both find themselves entwined within the novel's danger and its romance.

"The Harp of Tairlaine" retained emotional significance for Carr into the twilight of his career, largely because its themes did. In *Deadly Hall*, Carr's penultimate work, he reimagines this short tale (under its revised title) as a novel written by his fictional counterpart, Jeff Caldwell. The dialog between Jeff and his love interest, Penny Lynn, concerning it and the author's historical romances generally, also clearly functions as a retrospective discussion between the much older Carr, a half-century professional novelist, and the aspirational, romantic spirit that remained within Carr through all those years:

> "...You chose the course you wanted, you wouldn't be put off or diverted by too much 'sensible' advice; and you've become the distinguished author you always wanted to be."
>
> "I'm not very distinguished, Penny. But I may make a living from it if I stay on the job."
>
> "Hasn't the work itself been a great satisfaction? All those books have been good, Jeff; two or three of them are awfully good."
>
> "Romantic foolery, for the most part!"
>
> "What's wrong with romantic foolery, if it's well done or realistic of its own kind?" Penny raised her eyes. "In *The*

---

2 This was an observation first published by Douglas Greene in the biography, pp. 142-144; he echoed and expanded on it in his 2021 introduction to the Penzler Publishers' edition of *The Eight of Swords*.

> *Inn of the Seven Swords*, for instance, I've never forgotten that
> fight on the battlements of Falworth Moat House. And the
> love scene with Lady Phillida in the garden might have been
> the garden behind Delys Hall..." (pp. 54-55)

As was the case for "The Kindling Spark" and the historical romances that followed it ("The Red Heels," "The Dim Queen," and "The Blue Garden"), "The Harp of Tairlaine" is colored by its yet-immature author's disposition to view love hopelessly, even tragically. The teenaged writer had himself so far only experienced disappointment in love at the time he wrote this tale; so for suitors in Carr's early narratives who are not romantically disappointed ("The Blindfold Quest," "The Cloak of D'Artagnan," "Candlelight: A Ghost Story of Christmas"), as we have seen, romance comes only at each story's end in the form of a promise. The young Carr, without any success himself yet in romantic love, has no idea how to describe and incorporate it as a subplot.

Given this, "The Harp of Tairlaine" is somewhat too obvious in its sympathetic bitterness concerning Lady Joan's disparagement of Michael as undeserving of "the blood-red of romance." (Note, too, how this story, with its white and red imagery of commingled blood and love, anticipates the use of the same imagery, more emphatically, in "The Blue Garden.") The dramatic ironies Carr counterpoints with the language of Joan's rejection—that the "feminine" poet once saved the life of the bigger, burlier Gareth by plunging "into a boiling sea to rescue a friend" (and which is mocked in the first moments Gareth and Joan see one another: "Then the deep tides swept Joan to the center of the room, where Gareth caught her"); that it is Tairlaine himself who conceives the plan "to sway empires, with a brain to plan and a heart to dare"; that Joan erroneously imagines Ardell, not Michael, "a brave man...to risk so much"; and that it is Tairlaine's plot to save King Charles which results in the Lady's own rescue—are too precisely crafted a set of matches between protestation and circumstance to be fully effective storytelling elements. But what lovelorn teenager was ever subtle?

Disappointment in love differentiates Carr's early works from his professional novels. In those, Carr's surrogates (and non-surrogate lead characters alike) almost unfailingly find romance. A likelier romantic dilemma for the adult author's protagonists is the choice (as noted in the introduction) between two lovers—and consistent with the tradition of literary romance, generally, one prospective lover is the virtuous and better choice, the other often, despite appearances, a "mercenary and cold-hearted virago" (as Carr describes the type in 1967's *The House at Satan's Elbow*, p. 209).

"The Harp of Tairlaine," like "The Riddle of the Laughing Lord" before it and "Pygmalion," which follows in 1927, examines the artist allegorically. These three stories do so in incrementally increasing, elaborate manners. This middle story's allegorical conceit is governed by a metonymy: the titular harp represents the poetic spirit and power of its bard, indeed, the cultural power of ballads generally.

With respect to ballads, note that Michael Tairlaine's plaintive song in the story's second section may have been part of an early draft of Carr's poem "Poets' Isle," published in *A Book of Hill School Verse*. Compare Michael's lay to the second stanza of Carr's finished poem:

> If this could be!
> From out the sea to raise the crystal spires
> Of cities dimly known to me,
> Where move the shapes of fantasy
> And bards of dreams in fancy free awake their sleeping
> lyres—
> If this could be!
>
> —
>
> Builder of dream-spun cities,
> Maker of minstrel men,
> Harp of the deathless ditties,
> Weaving a song again—[3]

The subject matter and language are very similar indeed; where Michael's tune departs from Carr's poem is in its rhythm. Carr's poems usually lack emotional depth, but they are unfailingly incantatory, having strong, regular meters and refrains constructed mnemonically—too much so, really, which is typical of amateur teenaged poets, but the poems are clearly written to be remembered easily and recited. The metrics of Michael's song are less consistent, less obvious: while there is a lyrical rhyme scheme (the pattern by which verse lines rhyme)—A-B-A-A-B-A—the bard's line lengths are inconsistent: a line of dimeter (two total stressed syllables) followed by a line of pentameter (five stressed syllables), then two lines of tetrameter (four stressed syllables), a very long heptameter line (seven stressed syllables), and finally the repetition

---

3 *A Book of Hill School Verse*, p. 10.

of the opening dimeter line.[4] This really requires a musician to make rhythmic sense of it through the composition of a compelling melody. Michael's lyric does not read attractively on the page. "Poets' Isle," in contrast, is much neater and more available to the ear: an A-B-A-B rhyme scheme delivered in trimeter. One might argue, though, that in context, Michael's musical plaint, with its irregular metrics, forces the reader to slow down, to read the words, and to connect them emotionally to Tairlaine's situation.

In any event, Carr's use of music in "The Harp of Tairlaine" is more than ornamental. In addition to enhancing the seventeenth-century atmosphere and layering Michael's character, Tairlaine's verse demonstrates the influence of Macaulay upon the story's young author. Tairlaine's harp has the power to soothe and console, to conjure romance by candlelight, but as well, to incite revolution:

> There...stands the harp of Michael Tairlaine. With it I may speak to the people who are ripe to revolt. Do you effect the escape of Charles; I will ride from York to Cornwall and weave a song to set their hearts afire.

It is not only Macaulay's emphasis on the connection between ballad and history according to which the reader can observe the historian's influence on Carr's short historical work. The seventeenth-century England Carr evokes in "The Harp of Tairlaine" traces back to Lord Macaulay's twelfth-century Provence:

> ...the most flourishing and civilized portion of Western Europe...in no wise a part of France...It was there that the spirit of chivalry first laid aside its terrors, first took a humane and graceful form, first appeared as the inseparable associate of art and literature, of courtesy and love...A literature rich in ballads, in war-songs, in satire, and above all, in amatory poetry amused the leisure of the knights and ladies whose for-

---

4 The reader might speculate that there is an editing mistake, that the heptameter line should be broken into two, a tetrameter line followed by a trimeter one. This would adjust the rhyme scheme to a very regular A-B-A-B-A-B-A, as well. The difficulty is that Carr clearly intended otherwise. Both times the story was printed, the first letter of each line was capitalized, but the word "awake," which would start the new line, was not—and both times, although the line's physical length broke across printed lines, it is clearly typeset as a single, longer line, not as two.

> tified mansions adorned the banks of the Rhone and Garonne.
> (pp. 1505—1506)

So "The Harp of Tairlaine" is an early demonstration of Carr's subscription to Macaulay's Romantic interpretation of history in which ballads, poetry, texts, period detail, and dominant figures ("great men") come together to revivify the past for us and help readers to understand its truths and lessons in a more evocative and personally felt manner—a greater truth than that possible to convey through the bare recitation of historical incident and fact.

While Macaulay's influence is one of perspective, an inspiration of content behind Carr's story and its metonymic harp is Thomas Moore's, "The Harp That Once Through Tara's Halls," a broadside ballad[5] later collected into a volume of Moore's Irish melodies. (This Thomas Moore, an Irish writer born in 1779, is not to be confused with Saint Sir Thomas More, the Englishman martyred by King Henry VIII in the sixteenth century.) Moore's ballad, written from nationalistic sentiment while Ireland was under English rule, summons recollection of the Hill of Tara, traditionally identified as the inauguration site of Irish high kings:

> The harp that once through Tara's halls
> The soul of music shed,
> Now hangs as mute on Tara's walls,
> As if that soul were fled. —
> So sleeps the pride of former days,
> So glory's thrill is o'er,
> And hearts, that once beat high for praise,
> Now feel that pulse no more.
>
> No more to chiefs and ladies bright
> The harp of Tara swells;
> The chord alone, that breaks at night,
> Its tale of ruin tells.
> Thus Freedom now so seldom wakes,
> The only throb she gives,
> Is when some heart indignant breaks,

---

5 A broadside ballad was one printed on a single, inexpensive sheet of paper, usually featuring a popular theme, common in Britain and Ireland beginning in the sixteenth century, and then as well in America, through the nineteenth century. They were printed cheaply in high volume and sold for a penny apiece, or a few pence.

To show that still she lives.[6]

In Moore's poem, the harp's decline into silence is likewise the decline of the unalloyed Irish culture.

Carr must have found Moore's *Irish Melodies* on the shelves of his father's library, and he likely revisited Moore's poem often. For instance, Carr wrote an ode to Moore in April 1924, "The Voice and the Harp," which is somewhat in the style and spirit of Moore's own poem:

> Here's a health to the fair land of Erin,
> From Columbia over the sea,
> And soon may the flag of her fathers
> Be raised over Ireland free.
> And here's to the bard of the nation,
> Be his memory green evermore,
> For naught has done more for her freedom
> Than the voice and the harp of Tom Moore.
>
> The voice of the singer is silent,
> The hand of the singer is dust,
> But the thoughts and the hopes they awakened
> Come down through the years as a trust.
> Here's a glass to the songs that he gave us,
> The world is repeating them o'er;
> And we hold as a heritage sacred,
> Each strain from the harp of Tom Moore.

Carr demonstrated the place for "The Harp That Once Through Tara's Halls" in his memory and heart by alluding to it in multiple college writings—poetry, prose, and fiction—and then, across the years. Carr draws upon it decades later, in *Panic in Box C* (1966): Kate Hamilton, asked to cast her recollection back nearly four decades, disclaims, "I'm not the harp that once through Tara's halls, you know" (p. 191).

As to his college prose, in March 1925, only a month before publication of "The Harp of Tairlaine," Carr further apostrophized Moore, and other patron Hibernian spirits, in an essay, "The Land of Lost Causes," printed in *The Hill Record*:

______

6 *Irish Melodies*, Longman, Green, and Co. (1867), p. 6.

> Oh, Ireland, mother of the mighty dead, land of O'Neill and Wolf [sic] Tone, of Emmet and Burke, of Goldsmith and Moore, look upon the works of thy sons and be proud[7]

"The Land of Lost Causes" also alludes specifically to Moore's "Harp," observing:

> The leaders stand beyond the reach of mortal hands, looking down upon the land where Tara's silent halls are visited only by the moonlight and the ghosts" (p. 8).

"The Harp of Tairlaine" is in essence a fictional exploration of the themes in "The Land of Lost Causes"; although Carr's "Harp" is a story of the minstrel's fealty to Charles, and "The Land of Lost Causes" a paean to the island of the young author's ancestry, the essay's opening paragraph nonetheless offers a tone and setting readers of the short story will quickly recognize as the story's antecedent:

> Minstrels have sung its fame in smoky banquet-halls, where the wolf-dogs snarled and the chain-mail clinked and the long bright swords gleamed back the firelight. They have sung its fame across the great ocean, and sad eyes smile at the songs which rise in the moonlight and vanish like the peat smoke...They tell of crushed ambition and hope gone out like the peat-fires...They tell of the gallantry of men who fought to the end for an ideal—perhaps for a phrase. And in its dark story the sob of the harp rises to a triumphant cry in the lilt of Irish laughter and the smile of Irish tears....The gallant nearly always fail, because they take the greatest odds. (p. 8)

Indeed, the closing words of "The Land of Lost Causes" might easily have been a draft on the end of "The Harp of Tairlaine":

----

7 *The Hill Record*, March 1925, p. 9. All subsequent excerpts are drawn from the same edition. Regarding the other figures named: Hugh O'Neill, Earl of Tyrone, led the Irish Clans against the English during the Nine Year's war. Theobald Wolfe Tone (Carr or his errant editor unfortunately wrote, "Wolf") was an eighteenth-century Irish separatist who was exiled and then brought back to Dublin to face a court martial. He escaped the hangman by an apparent suicide. Robert Emmet was an Irish Republican (and rebel) during the late 18th and early 19th centuries. Christopher Patrick Burke, only eight years Carr's senior, was an Irish Revolutionary noted for his twenty-three-day hunger strike. He died in 1964. Goldsmith is of course Oliver Goldsmith, the writer.

And in the hearts of the world that great message of music
everlasting has remained and shall remain until the harp falls
from the hand of the minstrel, and the lips of the singer are
dust. (p. 9)

Tairlaine's harp is, within its own tale, like Moore's harp, a spiritual
manifestation: of human song, of ballads, and of passions such as love
and laughter. This is not trivial. Tairlaine's thoughts concerning these
are Carr's own:

We shall be playing a dangerous game with a dangerous foe,
but the Puritan must fall, for he has forgotten how to laugh.
It is fatal to scorn laughter; it is fatal to scorn song. Charles
is a fool, but he is a great man, and all great hearts are fools.

Michael conjoins the "foolishness" of laughter and song with the "foolishness" of patriotism, and even the "foolishness" of greatness. It is the
same "romantic foolery" that Penny Lynn will defend in *Deadly Hall*,
published forty-six years later. It is Macaulay's satire, which with courtesy and love, is a part of chivalry. This triad of laughter, song, and
cultural pride are among Carr's indispensable themes, and which in
the young author's eyes makes the story's closing image so meaningful:
the destruction of the harp of Tairlaine is in the greater allegorical sense
the destruction of truth and gallantry. It is even, just as the silencing
of Moore's harp is the silencing of Ireland itself, the precipitating loss
confirming the destruction of the English monarchy: had Ardell not
betrayed Michael's plan, the king might have been saved.

Michael's passionate belief in the indispensability of laughter is not
a rhetorical artifice; it is genuinely felt by his author. Carr is a richly
ironic author. While the signal manifestation of irony in Carr's detective novels is situational irony—the unexpected outcome that provides
the climactic satisfaction in all great detective fiction—many of Carr's
detective novels are saturated with humor (itself a product of irony,
whether formulated verbally, situationally, or dramatically). Carr's creative need to intertwine mystery with laughter was so unrelenting that
he assumed the pseudonym Carter Dickson to create his major series
detective, H.M. (Sir Henry Merrivale), perhaps crime fiction's greatest
comic detective. Nearly all of H.M.'s two dozen adventures (twenty-two
novels, a novella, and a short story) are as risible as they are perplexing,
intermingling not only the mysterious, but on occasion even the Gothic

and the otherwise terrifying, with the slapstick—and in demonstration of Carr's writerly accomplishment, nearly always successfully.

Nor was laughter for Carr merely the jester's bells. Carr's elevation and lifelong exploitation of the adolescent as one of the two essential ingredients combining to create "the best of entertaining interchanges between characters" is not a persistently immature remnant of his juvenile temperament—in fact, often enough, it is not so little as that even in his actual juvenilia. Recall the young author's credo in "L'Envoi" (the concluding remarks) of "The New Canterbury Tales," published the month before "The Harp of Tairlaine": "if, when the dim window falls, it causes one person excitement or laughter, our experiment in pure romanticism will have been a success." For Carr, as for the classic dramatists, comedy and tragedy were only two masks, never far separated, but instead simply two moods of a changeable face.

Although Carr's invocation in "The Harp of Tairlaine" of the artist's heart is more personal and more penetrating than in "The Blue Garden," that relative level of penetration is fitting to the goals of each story. In both, shallowness is ruinous. In "The Blue Garden," superficiality is the point: the shepherd Francesco deceives himself that he is a poet, that he loves Joanna, and then that Lucrezia loves him. That none of these is true leads to Francesco's disfigurement in both face and spirit, to his transformation into the bellicose, ultimately destructive Il Duce.

In "The Harp of Tairlaine," superficiality resides in the lustful self-interest of Ardell and Lady Joan Gardline, which those two confuse with virtuous love. Their faults nullify Tairlaine's genuine virtues, heartfelt love and selfless patriotism. In fact, when the Lady Joan rebukes Michael's love by insisting that a woman "loves one who can sway empires, with a brain to plan and a heart to dare...who stops at nothing," she is explaining Lucrezia Borgia's character as accurately as her own, unknowingly putting her finger on the pernicious bent of character that, in both tales, leads to tragedy—not merely personal tragedy, but even to the overthrow of the state, which cannot survive without unalloyed virtue defending it. What's more, Carr plays knowingly upon another irony: the etymology of virtue, which in its original Latin sense refers not to integrity or ethics, but to masculine valor, strength, and merit. Later, medievalism and Romanticism would help transform virtue into its modern-day sense of (ungendered) moral perfection. In this story, Lady Joan and Ardell's misunderstanding of feminine versus masculine traits inhibits their recognition of Michael's authentic virtues.

The greater emotional resonance of "The Harp of Tairlaine" than "The Blue Garden" is because, in Michael, the tragic becomes intimate:

intimate to the author, whom the bard represents with his sensitive manner and artistic mien—and given of the consequent exploration of Tairlaine's inner life (which has no cognate in "The Blue Garden"), to the reader, too. The reader feels all three of the circumstantial loss, the allegorical loss, and the personal loss.

Carr the professional novelist remembered not only this story, but its fallen bard by giving him a namesake "descendent," Dr. Michael Tairlaine, in *The Bowstring Murders*. In that novel, Dr. Tairlaine voices a complaint, one of the highest importance to Carr, which serves as a key theme throughout his works:

> "What pleasures have I ever got?" the tall, frail man demanded. "Why can't I dance and sing bawdy songs and play the rowdy like any sane human being? Did I ever have any childhood?—and now I'm old. It took me this sabbatical year to realize how old. And what adventures did I ever have?" (p. 4)

Dr. Tairlaine reappears in *The Red Widow Murders*...

> ...as hopeful as a boy playing pirate. Hopeful—it might be as well to ask himself—of what? Of adventure tapping his arm in a London mist, a shadow on a blind, a voice, a veiled woman? They did not, he thought in his muddled, kindly way, wear veils nowadays.[8]

It is in this unity of laughter (even bitter laughter), of romance, and of the pursuit of Adventure in the Grand Manner that the reader comes best to recognize Carr, not only in these early historical tales, but throughout his career, whether through Carr's detective, adventure, fantasy, horror, or historical fiction.

---

8 Douglas Greene first made this observation in the biography (p. 130), but it is so suitable that it needed to be borrowed here.

The Red Heels (1926)

Monsieur de ma Belle Dame, whom they called the ugliest man in France and its greatest lover, was drunk again that night. There were two other men in his room, and the candlelight lay on them like a veil of yellow gauze in which blue wreaths of smoke were tangled, but all three stood out sharp and distinct as painted dolls. Monsieur de ma Belle Dame himself resembled a clockwork man; he sat at the table with one thin arm across it, his eyes glassy as marbles. Hair strayed down over his long face, like straw pasted there. And he sat propped sideways, staring at Vandeliers.

Vandeliers—Pierre Vandeliers of the rue St. Antoine—was a kind of adviser who sat on Danton's[1] shoulder. He was a great hulking schooner of a man, fat and broad-mouthed and complacent. In the firelight the rings on his fingers glittered against the white skin as he sat piled in the chimney corner. Vandeliers was not drunk, and he smiled upon the other two, the third of whom sat near the door with his head between his hands.

"I wonder," said Vandeliers, "I wonder to what I owe this invitation to your charming quarters, my friend."

When Monsieur replied he did not move from his sideways position, nor did his eyes move in their stare.

"Time enough. Oh, time enough. See!—We have the whole evening, and you with scarcely a drink in you—" Abruptly he drained his mug, and set it down with a thud.

"Monsieur must know that my time is valuable."

"Oh—to Danton?"

"To the republic." There was more than impatience in Vandeliers' tone now. He moved with a little jingle of sword-belt, and his face shone and glistened in lumps of fat. "To the republic," he repeated. "We Mountainists[2] are honored to count you among our number, are we not?"

---

1   Disfigured in youth by smallpox and accident, Georges Danton lifted himself out of an obscure law practice through renowned oratory. He became a leading figure of the French Revolution, credited with key roles in overthrowing Louis XVI and forming the First French Republic. Danton was appointed Minister of Justice in 1792, but only lasted in that role scant months. Subsequently, he dissented against governmental use of violence, exacerbating his political rivalry with Robespierre and pleading for an end to the Terror. Danton actually announced its end in March, 1794, which led to his swift arrest, trial as a conspiracist and royalist, and his execution.

2   The Mountain resulted from the political merger in 1792 between the Jacobins and

"Name of God, yes! You are absurd, mignon.[3] Does one keep one's head from thirsty Madame Guillotine otherwise? Now," cried Monsieur, beginning to laugh, "now, you damned spy, go back and tell *that* to your master!...No, no, I was joking. I am an extremist, yes. But I wonder how long it will last, this wholesale murder. Daily it grows worse..."

"Well?"

"Well! Our party, my dear Vandeliers, cannot remain in supremacy forever. Robespierre is the most unpopular, and hence he will remain supreme longest. Danton—pah!"

"So long as Danton's oratory grips the people..."

Monsieur struck the table, making the candlelight jump and quiver. But he did not shift his lopsided position, and his eyes were still glassily set.

"Oratory!" he cried. "Does oratory tame beasts, I would know? Oratory! Why, there now sits a greater orator than Danton!" He gestured toward the man by the door, but he did not turn. The man by the door lifted his head, so that the far beams of the candles fell on his face and showed that it was even more befuddled than Monsieur's own. It was a terrible face—terrible because it was so superbly handsome. Blond as a seraph, with the careless dash of a drunken god, and eyes that were netted in red. The eyes regarded Monsieur vaguely.

"Oh," Vandeliers grunted, "I had forgotten. The American! Yes, the American pariah, who could not even handle his own affairs. Men such as that must not handle whole nations. Has he, then, been sober one moment since he has been in Paris? I ask you, Monsieur!"

The young man did not speak. Monsieur leaned forward with a sudden falling motion, like a toy.

"Vandeliers, you never fell from a great height. If you had, it would have broken every bone in your fat body...You wanted to know the reason why I asked you here tonight; eh, is it not so? That is well. Now," he said deliberately, "is it you who has been causing agitation for the execution of our late queen, Marie Antoinette?"

"It is time," returned Vandeliers harshly, "to do away with these royal harlots."

"Ansmith," said Monsieur, "lock the door."

Cordeliers. Danton became president of the Club de Cordeliers in April 1790, leading it until after the monarchy's overthrow in 1792. Danton was also a dominant voice in the Jacobin Club, where political differences between him and Robespierre were evident as early as 1791.

3 "Mignon" means, "cute." Monsieur is good-naturedly belittling Vandaliers.

The words fell with terrific heaviness. Vandeliers surged to his feet. He laughed, but he could not quite control his voice.

"Your affairs of love are well known, my friend, but I confess that I scarcely thought—"

Monsieur shot to his feet, soaring to his great height that made him thin and awful—a skeleton in uniform. His body was balanced on his long arms, hands spread out on the table.

"Come, is it not a merry jest," he said, "is it not a merry jest that the guillotine will never dance for you? You will die in a much more artistic manner...What! Have you no thanks?..."

Vandeliers was clearing his throat, fumbling his cravat and scratching at the hilt of his sword.

"You madman!" he shrilled, groping in the chimney corner, "Oh, you madman! Danton shall hear of this, I warn you—you madman!—"

"Ansmith," said Monsieur, "lock the door."

The young man with the twisted beauty got up and half fell against the door, pawing at the key. Monsieur wrenched the table to one side, so that it toppled with a crash, spilling the candles and leaving only one dim light on the mantel. Vandeliers was under that light, a fat mountain blundering backwards in a blotch of shadow. Then Monsieur drew his rapier.

"For not being able to distinguish between a real affair of love and something obscene," he said; "for that, pray le bon Dieu, Vandeliers. Pray to Him!"

Vandeliers had twitched off his hat and whipped his sword from its sheath. The candlelight ran along the blades like fire; it touched the lace at the men's wrists as their shadows whirled and bobbed on the ceiling. In the fireplace the wood was crumbling to red embers; by its glow Vandeliers could see Monsieur's long legs in their white stockings go flashing about with a kind of awkward grace. He could see, too, the face of his opponent, with its painted wrinkles and the eyes that never moved from the tips of the swords. But he saw that, he heard the stamp of feet, the tiny terrible *ring,* and the sob of his own breath only a moment more.

Monsieur lunged just once, under the guard and up cleanly through the heart. On the wall his adversary's shadow shriveled up, tumbling sideways against that wall. Then Vandeliers, all in a lump like a piece of clay in uniform, slipped to the floor. One hand, thrown out into the fire-glow, kept sprawling and picking at the boards...

In the corner, Ansmith raised his head. When Vandeliers fell he had been leaning against the door and laughing a little. Monsieur was kicking at the wounded man, whose hand writhed and clutched at his leg like a trodden worm, and he was muttering things that made Ansmith feel a jab of pity.

"Poor devil!" the American said, "poor devil..." and added querulously: "Give him some water, can't you?...Stop it, do you hear? Stop it!"

Monsieur was still cuffing him. Vandeliers began to cough horribly and noisily, as though there were water in his throat. Though the American was very drunk, he felt a wave of sickness; vaguely he tried to motion Monsieur away—then he lurched out of the door. The picture of the scene in his head was a distortion of shadow and glare, with Monsieur's great shape blocking out the fire over the twisting body; nevertheless he could still hear Vandeliers coughing...

II

Those were mad times. When life is so short, when La Guillotine's bright blade may sever its thread in an instant, when each glass of wine may be one's last— who will care then? Drink the wine in the old rook's city, lurch in the gutters that are stickily damp, kiss the prostitute who reels against you and pats your cheek with hands that have been in dead men's pockets a while ago!—Drink the wine under the leering red eyes of the torches, kick at the bodies lying all headless before La Guillotine's feet! Who will care ere the clock ticks once? Who will care?

They were singing "La Marseillaise." The song marched in splendor through the streets, like a great dead army whose feet beat time in thunder. You could see the soldiers stalking, phantoms in the crowd, and the spurs of the old horsemen went flashing past, for all the ghosts were out of their tombs now. Here was a world gone mad, specter-filled, as when the lances of Burgundy's cavalry drove in spurts of steel through the ancient lanes. For Paris had tasted the terror.

"Behold," said Mademoiselle Aubley, who was standing by the window, "behold, they make very merry, Monsieur le Dictateur."

She stood there, with a dim ghost of her reflected in the windowpane, one white arm motionless on the shutter. The elfin glow of the candles was reflected in the pane, too, crowning her hair—hair that was startlingly, incredibly black. You noticed the profile above the sweep of crimson gown, but you could not have described it.

"Is it not strange," she added, "that such a man as Danton, a leader of the people, should withdraw to the very outskirts of his city when down there...those madmen! Is it not strange?"

Georges Jacques Danton was out of place in this apartment he had obtained, for his swaggering, bullying dash smashed in on the delicate tone of it. He stood there, a mountain with a great pock-marked face, carrying his hair like a banner, an untidy figure that was full of power. He stared at her, framed in the opposite side of the room. Then he walked to a table in the center and drained a glass of wine.

"Denise Aubley," he told her, "you are either a very clever woman or a most empty-headed fool..." He set the glass down idly. "No, Denise Aubley, you are not a fool. One does not so easily bestow favors, even on Danton. You want something. What is it?"

She turned, white and scarlet against the dark sheen of the glass. She was very intense when she spoke. And she was as brilliantly alive as a flame.

"Why, yes, there is something I would have; is it not natural? For what purpose do we women exist, if not for wanting something? You die, finally, because you cannot give us our last wish. But you can grant me a favor—one small favor, which is nothing to Danton?"

"Eh bien!" muttered the big Frenchman, staring at her.

"Monsieur, you are King. You are Herod, you are Tetrarch. And all I ask is a head."

"Hein?" said Danton, and repeated: "Eh bien! Whose head?"

"Once," she answered, very persuasive, "a woman flogged me. Because I was very young, and very beautiful—yes, that is true—I was taken from my mother, whom my father had deserted. They made me—ah, they made me a fine lady! They feasted me, and gave me silks. To have me near him, a kind king put me in attendance on his wife. Gracious Marie Antoinette!" cried Mademoiselle Aubley, and laughed; "Angel's face, and pig's soul! Slothful, you may see, and uncertain of temper... All this is well. I have been successful in this life. But she flogged me, monsieur, from jealousy of an Englishman. That I do not bear. No, that I cannot bear..."

Danton's big laughter boomed.

"The head of our queen! Why, freely, mademoiselle! I give you that which must be your due in any event! Listen, then: tonight she goes before a secret tribunal, to be faced with all her crimes. Had you not captivated me, and made me bring you here, I should have been there. She will be convicted, rest assured...Bien, mademoiselle, you interest me! I swear you interest me. Nor had I conceived that such was your history. Pardon me—you are French?"

For the first time Denise Aubley smiled. The tension faded from her.

"Corsican, if it matters. I was born there; my father was French."

"So? He must indeed have been fortunate to be the father—"

"M. Danton," she said, and was very impatient, "come, you do it quite badly!—But you are right; I am singularly graced in the matter of a father. A royalist fool and philanderer; his name does not matter since even living people are of so little value now. You know him as Monsieur de ma Belle Dame. He is called the ugliest man in France and its greatest lover..." Abruptly she paused, meeting the stare of the man in whose eyes there was fire. There was an uneasiness of silence, tense as an indrawn breath. Then she said coldly: "Well, M. Danton? You don't fancy, eh, that I shall go back on the bargain?—or is it just possible that you are afraid?"

She laughed like a ring of glasses, and there was witchcraft in her face. Danton's shadow rose, and moved forward across the candlelight.

III

When Denise Aubley left the house and entered the coach that awaited her, it was very late. A low moon distorted all Paris to white imagery; she adjusted her attire with composure and held up a mirror to catch the dead white of her face in the moonlight. Then she settled back with composure...

It was the sound of the rain drumming on the roof of the coach that roused her from a doze. Gusts of it blew through the curtains, and on the roof she could hear the driver's maledictions swept past by the wind. Hollow thrummed the wheels, as though the coach were in a great box, but when she looked out she saw that it was the *Place de la Revolution*. All deserted now, in the hush before dawn...

There was a leap of lightning, whitening the sky and slashing across it the black profile of La Guillotine, standing up against the *Tuileries* with its blade new-washed. Mademoiselle cried out—it was no bit of imagination, nor did she drop her eyes when she saw a man on the platform before the knife, arms outstretched and motionless, weird with face upturned. Then it was dark.

But Mademoiselle did feel alarm when the coach bumped something soft. The horses clattered and plunged in a burst of abuse from the driver. Denise Aubley was not prepared for the arm that was thrust through the window of the coach; even less was she prepared for the voice that came to her.

"Your coach is well known to me, Mademoiselle. I have watched it often. For the sake of an old acquaintanceship, will you receive a drunken child into it?"

There was a tinder-box inside. Denise Aubley thought she recognized the man who stood there, head framed in the window, but she was not certain until the spark caught the candle. Through the curtains a strange face shone up at her, dripping water and with stringy black hair plastered against its leanness. It was pale, like a student's, and the eyes were very brilliant.

"Come, come, my dear," the stranger said impatiently, "the greatest man in France lies just out here, racked with coughing. He will take his death if you do not assist him."

"So," Mademoiselle observed idly, "you are here—in Paris—"

"Yes, yes! An artillery officer once upon a time; not the world conqueror we pictured in our dreams. Come now; will you help him?"

"This is very strange," went on Mademoiselle, still idly. "You have no word for me, then—"

For answer he pulled open the door. Then he trundled a slim and twisted figure over the step. The face fell back, white against the scarlet of the cushions. Rain made it shiny, like wax; the eyes were closed. Mademoiselle twitched away.

"Name of God! You expect me to carry—this?"

"Why not, Denise? See," cried the man, and laughed, "he is very handsome!...Listen, Denise, you were pleased to say you loved me once. For the sake of that, carry him. It is Ansmith, the greatest orator these ears have ever heard. Drunk—bien! What of it? We may need him. He can be very useful in this hubbub, very useful. We cannot afford to have him die."

"Yes," the woman agreed, "he is of great beauty...Well, then, what of yourself? Really, you treat me vilely! What of yourself?"

Her companion pushed back his dripping hair.

"Oh, no condolences, if you please! Quiet, do you hear? You never, if I remember, cared particularly to hear about me in Corsica, eh? No, you did not."

"You will ride—"

"No, I will not ride! You irritate me more every moment!"

"Well, go, then!" she snapped. "You are much of a spoiled child, I see, who is too precocious and ought to be whipped. No, I shall not throw your friend into the street..."

"As you did me?"

"As I did you! Why, ohé, Monsieur, I had my way to make in the world as well as you! If I were to become a fine lady, could I idle my time with one who was to be nameless? For you will ever be nameless. Good-night, Monsieur. The rain is cold."

The man turned his face from the window. Very slowly the wet fingers dropped from the window ledge.

«He lives at Les Trois Coquins, rue Royale. I am very grateful...Yes, I suppose I shall be nameless..."

The woman blew out the candle with an air of finality.

"Good-night, M. Bonaparte...Cocher, en avant!"[4]

The hand was wrenched from the window-ledge as the coach moved away. And the lightning showed Mademoiselle's late companion motionless, looking into the rain.

IV

They found Monsieur de ma Belle Dame in the morning across the table, delirious and fever-flushed. Rain smeared the windows, so that the figures of men moved dusky against gray light when Vandeliers' body was taken downstairs. Nobody spoke then. Nobody ever saw him again.

Monsieur they put into the big bed, where he lay ugly and stupid and with no strength to his sword-arm. The aubergiste,[5] of course, would have taken his money, but an officious lieutenant of artillery, a quick-tempered little man who looked as though he were responsible for the world, had appeared that day to take charge of affairs. Mine host remembered having seen him before at Les Trois Coquins. So mine host did not dare.

All day, while the rain swelled Paris's sewers, the little man with the pale, brilliant face stood at the window. This man was hating France. More, he was hating Mademoiselle Aubley.

A candle burned at the bedside, and by its light the physician was cleaning his blood-letting instruments. He wore a battered cocked hat, which shaded his face. The shadow did not move as he spoke to the man by the window.

"Come, is it not a pity, Monsieur?—Look at him! I knew him once, when he was the beau gallant everyone wanted to know. He was fascinating then, and loved by all the ladies."

"I knew him too," said the Corsican. "Well! His condition is dangerous?"

"Dangerous? He is dying, Monsieur."

The room was naked, except for death. But death was sitting quietly, and had not yet lain upon the bed.

"—yes, he is dying," pursued the medical man. "You knew him, you say. Has he relatives?"

"He once had a wife and a daughter. The wife is dead; the daughter—"

"Voila! I understand." Thoughtfully the doctor wiped his hands on a handkerchief. "Yet he was kind; he was the kindest man alive. You know

---

4 This translates, "Coachman, onward!"

5 An aubergiste is an innkeeper.

the young American who lives here?—eh, and who has not appeared today?...And what is this man's name, Monsieur, his real name?"

"You will need it," said the other, "on the death certificate, I suppose. Well, it is Jean Aubley."

"Oh, the devil!...Why, this is news indeed! He is, perhaps—the father of L'Aubley?... What! You have not heard of L'Aubley?"

"I have been away many months. Bien—speak up!" cried the Corsican, turning. "Who is she?"

"They connect her name with the names of dukes. She was an aristocrat, they say, once upon a time. But now she is a good citizeness; too good, my friend, for they mention her name now with Vandeliers, even with Danton, though she is the mistress of M. Fouquier-Tinville. Yes, it is best gossip now. She has a motive. Listen, Monsieur, you know of the trial of this Austrian queen of ours?

"Well," he went on, pointing with a lancet, "she has a hand in that. The evidence Fouquier-Tinville puts forward—secretly, her procuring! Witnesses—hers! Last night our queen went on trial. You must not repeat this, but we hear things! Because of L'Aubley, Marie Antoinette will go to the guillotine..."

"Hush!" His companion stole over to the bed and looked down. "A shock, you said, would kill him. A shock would kill him—"

Out of distances, out of gray rain, there was a sound. Death sat in the corner listening. The sound danced far down the rue Royale, creeping up in noises of hurrying feet, in shouts behind which there was a baring of teeth. And above it all they heard the rumble of wheels.

"It is the tumbrils," said M. Bonaparte; "yes, and there are drums..."

Drums! They twirled and thrummed under nimble fingers, a mighty rolling that swept past the windows in time to the beat of a march. Drums! The steady chorus drowned out the rattle of wheels, for mad voices were singing "La Marseillaise."

"It has wakened him!" cried the doctor. "Damnation!—It has wakened him!"

The lieutenant went to the window. Yellow light in one corner, with the doctor's shaded face and Monsieur's limp arm trailing out of shadow over the side of the bed—but M. Bonaparte did not notice. The limp arm stiffened, fingers quivering.

Drums! Thunder of them, tapping steadily through the song, tapping through the lumbering jolt of wheels, thrumming the pulse of war. A song to make men seize weapons and die, a song to hurl white faces to the guillotine on its weird crash and power, a song of whistling javelins and old fierce armies in battle-chariots, a song to swell the roar of plunging cavalry and scream the defiance of bugles. Drums!

"See!" the Corsican cried, and his shout smote the room where there had been only whispers, "See! It is Marie Antoinette going to the scaffold!"

The white arm over the bed lifted convulsively, fingers groping. It jerked backwards and knocked over the candle as it fell.

There was only darkness in the room now. M. Bonaparte stood motionless. Outside the drums beat time to "La Marseillaise."

V

Since Denise Aubley was M. Fouquier-Tinville's mistress, it was magnificently contrary to the etiquette of such matters for her to bring Ansmith to the apartment M. Tinville maintained for her. But then it had been slightly unfair to be with M. Danton earlier in the evening, and, besides, her past might always crop up—in which case, to have the ruling power of France and such a man as Ansmith for her allies was no small reassurance. Ansmith could help her if he were properly handled; moreover, he was very handsome. Which reason had prompted her to carry him to her own rooms instead of to Les Trois Coquins she did not stop to decide.

M. Fouquier-Tinville unquestionably would have been annoyed had he known that Georges Jacques Danton possessed a key to the apartment. He would have been annoyed even more by the number of such keys which were carried next to hearts. One does not maintain such a handsome suite of rooms for the edification of one's friends. Even Danton was given to caution in visiting Mademoiselle Aubley. Besides, there was his wife, who was most strangely jealous.

In the rue Royale the doctor had not yet even arrived at the room of Monsieur de ma Belle Dame that afternoon when Danton let himself into M. Tinville's house on the rue Odéon. He had waded through swift water in the gutters, he had been plucked at by a nagging wind which buffeted and fought him, spitting rain. When he stepped through the door he closed it softly, for he was a bedraggled sight.

This was another Paris—the behind-door Paris where were worn the brocades and jewels that must not be seen on the streets. Here were stairs that held the echo of tapping red heels; the lacquered fans of Fragonard, behind which there are eyes. Danton stood in the hall, delicate as the spray of a fountain and lighted by great clusters of candles like fiery fruit. Then he perceived that a fleeting air, light as romance, was peopling the hall with a ghostly minuet. The song fluttered from somewhere before him.

Danton laughed. He had heard that song once before, when he had met Mademoiselle Aubley. Clearly it was a part of her *repertoire d'amour,* an allure like a perfume, with which she stimulated one. Mademoiselle was entertaining a newcomer. That annoyed M. Danton.

He went forward, this big lumbering dictator, and down the hall he paused. It was dusky back there, and full of spindly furniture, but a lighted door made a frame for a picture. In the room beyond were many shining mirrors, and reflected in one he saw the picture itself, caught an instant out of old tapestries. The glistening top of the spinet, with Mademoiselle's fingers lying idle on the keys as she sat with her back to him. Her head was thrown back, and one arm was curved about the body of a man, whose lips were on hers.

"Pretty!" murmured M. Danton. "Exquisite!..."

In the mirror the man raised his head. Face strikingly handsome, in a careless way, but tired with an awakening more than physical. And he spoke with great intensity.

"I must go," he said; "I must go...but I shall not forget."

"You would go so soon——"

"I tell you," he interrupted, "I love you; I love you so damned much that I should have to kill you to express it. I do not know how to react to it; it blinds me. Because, you see, I have been in love before, but I have never loved..."

He stepped back and surveyed her steadily. "All last night I heard the heels of those red shoes go tapping up and down, and I saw your face. Do you know what it all said to me?——it said that there is still time to repair my life. Why, yes," he said, as though the idea bewildered him, "there is yet time to repair my life. I was killing myself, very slowly, up in a garret with the only friend I have ever had. Months I might have done great work...Yes, I will fight this murder..."

"Hush!—Your hands are feverish. Hush!"

"From now," he continued, rather wildly, "I will show them. Do you know the charge that exiled me? It was treason. But I will show them! For you, Mademoiselle!" He paused, and then said: "You have never told me your name."

"Nor shall I," she answered. "You might not care for that, my friend the American. After all, does it matter?"

In the hallway M. Danton mused:

"After all, does it matter?" And he withdrew into shadow.

Outside the afternoon deepened into a throb of drumbeats. The picture in the mirror had faded; the corridor lay empty and white under candle-shine. And this time the sound of "La Marseillaise" smothered out the opening of the street-door. Unfortunately, M. Fouquier-Tinville was returning.

In the corridor he stopped, smiling. She was at the spinet, this woman; he could hear her playing. He tip-toed down toward the lighted door beyond which shone the many mirrors, all flashing gold and silver.

Then, quite suddenly, M. Fouquier-Tinville's smile vanished. Framed by the doorway, mirrored in splendid hues, he could see a picture.

"Danton," said M. Tinville, and twitched off his cloak. "Danton!..."

The picture did not move, held by the tensity of its own characters. Outside the drums beat time to "La Marseillaise."

VI

Again at night there were three men in the room of Monsieur de ma Belle Dame, and again one was dead. The place had the smothered hush and oppression of a room filled with flowers, but there was only the naked bed over whose side trailed an arm. Under the candles at the center table Ansmith sat very dull-eyed and pale. He had been crying. He sat with one hand around a glass, slumped, and he was staring at death.

"He was kind to me," the American kept repeating until it grew ghastly. "...Oh, my friend, is it not a pity that he was kind to me?"

"Monsieur Ansmith must be a fearful coward," observed the lieutenant of artillery, who was standing by the window. He did not turn. "The man was murdered."

The glass rolled from Ansmith's grasp and shattered on the floor.

"Murdered," repeated his companion, coming to the table and looking at him steadily, "killed this afternoon—by what a woman did to him. Is not Monsieur Ansmith a coward," he added with fine contempt, "to stand that?"

Ansmith looked very much like a child now, a spoiled, stricken child. Still he did not speak. His eyes met the lieutenant's with the mute appeal of a sick dog.

"In Paris there is a woman," went on M. Bonaparte. "She is possessed of some devil—stop! I know it is splendidly absurd to say that. But it is true...And you know why that poor shattered thing on the bed was dying, eh? Because they were hounding Marie Antoinette, because this woman was hounding her, though he never knew her name. Yesterday it was this woman who killed him. For when Marie Antoinette passed out there in the death-cart, he arose and followed her, though his body lay there on the bed."

M. Bonaparte went to the bedside, and in his theatrical way he made a military salute. When he spoke again his voice rang like a chord of music:

"The last of the gallants! The last of the old regime, Monsieur Ansmith, who put a higher price on a dream than on a kingdom, who died for a love they could never win. Foolish—and splendid, monsieur!"

Ansmith was too befuddled to see the awkwardness of his acting, nor did Ansmith know that he was being hit in his most vital spot. M. Bonaparte continued:

"Dying, he was, and calling for you. And you never came. Do you remember him, my friend; how good he was?—how he used to care for you, and quiet you when you were insane?" He paused, and looked speculatively at his companion.

"Damned cheap sentiment!" cried Ansmith, but there were tears in his eyes again. "Well, was he not a friend to you also?"

"Pah! What am I, my friend? A sous-officer, waiting to be squashed out by a cannon-ball at any moment!—Why should one care for me? He loved you, Ansmith, but you were not here; you had forgotten when he cried out for you to avenge him—"

"Avenge him?"

"Against the woman! Do you know who she is? She is Denise Aubley!"

"Oh, do I care? No, no…I have never heard of her," said Ansmith wretchedly.

"What? You do not know her?" They were both silent; then the officer shrugged. "Eh, well…it does not matter; I had thought differently. She was once a companion of the aristocrats, who swore she hated these people on the streets. There is enough evidence to send her to the guillotine. Now, you are an orator; they will listen to you at the revolutionary tribunal. Remember that he wanted you to do this!— I? Why, I could not frame a decent sentence."

There was a kind of swaggering bravado to Ansmith now, thin and cheap, but very dangerous. He took another drink and went bullying round the room, tearing off his phrases like an actor in an emotional scene. Between the two they both seemed painted things on an ugly stage. But the stiff arm over the bed was too real.

"Denounce her?" the American shouted; "yes, I will denounce her! I will take your evidence and go before the tribunal, and it shall be my supreme effort. Listen, Monsieur, this afternoon I was in love. I swore that I would make myself great—I promised her that France should ring with my name. Bien, it shall! For her, it shall!"

"In love?" M. Bonaparte asked oddly.

"Yes, it is not strange? She found me—well, I do not know where. But she too was kind to me. I do not know her name, for she refused to tell me. She wears red shoes, Monsieur; they are wonderful red shoes, and always when she is near I can hear them tapping. Red heels, the

Lady of the Red Heels. I know her by that. Is it not a clever fancy?...
Why are you laughing?"

The thin, pale figure, rather like a ghost as it stood erect with eyes very
bright, had broken its illusion by bursting into laughter. M. Bonaparte,
in a rollicking mood, caught up a glass from the table and flourished
the bottle.

"Wonderful red shoes!" he said. "Why, then, I drink to your Lady of
the Red Heels; may she approve your great resolves, say I. And I drink
to the last of the gallants, since we grow symbolical. The last of the gallants!" He put the glass to his lips, and then said: "Yourself!"

VII

Drums! Rattle and skirl of drums, like a million tiny feet marching
the streets. October, with great wild winds that go winging over Paris,
carrying the drumbeat. Shoutings during the morning—then in the rue
Odéon, silence. Silence, where it does not belong, as though the whole
world were congregated elsewhere. Silence terrific in its import.

And in the room of the mirrors, alive with candle flames, Mademoiselle Aubley stood very nervous. It was horrible, because she did
not know why. Outside was only silence, tossed by boisterous winds.

"Jeanne!" cried Mademoiselle Aubley, vivid in her scarlet gown by
the marble of the fireplace. "Jeanne! Come here!...I am afraid!...

The femme de chambre, a gray sullen girl, hesitated on the threshold. It was only that pale, black-haired statue by the fire, but it alarmed
her. The fire did not heat the room. Mademoiselle's eyes were fixed.

"Jeanne," she demanded, "why is it so quiet?"

"They say the tribunal is meeting, Mademoiselle..."

"The tribunal? Yes, yes," answered Denise Aubley, smiling and adding hastily: "All our friends are there, Jeanne. That is why it is so lonely.
Bring wine."

She moved around the staring room, so brilliantly lighted that the
effect was disquieting, as when one kindles all the lamps at night to drive
away darkness, knowing that darkness is nevertheless outside. Her red
heels tapped on the parquetry as she went to the spinet. She sat down,
and picked at the keys, but when she found that she was playing the
old minuet she rose quickly...

Was it the drums again? Or hoof-beats? Now a key rattling at the
lock of the street-door, and then the slam of the door went booming
up in echoes. Footsteps sounded in the hallway. She was standing there
a bit terrified when Ansmith opened the door.

"Mademoiselle," he greeted, and there was a quick uneasiness to him also, "forgive my coming here…I rode hard…It scares me. I do not know whether I have done right."

"What ails you? What is wrong?" She was not yet reassured, and went to him.

"It was not glorious. It was horrible! All those faces tossing out there, screaming! I am afraid they will do her violence when they go to arrest her. My lady, your orator's glory is very empty."

"Why, what can you mean?"

"I denounced a woman! Well, it was a duty; my friend's dying wish…I did not see the woman, but I could fancy her. Listen!—you can hear the noise now, if you strain your ears. They are going to arrest her."

She kissed him, meeting unresponsive lips.

"Who—who is this woman?"

In the hallway the femme de chambre, returning with wine, heard the drums again, and the tapping of heels. But suddenly she heard someone screaming. She had heard people screaming like that, and it had always been on the steps of the guillotine. When she entered the room Mademoiselle was standing with her back against the spinet. Her lips were drawn back, and her eyes were terrible as an army in battle.

"Yes," Mademoiselle was crying, "you see it—they are coming for me! They are coming for me, as you meant they should. Yes, I am Denise Aubley!"

"Well—" said Ansmith vaguely; "well—"

The woman was growing hysterical. But she spoke to Jeanne:

"In the next room—M. Tinville's dueling-pistols. They are in the escritoire. Bring me one, do you hear?"

"You are not—" Ansmith cried.

"Why, no! I am not a coward…Don't you hear them now, your men? Outside in the street? I am going to fight them. Bien," she said, shaking free from his grasp, "why don't you go? Why don't you leave?"

"I swear to you—"

"Let me go! Did you not hear?—Tinville's pistols! This is his room, these are his possessions. I was not serious with you…No, nor did I ever care."

"Jeanne," Ansmith commanded, and laughed. "The pistols—bring me the other."

He turned. A moment later she heard the bar fall across the street door. The thoroughfare was full of marching feet, bursting with sound. Somewhere upstairs the glass of a window spattered and crashed.

A terrified girl handed him the case of pistols as she returned. Carefully, he locked the door of the mirror room. His throat throbbed, but he was smiling, turning the weapons over in his hands.

"Oh, what the devil, my dear!...Let me see, 'Foolish—and splendid, Monsieur!' those were his very words...Look, the pistols are loaded. Is it not fortunate?"

She turned to him, and struck at the proffered handle.

"You must not be found here! Stop this stage-play, I tell you! They will kill you too if they find you—"

"Take it!"—

"—you must go by the back way. Then they will not molest you."

He pressed the pistol into her hand.

"Don't you see, Denise? I cannot save you now, but I can remain. I can remain!"

At the street door they were hammering with the butts of guns. A heavier crash followed. Ribald shouts buffeted the walls.

Each curiously subdued, the two in the mirror room looked at each other. This time it was Mademoiselle who laughed, clearing her throat.

"Do you think," she pondered, "that they will kill instantly...I mean, shoot as soon as we shoot at them? I—can't stand torture; I can't!...I don't know what to do..."

"Oh, my God!" said Ansmith, faltering suddenly. He twisted the firearm with aimless hands; then he stood upright. The street door had been smashed from its hinges, shattering over in a plunge of gun-stocks and falling men.

"You wanted me to go a while back—" Ansmith went on breathlessly.

"Who was the man?" she asked; "who was the friend; *please,* who was the friend?"

"They called him Monsieur de ma Belle Dame. Why did you want me to go? Why?"

Hands pawed at the door from outside, wrenching the knob. The dark steel of a bayonet ripped through the wood.

"...Why did you want me to go?"

"Because," replied Mademoiselle, "I love you."

They stood with weapons levelled at the door as it burst in a gush of men. And the two pistol-shots came so nearly together that the flames of the candles flickered but once.

Notes for the Curious: "The Red Heels"

The reader is warned: This commentary discusses a key plot element of Carr's *Captain Cut-Throat*. If you have not read that novel yet, you may wish to do so before reading the following commentary.

———

"The Red Heels" as radiantly illuminates Charles Dickens' influence upon Carr as any of his other works. Carr would, throughout his career, demonstrate his affection for the Victorian novelist by drawing upon Dickens' novels, prose, and characters in his own. Occasionally, he would do so through simple admiration. For instance, in *Dark of the Moon*, Carr puts words of praise for Dickens and his contemporaries into the mouth of Alan Grantham, the protagonist:

> I maintain...that the Victorians wrote novels better than any-
> body before or since. One of their stock figures was the heir to
> an estate who isn't really the heir; if some curious personality
> turns up in the story after long absence from home, you can
> bet your shirt he's an imposter. (pp. 101–102).

Without revealing whether this was the case in any of Carr's novels, the returning heir was a stock figure he, too, employed in multiple novels, including not just *Dark of the Moon*, but *The Crooked Hinge*, *The Case of the Constant Suicides*, *The Sleeping Sphinx*, *The Nine Wrong Answers*, and *The House at Satan's Elbow*.

It is not only Carr's utilization of stock characters that recalls Dickens; Carr's echoes of Dickens are plentiful. Some are relatively subtle and seem-ingly minor, such as, later in *Dark of the Moon* (p. 131) paying tribute to both Dickens *and* Chesterton by having a character recite Chesterton's poem "When I Came Back to Fleet Street," which draws poignantly for a key image upon Mr. Pickwick's time in debtor prison; in *The Plague Court Murders*, the presence on either side of the portrait of Fouché in H.M.'s office of "a smaller picture of the only two writers H.M. would ever admit had ever possessed the least ability: Charles Dickens and Mark Twain" (p. 174); Carr's cribbing a line from *The Pickwick Papers* itself, only obliquely attributed and strictly for humor's sake, in *The Peacock Feather Murders* (1937);[1] Dickens' inclusion in a rant by H.M., in *Death in Five Boxes*, about how "some people can't let the dead alone" (p. 269);

---

1 The narrator, on p. 88, pointedly notes that a certain line in Dickens' novel *did not* come

when Carr (p. 54) supplies his own favorite works as a character's in *The Crooked Hinge*—the alleged returning heir, no less—*A Tale of Two Cities* among them; in *The Judas Window*, when H.M. speculates that the solution to the murder might compare to how Dickens intended to complete *The Mystery of Edwin Drood* (p. 201); when Sydney Carton (*A Tale of Two Cities*) is conjured in Carr's stage play, *Thirteen to the Gallows*;[2] in *The Sleeping Sphinx*, when Dickens serves (p. 169) as an unlikely witness from beyond the grave; in *The Cavalier's Cup*, when Congressman Harvey scratches out a reference to Dickens' Wilkins Micawber in a letter he is composing to his truculently American daughter (p. 224); and in "The Gentleman from Paris" (1950), basing the description of mid-nineteenth-century New York City on Dickens' own, from *American Notes*, Dickens' 1842 travelog.[3] Carr similarly cribs Dickens in 1959's *Scandal at High Chimneys* by observing:

> A pavement artist, hunched against the wall in the last Stretch of Oxford Street, looked up with blear-eyed glee from a colored chalk drawing of Napoleon Bonaparte and a couple of herrings. (p. 83)

This echoes nearly verbatim a passage from Dickens' "On Duty with Inspector Field," a source of interest Carr mentions in his "Notes for the Curious" following that novel's final chapter.[4]

Some of Carr's more salient uses of Dickens, crucial within the works where they appear, include: Mr. Benson, the choirmaster of Stoke Druid's St. Jude Church (*Night at the Mocking Widow*), whose openly remarked resemblance to Dickens' devious choirmaster John Jasper (*The Mystery of Edwin Drood*, Dickens' well known, unfinished murder mystery)[5] casts him into the reader's suspicions; H.M.'s carrying, in the

---

to mind for Sergeant Pollard, but might have. Carr's gratuitous allusion is strictly for the love of Dickens.

2 In Act II (no line numbers). The edition cited is *13 to the Gallows*, Crippen & Landru (2008), p. 139. All subsequent excerpts are drawn from the same edition.

3 Greene mentions this on p. 349 of the biography, in turn crediting the original observation to Gary C. Brockman.

4 This observation was made originally by James E. Keirans in his article "A Fascination with Napoleon: John Dickson Carr and the Emperor," which appeared in *CADS: Crime and Detective Stories Magazine, Issue 23* (May 1994), p. 21.

5 Carr had a lifelong fascination with who murdered Dickens' young Drood. In a 1949 letter to Lilian De la Torre, later published as "John Dickson Carr's Solution to *The

same novel, in "his good old suitcase a copy of *Edwin Drood*" (p. 158); H.M.'s mockery of Trollope in Dickens' favor, gibing, "Oh, my eye! One of these days I'd like to see a sketch called, 'If Dickens Had Written Trollope'" (p. 35); Carr's reclamation in *Scandal at High Chimneys* of the real-life private investigator and former police detective, Jonathan Whicher, from Dickens' 1850 *Household Words* article, "The Detective Police"...

> "Mr. Dickens, when he wrote some pieces about us in *House-hold Words* fifteen years ago, called me Witchem. The swell mob spelled Witchem with a B. I'll answer to any name that allows I've got wits in my head." (p. 88)

... the novel *Papa Là-bas*, Carr's antebellum New Orleans detection challenge to a historical United States senator fictionally turned amateur detective—and to the reader—with an impossible disappearance, an impossible murder, and the menace of Voodoo; and Carr's final novel, *The Hungry Goblin*.

In *Papa Là-bas*, Dickens allusions from the casual to the significant bubble to the surface: Carr records the emergence of a real-life gentlemen's club, The Mistick Krewe of Comus, from its antecedent, New Orleans' (also genuine) The Pickwick Club (p. 205); he drops mentions of *Bleak House* (Dickens' proto-detective novel, p. 120) and the Circumlocution Office of *Little Dorrit* (p. 98), published in 1857, the year preceding the one in which *Papa Là-bas* is set. Through the prescience of Senator Benjamin (the novel's detective figure), Carr even coyly designates himself Dickens' (and Poe's) unnamed successor:

> "Into *Bleak House*, some five years ago, the same author wove a full-scale murder mystery as an important part of his plot. The chapters dealing with the death of old Tulkinghorn, and the surprising identity of his assassin, form a separate entity which may be read by itself. Though it's a device invented for the short story by the late Edgar Poe of Virginia, and soon abandoned by him, let's hope it won't be lost. Let's hope Mr.

Mystery of Edwin Drood" (*The Armchair Detective*, October 1981), Carr outlined his own answer, which deviated from the commonly held theories, and which was distinctly Carrian. Although he disagreed with Richard M. Baker's conclusion, published in *The Drood Murder Case: Five Studies in Dickens* (1951), in Carr's review of that book, "Did Dickens Murder Drood?" (*The New York Times Book Review*, March 25, 1951), he nonetheless concluded Baker's book was, "the best study of 'Edwin Drood' I have ever read" (p. 18).

> Dickens, or perhaps some younger writer, will give us a novel in which the solving of a mystery, through appropriately sensational events and with all the clues in sight, shall form the whole theme of the book. It might be called the novel of sensation or even, more fancifully still, the 'detective' novel. What a prospect!" (p. 120)

Senator Benjamin may have been channeling S.S. Van Dine, who in his introduction to *The Great Detective Stories: A Chronological Anthology* similarly declared, "Five years later, in 1853, came Dickens's 'Bleak House'; and in this novel appeared England's first authentic contribution to modern detective fiction."[6] In a comparable affirmation of Dickens' contribution to detective fiction—and of his influence upon Carr—a dozen years before *Papa Là-bas*, Carr observed that "Dickens wove a murder mystery into the somber length of 'Bleak House' (1853), twice misleading the reader with false suspects before his surprise ending..."[7] Of course, in an interview only a few years earlier with Robert Louis Taylor for *The New Yorker*, Carr had commented, "The majority of detective writers usually rest on the one big surprise...but I prefer the double. It's more ingenious."[8] So we can number Dickens with E.C. Bentley, O. Henry, and perhaps Anthony Berkeley among those who taught Carr the value of the double surprise.

In fact, with characteristic Carrian cleverness, one clue to the solution of *Papa Là-bas* turns upon a Dickens reference.

Early in *The Hungry Goblin* (p. 17), Christopher Farrell (the perspective character) passingly compares his situation to that of the central character in Dickens' final Christmas ghost tale (of three), an 1848 novella titled *The Haunted Man and the Ghost's Bargain*. Later, Farrell and another character, Muriel Seagrave, warm their acquaintance through their shared admiration not only of Gothic novels, but particularly, of Dickens's *Bleak House* (pp. 186-187). Late in the novel (pp. 259-260), Carr even treats readers to a discussion between the novel's principals and Wilkie Collins (*The Hungry Goblin*'s detective) about Collins' personal relationship with Dickens. That conversation includes intimations concerning Dickens' planned next novel, *The Mystery of Edwin Drood*.

---

6 Published by Charles Scribner's Sons in 1927; the excerpt appears on p. 13 of that edition.

7 "Holmes Wouldn't Recognize It," *The New York Times*, Section SM, February 21, 1954, p. 10.

8 Robert Lewis Taylor, "Two Authors in an Attic" (Part I), *The New Yorker*, September 8, 1951, p. 39.

In fact, *The Hungry Goblin* itself is, albeit in the form of detective fiction, very Dickensian. In his review of it for *The New York Times*, Harold Schonberg, writing as Newgate Callendar, noticed all the novel's characteristic elements...

> The plot of "The Hungry Goblin" is extremely complicated, which will come as no surprise to Carr readers...Silly as [it] is...artificial as the layout is, naive as the characters are, there still is a residue of goodwill that is actually charming.[9]

...but somehow, Callendar failed to recognize these elements' intent and significance: *The Hungry Goblin* is not solely detective fiction, it is also an extended love letter to Victorian literature and, pointedly, to Dickens. Truly, some of the novel's less believable coincidences would simply have been typically Dickensian plot points had they appeared in one of that writer's novels.

Carr traced his literary descent from the Victorian giant both directly and indirectly. The earliest demonstration we have of the former is the fifteen-year-old's encomium to Dickens, particularly to *The Pickwick Papers* and *A Tale of Two Cities*, in one of his 1922 "As We See It" columns for the Uniontown *Daily News Standard*:

> ...read Dickens' "Pickwick." You can never forget Sam Weller or the genial Mr. Pickwick himself....It has been wisely said that a picture can do what words cannot. On the printed page there is nothing but cold type, which...before some may resolve itself into colorful picture...Take, for example, the final magnificent scene in "A Tale of Two Cities," wherein Sydney Carton delivers his great speech on the steps of the guillotine. The book-lover can see Carton pale, haggard, careworn, his cravat disarranged, his hair blowing about his face, yet with no sign of a falter in his gait and with the light of a martyr in his eyes...[10]

In a noteworthy demonstration of indirect descent, Carr cited the need to gather consideration of Dickens around what one of Carr's high-

---

9   "Criminals at Large," July 16, 1972, Section BR, p. 32.

10   "As We See It," Uniontown *Daily News Standard*, April 4, 1922, p. 5.

est idols, G.K. Chesterton, termed "the gigantic firelight of Dickens."[11] Chesterton wrote not just essays, but a book-length study about Dickens (1906), which Carr had certainly read, and which T.S. Eliot called the best that had ever been written on the Victorian. Chesterton's book was so influential in the early twentieth century, in fact, that he is credited with stimulating renewed interest in Dickens, who was at that moment no longer so much to the public's taste (or critically admired) as he had been during his own lifetime. Chesterton praised Dickens' artful and surprising balance of melodrama and realism, which he called "a queer mixture...deliberately dark and grim"[12] constituting Dickens' "second talent"—Dickens' first, according to Chesterton, being humor. Balancing these elements peculiarly is something Chesterton often emulated in his Father Brown stories, and which the reader finds so successfully done in many of Carr's novels. Chesterton saw some of Dickens' works as "nightmare novels" and called Dickens' darkness "a certain sort of horror"—which it was, although in its Victorianism, it was social horror, not, as Carr's was in its Romanticism, fantastical. Carr shared with Dickens strongly, all the same, another characteristic, a tonality, Chesterton identifies as salient in the Victorian's work: "a sort of lurid conviviality."

In any event, while Carr needed no encouragement to love Dickens, that Chesterton did so before him only made Carr admire Dickens more. Carr wrote (without wearing the mask of Alan Grantham), "with Dickens and Thackery, this age produced the two greatest English novelists of all time..."[13] Carr could not help but wish to emulate those of Dickens' techniques that strongly resonated with him.

In "The Red Heels," the young author's affection for the Victorian novelist manifests itself as just that: emulation, specifically of a very affecting, distinctive novel. Consistently, whenever Carr borrowed anything from another author—an idea, a plot premise, a character—he never did so slavishly or unimaginatively. Carr's borrowings are instead graceful balances between echoes and transformations; that is the case for this story, which was inspired by *A Tale of Two Cities*. As "The Blindfold Quest"

---

11 Carr, *supra* note 5.

12 This paragraph both quotes and paraphrases Chesterton's article on Dickens from the entry he wrote about Dickens for the fourteenth edition (1929) of the *Encyclopedia Britannica*. Chesterton's entry, unsurprisingly, is not limited to being a fact-driven documentation of Dickens, his life, and works (although it touches on those), but is instead a literary-appreciative essay about Dickens drawing on some of the same points Chesterton made in his book and essays.

13 In Carr's "Notes for the Curious" appendix to *Scandal at High Chimneys*, p. 228.

had its origins so transparently in the Ruritanian adventures young Jack Carr enjoyed written by George Barr McCutcheon, Anthony Hope, and the Hanshews, and as Carr's early detective stories are so clearly imprinted with the influences of Poe, Arthur B. Reeves, Clinton Stagg, and Ernest Bramah, so "The Red Heels" is the young author's febrile expression of what Dickens provoked imaginatively in him.

The initial line of Carr's story subtly, stylistically imitates the celebrated start of *A Tale of Two Cities*. Both openings are constructed as antitheses, seizing the reader's attention with their apparent paradoxicality. The reader will doubtless recall Dickens', layered in parallelism:

> It was the best of times, it was the worst of times, it was the age of wisdom, it was the age of foolishness, it was the epoch of belief, it was the epoch of incredulity, it was the season of Light, it was the season of Darkness, it was the spring of hope, it was the winter of despair, we had everything before us, we had nothing before us, we were all going direct to Heaven, we were all going direct the other way—in short, the period was so far like the present period, that some of its noisiest authorities insisted on its being received, for good or for evil, in the superlative degree of comparison only.[14]

Carr's tale, more tersely, begins:

> Monsieur de ma Belle Dame, whom they called the ugliest man in France and its greatest lover, was drunk again that night.

Dickens' induction, exploring the lawless year of 1775 and its conditions corresponding between London and Paris, is more extended than Carr's, but Carr's story also explores, in more length and likewise in parallel construction of nearly musical prose, the anarchy of its own Paris, set only three years earlier than Dickens':

> Those were mad times. When life is so short, when La Guillotine's bright blade may sever its thread in an instant, when each glass of wine may be one's last—who will care then? Drink the wine in the old rook's city, lurch in the gutters that are stickily damp, kiss the prostitute who reels against you and pats your cheek with hands that have been in dead men's pockets a while ago!—Drink the wine under the leering

---

14 *A Tale of Two Cities*, James Nisbet & Co., Limited (1902), p. 3. All subsequent excerpts are drawn from the same edition.

> red eyes of the torches, kick at the bodies lying all headless before La Guillotine's feet! Who will care ere the clock ticks once? Who will care?

That is strong prose from a nineteen-year-old author. In fact, it is simply strong prose.

Carr also borrows and reshapes Dickens' Dover mail coach scene, the early plot springboard in *A Tale of Two Cities* that ends with Jarvis Lorry's famous, enigmatic response to a dispatch; his utterance becomes a theme for the novel: "recalled to life." In "The Red Heels," it is Denise Aubley's coach, like the Dover coach struggling through a dark rain, in which Ansmith is pivotally recalled to life: unconscious, he is handed over by Bonaparte into Mademoiselle Aubley's care.

Attentive readers will also have noted another detail borrowed in "The Red Heels" from Dickens: at its inception, the tale locates the revolutionary conspirators in the same Parisian neighborhood as the one centrally concerned in *A Tale of Two Cities*: Saint Antoine. All through the novel, Dickens endows the neighborhood with a chilling anthropomorphism that most readers (clearly including the young Carr) are unlikely to forget. "Saint Antoine and his devouring hunger" (p. 129) are often expressed simultaneously as an abstract personification and as a menacing collective, together corporealizing the neighborhood's mob mentality:

> Saint Antoine had been, that morning, a vast dusky mass of scarecrows heaving to and fro, with frequent gleams of light above the billowy heads, where steel blades and bayonets shone in the sun. A tremendous roar arose from the throat of Saint Antoine, and a forest of naked arms struggled in the air like shrivelled branches of trees in a winter wind: all the fingers convulsively clutching at every weapon or semblance of a weapon that was thrown up from the depths below, no matter how far off. (p. 257)

Carr, too, is attentive to the almost undead character of Paris's violent body politic:

> They were singing "La Marseillaise." The song marched in splendor through the streets, like a great dead army whose feet beat time in thunder. You could see the soldiers stalking, phantoms in the crowd, and the spurs of the old horsemen

went flashing past, for all the ghosts were out of their tombs now. Here was a world gone mad, specter-filled, as when the lances of Burgundy's cavalry drove in spurts of steel through the ancient lanes. For Paris had tasted the terror.

Carr's story borrows more than one metaphorical strategy from *A Tale of Two Cities*. The titular metonymy itself, of the red heels, with the repressive class conflict those heels represent, harkens back to a recurring, minatory metonymy in Dickens' novel, that of echoing footsteps:

> Headlong, mad, and dangerous footsteps to force their way into anybody's life, footsteps not easily made clean again if once stained red, the footsteps raging in Saint Antoine afar off, as the little circle sat in the dark London window. (p. 257)

Carr, experimenting with tone and mood during this phase of his apprenticeship, carries over into "The Red Heels" the sensibility and significance Dickens ascribes to every home in a great city during a time of turbulence. In *A Tale of Two Cities*, Dickens writes:

> A solemn consideration, when I enter a great city by night, that every one of those darkly clustered houses encloses its own secret; that every room in every one of them encloses its own secret; that every beating heart in the hundreds of thousands of breasts there is, in some of its imaginings, a secret to the heart nearest it! Something of the awfulness, even of Death itself, is referable to this. (p. 13)

Carr echoes this tone by casting a comparable secrecy around Denise Aubley's apartment:

> This was another Paris—the behind-door Paris where were worn the brocades and jewels that must not be seen on the streets. Here were stairs that held the echo of tapping red heels; the lacquered fans of Fragonard, behind which there are eyes.

Tinville has given Denise, his mistress, this apartment; in it, she regularly receives his rival, Danton, as a lover. Denise's installation there of the convalescent Ansmith, with whom she falls in love, ironically leads to her own betrayal. Because of this, the love nest in which Denise Aubley deliberately betrayed her lovers adds to its Dickensian air of secrecy that awfulness of Death: to conclude his tale, Carr converts Dickens' hundreds of thousands of beating hearts into the blunt, arrhythmic hammering of pistol butts at the outer door.

Ansmith is a dualistic character, Carr's sardonic response to the unlikely nobility by which Dickens links Sydney Carton to Charles Darnay. Because "The Red Heels" ends tragically, unlike its inspiration, Ansmith's duality is an inversion of Carton's selfless oblation to the woman he loves. Carton rescues and delivers Darnay to Lucie, recalling both of them to life, but Ansmith's misguided pretension to honorable conduct sentences himself and Denise both to death. Indeed, Ansmith's last thoughts, not revealed by Carr, might have been supplied, word for word, from *A Tale of Two Cities*:

> ...my love, the darling of my soul, is dead; it is the inexorable consolidation and perpetuation of the secret that was always in that individuality, and which I shall carry in mine to my life's end. (p. 13)

The outcome of "The Red Heels" turns consequentially, as *A Tale of Two Cities* does, not only on dualism, but on the plot device of confused identities. In Carr's tale, it is those of Monsieur de ma Belle Dame and his daughter. Note that this mirrored resolution of the two stories dependent upon confused identities amounts to more than a borrowed mechanism: it compels the reader to compare the implications of each story's ending and recognize a common concern. While one tale concludes happily and one calamitously, the corruptibility of institutions and governments, thematically and dramatically, resonates in both.

A reader of the mature Carr's novels may well find this theme surprising. It is inherent and frequent in Carr's juvenilia, a constituent of each of this collection's tales of the past. It is likewise a material concern in "The Kindling Spark," "The Deficiency Expert," and "The Haunting of Tarnboys." Questioning institutions and noting their corruptibility serves as subject matter as late as 1927's "The New Canterbury Tales," near the apex of Carr's apprenticeship. The mature Carr would contrarily relegate this theme, at most, to a plot point in his detective fiction, if any given novel addressed it at all. As Douglas Greene notes, Carr the many-years political conservative "almost never objected to a social structure" (p. 440).

Carr as he developed came to privilege dramatic perspectives (climax- and conflict-driven) over panoramic ones (those providing a broader view of life, and existential statements concerning it, through the experiences of their characters). This change traces the subsiding influence of Dickens' Victorianism, to the degree it influenced Carr as a writer—or as a historian. There is no stronger example of Carr's youthful taste for the panoramic narrative than "The Red Heels." Although Carr colors the story in the imagistic tropes of Romanticism and, as ever, tells the story tightly through the perspective of imperiled characters, "The Red Heels" presents a broad canvas on which he paints a Dickensian mob of the downcast and ordinary poor turned revolutionaries; an atmosphere of pessimism, doubt, and violence; and a discernible lesson about the dangers of an age—both the age in which the narrative transpires (as Dickens implicated in his opening paragraph of *A Tale of Two Cities*) and the author's own: a moment in history when widening class and economic disparity still sends societies into blood-smeared conflict with themselves. Carr's teenaged pessimism in "The Red Heels" is so powerful that although his admired Dickens usually comforted readers with joyful endings, in this tale, Carr does not.

Later, of course, in Carr's detective novels, he would comfort readers, too—but in doing so, he would be consonant not so much with Dickens' melodramatic Victorianism, but rather, with the fantastic romances of Dumas, Doyle, Scott, Cabell, and Stevenson. Every literary romance, by convention, has an optimistic ending.

There is one more point of interest worth considering: the relationship of "The Red Heels" to Carr's detective fiction. Recall that, in the introduction, the editor contends that the techniques and elements of Carr's writing, regardless of their genre, are essentially the same: Carr's fiction generally presents well-crafted language, an engaging level of (historical) detail, a consistent ability to evoke mood, atmosphere, and suspense—and always, the capacity to surprise. Now imagine if "The Red Heels" were rearranged to become a mystery story concerning several mysterious deaths following quickly on one another. First, the body of Vandeliers is discovered in the apartment of a man, Monsieur de ma Belle Dame who himself, hardly twenty-four hours later, dies raving in his bed. Quickly thereafter, Monsieur's passionate advocate, Ansmith, who denounced the woman to the tribunal he claims was responsible for that death, Denise Aubley, dies defending her against the vengeful mob Ansmith himself provoked. How are all these deaths related? Are they coincidence? Is there something, *someone*, more behind them? Perhaps Carr's blind Lieutenant Rene Lamar, late of the French air service and turned Carr's very first detective (appearing in "The Ruby of Rameses," later in this collection)—who asserts, "we blind men have eyes in our ears—our noses—our fingertips. In my profession, monsieur, sight is a handicap"—comes on the scene and sees what no sighted person could: behind all the deaths is a dark manipulator who instigated them in his jealousy of the beautiful L'Aubley and her handsome lover. It is a certain, obscure Lieutenant Bonaparte, spurned by Aubley because he seems destined to remain nameless—and were he apprehended by Lamar, perhaps he would have!

While the editor is no mystery author, it remains apparent that the elements of "The Red Heels" need only to be modestly changed to become a detective tale instead of a historical romance. Carr, of course, confessed that his historical romance novels were "really detective stories in disguise." In *Captain Cut-Throat*, as Tony Medawar observes in his introduction to *Speak of the Devil*, Bonaparte is similarly, and perhaps surprisingly, well informed concerning "a series of impossible murders among his own troops, massed in Boulogne and awaiting the command to invade England" (p. 21). In "The Red Heels," Napoleon's subtle responsibility for all the tale's deaths remains part of a historical romance, not a detective story; in *Captain Cut-Throat*, Bonaparte's shadowy presence looms over a historical romance that becomes a detective story in disguise. Carr's genres, sometimes, are thinly divided.

Tales of the Present

The Kindling Spark (1923)

This is the story of an inestimable service rendered by John Barleycorn.[1] If you didn't like the sentiment of Don Marquis's latest play,[2] then stop right here, for it will only put me in bad with you. Somebody—I've forgotten just who—told it to me. You must remember I'm only setting down facts. Anyhow, the thing occurred in the days when drunkenness was a disgrace instead of an evidence of wealth, and when they had a big fight every Saturday night at Fogarty's round the corner.

It was shortly after the Kaiser had gotten fresh and started a free-for-all in Europe.[3] Jimmy O'Brien was editorial writer on *The Times* then; throughout six days he whipped a typewriter in the din and glare of the city room, foggy as a London night with smoke and hideous with the chattering of the telegraph instruments. Jimmy was unique. He had gone in for newspaper work because he had thought that writing editorials would be about the easiest thing he could do; besides, there was a literary air about it that lent distinction. Michael O'Brien owned *The Times*. That was the explanation of his position, you see.

Jimmy had few illusions. One of them was that editorial writers could mold public opinion; that was a secret sense of power in which he exulted. He believed in the modern adage that no newspaper can print the absolute truth and live, but he clung to the frayed old one which said that the editorials were the backbone of journalism. Gree-

---

1 John Barleycorn is the subject of an English and Scottish folk song, personifying barley and the intoxicating beverages made from it, beer and whiskey. In the irreverent folk song, men set out to "kill" him first by plowing, sowing, harrowing, and throwing "clods upon his head," then afterwards of course reaping, threshing, and milling him. The song's refrain, though, assures the listener:
There's beer all in the barrel and brandy in the glass
But little Sir John, with his nut-brown bowl, proved the strongest man at last

2 Best known for *archy and mehitabel*, Marquis was a humorist, newspaper columnist, and author of poems, stories, plays, and novels. Carr refers to the 1922-1923 Broadway adaptation of *The Old Soak*, Marquis's 1921 novel relating the drunkard Clem Hawley's pre-Prohibition, nostalgic recollections. It was also adapted as a 1926 movie.

3 This story transpires on April 6, 1917, against the background of the U.S.'s declaration of war against Germany.

ley[4] would have congratulated him; McAlluster, with a longer nose for news than the best New York gossip monger, exercised his privilege as managing editor to hack mercilessly at the editorial page. Jimmy might have complained to his father, but O'Brien believed even less in his son than in the relic whose cigar resembled a smokestack and who could swear as artistically as Eugene O'Neill. Jimmy's editorials were good, as editorials go, but Jimmy himself was a failure.

He had always worn glasses and looked like an owl; that was one point against him. And then from early youth he had been long and lean. Thus his appearance had caused people to treat him as bookish and retiring; essentially a student; and one to look with sad amazement on those sophisticated youths who, at sixteen, made it their boast that, during the emancipation from that period in which they had enriched the Jigger Shop[5] and written home about how frightfully hard the work was, they invariably ate breakfast in a tuxedo. Jimmy had early damned himself irrevocably when he said that he didn't see why they should want to put on a tuxedo when they got up in the morning. Thereafter he was invited to dances to be singled out by misses known for close, swaying, breathless dancers that embarrassed him beyond speech; and made to display his awkward diffidence in the presence of gay young ladies who got him so rattled that he spilled demi-tasses and stuttered when he talked. In short, he was skirt-shy, sensitive, and utterly useless except to turn off pretty phrases from a typewriter—all because he looked the part.

His mother was Irish with a lineage as long as a kite string; his father's pedigree was not so lengthy, but he had once wrecked a saloon and quite a number of its occupants up on the Yukon in those days before the great god Mammon put a middle initial in his name. That implies something unbeatable. But neither his father nor his mother was able to bring that something out. The person who did was...but I am

---

4 Horace Greeley, newspaper editor and publisher, founder of the *New York Tribune*, popularized the motto, "Go West, young man, and grow up with the country." He served briefly in the U.S. House of Representatives, which position Greeley used to investigate Congress and publish the findings in his newspaper. Greeley was incumbent Ulysses S. Grant's opponent in the 1872 presidential election. During his long public life, Greeley championed numerous reforms, including an end to corporal punishment in the Navy, tariff reform, feminism, vegetarianism, economic incentives for laborers, emancipation, and after the Civil War, full political and economic equality for former slaves.

5 A jigger is a shot of whisky. The jigger shot was the British sailor's tiny daily portion of rum, ridiculed by being named for the smallest mast (the jigger) on a ship. Carr would also have been aware that nineteenth-century Irish immigrants building canals in the US received jigger shots. Jigger shops, of course, during Prohibition, served trifling portions of alcohol, often in creative disguise (for instance, added to fountain sodas).

getting away ahead of my story. What I wanted to say was that Jimmy stood studiously apart, brooding and sensitive; he wanted to be dashing and all that, but he didn't have the nerve. He had his reputation and he detested being kidded, which would assuredly follow if he tried to make a belated debut. Even at that he knew he should fail. He felt that he could be as romantic and gallant as the next one if he weren't so handicapped. It would be impossible now to blossom suddenly from a pale, modest white to the glaring vermillion you see on the covers of popular magazines. If only he hadn't wasted those years in Harvard by studying, there was Peggy Lynn...

Jimmy kicked a useless doormat viciously as he went into the high, narrow, dusty hall that marked the entrance to *The Times* building. The great, reeking presses were silent now; dirty men like gnomes toiled over their tangled surfaces as Jimmy glanced in at the door. A few stragglers outside the huge plate-glass window looked idly in through a plastering of bulletins in flaming ink. Those bulletins, pasted up hourly with some new smeary legend, spoke war, war, war. It was growing monotonous, this incessant threatening on the part of nations. War was not to be conceived of; it was something distant and remote, connected with pictures in history books and sprawling scareheads across the face of *The Times*. Oddly enough, it had created a stir in the city room lately. Why should newspapermen become excited over a mere...but, somehow, tonight seemed different. Something tingled even in the stifling, superheated air of the pressroom. The usual loungers outside the window moved uneasily; their number was growing, even though it was close to ten o'clock. An excited man with a rumpled tie brushed past Jimmy and bolted for the street. Outside a newsboy was bawling something incoherently; automobiles were drawing up at the curb, and people were babbling and gesticulating. A copy boy bounded down the steps from the city room; a door flashed open, and Jimmy heard the drone of the linotype rooms rise suddenly to a hysterical whir and click; then die to a mutter as the door closed again. That tense something in the air...

When Jimmy reached the top of the stairs and entered the city room he knew. It burst over him in a sudden surge, rushing out as he opened the door like a roaring torrent when the dam is broken. McAlluster was bending over the United Press wire, which gibbered madly like a live thing. He had lost his eye shade, and he looked a little wilder than usual. The operator's hand jerked along the sheet under his pencil. Beside him a rewrite man's fingers were mere flashing blurs above the keyboard of his machine. The city editor was straining forward over his desk. There were red glints in his eye and he sucked at his cigar spasmodically. Even the sharp staccato of the typewriters seemed forced, as though their operators were keyed up to catch the word that the United States had been drawn into the bloody whirlpool of Europe.

Jimmy flung himself over to the desk. Above the rapid pencil words stood out like fire on the paper, "...it was announced officially that a declaration of war with Germany had been..."

The appalling truth staggered him. War! Insane conflict with nations, possessing the deadly civilization of supermen and the little brains of animals, at death grips—and his country one of them! Now the whole significance of war smote him; once he had been deaf to the rumble of the great guns across the water, now...Blindly he turned the door. There would be no use of remaining. McAlluster would run an extra, the same as the afternoon edition save for the battle cry of America, its savage challenge to the Blond Beast,[6] regardless of the fact that enough blood must be spilled to dye the sea crimson as a result of that mad decision.[7] For mad it must be, Jimmy felt a cold, dry, bitter rage against those who would precipitate wholesale murder, as this must be, he pushed through the group that surged outside the building, eddying around the group that surged outside the building, eddying around the bulletin boards like the seething sea it represented. Down the streets a roar was swelling rapidly: the mad cry of a people aroused to arms. Automobiles were choked in the street, horns shrieking raucously; inside *The Times* presses were beginning to lumber. Jimmy shoved on through the swirling mass. Thoughts were crowding and jostling through his mind like the people about him. War would mean...it would mean a draft. Men would be forced to go whether they desired it or not. Jimmy shuddered a little. Tales had filtered back home, tales of things unthinkable. To lie like a rat in the blood and muck of a trench, with death whining in the shells and stuttering in the rifles; to venture out on the sodden red waste, where

---

6   Friedrich Nietzsche conceived this metaphor in *Thus Spoke Zarathustra* (1883-1885) and *On the Genealogy of Morality* (1887). "Blond beast" in the earlier work identified a lion, a symbolic threat of belligerence and violence. In his *Genealogy*, Nietzsche controversially and explicitly tied the phrase to the fair-skinned, fair-haired Aryan aristocracy. Nietzsche's metaphor was so persistently powerful that it became the nickname during WWII of Reinhard Heydrich, the high-ranking Nazi SS officer and architect of the Holocaust.

7   An oblique recreation, in contemporary diction, of Act II Scene II (61-64) in *Macbeth*:

> Will all great Neptune's ocean wash this blood
> Clean from my hand? No, this my hand will rather
> The multitudinous seas incarnadine,
> Making the green one red.

hell breathed in searing liquid fire and choking gas...it mustn't happen! And he was of the draft age!

Jimmy was trembling. People, shouting, reeled past him like dream figures; the up-flung glare of the electric signs mocked him like the flare of star shells. Faintly, he seemed to hear the pounding of artillery. Horrible...horrible!

He was growing desperate. That was why he pushed open the door of Kendrick's and almost threw himself in. He forgot himself—for the first time in his life. He wanted to do something reckless, something as a vent for the emotions that seethed inside him. Kendrick's had the reputation of being very exclusive and very risqué. So he went in.

Mirrors were shining in the blaze of light that flashed under the prisms of the great central chandelier. Cut glass glittered and scintillated in the yellow glory; the silverware gleamed against the snowy linen. Palms and rose lights; dull gold intermingling with seductive red; reeling frescoes; waiters moving ghostlike down the aisles of tables; the clatter of silver and a laugh-punctuated ripple of conversation; he was vaguely aware of it all as he plumped down at an unoccupied table. An obsequious water appeared like a genie at his elbow.

"Champagne," Jimmy said very steadily.

***

It was the third bottle. Jimmy let the liquid trickle deliciously down his throat. At first it had stung. Now it was as the mead of the gods is popularly supposed to be. Jimmy had slumped a little lower in his chair; a genial flush stained his pale, lean face; and he felt blindly, deliriously happy. If only they would choke the leader of that orchestra...and it was "The Star-Spangled Banner" they were playing. It was a dirty, low-down trick! He didn't want to get up.

Laboriously he pulled himself to his feet. Curious that it was so difficult to drag himself up when he felt so light...if those waiters didn't stop reeling like that they'd spill the soup...he shook himself irritably. Somebody had started to sing. Voices took it up; a sweeping roar of sound rolled like thunder through the restaurant: wild, free, and possessing a sort of savage exultation. It was all about the dawn's early light and the morning's first beam. Jimmy extended one arm as they did in the operas and bellowed "The Wearing of the Green"[8] so lustily that he

---

8 This was an Irish folk song, sympathetic to the rebels, which began as a street ballad in 1798 during the Rebellion. The symbolic defiance of wearing green, in as little as sporting a shamrock, was punishable at that time, even up to death. The song's refrain laments to listeners that, "they are hanging men and women for the wearing of the green."

lost his grip on the table and dropped suddenly, like a man hit by a bullet. The tablecloth streamed after him; china and silverware leaped in pursuit with a crash and tinkle that was like rubbing the magic lamp to the genie waiter.[9] Jimmy struggled to his feet. His glazing eyes opened wide, and he tried to hold himself very erect. Peggy Lynn!

The startled young woman was staring at him over the broad back of an escort. When Jimmy first saw her, her eyes were flashing blue lightnings that stabbed at him like a physical force. Her cheeks were genuinely red under the crust of rouge. She seemed about to rise; then her tense attitude relaxed, and she relapsed back into her seat. Jimmy saw it, and even in the delicious fog that enveloped his senses, he wondered. But another curious thing was manifesting itself to him. Cormack was with her; a sudden rage flamed up in him at that. Again he wondered. To his knowledge Peggy Lynn had never bestowed more than a casual thought on him. In those old, meek, retiring days that now seemed so far away he had watched sadly the horde of proud stags who had given up their antlers to her, but it had been only with sadness. He knew that he was outclassed, and he had accepted defeat with resignation. Yet here he was working himself into a glow of indignation because she was here with Cormack! Gone now was the last tattered vestige of timidity. Gone was his self-consciousness at the thought that flickered dimly across the horizon of his mind: that he was gloriously drunk. Gone was the knowledge of his saintly reputation. Jimmy O'Brien was coming out of himself.

"Peggy," he said sternly. He hung to the edge of her table as, after a breathless journey, he gained it, and stared accusingly at her. He had never dared call her "Peggy" before, but it didn't matter. He levelled an accusing finger. "Wha's this mean, Peggy? Wha's it mean?"

A crimson tide surged once more into the girl's face. Her eyes blazed as though there were a fire behind them. Cormack leaned back in his chair and laughed like an idiot! By this time Jimmy felt like smashing something.

"Jimmy O'Brien," Peggy began in a deadly tone, "you're drunk!"

"I'm drunk," Jimmy agreed earnestly. "I'm drunk." He flickered brimstone at Cormack as the latter choked again. Then he banged the table truculently. "Anybody here who dares to say I'm not drunk?"

"There is not," said Cormack brokenly.

"Jimmy O'Brien, you go home this instant!" Peggy was shouting. Jimmy blinked at her. She was almost on the verge of tears. In heaven's

---

9 The young Carr recurrently conflated alcohol and magic in his imagery; two years later, Carr scaled up the association as the central element of his fantasy tale, "The Gordon Djinn" (genie), appearing later in this collection.

name, what had come over her? Cormack was staring at her, too. Jimmy pulled himself up and spoke sternly again:

"I demand explanation. Explanation. Why are you here with him?"

"Good Gawd!" Cormack breathed. He gurgled ineffectually.

"I tell you I want explanation," insisted Jimmy.[10]

"You beat it!" ordered Peggy wildly. She started up. "I thought you were different, and you're just like everybody else. You..."

"Get away from here!" Cormack sponged off his smile. He jerked his head toward Jimmy's table. "You're a confounded nuisance, O'Brien. Vanish. Don't make a fool of yourself any more than you have."

"You have insulted me," Jimmy announced measuredly. "You have doubly insulted me." He righted himself with a jerk after a sudden dip and wagged a finger in the other's face. "You have insulted Miss Lynn... You have insulted...lots of people. You are no gentleman. In fact, you..." he thudded his fist on the table and caught Cormack's soup plate squarely on the rim, sending its contents flying into the other's shirt bosom.

"You...little plaster saint!" Cormack was on his feet in a flash.

In that instant the Jimmy O'Brien who had been made by environment dropped away. Something flared up inside him: it burned to a crisp the meek soul of him and surged out in a white-hot wave. Jimmy's Irish blood, ignited by alcohol, was on fire. He drove into Cormack head on. The latter reeled back against the table and vanished in a whirl of leaping china and heaving linen as the table crashed over. He was on his feet before the last glass had tinkled into fragments, and there was righteous murder in his eye. He flung up the wreck of chair and drove it at Jimmy's head as the latter closed in. It hurtled past Jimmy's shoulder and brought down a full-length mirror in a rattling shower of glass. He had jerked up a carafe as his antagonist drove into a clinch that sent them both reeling into a horrified waiter, expostulating with loaded tray held high. The negro's wild yell was punctuated by the clatter of shattering dishes and cut short when the three of them pitched headlong into the bed of a gay fountain rippling over a cluster of vari-hued lights. The thud of running footsteps was drowned out in a silvery jangle, and the flashing lights within the sheen of water sprang to bits. Jimmy staggered

---

10 Carr's ear for dialect as a professional novelist, whether in the form of a foreign accent, as a marker of economic or class status, or even of a historical period, served him effectively—but Carr also had a lowbrow, often humorous interest in the diction of drunkards, demonstrated here and in other early efforts such as "The Cloak of D'Artagnan," "The Gordon Djinn," and *Grand Guignol*. Carr's preoccupation with the culture of bibulousness continued into his early professional novels, notably including *It Walks By Night*, *Hag's Nook*, *The Eight of Swords*, *The Blind Barber*, *Death-Watch*, *To Wake the Dead*, *Death in Five Boxes*, *Fatal Descent*, and *The Case of the Constant Suicides*.

back beneath the furiously wielded carafe in his opponent's hand; then he met Cormack's sudden rush, and they plunged clear of the basin full and square into a second table whose occupants had risen in alarm. Thudding to the floor in the tangle of the tablecloth, they writhed in a dripping, swirling heap at the edge of the dance floor. A lightning twist, and they were up. Cormack was clinging desperately. He was taking terrific punishment about the middle. Jimmy drilled steadily away at the stomach and ribs, oblivious to battering jolts that were snapping back his head. People were pressing excitedly about him; somebody was shouting, and there was a flash of blue as a newcomer elbowed his way through the crowd. Cormack jerked himself free and spun round crazily, his face bruised and livid, his soggy coat ripped down from the shoulder, his shirt bosom crumpled shapelessly. He brushed one hand across his eyes, swayed, and leaped like a wounded tiger. Jimmy's arm whipped blindly in. The floor was lunging under his feet, and something warm and wet was trickling into one eye, but he knew that Cormack was going down. The impact of the drive quivered through his knuckles and shook him from head to foot. Cormack's head snapped back; he flung up his arms ineffectually, crashed into the crowd, and slid limply to the floor.

Jimmy looked wildly about. The people were pressing about him in a blurred riot of faces; that must be a policeman...but he had whipped Cormack. He wanted to shout; to get up on the tables and make a speech—and he was not drunk. The fight had suddenly cleared his brain. But he was just a little crazy.

A blue hulk loomed in front of him. Somebody seized his arm, dragging him forward; and somebody was speaking excitedly. He spun away.

"Get away from me!" he shouted. His wandering gaze encountered a table near him, and with a lurch he had gained its top.

"Hey!" he croaked in a voice he did not recognize. "Hey!" He blinked out over the crowd, and for that strange reason that sometimes holds men mute when a spectacle touches that vaguely defined line between the sublime and the ridiculous, they were silent. Then Jimmy knew himself. There was a spark in him, and it had been fanned into flame. Suddenly he began to speak.

"Gonna lick the Germans! Gonna whale the Kaiser! Whole gang gonna enlist! Let's sing..." The crowd was spinning, twisting, singing. Something roared inside his head, and the great yellow chandelier seemed to rush down on him in a whirl of blinding sparks, in the center of which, as the darkness crept across his eyes and he crumpled to the floor, was the face of Peggy Lynn, and there was that in her face which even he could understand.

Notes for the Curious: "The Kindling Spark"

To observe that Carr is an accomplished practitioner of suspense, one of the half-dozen rudimentary tools of the writer, is to observe the obvious—or it would be, were one referring to *dramatic* (or narrative) suspense, its more commonly understood form. Narrative suspense conspicuously suffuses Carr's detective novels, which every reader of his enjoys.

The defining characteristic of the other form of suspense, *literary* suspense, is *ambiguity*. Both varieties, dramatic and literary, withhold some knowledge or conclusion from the reader. The key difference between the two is that in a dramatic narrative (especially detective fiction, taking the form of a solution) the reader *expects* the unknown to be revealed or resolved, and the more specifically the suspense is resolved, the greater the reader's satisfaction; but in the case of *literary suspense*, the reader's enjoyment comes from the *opposite*: a *lack* of definitive explanation, which leaves the reader free to interpret by considering multiple potential meanings and their impact on understanding the narrative. As dramatic suspense is often a marker of genre fiction, ambiguity is often a marker of literary fiction, writing more likely to be admired academically, studied, and admitted to the curriculum.

As a writer of detective fiction, Carr almost never employed literary suspense. Carr had no special aversion to ambiguity, but the sorts of novels likelier to employ it were the "realistic" ones, often panoramic (concerned with a greater view of life) or contemplative. Carr generally disliked these kinds of novels. Of the authors who wrote them, the fifteen-year-old aspirant wrote:

> The author seems to delight in thinking of disagreeable things. He is continually telling one that happiness, like Solanio's reason[1], is as a grain of wheat hid in a bushel of chaff; one may search all day ere he find it, and when he does find it, it is not worth the search. It does not take an author but a pessimist to write such books; surely they demand no creativeness or writers' [sic] art, when their characters are but poor,

---

1 Salanio is a friend to the titular merchant Antonio in *The Merchant of Venice*. Shakespeare uses some of his dialog to illustrate the problems in the play (greed, vengeance, prejudice, justice), which Carr took to be the grain. Sometimes, as well—especially in bantering combination with the similarly-named Salarino—Salanio furnishes comic relief, which Carr takes as the chaff.

> weak attempts at what might be, and when they contain not the slightest shred of plot....It is our firm belief that it takes more writers' [sic] art to get out a really good detective story than a truckload of Fitzgerald's books.[2]

This was not a passing teenaged rebelliousness, either. The sixty-year-old author, in *Dark of the Moon*, only diaphanously disguises himself in an academic lecturer, Alan Grantham, a "reactionary conservative" whose "pet abomination," like Carr's, is mathematics (p. 23). Grantham assesses his own reputation this way:

> Because I can't admire our present-day sacred cows, the much-touted Prousts and Joyces with reputations overblown out of all proportion to their merit, I'm supposed to be an old mossback interested only in sensational melodrama or slap-stick farce. (p. 17)

That, of course, was exactly John Dickson Carr, who loved not only so many sensational writers whose influence is perceptible in his works, but at the cinema, Marx Brothers comedies. Earlier that same year—indeed, during the same period during which Carr was writing *Dark of the Moon*—he presents the same view of the metaphorical "literary market" without disguise in his personal correspondence, disparaging the same authors Grantham does: "Those nowadays quoted highest—Proust, Joyce, D.H. Lawrence, Henry James—I won't buy at any price."[3]

This is what makes "The Kindling Spark" such an unusual effort by Carr: it is a contemporary tale, a psychological tale, and a literary tale. "The Kindling Spark" also happens to be a very passable literary effort, particularly considering that its writer was all of sixteen years old. What is perhaps most intriguing about "The Kindling Spark" is the ambiguity of its ending: is the look on Peggy Lynn's face love or disgust? Is the story's ending a happy one, or tragic?

In the biography (p. 36), Greene (credibly) argues that "The Kindling Spark" is "a well-written but rather silly bit of adolescent daydreaming" in which Jimmy's drunken battering of Cormack sparks love: "Like the true woman she is, Peggy falls in love with Jimmy." In Greene's reading, the story is the young writer's act of wish fulfillment, and what "there was that in her face which even he could understand" is palpitating admiration. The nerd gets the girl.

---

2 "As We See It," Uniontown *Daily News Standard*, May 4, 1922, p. 8.

3 Letter to Nelson Bond, March 8, 1967.

Greene's reading is perfectly defensible, but the present editor reads the story's ending in the opposite manner: Peggy may never have had a romantic interest in Jimmy, but she admired his idealism, his integrity, his lack of brutishness. She "thought better" of Jimmy. Once he debases himself, the look Jimmy sees on Peggy's face in the closing line is revulsion.

In this reading, the "inestimable service" of John Barleycorn is not kindling a romantic spark between Jimmy and Peggy Lynn; it is disillusioning Jimmy. The "sentiment of Don Marquis's latest play," after all, with which Carr declares "The Kindling Spark" consonant, is not young love: it is the utility of inebriation. Being drunk makes each author's (Marquis's and Carr's) central character see the truth more clearly. The theme of "The Kindling Spark" is *in vino veritas*.[4]

In Jimmy's case, paradoxically, he could only finally realistically engage with and understand the world through sober eyes by first becoming intoxicated, which prompts him to shed the pretense, the principled illusions Jimmy holds about the power of writing and the civilized order of his society. The narrator inculpates Jimmy for these illusions. The declaration of war surprises and disturbs him, but it is becoming drunk that helps Jimmy, finally, cast off his disabling self-deceptions, which have rendered him ineffectual, both in his career and in love. Because Peggy Lynn admires Jimmy's uncommon idealism, her initial response to his common drunkenness, even before his brawl with Cormack, is repugnance: "I thought you were different, and you're just like everybody else."

The narrator, too, has already informed the reader, "drunkenness was a disgrace instead of an evidence of wealth, and…they had a big fight every Saturday night at Fogarty's." There is nothing unordinary or admirable in Jimmy's intoxication. Jimmy is not an even entertaining drunk; nothing amusing, let alone charming to Peggy Lynn, results from his confrontational drunkenness. Carr seems, however coincidentally, to offer insight into Jimmy's first bout with alcohol (and into inebriation generally) in another story, "That Ye Be Not Judged":

> …a man addles his wits when he gives himself to an evening
> of drinking—if it happens that he cannot afford to be with-
> out them he must pay the price, often a cruel one.

No, the estimable service of John Barleycorn, in the editor's reading, is more profound than fulfilling an adolescent fantasy of love. Jimmy's

---

4 Pliny the Elder, in the first century, documented what was already a Roman proverb: "in wine, truth": under the influence of alcohol, people see and state the truth without inhibition or evasion.

cruelly paid price is the loss of Peggy Lynn's regard, which if it did not bestow Jimmy romance, was also not pitiless indifference. John Barley-corn ushers Jimmy into maturity—pointedly, helping Jimmy attain the disillusioned view of the world all writers must acquire for their writing to be any good:

> In that instant the Jimmy O'Brien who had been made by environment dropped away. Something flared up inside him: it burned to a crisp the meek soul of him and surged out in a white-hot wave. Jimmy's Irish blood, ignited by alcohol, was on fire.

This is the exact moment of Jimmy's kindling spark (not the closing moment of the story), in which Carr grants Jimmy (who is, like his author, a youthful Irish writer) Carr's own spark, and by the same vehicles: recognition of an indifferent, even dangerous world over which the author's pen wields no material power; no longer within the cocoon of a privileged education, his feeling of being slight and unimportant in the wider world; the early (ab)use of alcohol; and the pains of early romance—fear of and desire for women, coupled problematically together.

In either reading, happy or sadly profound, Carr does more than a passable job drawing in Jimmy as a convincing, interesting protagonist, of cogently—and ambiguously—revealing the moment Carr's young character graduates from naïveté. This is ultimately more satisfying than if Carr had added another line, another paragraph, in which Peggy Lynn either explicitly embraces or openly repudiates Jimmy, delivering the reader either solely the silly adolescent daydream Greene sees or solely a final and emphatic, broken note of pessimism. The ambiguity elevates the quality of the story.

While Carr was engaged enough by its possibilities to experiment in "The Kindling Spark" with a strictly literary form—an experiment not yet concluded, since he would also write "The Riddle of the Laughing Lord," "Candlelight: A Ghost Story of Christmas," "The God of the Gloves," "The Devil-Gun," and "Pygmalion," which while they all feature degrees of genre coloring, also all leverage literary devices that Carr's mature work almost never does—what Carr seems to have learned from "The Kindling Spark" was that straight literary storytelling was of less interest to him than genre fiction: he preferred dramatic suspense to literary.

Candlelight: A Ghost Story of Christmas (1924)

I am going to tell you a story that could never have happened, which is possibly the only thing it has to recommend it. There will be no burglars reformed on Christmas Eve by angelic children, or wandering boys returning to the lamp in the window. But if you love Christmas for its own sake—for its kindly good cheer and merriment— for the warmth of old hearts grown young—then you will not object to the maddest unrealities. In the chime of the midnight bells and the roar of the Yule-log—while the snow drifts against the windows and the white candle-flames smile in their Mona Lisa fashion—we shall banish the things that are...

Once a year the Trio Club met in Danforth's room—high up in the stolid old rookery which had housed five generations of Danforths. The glare along the sky that marked Pittsburgh could not be seen from its windows; it was aloof in stone dignity, hearing the clamor of the city from afar. On the road before its doors the traffic flowed smoothly. It bothered nobody, nor wished to be bothered.

Just now Danforth was thinking about his house. The image of its chill austerity loomed in his mind, superimposed on the faces of his two fellow-members of the Trio Club. He sat at his desk in the green-carpeted suite, tucked under a wing of the Frick building, and he was scowling at the inkwell. His stenographer, slipping past the door, saw an oldish young face atop his athletic figure— a severe face, like a Puritan elder's, with scanty and unkempt hair. And yet his aspect was not unpleasing, especially when he spoke in the rich voice, which had swayed so many juries. Holmes Danforth could talk like a wizard, with a power over words that was uncanny. Just now, however, he said: "Damn the radiator!" and kicked at it as he got to his feet. Then he went to the window, shivering.

It was snowing—dim and swirling out of a hard, chill sky, gray as slate. The flakes drifted white into the nooks and crevices of buildings. They sifted down into the gulf of Fifth Avenue, where cabs with glistening tops crawled like flies and yellow light lay across the wet, shining pavements with their tangle of pedestrians. All around, windows showed lighted oblongs against the gray. Two o'clock in the afternoon...the day before Christmas...and the Trio Club had its annual meeting that night...

Danforth scowled again, jingling his keys. He wondered what he should tell the other two at the meeting. The confession was inevitable—it was an invariable rule of the Trio Club that however far and wide its members might be scattered during the years, they must disclose their innermost hearts to one another when they met. For ten years they had done it—since they were kids—and always it had been the same jumble of half-fulfilled ideals. Now Holmes Danforth, at twenty-eight already old and crafty in the ways of the bar—a powerful speaker with an unerring genius for cross-examination—was at a loss. He was stolid and prosperous. Disconcertingly, he was in love.

He wondered how the others would take it. They would try to be sympathetic, of course, but they would laugh at him. There was Richards—lean, steel-fingered Richards, with his steady eye that seemed forever on the sights of a rifle. Richards, with his sun-cooked face and his wind-buffeted hair—Richards, sportsman and wanderer, who boasted that he had been or would go wherever man had been before him. At nineteen he had been expelled from college for drunkenness; and since then he had been climbing over the steeps of the world, glorying in it—but never failing to return on Christmas Eve. Undoubtedly Richards would smile slyly at his pipe...Danforth stirred. Then there was Barrisdale, insignificant and sharp-tongued, who wrote a bit and had a good time without exerting himself. He would make a joke about it...

With a sigh Danforth went into the outer office and dismissed his stenographer. Still, he had work to do...one mustn't neglect the neat and punctual discharge of one's duties...but how the *devil* was he going to break it to them about Jane?

II

When Danforth came out of the building, he felt vaguely that there was a spirit abroad like a ghost of holly, but it passed him by. In the wintry dusk the shop windows blazed with light, and the white specter-shapes of snow brushed past, vanishing in the slush. A babbling roar beat up to the electric signs, which seemed to be moving feverishly. Ruddy faces were pressed to windows, where weird, gorgeous tableaux were set out, and wax figures nodded with a goggle-eyed leer at children; other and older ruddy faces were thrust from cars to swear at pedestrians. And yet, dominating the intent look on the faces that bobbed past, was a kind of eager cheerfulness that shone over parcels; that pushed up a battered hat from its eyes and grinned.

Danforth was thinking of other things as he pulled up the collar of his coat against the spiteful wind and ventured on the slushy pavements. Shoppers banged against him and hurried on. There was a rushing sound as of many waters. He struggled through the press, heartily glad he was out of the throngs, which jammed the stores he passed. Nonsense, all this fuss...

When he got to the parking yard, where his car stood muffled against the cold, he was chilled to the bone and his hands felt numb and brittle. The relentless snow drove into his face, cloaked the arc lamps whitely, sifted over the city with silent insistence. He swore as he eased the big roadster down into the street, treacherous and slippery, with ghosts of people darting across it—with the blinding glare of headlights bursting suddenly in his face and then vanishing. It was not until the cold motor was humming smoothly into the outskirts of the city that he shook off his irritation. Along here the streets were white and quiet; naked trees glittered when the light of the lamps struck them. Christmas...!

Through the black skeletons of trees the house glowed at him. He swung the car into the drive, hurried it to the garage at the back, and stamped around to the front. All the windows were lighted; he could see the candle-flames. Baylor had followed his instructions; candlelight all over the house. And there were round wreaths of holly in the windows, too. Danforth felt himself bounding with expectation. Had Richards and Barrisdale come yet...?

He thumped his shoes on the mat, unlocked the door, and went into the dim hall, speckled with candle flames reflected in old mahogany and alive with crawling shadows. Baylor, young and genial, came bursting up to him.

"Everybody here, Mr. Holmes," he said, taking Danforth's coat. "Sh!" he went on, suddenly lowering his voice; "they in the library—want to surprise you." He grinned gleefully and went on almost at a yell; "All up in their rooms, sir! You'd best go to the library..."

Danforth hurried across to where a bright yellow path lay on the floor, streaming from the open library door. He sniffed the air appreciatively. Turkey!...

They pounced on him when he went in, clapping him on the back and shaking him until he was breathless. Richards, tall and powerful, Barrisdale with the laugh in his eyes. Then they joined hands and danced around the table in the big, black old room, with its towering rows of books and fire leaping at one end. In the candlelight—bright, unwinking flames reflected in mirrors all over the room—there was a witchery about the place. The fire gleamed on the leather chairs in front of it.

"A right guidwillie-waught!"[1] said Danforth, getting a decanter with trembling fingers and pouring out drinks. "Auld lang syne!"

"Auld lang syne!" repeated Richards, and gulped down the toast. "This," he went on, "is a proper dramatic gesture in the movies." He snapped the stem of the glass and flung the remnants into the air hilariously. "Many like it!"

Barrisdale had dropped into a chair.

"Everything about ourselves!" he said. "All of us must tell! Lord, you're looking great, Holmes!—and you, of course, Bob."

"Ought to," Richards told him, juggling another wine glass. "Just blew in today on the 'Reliance'—Africa. Horrible season— no luck— God!" He was excited, and showed it.

"As for me," Barrisdale announced. "I came out of nowhere and am continuing as was. No, sir, not a bit of progress. I've got a new novel out in January, but it's a silly thing...How about it, Holmes?"

Danforth lit a cigar and watched the smoke writhe toward the ceiling.

"I," he said solemnly, "have met my ideal..."

The others were silent. The wind snarled in the chimney; the firelight leaped on Richard's rugged face as he sat there inscrutably...

"You mean," Barrisdale spoke, "that you have fallen—married or engaged or something?"

"I have met my ideal. After all"—Danforth shook himself fiercely—"why should we scoff at—at love? The greatest thing in life?"

Barrisdale lit a cigarette carefully.

"I do believe you're right," he asserted. "I've often wondered whether I had the money." He laughed in a soft and inoffensive way. "I think I could write a novel about you and the way you look at it, Holmes. Congratulations. How about it, Bob?"

"You might say in your novel—something about me," answered Richards, clapping his knees decisively. "For—I have the same thing to report."

"My God!" said Barrisdale blankly. "You—in love—desperately— or something?"

"Desperately. Yes, It's true. Fact is, I need somebody to sort of chain me down. One that'll keep rein on me, and at the same time be lively— d'ye see?"

"And I," put in Danforth, "need to be waked up a bit. I'm getting to be an old fogy. My law practice is absorbing me. Now, Jane—Jane's

---

[1] This means "goodwill drink." The revelers are citing the original Scots language of Robert Burns' "Auld Lang Syne."

her name— she's been away for a time—haven't heard from her for a while. But, I'm worried!" He saw he had a sympathetic audience and he launched whole-heartedly into his theme. "She's been—reticent. I can tell it, I'm half afraid she's met somebody else on that trip..."

"Jane!" repeated Richards. Elaborately casual, he leaned over and flicked his cigarette ashes into the fire. "Do you mind telling me her last name, Holmes?"

"Wainwright. Jane Wainwright. And—"

"Holmes," Richards said, and towered to his impressive height, the fire glimmering in his eyes. "Holmes," he said again, swallowing hard, "I think—I think something's wrong. Hell's fire!" The words exploded suddenly. "We've gone and tumbled for the same girl!"

And Baylor, when he came in to announce dinner, saw Barrisdale leaning back in his chair, laughing, with a light on his teeth.

"I think," he told them, "I think I shall really write that novel, after all."

III

And now it is almost midnight. Our Trio Club is in a very old house, we must remember. Over their wine they are brooding on Christmas—and a woman. And as the clock chimes in Christmas, ghosts people the halls, stepped down from the ancient portraits to smile out of the dead years...

In six-and-twenty huge fireplaces great roaring piles of logs sent furious blazes streaming up. The warm light bobbed genially on the walls. "Christmas!" it sang. "Christmas! Here for Christmas!"

The slim candles nodded back in their orderly arrays in the rooms, spangling the dark furniture. The green wreaths crackled to the heat; like ruddy cheeks the holly berries glowed. '"Christmas!" sang the tea kettle in the library...

Outside the moon glimmered on the snow. There was a crunching and jolting of the high coach, a floundering of the horses in the snow. But it drew up magnificently in front of the house, harness bells jingling. The long whip curled and cracked. The horses' smoking breath blew out on the moonlight.

Crash! went the big front door, letting a flood of light gush down the steps. A chorus of shrill cries tore the moonlight to bits; little white figures went bounding down in the snow. There was a flurry of coats and mufflers. Ruddy faces shone in the light of the coach lamps. The coachman stood patting his stomach, a huge smile on his countenance. Boxes were flung from the roof. Turkeys cackled and protested...

Back surged the white wave into the house. Everybody jumped, and the candle-flames did, too. Jim was back from school—big, handsome Jim, with his pockets stuffed full of toys and a covey of the children hanging around him, stamped through the hall.

There was a beaming mother and father, jolly as the jovial apple he was munching, and a whole parcel of aunts and uncles, all babbling.

Suddenly they fell silent, as of one accord. A voice was raised—through the house—a voice low and sweet as the chime of Christmas bells; a haunting echo of some divine song, with a violin breathing dim accompaniment.

Si-lent night, holy night
All is calm, all is bright—

Through the song it drifted sweetly, and wandered into silence again—while Jim stood mute with one of the children in his arms. Then the singer appeared at the door of the library, the candlelight bright in her violet eyes, her white frock gleaming, and the old gray-haired fiddler after her. Winter following Spring, doddering.

With a bound Jim has grasped her hands, and they are all babbling again. They sweep into the library, where the fire roars loudest of all, and chestnuts pop on the hearth. They do not seem to see three figures that sit slumped around the blaze like ghosts, huddled there with dead cigarettes in their hands, like ambition gone out. Not they! They are snuffing the odor of turkey—a huge turkey with a knife in its breast. Kindness and good cheer—happiness!

The doors to the dining room are flung wide; the candlelight waves on gleaming glassware and goblets that smile with wine. The smiling of the wine is reflected. Happiness—poured from a brimming cup...

The shouts ring through the house. Some of the children have procured old costumes— buckled shoes and cocked hats, and swords of a fashion of thirty years gone by. They are making a parade of them. And grandfather on his rickety legs is trying to catch his granddaughters under the mistletoe, a grotesque figure wabbling about. Withered hands that once were strong—faded eyes that once held the sunlight...returned!

But what is this? In a corner of the big library, violet eyes look up at Jim, handsome with his tall stocks and his curling hair—impressive, too.

"That is final, then?" he says, smiling down at her.

"Final," she answers, very low. "I'm sorry, Jim, you-—you aren't like me, you see—"

"I need to be quieted down," he tells her, still smiling. "You know that you could do it. Keep me under control."

"Is that an excuse for marriage?" she asks accusingly. "I don't think I love you, Jim—for you to ask me because of that would be selfish, don't you see?—for love is the only excuse. I'm sorry, at this glad time..."

"I brought it to myself," he replies, laughing aloud this time. "Well, the Danforths are sportsmen. We shall see that they keep their reputation." There is a poignant something in his face even as he laughs. He steadies himself against the table. "I have made my bet—and lost. Shall we dance?"

The echo of a carol drifts amid the laughter.

IV

Danforth raised his head. The candles were low in their sockets, sputtering with wide sheets of flame. The light wabbled around the room in the gray and ghostly twilight, for the fire had sunk to ashes. Barrisdale shivered and he glanced up, too, mechanically putting his dead cigarette to his lips.

"Lord!" said Richards shakily. "We ate too much after dinner!"

Solemnly Danforth got up and stirred the fire with a poker. He set the decanter before his friends. "Help yourselves!" He looked at his watch. Three o'clock! "So—Merry Christmas!"

"Merry Christmas, indeed," growled Richards. He rose and moved uneasily. "Holmes—I wasn't asleep. I've been thinking a lot. And I don't think Jane is the girl for me. Now you—"

"Wait a minute," said Danforth with his glass half lifted. "I was just going to give a toast to your—your happiness. For I think that I—"

"Oh, damn!" exclaimed Richards. "We'll both give Barry a toast! We'll drink—"

"Suppose we drink," suggested Barrisdale, quietly, "suppose we drink to Jane Wainwright. For I wanted to tell you—she's engaged to me..." He held his glass aloft. "To Jane Wainwright?"

"To Jane Wainwright," replied Danforth, and laughed in a queer way. "We Danforths always were sportsmen...'Shall we dance?...'"

Notes for the Curious: "Candlelight: A Ghost Story of Christmas"

The reader is warned: This commentary discusses the plots and reveals the endings of two O. Henry short stories, "Helping the Other Fellow" and "The Trimmed Lamp." The reader may prefer to read those first.

—

The modern Anglo-American reader is conditioned to expect that any Christmastide story (especially if its title declares that it will feature ghosts) will follow in the spectral steps of Dickens' "A Christmas Carol," which was as ubiquitous a century ago when Carr wrote "Candlelight..." as it is today. As Carr's detective fiction usually does, this story subverts the reader's expectation: "Candlelight: A Ghost Story of Christmas" demonstrates not the influence of Dickens upon its young author, but that of O. Henry.

Carr coyly warns the reader of as much with the story's initial remarks, addressed directly to the reader. While the premises of the Yuletide stories the author disavows—burglars reformed on Christmas Eve by angelic children and wandering boys returning to a lamp in the window—are not *actually* the plots of O. Henry stories, they are very Henry-esque premises—as is the tale "Candlelight..." itself tells.

It should be noted, too, that in his commitment to "the maddest unrealities" and what Carr considers possibly the tale's only virtue—that it is untrue—the reader hears once again Carr's commitment to the tenets of Romanticism—indeed, as Coleridge originally formulated it, "the power of exciting the sympathy of the reader by faithful adherence to the truth of nature, and the power of giving the interest of novelty by the modifying colours of imagination."[1] This short sketch, so otherwise completely unlike Carr's detective fiction, shares these same prevailing principles with his detective fiction—the primacy of the imagination, its power to generate an absorbing mood, and yes, a surprise ending—because it reflects, more broadly, what is characteristic in Carr's disposition and his writing. The writer's viewpoint and ambitions extend beyond the puzzle mechanics in any given novel, however brilliantly those are usually executed.

But as to any explicit Dickensian influence as against O. Henry's, the "ghosts" in this story, the engrams of ancestors that bring the living

---

1 *Biographia Literaria*, p. 174.

Danforth a lesson of love, these are not Dickens' chilling conjurations. The ghosts of "Candlelight..." are genial, even wistful in their conciliation of any potential distress from Jane's rejection of Holmes Danforth. That peculiar geniality, a climax without crisis, the characters and circumstances Carr sketches are all, to any reader familiar with Henry, quite consistent with, even evocative of, Henry (whom Carr numbered among the five writers most influential upon him, and in agreement with Hugh Walpole, Carr considered "the father of American literature").[2] In fact, the ending of "Candlelight..." is a pitch-perfect "tearful smile," that well-known, tragicomic method by which Henry carried off the endings of so many of his own stories. Additionally, it is more reflective of Henry's most famous Christmas tale, "The Gift of the Magi" than it is of "A Christmas Carol," in as much as the resolution turns on the mutual affections of the principal characters. "The Gift of the Magi" even features another technique Carr encountered as a teen in Henry's *Cabbages and Kings* (and probably in Bentley's *Trent's Last Case*): the double surprise.

There are more than generalizations concerning tone and high-level mechanics that uncover Henry's influence upon Carr's vignette. Carr—probably quite consciously, but nonetheless characteristically—borrows in his Christmas tale elements from specific O. Henry stories, refashioning them distinctly into his own. This begins with Carr (as we have seen in other works, and with other authors) appropriating a couple of key characters' names in "Candlelight..." from Henry. The names are only the first in a largely subtle series of recursive echoes running to styles and themes, in both the stories from which Carr borrows and the stories underneath those. As one peers below the seemingly gossamer surface of "Candlelight...," one perceives a literary lineage several levels deep, all quietly disguised.

Jane Wainwright, who appears by name only, takes her surname from O. Henry's "Helping the Other Fellow" (1908, collected in 1912's *Rolling Stones*), a story within a story in which a key theme is the tension between personal gain and finding love. Jane is the antithesis of O. Henry's *Clifford* Wainwright. In "Helping the Other Fellow," the main character, Trotter, meets Wainwright, whom "Colleges had turned...out, and distilleries had taken...in."[3] Nonetheless, Trotter recognizes him as

---

2 The fifteen-year-old Carr wrote an encomium to Henry, making the argument for Henry as a writer of genuine literature, in his column "As We See It" for the Uniontown *Daily News Standard* on August 18, 1922, p. 4.

3 O. Henry, *Rolling Stones*, Doubleday, Page & Company, 1916, p. 40. All subsequent

"the smartest man on the whole coast, but kept down by rum" (p. 46). Clifford declares that he hates "to see fools trying to run the world" (p. 42), and in the South American country where the two meet, believes he can better his fortunes politically. Trotter, though without means or status, determines to help his new friend and does so by forcibly recovering him to sobriety. Trotter abducts Wainwright to the shack of Timotea, a "mighty wise girl" (p. 46) he has met, where they nurse Clifford off his addiction to rum. Afterward, Wainwright secures a position as private secretary to the country's president at "20,000 Peru dollars a year" (p. 47). Initially, Clifford helps the republic pull out of its debt and prosper—but then he relapses into drunkenness, sells state secrets, and is executed by a firing squad for treason. Trotter muses, "Ain't it funny how we can't do nothing for ourselves, but we can do wonders for the other fellow?" Moved by Trotter's unselfishness, the unnamed narrator of the framing story, in his own turn, offers to secure Trotter a well-compensated position back in the United States. Trotter rejects the offer in favor of love, choosing instead to live impoverished with Timotea.

The closing line of Henry's story ("Can thim that helps others help thimselves?") is drawn from Kipling's "With the Main Guard" (1888). Kipling, of course, was another favorite of Carr's. Henry openly credits Kipling in the framing narrative:

> As usual, I became aware that the Man from Bombay had already written the story; but as he had compressed it to an eight-word sentence, I have become an expansionist, and have quoted his phrase above, with apologies to him and best regards to *Terence*.[4] (p. 39)

In fact, "Helping the Other Fellow" borrows its device of the framing narrative from "With the Main Guard," which in turn, "Candlelight: A Ghost Story of Christmas" borrows from both. Carr's apprenticeship fascination with the framing narrative is manifested most strongly in 1927's "The New Canterbury Tales"; professionally, Carr draws upon the technique in *The Blind Barber* (1934) and *The Arabian Nights Murder*.

The closing line Henry draws from Kipling and his story's lesson of a selfless regard for others is an inheritance of spirit in "Candlelight...," resonating in the magnanimity between Carr's trio of friends. This borrowed spirit and the specific acquisition of Jane's surname are

---

excerpts are drawn from the same edition.

4 Terence is a character in Kipling's "With the Main Guard."

transformations of the sort Carr performed whenever he took the works of others as inspirational sources, familiar to readers of works in which Carr openly appropriated elements from Chesterton, Poe, M.R. James, Stevenson, Melville Davisson Post, and others. As here in "Candlelight...," this was a lifelong penchant of Carr's.

Henry's influences (in this story and generally) included not only Kipling, but in common with Carr: the Bible; mythology; with both Carr and Stevenson, the Arabian Nights; Guy de Maupassant (whose own surprise endings were probably his most overt influence upon Henry); and Anne Partlan, a progressive writer whom O. Henry openly credited. Her underclass short-story protagonists included students, shop girls, and artists. Partlan was one of the inspirations who determined Henry to make "the four million"[1] the subjects of his own stories. Henry sought Partlan out when he arrived in New York, and they became friends. She introduced Henry to working-class people she knew, some of whom served as models for characters in his stories.

The second name in "Candlelight..." significantly borrowed from Henry is Danforth, which is the surname of Nancy in Henry's "The Trimmed Lamp." In that story, Nancy recognizes that marriage for the wrong reasons is a mistake; she rejects multiple wealthy suitors while awaiting genuine love. Instead of a millionaire, she chooses Dan Owens, who is possessed of modest $30/week earnings, but of a great heart, and whom Lou, Jane's fellow shop-girl and friend, rejected. Lou is herself a fortune seeker in marriage, chasing millionaires and puzzled by Nancy's rejection of them. One day, Lou returns to the shop after some days' absence "in costly furs, flashing gems, and creations of the tailors' art."[2] Lou has landed herself her own millionaire, but when she learns that Nancy will marry Dan, she breaks down "sobbing turbulently" (p. 21), only then realizing what she has lost, and holding her newfound financial security cheap by comparison.

The ghosts of the past in "Candlelight..." echo Henry's only-indirectly narrated episodes between Nancy and her suitors. Jane's unnamed analog rejects Jim Danforth because she doesn't love him: "love is the only excuse."

In fact, were the narrative perspective of "Candlelight..." piv-

---

1 While the context should be clear here, that "the four million" is everyday people, for a full explanation of this term and its significance to Henry, please see the commentary following "The God of the Gloves."

2 O. Henry, *The Trimmed Lamp and Other Stories of the Four Million*, Doubleday, Page & Company, 1915, p. 20. All subsequent excerpts are drawn from the same edition.

oted, making Jane Wainwright its protagonist, her story would be a direct retelling of Nancy Danforth's: Jane's rejection of the well-heeled Danforth and Richards in favor of love with the impecunious writer Barrisdale (of course, a surrogate for Carr) is exactly the plot, with a similar concluding irony, of "The Trimmed Lamp." (And it is Trotter's story, Trotter's lesson, as well.)

"Candlelight..." also emulates "The Trimmed Lamp" by adopting its underlying metaphor of the parable of the ten virgins (Matthew 25:1-13):

> "Then the kingdom of heaven shall be compared to ten maidens who took their lamps and went to meet the bridegroom. 2 Five of them were foolish, and five were wise. 3 For when the foolish took their lamps, they took no oil with them; 4 but the wise took flasks of oil with their lamps. 5 As the bridegroom was delayed, they all slumbered and slept. 6 But at midnight there was a cry, 'Behold, the bridegroom! Come out to meet him.' 7 Then all those maidens rose and trimmed their lamps. 8 And the foolish said to the wise, 'Give us some of your oil, for our lamps are going out.' 9 But the wise replied, 'Perhaps there will not be enough for us and for you; go rather to the dealers and buy for yourselves.' 10 And while they went to buy, the bridegroom came, and those who were ready went in with him to the marriage feast; and the door was shut. 11 Afterward the other maidens came also, saying, 'Lord, lord, open to us.' 12 But he replied, 'Truly, I say to you, I do not know you.' 13 Watch therefore, for you know neither the day nor the hour."

Both Carr's and Henry's stories turn the Biblical parable's metaphorical plot into their literal ones: in each, the kingdom of Heaven is marriage, and it is the wise virgin who trims her lamp and watches prudently until the day and the hour of her happiness.

Because "Candlelight..." is such a slight, seemingly diaphanous tale, that there are further, subtler influences identifiable beneath it is surprising—but there are indeed, including, pleasingly, two of the young Carr's own preceding works, if not three: if the reader sees Holmes Danforth as an improved draft upon the young author's unnamed protagonist in 1922's "The Will-o'-the-Wisp," both lawyers, then the reader's suspicions are consonant with the editor's—and both characters, critically, fall into dream-states comprising the inner narrative of each story within a story.

Either way, the first of the two certain callbacks to Carr's earlier works will be familiar to readers of *The Kindling Spark*. Carr's presentation in "Candlelight..." of a trio of friends, with one of the story's tensions being their competition for the love of the same woman, is a revisitation of "The Blindfold Quest," written a year earlier and concerning another trio, of traveling friends, two of whom during their Ruritanian adventure become involved in a love triangle. Both stories end with a surprise twist concerning which friend wins the woman's love.

"Candlelight..." also revisits, as fiction, a theme from Carr's non-fiction essay, "Christmas Spirit," which he had written a year earlier. As "The Harp of Tairlaine" found its theme and inspiration in the language of Carr's preceding essay, "The Land of Lost Causes," so "Candlelight..." follows on the language and themes of "Christmas Spirit," in which he wrote:

> The firelight! To every person among us a wood fire has its genial charm. In his bachelor's book Ik Marvel has painted his fireplace as a glorious gate, out of which bright-eyed brain folk troop to keep him company, and some of that love of flames is inherent in every man...With what blissful content do we watch the struggle of the Christmas blaze, when the wind stirs in the chimney and the snow brushes the window panes with ghostly fingers! What a wealth of memories, warm and ruddy as the friendly flames, rise from the logs—and vanish with the smoke! Who does not see the faces there—ghosts? The faces that smile may be dust; the voices that whisper above the crackling wood long silent, the shadow-reunions forever gone, but the satisfaction is there—the satisfaction of
> "One who cons at evening o'er an album all alone
> And muses on the faces of the friends that he has known."[3]

The conclusion of this passage quotes the opening lines of James Whitcomb Riley's *An Old Sweetheart of Mine*, which is itself an evening reverie in flickering light that Whitcomb terms "a fragrant retrospection."[4] Riley continues:

---

3 *The Hill Record*, December 1923, pp. 5-6. All subsequent excerpts are drawn from the same edition.

4 *An Old Sweetheart of Mine*, The Bobbs-Merrill Company (1902). The edition's pages are unnumbered, but this is on what is p. 23 of the main text. The next excerpt is on what would be p. 24.

> So I turn the leaves of Fancy, till in shadowy design
> I find the smiling features of an old sweetheart of mine.

So in "Candlelight..." Carr is drawing, as it were, upon an echo of an echo.

"Candlelight..." further follows the lead of "Christmas Spirit" by adopting the essay's concluding mood: "The empty dining room is mocking with the suggestion of those who have gone" (p. 6). While in his essay Carr refers to the only-just-concluded Christmas-Eve feast, not to anything supernatural, in "Candlelight..." the long-ago feast becomes the setting in which the ghosts revive briefly in Danforth's dream to guide him. Their lesson enkindles his gracious concession to Barrisdale: "Shall we dance?"

There are even more echoes of echoes: note Carr's reference in "Christmas Spirit" to Ik Marvel, a pseudonym of Donald Grant Mitchell. Mitchell's 1850 *Reveries of a Bachelor*, which was wildly popular in its day and reprinted into the early twentieth century, includes four "reveries" on different themes. The first reverie, concerning marriage, is an influence that carries through into Carr's "Candlelight..." almost as silently as a ghost. The reverie's title is "Smoke, Flame, and Ashes." As in Carr's story, the reverie's meaning emanates nearly invisibly on waves of heat from the story's hearth:

> Something—it may have been the home-looking blaze, (I am a bachelor of—say six and twenty,)...had suggested to me the thought of—Marriage.
>
> I piled upon the heated fire-dogs, the last arm-full of my wood; and now, said I, bracing myself courageously between the arms of my chair,—I'll not flinch;—I'll pursue the thought wherever it leads, though it lead me to the d—(I am apt to be hasty,)—at least—continued I, softening,—until my fire is out.
>
> The wood was green, and at first showed no disposition to blaze. It smoked furiously. Smoke, thought I, always goes before blaze; and so does doubt go before decision: and my Reverie, from that very starting point, slipped into this shape:—....A wife?—thought I;—yes, a wife![5]

As one reflects upon all the sources and sources of sources behind Carr's little Christmas carol—O. Henry, Kipling, two or three of Carr's own earlier works, James Whitcomb Riley, and Donald Grant Mitchell—

---

5 *Reveries of a Bachelor*, Baker & Scribner (1851), pp. 18-19.

what astonishes is how *original* and *underivative* the seventeen-year-old's vignette is: despite all these inspirations behind it, "Candlelight: A Ghost Story of Christmas" remains distinctly Carr's own creation, with its own freshness. This is, after all, the same writer whose earliest stories, of horror and mystery, not long behind him when he writes "Candlelight...," were too openly indebted to, and too imitative of, Edgar Allan Poe.

In fact, if Dickens' chestnut, so immediately expected because of the story's title, is echoed within "Candlelight..." at all, it is heard only indirectly, mediated by the encapsulation Carr offered of Dickens' classic in "Christmas Spirit"—not according to Scrooge's epiphany, but rather, according to the already spiritually enlightened perspective of another character, Fred: "'A kind, forgiving time,' Scrooge's nephew called it" (p. 6).

"Candlelight..." concludes in this same mood. In "Christmas Spirit" Carr declares, "There is no happier night in the year" (p. 6). Despite their unknowing romantic rivalry, that is indeed what Carr's Trio Club makes of Christmas Eve. Barrisdale, the slight writer (and Carr's stand-in), wins the girl, but his friends celebrate him rather than resenting him.

This Henry-esque ending ensures that "Candlelight: A Ghost Story of Christmas" is a comedy, not a tragedy like the other early stories in which Carr's main characters, also disguised versions of himself, struggle with romance: witness in this collection alone, "Héloïse," "The Blue Garden," "The Harp of Tairlaine," "The Red Heels," and of course, "The Kindling Spark." And as was the case with "The Blindfold Quest," because the young writer still had yet actually to experience romantic success in his own life, while each of the narratives of disappointed love is unhappy in its own way, all the young Carr's happy endings are alike: they hold a forthcoming *promise* of love, beyond and outside the narrative, which because of Carr's personal inexperience cannot yet describe any of love's innumerable and delightful, significant insignificances.

The God of the Gloves (1925)

In the star's dressing-room back-stage, Streak Martin sat with his feet on the table and his stocky body swathed in a flaring bathrobe. He was grinning maliciously, and a grin only showed his chopped face off to worse advantage by baring the gold of his teeth.

"I'll get 'im." His close-cropped head bobbed. "I'll get 'im so good he won't step into the ring again in a hurry. He's too old to fight, anyhow."

"You'd better not be too sure," said Mickey Donovan, brushing the smoke away from in front of his face with a languid hand. He looked wisely at his companions in the dressing-room. "He might surprise you—*I* wouldn't be surprised if he did. He ain't down and out yet, not by a long shot!"

Martin's expressive neck jerked his head away in a twitch of disgust.

"Aw, don't tell me!" the fighter snapped. His birdlike eyes fixed Donovan like the ancient mariner's. "He's old. He's clean through. Hell! I wouldn't even need to train!"

"You be careful," warned Michaels, the lightweight champion's manager. "This is only a set-up, but you be careful, Streak. Just have a look at that gang out there in the theater. Just look at 'em!" He made vain attempts to light his cigar, and the words struggled out: "A bunch of miners from the works. Drunk and out to see execution. They threatened to kill two of the prelim boys for stallin'—an' my God! They were tryin' to kill each other so's to get on more fight cards. If you put McFarlane on the floor in one round..."

"Don't you worry about that," Martin advised. "I got somethin' to settle with McFarlane myself. You watch me. He ain't good for three rounds with the worst pork-and-beaner in town... much less me. He was lightweight champ once, an' he knows how it feels. I'm goin' to just cut 'im up—like that!" The big feet came down on the floor with a crash, and Martin's hand sliced the air.

Michaels' red face, glistening with perspiration, wore a puzzled look.

"I don't know what you got against this bird. But go to it. The referee is a friend of mine...Don't get too raw, because there may be some ham newspapermen here. But the crowd don't know the difference, and they want a nice fast bout with a split mouth and a nose lop-sided. A little blood stuff. You get me...Come on, now; it's way past time for the thing to start. You don't want to get to the ring too early, but McFarlane'll be there already, and that bunch'll pull the theater down if you keep 'em waitin' long. Git off that chair!"

The little procession clumped through the damp, musty hall, with its sickly electric bulbs and scrawlings on the once-white walls, and up to the first floor of the theater. An atmosphere of bareness and desolation, of dirt and mustiness, pervaded the big stage. The curtains were up and the props pushed away; the back brick wall loomed nakedly through the tawdry gilt of the proscenium arch; and on the stage a ring had been hurriedly set up. Draughty and dimly-lighted, the bleak auditorium was seething with excited people, seen mistily through streaks of tobacco smoke. Echoes flung and tumbled about the little group as it wended its way up to the stage. The odor of stale tobacco and the reek of garlic and sweated bodies seemed to act like a tonic upon the champion. He opened his petals and smiled like a distorted, gold-toothed flower upon the assemblage. Somebody hurled a bottle ecstatically into the air; a smashed straw hat was travelling and bounding over the long aisles. A surge of whiskey-laden air burst over Martin and his retainers like a wave as the entire crowd swung round to greet him and swear affectionately at him. Dim hands groped in the aisle; jostling bodies whirled; the owner of the smashed hat was shouting out anathema in a high-pitched key...

Almost alone, seated quietly in his corner of the ring, sat Old Bob McFarlane. He was staring out over the many moustaches and the riot of heaving faces. Even in the superheated air of the theater he shuddered a little. It was age. Tonight was the last.

He looked reflectively at his hands—once the most dangerous hands in America. But they were slower now; they felt brittle. The lightning brain moved haltingly, like an unoiled machine. He felt slightly befogged, and he knew that his knees were not quite steady. Age—seen in the shadows behind the blinding glare of the calcium lights; heard in the clang of the prophetic bell. Age—looming beyond his failing guard, peering over his upraised arm; remorseless as the terrible right hook that had lost him the championship at Denver five years ago. The old was going down before the new, while the years tramped on, iron-hoofed.

He paid scarcely any attention while the referee conferred with his own manager and Michaels, and the handlers bustled ostentatiously about, rattling buckets and tossing towels. He did not see Martin's steady, intent grin. His fine eyes were looking at past glories as his hands were held out listlessly to be taped. Dim figures blurred before him; voices hummed; his feet shifted mechanically on the canvas. Thoughts raced through his mind. He did not see the hysteria in the face of the slim boy who was fighting to get nearer the stage.

It was the bell: clanging, electric, whirling away his cobwebby fancies and flinging him into the hard glare of the lights over the ring. There was a scant instant when he realized that he had not remembered the clearing of the ring, the brief moment when he had touched gloves with Martin; it was all hazy and indistinct as past years until the searing flash of the gong brought the champion's sardonic face dancing before his eyes, with the referee bobbing in the background.

In the orchestra pit, with the protecting arm of his companion about his shoulders, the white-faced boy watched the champion cut loose dazzlingly. Intent, grim-faced, he swept McFarlane against the ropes, his left stabbing at will into the older man's face. With a glimmer of old-time footwork, McFarlane maneuvered free, landing only lightly. Again Martin bored in; hooked left and right to the wind; and slashed his opponent's eye with a cleverly timed jab before McFarlane covered up. The blood spattered Martin's white trunks, and a concerted roar shook the roof of the theater.

Again and again before the gong terminated the nightmare of the round Martin's merciless glove cut and hacked. There was no knockout in those punches; only rending power. McFarlane, blind and drenched crimson, fell into his chair—slumped lifelessly there like an ill-stuffed laundry-bag, while handlers buzzed like flies around him, and Martin stared calmly and grimly across at his crumpled adversary.

The boy in the orchestra-pit was tearing at his hat.

"My God!" he said huskily. "This can't go on! He—he's too...Martin is trying to kill him! Can't you do something?"

His companion looked back at the roaring crowd. Higher and higher had mounted the fight hysteria, like a blood-lust.

"I'm afraid not." His voice was strained and low.

"Only the referee can stop it—unless the sponge is thrown up."

"He won't do—that," breathed the other. "That's his boast...He won't throw it up...and unless he does...*There's the bell!*"

As though in a mad mist the second round swept after the first. Drilling mercilessly, the champion sent the blood spurting in a spectacular attack that brought the audience to its feet with a roar of wordless amazement and approval. No longer was the taller of the two battlers immaculate and handsome, somber with a tinge of gray in his hair. He was a shifting, stained hulk, countering feebly before the whirlwind of blows that hurled him from pillar to post. Time and again the referee glanced at Michaels, stolid near the ropes with a cigar wagging rhythmically in his mouth, but always the manager shook his head.

Desperately the youth in front strove to mount to the stage. The growls of those about him were drowned in the hysterical sweep of sound as a grazing uppercut clipped McFarlane's chin, snapping back a face that was ghastly under the white heat of the lights. Martin's powerful body surged under, burying his glove in the pit of the older man's stomach. Toppling, he staggered forward as the champion's fist whipped in again, and as the boy in front sprang to the stage McFarlane crashed headlong to the canvas, to lie there quivering...

The gong tapped, and while the youth stared, half hypnotized, handlers bore McFarlane to his corner. They dashed water into his face; they thrust a lemon between his bruised lips and put stinging ammonia under his nose. Feebly he rallied. The room was swimming...somewhere distant, they were talking about throwing in the sponge. A fire flickered out of the ashes.

"No!" he said forcibly, sitting up straight and looking at Martin through his swollen eyes, "You won't throw up the towel, Tom...you won't; you've got to promise me..." His eyes wandered in search of his manager and encountered the spindle-like figure of the youth, tense and quivering beside him.

"What—are—you—doing—here, Dinny?" The words came a little gaspingly, like those of a man in a delirium. He brushed a crimson glove across his eyes and strove to hold himself very erect in his chair.

"Dad!" The word was wrung from the boy. "Dad, I had to come... He's trying to kill you! Oh, Dad..."

"Now, Dinny, you go home—go—home," McFarlane went on ramblingly, essaying to smile. "Just—go—home. I'll attend to this..."

Aimlessly Dinny McFarlane stumbled toward the ropes as the bell sent his father forward. The champion was speaking, low and snarling, as he smashed the battered mouth again and crossed with a murderous right to the eye.

"You never thought I'd beat you, did you? You—who taught me all your tricks!" Viciously his lightning glove darted in again. "I'm just gettin' you tonight. This is your last fight, Bob McFarlane!" He took the older man's weak right to the head and flicked in his serpent's-tongue left. Carefully he thudded McFarlane's heart, and the latter's knees crumpled like paper. Into the ropes plunged the other...

Dinny McFarlane, disregarding the referee and the barking Martin, dove through into the ring as his father slid to the canvas for the last time. Eyes on fire, mumbling and swearing, he bent over the older man, huddled with one limp arm outflung. From the twisted lips faint words breathed up:

"He—didn't—make—me—throw—up—the towel... He didn't..."

II

The final edition had gone to press. Far below, the big presses were thundering and grinding; gone was the fierce beat of the newspaper's pulse in the city room. Forlorn as some vast, unkempt apartment struck by a whirlwind of papers, that was deserted except for O'Neill[1] and Dad Kenwood.

The sporting editor sat at his desk, feet on it and pencil playing an idle tattoo on the green-shaded lamp. Kenwood, thin shoulders hunched, gaunt neck outthrust, spoke with low intensity, beside him.

"I've told you about this kid before," the old lawyer said. "Now—is there any chance of dating him up with Martin? Mike Michaels won't even consider it. If you could do a bit of razzing in your column..."

"What I'd like to know," O'Neill countered, pulling at his small, neat moustache, "is why this McFarlane boy is so intent on meeting Streak. He's clearly not in the lightweight class—and he hasn't fought in six months, either. He's just trailed around doggedly trying to get Michaels to sign him up for a bout with Martin. I don't know that I blame Mike. He couldn't whip Streak, but he'd give too much trouble for the kind of soft set-up Martin wants on his tours. If the papers were howling, I suppose they *would* have to give in. But McFarlane's unknown, and, anyway, he's no contender for the title."

Dad Kenwood snapped shut his old cigar case viciously.

"Good Lord! Don't they ever think of fair play? Don't they ever think of giving anyone a chance?"

"Nobody," responded the other dispassionately, "is in the game for his health. They don't give a whoop about anything except it gets the money. After all—why should they? It's a business, you know."

"Seven years ago," Kenwood told him, the lines about his lean jaw becoming tighter, "I saw a bout in the old North End Theater. It was an exhibition fight in front of a mining crowd from the coal district

---

1 The teenaged Carr's closest friend at the Uniontown *Daily News Standard* was William O'Neil Kennedy, noted for his neatly waxed, spiked mustache. Kennedy, a writer, editor, and mentor to Carr, managed the sports pages, for which Carr received his earliest assignments—and which, frequently, since Carr received no byline, the teen filed writing as the persona "Ignatz the Oracle." Kennedy continued mentoring Carr, encouraging him to become a novelist. His letter of introduction in 1929 to Henry Tomlinson, Jr., a reader for Harper & Brothers, was the means of consideration that led to publication of Carr's first novel, *It Walks By Night*. Carr inscribed the first copy of it, a gift, to Kennedy.

for Streak Martin—who'd just become champion. Of course it was a set-up. Streak's still champion—seven years; think of it!—and he's still clever, but he was nearing his prime then. He fought Bob McFarlane... remember him?"

"Well?" O'Neill's newspaper sense was instantly on the alert.

"There had been a long row between them," the lawyer's voice droned on, "and Martin was out to get his man. It was awful! McFarlane's son saw the fight. And—believe it or not—up to that time, though he was well into his teens, he'd never seen his father fight. Bob didn't want him to; kept him at a swell school, or something. He was a shy, queer sort of kid—bookish, the way his father would have been if he hadn't thrown up education to fight. Well, he came to the theater that night..." Kenwood drew a long breath. "He saw it. And he knew Martin was out to chop Bob up. Do you begin to see what I'm driving at?"

"You mean—he wants to get back at Martin?" demanded O'Neill eagerly.

"He's set his heart on whipping him, yes; battering him from pillar to post in front of a big crowd; just—oh, I can't describe it. It's almost a murderous frenzy. For years he's been training. Bob died soon after the fight; he'd had some kind of trouble inside, and it about did for him. So the kid sets out on this fetish—obsessed. There's a pretty little thing named Kathleen who's crazy about him—and I know he has the makings of a lawyer—but, although he was never cut out for a prize fighter, he plugs away...and I must admit he's pretty clever. Yet he's ten pounds lighter than Streak; faster, but hasn't the wallop. He's just ruining things chasing a mirage."

"Then why are you trying to help him get a match with Martin?"

"For his own good, I think." Kenwood frowned out of the grimy window. "I—almost love that boy, O'Neill. And—I don't very often love people. I want to see him make good in the thing he can do. If he gets his bout—oh, I'll admit he can't whip Streak; nobody will till age gets him, just as it did McFarlane—but if Streak beats him badly, as he's bound to, he'll see how crazy his plan is. Yes, he's bound to give it up. It'll be a shock, but better that than wasting himself this way...What do you say? Will you give him publicity; clamor for a match...?"

"I'd like to meet your Dinny McFarlane, Dad," answered the sporting editor slowly. "This has the makings of a story—a long one. Of course, I'll have to manufacture a record and paint him up like a champ when I give him a write-up. But I'll do it; it's sports with an extra kick. Vendetta... Son a mankiller out to get his father's conqueror...Yes, I'll make Michaels take notice of him by yelling so loud—you know what a newspaper can do. What's more, I'll pass the word to the S. E. of the 'Trumpet' and the 'Blade'; besides, I can get in touch with the papers in neighboring towns. New contender for the lightweight title!"

Dad Kenwood went down the stairs quietly.

III

In the gathering dusk Dad Kenwood saw Dinny McFarlane's slim figure silhouetted against the windowpane as the young man stared down into the street. An auto horn blared faintly. The little city was sinking into evening lassitude.

"You're going to get it," announced the lawyer from the shadows near his desk. "Since you knocked out Blake in one round, you're going to get it. Very soon, too."

McFarlane stopped twirling the shade-cord. He whipped around.

"Yes, I'm going to get it! He can't deny me now. And I'll get Streak Martin—I'll get him, Dad—just you see..."

Kenwood sighed, and the old office chair creaked sympathetically. Now that Michaels, lashed by a dozen newspapers, had consented to take on McFarlane after he had with a lucky jab put out wobbly Slugger Blake in one round, the son of the one-time lightweight champ was steadily wearing his nerves to a saw edge. It would be a pity.

"And suppose you lose?" Kenwood asked softly.

"I mustn't lose. I mustn't. Martin *can't* get away with it!—You were there, Dad. You saw him!" The finely cut face turned away.

"And Kathleen—what about her?"

"We're about as good as engaged, I guess...If I win, I can do as you want me to and chuck the whole thing. If I lose...I'd hate to ask her to be my wife. But I won't lose; I want her there to see me fight—"

"Dinny!"

"Oh, yes, I do!" the other rattled. "I don't care! I'll win!"

Kenwood shifted uneasily. McFarlane could never whip Streak Martin; he knew that. But what if all the things he had counted on would go wrong, and that instead of accepting defeat with resignation...?

"I'm going now," Dinny said, drawing a long breath. "I want to go home and get to bed early. Nothing like keeping in training. When I can look back and say: 'Well, I've beaten Streak Martin; I don't need to keep grueling hours.'—that'll be great, Dad! Good-bye—you have work or something, don't you?"

"Yes, I have work," the lawyer lied absently. Apprehension turned him a little sick. Air castles might crush the builder when they came tumbling down, and Dinny McFarlane was rearing them amazingly. "I have a little something to do. Good-night, Dinny."

He fumbled with the top of his desk, nightmare figures dancing before him. He could not get the desk open, and he could not find the button of the drop-light, and so he sat there staring vacantly into the darkness, ever thinking...thinking.

Down the dusty stairs of the old office building tramped Dinny McFarlane. He went out into the hot, oppressive air which even with the coming of dusk had turned no cooler. The main street clamored only feebly, as though it were dying. Even the shop-windows seemed to sag—humid and gasping for breath. At supper-time only a few pedestrians were abroad; an auto limped wheezily past, and a blast of suffocating air gushed out of a clattering restaurant as Dinny passed. Coal-dust seemed to press down on all sides, like a spirit of the ovens.

Dinny turned off into a side street and mounted the steps of the heavy, stolid boarding-house where he roomed. In the dim hallway he groped toward the steps; a baby shrilled faintly at the back of the house. He tramped up to his room, shut the door carefully, and turned on the lights. Standing with his back to the door, Dinny let his eyes wander over the comfortable furnishings—easy chair, lamps, books...to come to rest on two photographs on the bureau. One was that of a girl, a tantalizingly pretty girl with an Irish laugh in her eyes and an Irish quirk to her lips—vivid as though she were alive in the frame. His somber eyes lingered a moment on that; then they moved to the almost boyish face of the photograph next to it. There was the same delicate contour, the same eyes; but there was something in Dinny McFarlane's face that was not present in his father's.

For dragging minutes the young man stared across at the picture. Somehow since he came into that house it seemed to him that he had dwindled; shrunk within himself. Slowly, a little dazedly, he looked down at his thin hands and wrists, and the hand that he clenched in his spasmodic way quivered—but it did not quiver with anger. He walked to the mirror and stared at his lean, white, tense face. It was as though he were awakening, like one who strives to ascend mountaintops and suddenly finds himself paralyzed; a ringing hollowness...Dinny McFarlane dropped into a chair and let his head fall in his arms.

IV

Thronged, overflowing, bursting with sound and people, the North End Theater roared its reception to the champion. A little older, a little heavier, a little more self-satisfied, Streak Martin waved a casual hand and climbed through the ropes. Then he frowned, drawing down his bristly scalp over the eyebrows. Dinny McFarlane, swathed in a bathrobe, sat in his corner, eyes fixed steadily, intently on the champion. Behind him stood Dad Kenwood, chewing a cigar, and O'Neill of the

News. A little further back, in the shadow of the wings, a slight figure bent forward, eyes shining out of a shadowed face.

"Cheers!" said Martin. "There's the Killer himself." He put his arms akimbo and surveyed his opponent, a gleam in his ugly eyes. Behind him Dinny could see Michaels' fat face, and it wore an inexplicably worried look. A bullet-headed negro in a dirty red sweater, Martin's second, was watching the champion furtively.

"Out to murder me?" asked the champion, raising his voice. The tumult in the hot theater subsided. Every person in the blurry crowd beyond the glare of the ring lights was silent, watching the figure in the middle of the roped arena. "Out to murder me?" Martin repeated. "My God! The nerve of the kid!" He twitched off his bathrobe with a surge of his powerful shoulders, and Kenwood's teeth clamped on his cigar. Streak Martin was in perfect condition. McFarlane's last hope...

"Oh, play ball, Martin!" It was O'Neill's crackling voice, and it held a jarring ring of common sense. "Never mind the grand-stand stuff; you aren't scaring anybody!"

Streak Martin flickered red at the sporting editor. He made a superb tableau standing there, sharp against the light, with wreaths of tobacco smoke drifting about him.

"Oh, you! You and your pet!" he snapped. Then he turned and walked to his corner, while a sudden roar burst across the stage, through which one cry ripped like a knife-thrust.

"Go get 'im, kid!"

It tingled in McFarlane's ears as Michaels bustled over to oversee the taping of his hands, and the slim referee bellowed the announcements.

"There's something funny," Kenwood muttered; "something funny in the way..."

The clash of the gong cut him short. One glance McFarlane cast over his shoulder at the wide eyes and parted, quivering lips of the girl in the wings; then he slid forward, flinging off his bathrobe. In comparison to the champion, he looked almost puny. By mutual consent the formality of shaking hands had been done away with; handlers skipped from the ring with a clank of buckets; the stools were whisked away; and Dinny McFarlane was face to face with the onrushing future.

Lightnings were leaping in Martin's eyes as he whisked forward on the offensive. Twice his glove flashed and thudded on the other's guard; McFarlane landed lightly as he retreated. The champion missed a vicious left to the face before he connected solidly with the young man's middle. An instant McFarlane's guard seemed to crumple; Martin, pressing his advantage, swept him toward the ropes, his short whips drawing blood from his antagonist's nose. Again he hooked left and right in lightning succession, but he covered slowly, and the other's return smash over the heart shook him visibly. An instant of swift maneuvering, and his glove was dancing in McFarlane's face once more. Yet he seemed to be slowing up; he tore Dinny's eye with one of his stabs, but fumbled his retreat and took terrific punishment about the body. Boring in eagerly, McFarlane missed twice before Martin, countering, drove him to his knees as the bell jangled sharply through the surf of sound.

McFarlane was panting as he went to his corner, and his knees shook. Kenwood had torn his straw hat to ribbons; he looked wild-eyed, mumbling over his cigar. O'Neill was shouting out something incoherently; he bustled about Dinny as the latter fell upon his stool, whipping the crimson from his face. Hysteria pulsed through the spectators; their sympathies had turned to the spindle-legged lad who was slowly wilting under the champion's attack.

Bulking over the reddened body of the champ, Michaels was speaking swiftly:

"You can't stand it much longer; oh, you *would* go on a bust...you cheese champion!... Here; take this...No; in your glove!"

"Go 'way!" Martin said a little dazedly, shaking his head as the other fumbled with his glove. "I'm all right; the Turkish bath got me on my feet today; it was bad booze anyway...What in hell are you doin'?"

"Shut up!" Michaels smoothed at his glove. "It's the hypo syringe; in the pocket under the stitch! You ain't good for much more; you showed you'd been shot, shootin' your mouth off in front of all them.—I been feedin' you on stimulants, and you know it! Clinch with the kid, and get him with the hypo. It'll make him groggy, and then goal him! Damn it—shut up! I know what I'm doin'! He's wobbly; he won't know...A little more of this, and he'll put you on the floor! Careful..."

He spun round as the bell sounded. Kenwood was staring straight across the ring, with a glimmer of something dimly guessed in his mind. Michaels dove between the ropes; in one searing flash he knew that the old lawyer had divined...

Thud—thud—the gloves were whirling in mid-ring; McFarlane with his patched face white and intent; Martin shifting, countering, blocking; now and then lashing in his deadly left. Kenwood, brandishing his shattered hat, was shouting something that was lost in the crash of the cheering. Twice Martin smashed his opponent's guard and drove him to the canvas; each time he tottered up. Even Michaels knew that there was no need of the hypodermic syringe—McFarlane was crumpling, and the manager realized with a hot rush of anger and chagrin that he had exposed himself needlessly to the danger of detection. Martin knew it, too; for he was himself again, sweeping the battle onward mercilessly. One of McFarlane's wild swings ripped his chin; the champion's return spun him against the ropes, to reel drunkenly into a terrific right. The younger man groped for a clinch and clung despite the short-arm jolts to the body. The house surged to its feet, calling madly for a knockout...

Then it happened. Martin stiffened before the other's flailing arms, wrenching to disengage his right hand. He looked dazedly over his opponent's shoulder, seemed to strive to push McFarlane from him, and gave when one of McFarlane's failing punches connected with his body. Dinny could feel the big body shake. He flicked in his left, and countered feebly as Martin leaped like a dying tiger. Up streaked McFarlane's arm in a last despairing jab; blinded and with the dripping face blurred before him, he whipped for the champion's jaw. He quivered as the glove shocked; his knees buckled, but in a swimming haze he saw the mountain of flesh surge and pitch to the canvas like an avalanche. Then, as one glove strove to clear the warm, thick blindness from his eyes, he stood tottering...

A white arm rising and falling...the drone of a count... then somebody had flung up his arm, and the roar of cheering shocked over him like a physical force. Dimly he saw O'Neill hurl a bucket into the air like a lunatic; wild-eyed and disheveled, Dad Kenwood had pushed into the ring, leaped over the fallen champion, and seized Michael's arm. He had not heard what the lawyer said to Martin's manager; he knew only that warm, soft arms were about his neck, and that a wet face was pressed to his own besmeared one. He heard only Kathleen sobbing out something...

"Yes, you did!" Kenwood shouted into the manager's ear. "The hypo is in his glove—and if he hadn't got it accidentally jabbed into himself while they were clinched he'd have my boy on the canvas now...Just try to do anything! If you ever say a word I'll have you run out of the business, and you know I can prove it, too! Not a word to McFarlane; oh, you can have your title—he's through with prize-fighting. But you know how to keep mum, Mike Michaels!"

And, stumbling through the wings, pursued by a hysterical crowd, Dinny McFarlane was mumbling into attentive ears.

"I beat him, Dad...didn't you see me beat him? I beat him, Dad. Now it's Kathleen and the work I was cut out for...But I beat him, Dad; didn't you see me?"

Notes for the Curious: "The God of the Gloves"

The reader is warned: While this commentary does not reveal the solution to any of these novels, it mentions some key plot elements from Carr's novels *The Nine Wrong Answers*, *Behind the Crimson Blind*, and *Fear is the Same*. If you have not read these, you may wish to do so before reading the following commentary. Also of note: this commentary reveals the ending of O. Henry's short story "A Harlem Tragedy" and most of the plot points of his ""Little Speck in Garnered Fruit." The reader may also prefer to read those first.

—

While not humorous, "The God of the Gloves" is a story strongly in the style of O. Henry: its simple dramatic premise, its focus on characters of modest social standing, their vernacular voices, and its concluding irony all illustrate the short-story writer's influence. Henry's championing of commonplace people as fit protagonists, whose experiences occasionally touch the remarkable, put him in the same camp with two of Carr's other cardinally influential writers, Robert Louis Stevenson and Brian Oswald Donn Byrne. The choice of the common protagonist distinguished these three from the established literary writers who chronicled the moneyed class, and whom Carr favored less, such as Henry James and Edith Wharton. Carr's admired trio often elevated their everyday subjects from sublunary insignificance into narrative significance by wrapping them in the language and echoed circumstances of mythology. With Donn Byrne, this took the form of Hibernophilia, a celebration of Irish culture and characters and the recounting of Irish myth and folktale; Stevenson and Henry both appropriated another Carr favorite, the Arabian Nights, which they used to transform begrimed and prosaic, modern metropolises into settings of higher romance where (as Chesterton praised Stevenson):

> men's souls have stranger adventures than their bodies,
> and...that thrilling mood and moment when the eyes
> of the great city, like the eyes of a cat, begin to flame in
> the dark...[2]

The contradistinction to James and Wharton is not arbitrary. What Henry, Stevenson, and Brian Oswald Donn Byrne (also an inspiration

---

[2] G.K, Chesterton, *The Defendant*, R. Brimley Johnson, 1901, p. 121.

behind "The God of the Gloves") taught Carr, in contrast with the tales of society and the well-to-do penned by the literary novelists, Carr put a quarter century after "The God of the Gloves" into the mouth of Congressman William Tecumseh Harvey, "of the 23½ congressional district of Pennsylvania"[3] (just outside Pittsburgh). Harvey is based in part upon Carr's own father, Congressman Wooda N. Carr. Harvey declaims:

> Why, ladies and gen—that is, Chief Inspector—what is the ideal before which we should all humbly bow down? I may say without fear of successful contradiction that it is this same average man, the little man, the common man! This is so and shall forever last, immutable and immortal, wherever the torch of civilization casts its far-flung rays! (p. 108)

In particular, O. Henry's affection for ordinary subjects endeared him to Carr. Even more so than Carr's, Henry's characters are types, not fulsome literary characters. Less introspective than Carr's (and that is little enough!), Henry's characters are nonetheless drawn well and colorfully. Here is how Carr viewed Henry:

> ...O. Henry was something new when he began to write. His stories were never long; never tedious. He put the punch and the snap and the fire into the written word. Every line struck home. Every sentence was drawn from human nature; every character lifted off the street and set down on the printed page, with all his weaknesses. And then, sudden and dazzling as a lightning flash, there occurred that unexpected twist that gave the reader a real thrill; the surprise that every experienced reader looks for at the end of a full-fledged O. Henry story. O. Henry wrote literature. He wrote it because he probed to the heart of man with his delicate pen; because his characters think and do as we all think and do. Therefore, though he did not indulge in tedious morality; he did not use stilted phrases; was not verbose; he shaped with his master hand the destiny of American literature.[4]

It is apparent that in addition to going to school with Henry to learn

---

3 *The Cavalier's Cup*, p. 13. Carr's father represented Pennsylvania's 23rd Congressional district in the 63rd Congress, between March 1911 and March 1913.

4 "As We See It," Uniontown *Daily News Standard*," August 18, 1922, p. 4.

the value and best techniques for unfolding irony, the young author also learned from him how to leverage exposition, character descriptions, character diction, and character actions to bring these otherwise shallow personas to verisimilar life. These, of course, are not unlike the lessons in drawing character that Carr also learned from Dickens. Indeed, the two meet and reinforce one another in Carr's style, although ultimately, Carr bent towards Henry's naturalism more so than Dickens' heightened caricatures. All these techniques he learned from both are evident, and competently executed, in "The God of the Gloves."

Nor was the importance of the average person (one of whom in Carr's novels is frequently the perspective character, who makes each narrative of incredible circumstances accessibly credible to the reader) only a passing concern for Henry. In that, Henry may well have been unique in his influence among Carr's most admired authors. Brian Oswald Donn Byrne, like another Carr idol, James Branch Cabell, did not mind retelling a myth—although Donn Byrne would bring it down to earth with a sly humor that Carr also emulated. Similarly, while Robert Louis Stevenson often puts a young man at the center of a tale, the quotidian is never Stevenson's subject matter: what Stevenson bequeathed most to Carr was his love of "Adventure in the Grand Manner."

No, it was to Henry peculiarly among Carr's most influential authors that the everyman was essential, and the everyday was the story. This was so much so that the title of Henry's early story collection *The Four Million* (1906, and which served as the subtitle of some successor volumes) was a direct rebuke to The Four Hundred. The Four Hundred was a well-known list of the New York City social and economic elite during the latter part of the nineteenth century ("The Gilded Age"), conceived and maintained for the *New York Times* by Ward McAllister, a relation for a time by marriage and a friend to the preeminent Astor family. In McAllister's view, the list of bankers, lawyers, brokers, captains of industry, old money, and tastemakers were the only four hundred people who mattered among New York City's population of four million. They alone belonged in the ballrooms and drawing rooms of high society; they were fit subjects of interest. While The Four Hundred's cachet passed along with The Gilded Age, the Anglo-American preoccupation with status, wealth, and influence has not: even in the present day, the Forbes 400, a descendant of McAllister's list, betrays the ongoing rivalry of influence between the elite and the egalitarian in Western capitalist democracies.

But O. Henry was having none of it, not from James, not from Wharton or other chroniclers of the influential, and certainly not from McAllister. Henry's stories were about the other, ordinary four million residents of New York City, uninteresting to McAllister and the novelists of privilege. However fantastic his narratives, in comradery with Stevenson, G.K. Chesterton, Doyle, Poe, and others, Carr nonetheless always followed Henry by peopling his novels with relatable, ordinary leads. In fact, the fifteen-year-old Carr, in his column "As We See It" for the Uniontown *Daily News Standard*, also followed Henry's lead in mocking the Four Hundred by suggesting that were an author to write a book...

> ...giving a sensational account of the fight when Lord Hokum came home drunk and crowned Lady Hokum with the umbrella stand, and, in a final blaze of glory, telling how society split into two factions over the divorce and the hero and the heroine thus wormed their way into the Four Hundred: then he could retire and live happily ever after...[1]

In his introduction to *The Door to Doom*, Greene points out that, "Carr was less interested in whether a story is probable than in whether it is entertaining and believable....Carr...made his stories believable by a punctilious attention to detail."[2] This is true—but Carr also made his tales believable by filtering them through the perceptions and sensibilities of the kinds of everyday, sympathetic characters Carr learned to create, in part, from O. Henry.

With respect to subject-matter influence, while Carr had taken a real-life interest in boxing during his internship as a sports writer for the Uniontown *Daily News Standard*—by "the time he was fifteen, he... had emerged as an expert on prize fighting"[3]—Henry helped whet Carr's appetite for the sweet science as a subject of fiction through Henry's incorporation of boxers and boxing into his stories, whether as characters or metaphors. For instance, the framing imagery of Henry's short story "The Duel" is pugilism:

> ...every man Jack when he first sets foot on the stones of Manhattan has got to fight. He has got to fight at once until either he or his adversary wins. There is no resting between

---

1 "As We See It," Uniontown *Daily News Standard*, May 4, 1922, p. 5.

2 *The Door to Doom*, p. 10.

3 Robert Lewis Taylor, "Two Authors in an Attic" (Part I), *The New Yorker*, September 8, 1951, p. 42.

rounds, for there are no rounds. It is slugging from the first. It is a fight to a finish.

Your opponent is the City. You must do battle with it from the time the ferry-boat lands you on the island until either it is yours or it has conquered you. It is the same whether you have a million in your pocket or only the price of a week's lodging.[4]

A bit disturbing in its darkly comic take on domestic abuse, "A Harlem Tragedy," introduces the reader to a certain Mrs. Cassidy, who cheerfully flaunts her bruises to an upstairs neighbor, Mrs. Fink with "the air of Cordelia exhibiting her jewels,"[5] then wryly explains that she tolerates her husband Jack's beatings because he makes it up to her in gifts:

Jack's got a left that spells two matinees and a new pair of Oxfords—and his right!—well, it takes a trip to Coney and six pairs of openwork, six lisle threads to make that good.... Sometimes I take the count in the first round; but when I feel like having a good time during the week or want some new rags I come up for more punishment. (p. 161)

In her improbable jealousy, Mrs. Fink tries to cultivate her own domestic bouts (and rewards) but fails: "she was ready to throw up the sponge, tired out, without a scratch to show for all those tame rounds with her sparring partner" (pp. 163-164)—and that failure, ironically, supplies the "tragedy" of the story's title.

Characteristically, if more passingly, in "The Princess and the Puma," Ripley Givens, a cow-hand who desires to marry Josefa O'Donnell (the titular princess), daughter of the local cattle king, throws himself between her and a Mexican lion planning to make a meal of her. Ripley, wrestling with the cat, has the cool wit to remonstrate with it by citing the rules of boxing: "Let up, now—no fair gouging!"[6]

Among Henry's actual boxers is Kid McGarry (the story is "Little Speck in Garnered Fruit"), whom we meet in the early days of his

---

4 O. Henry, *Strictly Business: More Stories of the Four Million*, Doubleday, Page & Company, 1910, p. 295.

5 O. Henry, *The Trimmed Lamp and Other Stories of the Four Million*, p. 160.

6 O. Henry, *Heart of the West*, Doubleday, Page & Company, p. 251. All subsequent excerpts are drawn from the same edition.

marriage, a marriage happier than the Cassidys' in Harlem. On their honeymoon, McGarry's bride contemplates their love:

> There was no welter-weight from London to the Southern Cross that could stand up four hours—no; four rounds—with her bridegroom. And he had been here for three weeks; and the crook of her little finger could sway him more than the fist of any 142-pounder in the world.[7]

In a typically O. Henry premise, when McGarry's bride expresses a craving for a peach—months out of season and unavailable at any grocery—the boxer pursues a desperate strategy. He tips off the police and leads them in a raid against an illegal gambling house, counting on finding among its luxuries fresh peaches (imported expensively from other climes). There, McGarry matches his skills against the proprietor:

> Denver Dick had graced his game with his own presence that night...when he saw the Kid his manner became personal. Being in the heavy-weight class he cast himself joyfully upon his slighter enemy, and they rolled down a flight of stairs in each other's arms. On the landing they separated and arose, and then the kid was able to use some of his professional tactics, which had been useless to him while in the excited clutch of a 200-pound sporting gentleman... (pp. 45–46)

After vanquishing Denver Dick, McGarry uncovers a single unconsumed peach to take home as a love prize to his bride.

In Henry's "Hygeia at the Solito" (1907), "Cricket" McGuire, a consumptive ex-featherweight prize fighter given six months to live, finds unlikely convalescence and redemption in Nueces County, Texas. Of note, Cricket is an autobiographical echo: William Sydney Porter (Henry) himself, upon his physician's advice, moved to LaSalle County, Texas in 1882, where he lived for two years on a ranch owned by a man named Richard Hall. Porter's health improved, and he moved afterward to Austin, where he lived until he was indicted for embezzlement in 1896, subsequently fleeing from those charges to New Orleans and on to Honduras—which became the source material and predicate to Porter's early writing career, as well as the reason for adopting his pseud-

---

7 O. Henry, *The Voice of the City*, Doubleday, Page & Company, 1918, p. 40. All subsequent excerpts are drawn from the same edition.

onym of O. Henry (as Porter, who began writing stories in prison, was concerned nobody would buy stories from a convict).

Carr may have drawn specific plot inspiration not from Cricket himself, but from one of that character's utterances: an early discussion between him and Curtis Raidler, the cattleman who takes in the pugilist to convalesce, includes this exchange:

> "You're from the No'th, ain't you, bud?" he asked when the other was partially recovered. "Come down to see the fight?"
>
> "Fight!" snapped McGuire. "Puss-in-the-corner! 'Twas a hypodermic injection. Handed him just one like a squirt of dope, and he's asleep, and no tanbark needed in front of his residence. Fight!"[8]

It seems possible that Cricket's metaphorical disparagement of the bout provided Carr inspiration for the actual climactic plot device in "The God of the Gloves."

Brian Oswald Donn Byrne's plots had more direct influence upon that of "The God of the Gloves." His 1915 collection *Stories Without Women (and a Few with Women)* includes two boxing tales, "An African Epic" and "A Man's Game." There is clear resemblance between the elements of Carr's story and those in "A Man's Game." Both pivot on cheating in a championship match. These two and Donn Byrne's other tale of the ring, "An African Epic," all put something greater at stake: all three stories focus on a turning point in the protagonist's life, cast in larger, interpersonal and social consequences, which themselves somehow hinge on the outcome of the boxing match. "The God of the Gloves" is, in this, an excellent example from Carr's apprenticeship of how he enjoyed borrowing premises from the authors and tales he relished and re-fashioning those premises into his own stories. In his professional years, Carr would continue doing this, most markedly in his radio dramas: he borrowed the titles and premises of fiction he loved by Stevenson, Poe, Chesterton, Conan Doyle, Ambrose Bierce, and Melville Davisson Post, and reworked them all by constructing his own, original plots.

Carr also clearly took delight in emulating Donn Byrne in the dramatization of every thrust, feint, and parry, carefully, technically observed—just as the feints and thrusts in the fencing matches Carr narrated in his period stories and novels were written with the authority of an expert. Carr saw boxing and fencing in the same light, each

---

8 O. Henry, *Heart of the West*, p. 94.

a duel of honor between two men of chivalric skills (or what should be chivalric). Carr's use of boxing, though, did more than advance the narrative with exciting action: it provided a mimetic pacing. Following the lead of Donn Byrne's stories, "The God of the Gloves" metes out its plot and character revelations blow by blow.

As he did fencing, Carr showcased pugilism in his professional writing; "The God of the Gloves" is the starting point of boxing as a motif throughout his works. Although he narrates bouts inside and outside rings, Carr nonetheless differentiates his own detective fiction from hard-boiled detective stories, which he contends characteristically rely upon fisticuffs, while his do not: "When the hero goes into action, he uses his brains and not his fists completely to shatter and destroy the villain..."[9]

While Carr often honors his own precept—for instance, with the climax of *The Eight of Swords*, Carr does *not* succumb to any temptation for his amateur middleweight pugilist, Hugh Donovan, to showcase his boxing skills—sometimes, a Carrian hero's victory is, in fact, with fists. Carr's earliest incorporation of boxing as a set piece after "The God of the Gloves" is in *Devil Kinsmere*, also his first historical novel:

> ...Uncle Godfrey drank a bottle too many, as old gentlemen will do. He got up on the table and offered even money on his nephew to crack the skull of any man in Somerset within half a stone of his weight. Whereupon a visiting landowner from the Mendips instantly offered two to one odds on a promising carter of his village, and a match was arranged (under terms of the most absolute secrecy) at Blackthorn....You will, of course, anticipate what occurred. (p. 23)

The reader may or may not anticipate what occurred, but it will not be revealed here!

There is a pair of similar boxing matches, which as in *Devil Kinsmere* are simply set pieces for the sake of entertainment, in *Night at the Mocking Widow* (pp. 143–145). The widow Virtue Conklin describes to H.M. how a personality conflict boils over into two amateur bouts, gloves and all, at the village pub between (of all people) the vicar, the Reverend James Cadman Hunter—one of two surrogate characters for Carr in the novel—and two locals (whom he boxes one after the other). The fights are refereed no less, by Gordon West—Carr's other surrogate.

More significant to the novel in which it occurs, in *Scandal at High*

---

9 Letter to James O'Brien, April 22, 1955. Also cited by Greene, p. 345.

Chimneys, set in Victorian England, a climactic brawl in which the protagonist uses his fists to dispatch an antagonist, not his wits, precedes the revelation of the murderer's identity. Clive Strickland, confronts his louche adversary, Lord Albert Tressider, at London's Alhambra Theatre. Earlier in the novel, Carr had pointedly informed the reader that the theater echoes with the memory of celebrating "Tom Sayers, retired former Champion of England" (p. 161). Although Carr confers upon neither Strickland nor Tressider any formal training as a fighter, when the two close with one another and begin exchanging blows, the crowded room cries out with, *"Make a ring! Make a ring!"* (p. 202)—and the crowd does. Next, as Carr delivers a clinical description of traded fists, the crowd roars its same old chant with which, in times past, it had cheered on that boxing champion Tom Sayers:

> "Hit him on the boko!
> Dot him on the snitch!
> Wot a lovely fighter—!
> Was there ever sich? (p. 203)

In 1952, Carr turned to boxing in both his novels. *The Nine Wrong Answers*, as "The God of the Gloves" does, links the protagonist's psychological and circumstantial difficulties; Bill Dawson, the novel's hero, can only resolve them by fighting his way through them. This is despite Bill's own belief in Carr's distinction:

> When you get into trouble, Bill thought, you must get out
> of it by using your brains; not by the dreary fictional pana-
> cea of a slosh under the jaw. (p. 77)

Dawson finds himself disadvantaged by an inability to overcome a deeply ingrained self-restraint. In a flashback, Bill recalls the admonitions of his trainer against Bill's inhibitions:

> Look, kid. What boins me is, ya *got* the punch. In both hands,
> like I loined ya. I got ya drilled, see, in what kids and ama-
> chures never loin: slam straight into the body; only a coupla
> head-punches till ya got him soft. Look kid. If ya'd wade in
> and sock, like I said, ya'd smear the son-of-a-bitch all over
> the canvas in the foist round. But ya won't do it. Ya can't get
> mad....I'm tellin' ya; that's all. Sure you can get sore, plenty
> sore. But ya can't get blind *mad*. And ya pull punches, kid,

even when you don' wanna. Ya just can't bear to hurt anybody. (pp. 110–111)

Bill finally realizes for himself what young Dinny McFarlane had more
quickly understood:

The underlying truth is this. Every man, a few times in his
life, must burst out of his surroundings—either physically,
or mentally, or spiritually—and for a brief time he must riot;
or else he will go mad in his tidy house. (p. 256)

It is his new self-awareness that helps Bill become a fighter in his own
cause, figuratively (engaging in a literally deadly battle of wits with the
book's antagonist, old Uncle Gaylord) and actually: Bill's breakthrough
begins with a pugilistic beatdown of Uncle Gay's sadistic manservant
Hatto, a former wrestler and capable boxer, who enjoys a considerable
size and reach advantage over Dawson:

"Now, J. Hatfield," he said, "can you only wrestle like a
dog? Or can you box?"
"I can do both. But if I box, young man, I will kill you.
I have greater height and reach; I can stand away and smash
your face off. I am two stone heavier. I think you can remember I am in very good training..."
....What happened did not take long...It happened in three
minutes and four seconds, only four seconds longer than an
ordinary professional round. Almost any referee would have
stopped it by the end of a minute. What happened was the
near murder of Hatto.
Not a man spoke during the fight...If any voice spoke
then, it was only in Bill's imagination.
*"Now ya doin' it, kid! Now ya doin' it! Smear the son-of-a-
bitch all over the canvas!"*
....Hatto's head snapped back, his bloodied face and shirt
front flung upward. Still another instant he swayed; then,
as though something had jerked loose every sinew from his
body, he fell straight backward...
....Bill, dazed, looked down at his gloves. Then he looked
at Hatto, who lay across the board with his head hanging
down over one end and his knees and feet dangling down
over the other.

> ....Again, Bill looked at his gloves, and shuddered. He tore them off and threw them away.
>
> "A cheap victory!" he said.
>
> It was as though that strange mood, which since afternoon had been closing in on his senses for murder or near murder, were now floating away; only to be replaced by a calmer mood which required eyes and brain.
>
> "After all," he mused aloud, "my main business here is with Gaylord Hurst. Yes, Mr. Gaylord Hurst!" (pp. 253–255)

Bill, who in Carr's phrasing had used "his fists completely to shatter and destroy" one villain, afterward goes on, similarly liberated in thought and consistent with Carr's principle, to use his brains, not his fists, to defeat the other.

A key antagonist in Carr's second 1952 novel, *Behind the Crimson Blind*, is G.W. Collier, a sour, bad-intentioned former prize fighter turned lawbreaker and the front-man for a criminal known only by the moniker Iron Chest. It is easy to imagine Streak Martin as, to some degree, a rough draft of Collier. While Martin's never-clearly-expressed motive for tormenting the elder McFarlane is one Carr the mystery novelist would not have left undeveloped, in "The God of the Gloves" it is less important. Martin's is simply a rotten nature. Even if the reader knew the particulars of his enmity toward McFarlane, it would not legitimize his brutality. In *Behind the Crimson Blind*, Carr provides credible motivation for Collier, but like Martin, Collier is also simply cold-blooded and pitiless.

As in "The God of the Gloves," *Scandal at High Chimneys*, and **The Nine Wrong Answers**, a boxing match (set in an impromptu ring, with gloves, and refereed by Carr's series detective, H.M., himself) with Collier is the novel's penultimate confrontation. Collier is indeed, contrary to Carr's epistle to James O'Brien and like Hatto, put down with fists, not wits. In 1952, there seems to be a consistent suggestion in Carr's fiction: while the protagonists overcome the ultimate villains (Uncle Gay, Iron Chest) in mental duels, pugilism serves very well for dispatching their henchmen.

Carr also slips boxing as a key element into one of his Sherlock Holmes pastiches, "The Adventure of the Wax Gamblers" (collected in 1954's *The Exploits of Sherlock Holmes*). In Carr's homage, Holmes (credited as a master of the eclectic martial art baritsu by Doyle in 1903's "The Adventure of the Empty House") accepts a boxing match with Bully-Boy Rasher, a professional middleweight fighter, merely for sportsmanship. "Having broken Rasher's hanging guard and survived" (p. 60), Holmes surprises all—spectators, oddsmakers, and professional gamblers—by knocking out the pug. This episode, which opens "Wax Gamblers," is a different and more bracing prologue than Doyle's usual series of startling deductions by Holmes when greeting new clients. It is also the direct springboard into the main plot of "Wax Gamblers," not an unrelated preliminary. So Carr's use of boxing, as in the other narratives, is not extraneous.

Fear is the Same, perhaps one of Carr's more greatly underappreciated novels, and his only historical romance written as Carter Dickson, features pugilism at its climax. Leave it to Carr to make even the expected unexpected and exciting: Philip Clavering, a former professional boxer and the novel's hero, laces on his gloves to contend against not one, but two opponents—two swordsmen. For Carr, the accomplished amateur fencer and student of boxing, there could be no more delectable match to narrate feint by feint, blow by blow, than the boxer versus the bladesmen.

Like Bill Dawson's, too, and as in "The God of the Gloves" and in Donn Byrne's boxing stories, Clavering's fight has ramifications outside its ropes: the identity of a murderer; Clavering's own freedom; his chance at happiness with the woman he loves; even national political consequences—and like Dinny McFarlane and Bill Dawson, Clavering must overcome his own, self-limiting psychological barriers:

> "Do you guess now why I hated my work? It was 'the crowd.'
> Every time I landed a solid punch, I was hitting 'the crowd.'
> Every time I knocked out a man, and knew he was gone the
> second he hit the canvas, for an instant I had knocked out
> 'the crowd.' Those two swordsmen in the ring now, whom I
> own I hate, are 'the crowd.' What's a championship, Jenny?
> It's only murdering 'the crowd.'" (p. 231)

In short, Clavering (more than thirty years after Dinny McFarlane), who hopes to go on and become a teacher of history or English, is an "older and wiser" surrogate of his fifty-year-old author, just as Dinny, struggling onto the path of his adult life and livelihood in a manner contrary to the guidance of his seniors, was a surrogate for the eighteen-year-old who created him. Both tales and a number of others in between demonstrate that pugilism, a duel of honor, so apt as a symbol for personal struggles, remained a theme of resort for Carr across the whole span of his career.

Pygmalion (1927)

"Mr. Ferguson isn't in? Oh, all right, I'll just walk through to the studio and wait for him. You needn't trouble to show me the way. Thank you."

Joan Ingram spoke decisively. She walked across the hall and down the passage, and so out and across the yard to the studio. She opened the door and went in, closing it quietly behind her, and stood for a while motionless on the doormat.

The room looked bleak and pallid in the light of the late winter noon. The fireplace was a heap of charred black wood and grey ashes. An easel, draped in a dull white cloth, loomed up in the center of the floor, like a patient, watchful phantom. On the walls hung, here and there, pictures in gold frames, lost and pale in the gathering dusk. Everywhere, there was litter and confusion; empty packing-cases, a broken, bursting divan, tousled cushions, straw, crumpled-up tubes of paint, lying about the floor.

Joan Ingram looked out of place in this ghostly, untidy room—a virginal Diana, golden-haired, young blood eloquent in her cheeks, grey eyes steady and clear; slender, erect, alert. She glared at the comfortless disorder of the studio with a frown, half amused, half scornful. All this would be altered, for Luke's sake, when they were married. When they were married? She frowned again. If they were married, rather. She remembered why she had come. As she pulled off her gloves, she gazed curiously across the room at a door, shrouded in a green baize curtain. Yes, she was jealous. She hated secrets. She pulled a key out of one of the pockets of her fur coat and stared at it, without seeing it.

Then she walked quickly across the room, and pulled the green curtain on one side, and inserted the key in the lock. It turned.

She paused. What right had she to come prowling like a thief into Luke Ferguson's studio, to wrest his secret from him, behind his back? Wasn't it dishonorable —stupid jealousy—unworthy of her? She walked back to the crazy divan, deep in thought, her head bent. She dropped her gloves on the divan listlessly, still thinking and frowning. Then she raised her head with a sharp, decisive sigh, shaking herself free of doubt. She took off her hat and threw it down beside the gloves, and then her coat across the gloves and hat.

She walked round the walls of the studio, gazing at the pictures. "Always landscapes!" she sighed impatiently; "always trees and skies and clouds! Never faces! Why doesn't he go back to faces? Everyone knows that he is a portrait painter. He does these things all right, but everyone says his faces were wonderful. Why can't he finish his portrait of me? Why won't he let me see it? Has he lost his skill?"

She turned and looked at the model-stand with the high-backed antique chair upon it. How many hours had she spent, sitting there, silent, unmoving, while her lover toiled at his canvas? It had been happiness at first—the tense, creative silence, the flickering sound of the brush, the cries of children in the distant, noisy street, her lover's dark eyes flowing over her face and throat and shoulders, like a warm tide of summer. Then it had been pain. The dark eyes became dreamy, blind, unseeing; they gazed through her, beyond her, with faint suspense and splendor and regret; the children's voices fainted into thin air; the brush fell to the floor; silence had straining, ghostly ears, straining ghostly eyes—for the vision, for the voice. Once or twice, she had stirred, had spoken, and then her lover had slowly wakened from his trance, gazing at her with a puzzled frown.

And when she went to look at her face on the canvas, it was always blurred, always sightless.

"My dear, I can't do it, somehow," he had said; "I can't get your face. Your eyes..."

She had insisted on his painting her portrait as a wedding gift. She had her own good reasons for making this demand. She and Luke Ferguson had met casually at some social function. She had been unaccountably drawn towards this dreamy, absent-minded artist. He had seemed to respond. Other meetings had followed, and in the end, quite suddenly, Luke Ferguson had asked her to be his wife. She had been proud, she had been happy. Luke Ferguson was a man well worth marrying, and there was mystery about him.

"Do get him to go back to portrait painting," her friends had said, on hearing the news; "Why, don't you remember, Luke Ferguson was all the rage ten years ago. No one could do eyes better than he did—you know, angular and heavy-lidded. They were always more alive than all the rest of the face put together."

And *his* friends had said, "If you can get Luke to chuck all these second-rate landscapes of his, and take to portraits again, you will be doing him a good turn, and you will be doing Art a good turn, too."

"It's one of the great mysteries," others had told her with knowing smiles; "Why, almost overnight, Luke Ferguson turned from portrait painting, which brought him in thousands, to landscapes, which any silly boy could paint. A disappointment, somewhere, I should suppose."

Joan had set herself to work to sound this mystery, for Luke's own good. And, for his own good, the first task that she had laid upon him was a portrait of herself. But the mystery was still there. The portrait was not yet finished.

She walked over towards the easel, and pulled the cloth aside impatiently, and stared at the face upon the canvas in the winter-laden gloom. Of course, it would be an empty blur, without eyes, still! But was it? Two dark eyes seemed to be staring back at her with a steady gleam. She drew back in surprise. Then went to the wall and turned up the lights and came back to the easel.

Yes, there was her face, radiant, cold, dauntless, unutterably pure in outline, crowned with golden hair. But whose were those dark green eyes, staring back at her with a restless, furtive mockery—the eyes of Astarte[1] in the face of Diana?[2] *Her* eyes? Anger, pride, humiliation, surged through Joan like a mad rush of sea. She raised her hand and struck the picture across the eyes.

For a moment she stood stunned, yet quivering, then she ran quickly across the room to the door behind the green curtain. Here was the answer to the mystery. Once she had come into the studio, unnoticed. This door was wide open. Luke was in the room beyond, standing before a picture in a gold frame on the wall opposite the door. At the sound of her voice, he had turned round sharply, with a white, startled face. Quickly he had come out of the room, had closed and locked the door and drawn the curtain. He had said nothing to her; she had not dared to ask. And he had never let her go into that room.

Joan pushed opened the door. She turned on the switch in the wall at the side of the door. The room was drenched in light...She saw her lover, white-limbed, his eyes ablaze, his lips parted on the fire of love and triumph...in his arms a woman, tawny, golden-limbed, sinuous, snake-like...with dark raven hair...her head was turned away from him...her eyes were alight with restless, furtive mockery...a long, sidelong, downward glance, half ashamed, half triumphant.

"My dear, I had no idea you were here."

Luke Ferguson was standing on the threshold of the studio, one

---

1 Astarte was a near-Eastern goddess of sexuality, fertility, and war. Biblical passages involving idolatry of her (and punishment) include: Judges 2:13-14 and 10:6-9; 1 Samuel 7:3-4 and 12:10; 1 Kings 11:5-13; 2 Kings 23:13; and Jeremiah 7:18 and 44:17-29.

2 Diana, goddess of the hunt, was also the goddess of chastity. She and Astarte overlap as fertility goddesses, but where Diana is a virgin goddess, worship of Astarte debases the sacred by commingling it with copulation.

hand still on the doorknob. Joan stood in the doorway of the mysterious room, staring back at him in tremulous silence.

A change came over Luke's face. He saw the big open door, the lighted
room, behind her. He lurched heavily across the room and gripped her
by the arm.

"What do you mean?" he said, shaking her roughly; "How dare you
come creeping in here behind my back?"

Joan faced him squarely. "Let me go," she said, coldly. He loosened
his grip. She went to the divan, and hurriedly began putting on her hat
and coat. Luke stared at her dully. When she had finished, she turned
to him.

"I have come to say good-bye," she said.

"But why?" stammered Luke Ferguson.

Joan pointed at the portrait of herself. "How dare you put that creature's eyes in my face!" she said, in a voice, quivering with suppressed rage.

"That creature?"

"Yes. In there. You've always loved her. Not me."

Luke Ferguson dropped on the divan with a groan, and sank his
chin on one hand.

"But, you don't understand—there is no such creature."

Joan looked at him, bewildered and incredulous; "I don't care," she
said at length, "but I won't be always second to that. Good-bye."

She turned and left him. For an hour Luke Ferguson sat brooding
on the divan. Then he rose and went through the door and stood gazing at the picture. He stood and gazed, and then suddenly he fell on his
knees, with his hands to his head.

"Oh, damn you!" he cried, hoarsely; "will you never come! And will
you never die!"

Notes for the Curious: "Pygmalion"

"Pygmalion," like "The Kindling Spark," while on the surface a contemporary literary tale, is also like that earlier story an uncommon experiment on Carr's part. "Pygmalion" is a psychological narrative bordering quietly on horror that also trades in ambiguity. The mature Carr had very little use for psychology, except, eventually, to the extent that psychology affected witnesses' perceptions: as Greene states the matter (p. 267), after Carr ceased to reject psychology entirely, he saw its role in fiction "as explaining the *how* rather than the *why* of human behavior." In "Pygmalion," Carr uncharacteristically (as he did in "The Kindling Spark") examines the psychological *why*.

The story's even greater experiment is that it is an allegory, which the reader might well expect given its title. "Pygmalion" is the most symbolic of Carr's early tales, probably his most symbolic narrative ever. In its deliberate layer of subtext reverberating underneath the surface and its playful pairing of persons and symbols, "Pygmalion" is related to Carr's two early horror stories, "The Riddle of the Laughing Lord" and "The Devil-Gun."

Perhaps the young Carr felt symbolism and psychological deviance were necessary ingredients of horror because that is what he learned from Poe.

While the Pygmalion myth (of the sculptor who isolates himself from the world and creates in ivory his idealized vision of a woman, Galatea, which the goddess Venus brings to life in response to his prayer) has been allegorically exploited countless times—the well-read Carr would surely have been familiar with works doing so by Dryden, Mary Shelley (hers subtitled "The Modern Prometheus," but very much a Pygmalion tale gone wrong), William Hazlitt, Nathaniel Hawthorne, William Morris, Henry James, Edith Wharton, George Bernard Shaw, Robert Graves, and even H.P. Lovecraft—it is perhaps only Shelley's and Lovecraft's Galateas who were anything like the one in Carr's story—at least, that is if the reader concludes the portrait in the room behind the green curtain is this story's Galatea figure. This is not necessarily the case. "Pygmalion," ambiguously, never declares in what form it conjures Galatea—or which character, in fact, is allegorically Pygmalion.

Either way, "Pygmalion" is an allegory of the artist. In the likelier reading, Carr's allegory demonstrates the incompatibility of the artist's unadulterated vision with ordinary persons' sensibilities (who expect comfortable art they recognize, with a capital "A"). The artist's vision is faithful to itself, not to others' expectations, even if, as in the story, that vision in its incomprehensibility is comparatively dark or seemingly twisted from others' perspectives.

Joan Ingram's "other friends" are proponents of the socially accept-able, unstartling, commercially negotiable craft they confuse with art. These friends cannot distinguish between an artisan and an artist. The sort of art they advocate would, if Luke Ferguson consented to create it, bring Luke stature, recognition, and remuneration. Portraits especially, which by tradition glamorize and valorize their subjects, reinforce the social order so important to these unnamed friends. The affluent com-mission portraits, after all, to exalt themselves.

It is evident that Luke has abandoned portrait painting because it became too revealing of his undisguised artistic sensibility, which to the average eye would be frightening, grotesque. Were Luke to paint por-trait subjects honestly, their portraits would reveal what Luke sees in his subjects, rather than flattering them by depicting what they see in them-selves. In this, Luke was in danger of becoming the tragic version of O. Henry's comic artist, Sherrard Plumer. Like Luke, Plumer was once in vogue and then abruptly fell out of fashion. He explains his downfall:

> I soon found out what the trouble was. I had a knack of bringing out in the face of a portrait the hidden character of the original. I don't know how I did it—I painted what I saw—but I know it did me. Some of my sitters were fearfully enraged and refused their pictures. I painted the portrait of a very beautiful and popular society dame. When it was fin-ished her husband looked at it with a peculiar expression on his face, and the next week he sued for divorce.[3]

Understanding his dilemma, to avoid shocking and displeasing his audi-ence, Luke has turned to painting bland landscapes. In Carr's allegory, Luke's is showing the face of conventionality an artist assumes for meet-ing the uninitiated.

Macaulay deliberated over this same predicament in portraiture:

---

3 O. Henry, "A Madison Square Arabian Night," *The Trimmed Lamp and Other Stories of the Four Million*, p. 28. Note that this story, one in which Henry overtly works an Arabian Nights metaphor, would likely have been among Carr's favorites. This makes the possibility greater that he borrowed Plumer's troubling insightfulness consciously and bestowed it upon Luke.

> Any man with eyes and hands may be taught to take a likeness.
> The process, up to a certain point, is merely mechanical. If this
> were all, a man of talents might justly despise the occupation.
> But we could mention portraits which are resemblances,—
> but not mere resemblances; faithful,—but much more than
> faithful; portraits which condense into one point of time, and
> exhibit, at a single glance, the whole history of turbid and
> eventful lives—in which the eye seems to scrutinise us, and
> the mouth to command us—in which the brow menaces, and
> the lip almost quivers with scorn—in which every wrinkle is
> a comment on some important transaction. (p. 6497)

Carr knowing Macaulay so well, this distinction between taking a likeness and painting a portrait may also have partly inspired the central problem of "Pygmalion."

Luke's genuinely artistic vision clashes with commercial art because the young Carr's does. This rejection of an expected social order, though, is not that same fear of the corruptibility of institutions in "The Red Heels." Rather, the artistic temperament of this story's allegory is the same one Carr propounded as a young newspaper columnist:

> Why must an author see the world through smoked glasses to
> be called a realist? Why is the market flooded with stuff such as
> *Main Street*, *Potterism*, and *The Beautiful and the Damned*? And
> prodigious wonder, why do these books rank as best-sellers?[1]

To Carr, contemporary literature, pursued cynically for profit and recognition, is corrupt. He elaborates on the problematic connection between "realism" and commercialism in the concluding section ("L'Envoi") of "The New Canterbury Tales":

> Realists are the people who look in a mirror and get disgusted.
> They are the ones who will explode all your fine ideas. They
> would pull down Kenilworth Castle[2] and substitute an effi-
> cient gas-station; they would take the Lorelei[3] off the rocks

---

1 "As We See It," Uniontown *Daily News Standard*, May 4, 1922, p. 8.

2 Built in the early twelfth century, Kenilworth was a storied royal castle for most of its existence. It was dismantled in 1650, but its romantic ruins have been preserved since that time.

3 In German mythology, sirens of great beauty living upon a Rhine rock; as in *The*

and substitute Margaret Sangers[4] and Carrie Chapman Catts.[5] Your realistic author has begun to notice a protuberant stomach and weakening eyes, so he goes right merrily to work and writes a novel exposing something as sordid. It is considered a great novel; he is awarded the Pulitzer or the Nobel prize, which he refuses. Aesop once wrote a fable about this, and called it The Dog in the Manger.[6]

In "Pygmalion," Luke's friends, neighbors, and even his fiancée, Joan, are such realists. Joan sees the portrait she demands of Luke as currency of their love, a public subsumption of his artistry to their conventional, wedded relationship. Joan believes this is "for Luke's own good."

When Luke attempts to complete the area of Joan's portrait—her face, her eyes—that to him convey the most intimate insights of painting, he cannot do so with authenticity. There is even the hint by Carr that Luke previously blurred Joan's face because her "artistic" demands of him blended themselves indistinguishably—and Joan herself—with those of the faceless and unnamed others, the "friends," who somewhat self-interestedly push him toward commercial success and repute. Luke Ferguson's reascent, after all, would reflect well on them, the circle of "intimates" to Joan and him.

From this angle—the "less likely" allegorical reading—the story's title can be read as an ironic inversion of the classical myth in which the artist's work is so lifelike and beautiful that it comes to life. In this unlikelier allegorical interpretation, it is Joan and her friends who attempt to be "artists," to sculpt Luke into their unexceptional, everyday vision of

---

Odyssey, the Lorelei attract passing mariners with irresistible songs, causing the mariners to wreck their ships upon the rock. The Lorelei were a favorite allusion of Carr's, and he used it repeatedly: in 1922's "The Will-o'-the-Wisp"; in "The New Canterbury Tales" and "The Deficiency Expert" (both 1927); and in *The Gilded Man* (1942), on p. 249.

4 An American nurse and birth-control advocate, Sanger campaigned against the Comstock Act, which criminalized contraceptives. Carr of course would have found her to be a very unromantic figure.

5 Carrie Chapman Catt was an American women's suffrage leader who, as two-time president of the National American Woman Suffrage Association, campaigned for the Nineteenth Amendment to the U.S. Constitution, which granted women the right to vote in 1920.

6 The moral of Aesop's fable, in which a growling dog unnecessarily drives a hungry ox away from hay, is "Do not grudge others what you cannot enjoy yourself."

what he should be. Luke, their Galatea, will regain "life" by becoming "all the rage" again after ten years of social insignificance (lifelessness).

In the likelier allegorical reading, with Luke as Pygmalion, Galatea is his darkly sexual painting: a depiction redolent of Astarte, the Canaanite goddess of sex, fertility, and war, who displaces Joan's staid expectations of Diana imagery, Diana whose name derives from turning darkness into heavenly daylight,[7] and who is a chaste hunter, an idealized object of love, the protector of virgins. Luke's vision is too untamed, too conflicted with Joan's and that of the unnamed friends to serve as "Art with a capital A."

Luke's frustrated recognition of this problem is an attention-grabbing antithesis, a paradoxical expression of his own conflicted feelings: "Oh, damn you...will you never come! And will you never die!"[8] This utterance is one stylistic demonstration of Carr's frequent reliance upon antithesis, and upon contrasts generally, when he wishes to conjure emotional difficulties and juxtapositions between characters—or between characters and settings, by which Carr evokes a striking mood. Examples in his mature detective novels are numerous, but Carr began developing this technique in his early stories. Consider, for instance, his more overt and frequent use of antithetical contrast in "The Riddle of the Laughing Lord" and "The Devil-Gun."[9]

Of note, the two allegorical interpretations concerning which character(s) might be Pygmalion, and which figure Galatea, are not irreconcilable; unlike the ambiguity at the end of "The Kindling Spark," the reader can accept both interpretations simultaneously.

Luke's finished portrait of Joan represents the artist's attempt to meld the vitality of his art, Astarte-like, with society's, most pointedly with Joan's, conventional expectations—and at the level of the story, somehow subserviate his artistry to their relationship. Luke's unspoken fantasy is to engender in his fiancée a living connection to his muse, unifying the artist's life, love, and art—but he cannot. The portrait, Luke's attempt, is neither wholly Joan nor wholly his untransformed serpentine paramour. It affronts Joan's chaste decency, affirming that,

---

7 The name Diana traces back to the proto-Indo-European root dyeu, "to shine."

8 The wonderfully anguished antithesis concluding the story pleased Carr so much that, however consciously or not, he echoed it more than a dozen years later, when he ended the second chapter (p. 30) of *The Man Who Could Not Shudder* with the protagonist's self-contradictory exclamation, "Why the devil couldn't it happen next day? Why the devil should it ever have happened?"

9 Both these stories were published in *The Kindling Spark* (Crippen & Landru, 2022).

allegorically, genuine art cannot be an aesthetic compromise between artist and audience. When Joan looks at Luke's unfiltered art, she sees only a "woman, tawny, golden-limbed, sinuous, snake-like...with dark raven hair," a lubricious, bestial figure repulsive to her. Joan perceives only the painting's surface, not its underlying meaning.

For Joan, Luke's fidelity to art is an infidelity to her.

Luke, for his part, expresses intimacy with his muse as coital; he underscores it with the visual suggestion of myth, which implies its eternality and power. Luke cannot embrace art with the chaste, conventional—and surface-level—adoration Joan demands.

Her break with Luke leaves the artist, allegorically, alone and lonely, looking to find in the world he occupies some material manifestation of his muse that he can embrace passionately and without disguise. But the story's allegory demonstrates that artistic truth cannot take a comforting form; so as Luke despairs, the closing lines affirm paradoxically that the artist's ideal can never come fully to life, but neither can it fully die.

The story's three progressive portraits (Joan's unfinished portrait, Joan's finished portrait, and Luke's mythic lover), as Luke conceives them, align rather neatly with James Branch Cabell's sexualized conception of the male-female relationship (to which Carr subscribed): "domnei, or woman-worship...a man's mistress [is] an ever-present reminder, and sometimes rival, of God" (p. 49). Each of the portraits in "Pygmalion" corresponds with one of Cabell's seminal:

> "white witches" who could help, but not hurt; "black witches," who could hurt, but not help; and "gray witches", who could do either at will....in dreams man has shown no aversion to the witch-woman...but, to the contrary, man has always clung, with curious tenacity, to the notion of some day attaining the good graces of that fair-haired and delicate-voiced witch who is a bane to men, and yet sometimes takes mortal lovers. (pp. 61–69)

Joan's innocuous portrait, as she would have it completed, is a white witch; Luke's smoldering, undisguised muse is a black witch; what Luke covets and tries to summon with Joan's finished portrait is a gray witch—who will never, unfortunately, actually come into Luke's life, although his desire for her will never die.

We hear Carr's own, echoing desire not just in the works of his apprenticeship, but in the professional novels, too...all throughout his career. Thirty-eight years after "Pygmalion," in *The House at Satan's*

Elbow, the fifty-nine-year-old novelist once more draws directly upon the Cabellian framework he finds so persuasive, reiterating the same urge the younger Carr demonstrated:

> Each man of imagination searches throughout his life for the witch-woman, the siren, the charmer who shall unite all qualities in one flesh. I think I have found mine; I could die happy if I were sure of it; and yet—who knows? Who can ever be sure? (p. 185)

Carr summons this metaphor four years later, with an interesting twist, in *The Ghosts' High Noon*. In that novel, Carr has a woman herself, a respectable one, embrace Cabell's feminine taxonomy: "Remember me, Mr. Blake, if you remember me at all, as an old witch who used white magic in prophesying only for people's good" (p. 197).

Finally, two years after that, Kit Farrell, the protagonist of Carr's last novel, *The Hungry Goblin*, regularly refers to his love interest, Pat Denbigh, as his "Circe," the witch-woman in Homer's *Odyssey* who seduces Odysseus's men with her sexuality and then, in an overt allegory, magically transforms them into swine.

Beyond the uncharacteristic allegory of "Pygmalion," more characteristically of Carr, Luke Ferguson serves as another of the young author's literary proxies. Like most creative teenaged boys, Carr was torn between passion for his art, his desire for women, and a very impractical wish, somehow, to unite them. Luke's feelings came authentically to Carr.

All this subtext unsubtly present in "Pygmalion," Carr's dabbling with symbolism and ambiguity, the story's unusual precedence of psychology over circumstance, is an experiment upon which Carr would not build. The more durable influences upon him—Chesterton, Stevenson, O. Henry (whom he would continue to echo, but with more fidelity of tone than the one echo in this story), Doyle, Dumas, and even Thomas and Mary Hanshew, whose Man of the Forty Faces, Cleek, undertook wildly imaginative adventures told hilariously—would prevail, and Carr would more and more focus on his youthful dictum that...

> ...it takes more writers' [sic] art to get out a really good detective story...the author's chief aim is to amuse. If he can create a new and ingenious plot, create a tense undercurrent of suspense that carries the reader along in spite of himself, and then produce a climax [that leaves the reader] breathless while he naively explains away all the seemingly unsolvable puzzles

that have added zest to the story—then [he has] written a good mystery novel.[10]

Nonetheless, "Pygmalion," like so many of Carr's other early experiments in genre, is gratifying reading, and in that, despite its minimal plot and uncharacteristic psychological focus, accomplishes Carr's chief aim.

---

10 "As We See It," Uniontown *Daily News Standard*, May 4, 1922, p. 8.

The Deficiency
Expert (1927)

"Undoubtedly," said his father, "you have made a mess of it."

Rinkey Donovan tried to look uncomfortable.

"I have here," his father went on, "a letter from the president of your college." He puffed out a cloud of smoke like a dragon, and attempted to seem dragon-like. But it was difficult, for he was stout and bald-headed and genial, and he worshipped Rinkey.[1] "A letter—" he repeated uneasily, and waited for his son to speak. He did not relish his task; he had kept the letter by him for over a week before he made up his mind to get violent. Remembering, he scowled.

"Well, dad?" said Rinkey, wondering what the old hod-carrier[2] had written.

"Rinkey, you've been a great disappointment to me," the elder Donovan blurted out. "Now, all these fool things you did—unnecessary! Now, what was the sense of printing those ridiculous things about the professors in your college newspaper? That was unnecessary! Then there was the time you bribed your local constable to arrest the dean on a charge of bootlegging, and you and your Skeptics Club went around singing 'Hail, Hail, The Dean's In Jail,' or something. The president has tabulated sixty-four offenses here, and says these are only smaller ones."

Rinkey sighed, and waited. The elder Donovan sat rubbing his nose and looking thoughtful. On the walls of the library there were big pictures of dead statesmen, so that he seemed part of a ghostly political conference.[3] He scratched his head and continued:

"He says, Rinkey, that you have absolutely no sense of values. He regrets, of course, the necessity for any step he may take; they always do. He says that you are probably the biggest liar in the United States, including the District of Columbia. He says that you have persistently

---

1 Rinkey's father resembles, naturally, Carr's father Wooda (Greene, p. 60).

2 A hod-carrier is a laborer in masonry. The hod is a three-sided box for carrying building materials, usually mortar or bricks.

3 Carr's father represented Pennsylvania's 23rd Congressional district in the 63rd Congress, between March 1911 and March 1913. The elder Donovan's office is modeled on that of Carr's father.

overturned everything that is noble and good in the college. But he says you have a brilliant mind—hm."

"Soft soap," said Rinkey. "Must be dirty water somewhere around. Well?"

"And he suggests that you withdraw. That you do not return this fall."

Rinkey looked down at his hands.

"I'm sorry, dad," he said.

"You have been a great disappointment to me," the elder Donovan told him, and sighed like a steam shovel. "I gave you all these opportunities because I thought that you had something in you. Now you've just thrown them all away. What am I going to do with you?" he went on plaintively, because he did not believe what he was saying. Inside him he was proud of Rinkey, and at the Elks' Club he was in the habit of referring to 'these damn tame little rabbits who haven't a damn thing in 'em!' He continued: "This will just about kill your mother...Hm, now. There's this liar business. What's he mean by that?"

"Oh," said Rinkey, "it wasn't lies; it was art. It was the *Record* and the way I handled it. As a matter of fact, there wasn't a word of truth in the paper from cover to cover except the date, and we juggled that sometimes. But the news stories were humdingers. Yes, sir, we had the biggest circulation of any college paper in the world. Lord, everybody was buying it! We got to rivalling the city papers—"

"And it was all lies," observed his father looking at him curiously.

"It was the popular conception of a newspaper worked up a hundred times. It was art. Look here, dad: do you think people are going to stop buying a newspaper because it's full of lies? They won't. They'll buy two copies; they'll buy three or four. Why, it's a revolutionary movement in journalism!"

"I'm not so sure," remarked his father. "It's been done in politics for a thousand years."

"And that," said Rinkey, "is what you're going to give me to do."

He studied his father's jovial red face, with its bald head fringed in red and its peering look over the glasses. The face became startled, and the stomach puffed out.

"Oh, Lord! No! Not that, Rinkey—"

"Now, listen," said Rinkey, becoming excited and pressing his point with the relentless zeal of a lunatic. "You own the *Bulletin* right here in this town, don't you? You want to see it a good newspaper, don't you? Yes. Well, it isn't, because all it does is try to take a fall out of the other political party. It's awful!—"

"No!" cried his father explosively, like a boy refusing castor oil.

"You're going to give Colaway a vacation, first of all. He may be a good editor, but he makes the news stagnate. What you ought to do is put me in charge for a few months, and the people who don't like it can spit on their hands and choose their own weapons. I'll lie, certainly. I'll lie," proclaimed Rinkey, "until the heavens split and the graves give up their—"[1]

"You figure on meddling with politics? Look here, now," said his father weakly.

"—dead," said Rinkey. He became persuasive. "Why, *consider* the advantages to be derived. Your own candidate for Congress goes up this fall. And you know that in this state he hasn't a prayer in God-help-us unless something can be done to sweep the heavens with fireworks and twenty-dollar bills. Just think! A triumphant victory, and Billy Mugson, the honey-voiced orator, your own choice, swept to Washington, charioted in green fire and bursting adverbs! Just think!"

The elder Donovan listened with patience, hands folded across his waist. His son stalked up and down among the bookcases and the solemn portraits, his face set and serious while his ideas flowed in a crazy stream, like a Puritan elder singing a jazz song. He began to resemble a good-natured goblin, with tousled reddish hair and a homely, appealing face. Finally his father sighed.

"I think," he opined, "that you are going to be a most magnificent deficiency expert."

***

The Humberville *Bulletin* office stood as it had stood for forty years, dusty, stuffed with forgotten files, thrumming and lumbering with the old flat-bed press at the back. It stood at the corner of grimy streets from which main traffic had been removed—opposite a vaudeville theater, it was remote and thoughtful among hot-dog stands and the back entrances to stores. Squealing, darting newsboys were its fauns, each faun having a secret ambition to drive Mike, the town patrol wagon. Its verdure consisted of boxes and packing cases, where the little fauns whooped and danced and thumbed their noses. Furniture vans got into a swearing jam there, paper whirled in brisk winds, dust blew, and *rattlety-tum* went the music from the vaudeville theater. Amid all this bang and chatter, mixed with frantic reports from a garage, smoke-blasts and

---

[1] This is a wonderfully comic reference to Revelation 20:13: "And the sea gave up the dead which were in it; and death and hell delivered up the dead which were in them: and they were judged every man according to their works." Note that the latter part of the verse, which Rinkey neglects to consider, becomes one of the driving tensions in this story.

mechanics addressing a drowning carburetor, the *Bulletin* office was a forlorn place. It was a relic of the old battling days of politics. About it clung the smell of ancient beer-bottles, the ghosts of yelling torchlight processions.

But the last of these glorious traditions was passing. A sprightly new Chamber of Commerce in the up-and-humming Humberville (slogan, "Humberville Hums for Humans") was daily inserting some new res-olution approving something in the *Bulletin*. Now once upon a time along the national pike the stage-coaches had brought tall-hatted men; Clay of Kentucky and the beefy Lafayette swaggered through when Indi-ans were yet in the mountains. There had been the stage-coach races, the drinking bouts; there in the White Swan Tavern old Tom Fossit was boasting how he had put a musket-ball through the head of Gen-eral Braddock when the redcoats strutted down the mountains into the Indian ambuscade. In those hills young Washington had fought his los-ing fight at Fort Necessity.[2] Old days, great days!—gone with the cocked hat and the minuet-music. Instead, from the vaudeville theater across the street the linotype men in the *Bulletin* office heard the ripple of a piano, a pleading husky voice upraised in song:

> *"I am Sir Gal-a-had,*
> *And, if I'm ver-y bad*
> *Who'll wash my TIN un-der-shirt?"*

Rum-tiddlety-tum skipped the music, and ended in a plink as the whir of the linotypes drowned it out again. Ed Miller, the foreman, heard it occasionally, and swore at it sometimes, but heavier matters were on his mind. Ed was a sullen-looking man with broken teeth and China-blue eyes. He had lived long enough in the hot greasy air of the composing room to abhor liberties with the paper, and at present things were being hurled about in the *Bulletin* office in a way that staggered him. The wildest news stories were dribbling through Ed's hands; they infuriated him, they made him chew his pipe-stem until he felt he must have the thing out.

He had the mien of a bespectacled Jove when he stalked up to the city room that afternoon. He left the banging, the rush of feet and the *tap tap* of the hammer that wedged the forms, and Ontko, the ad man,

---

2 Fort Necessity is not much more than ten miles from Uniontown, which affirms that Humberville and its newspaper are thinly disguised versions of Carr's hometown and its local newspaper, on which he worked as a teenager.

quailed when he saw him pass. There were only two people in the city room, though the door to Colaway's tiny office was closed and voices issued therefrom. At the city editor's desk sat O'Neil, an Irishman who looked like a German and who stuttered;[3] beside him was Rinkey Donovan, admiring the afternoon edition. They saw the avenger, and were uneasy.

"Look here," said Miller ominously, holding up the final edition. He stood there in the dusty light, among forlorn typewriters and cigarette stubs on the floor like a light snow-storm.

"W-what's the matter?" asked O'Neil.

Miller exploded, and told them. His wrath blew across the room; the light on his glasses made his eyes terrible; he smote the desk, and finally demanded the purpose of these lies, pointing out the awful consequences when Colaway, the managing editor, should return from his vacation.

"N-now listen, Ed," said O'Neil, "this is p-perfectly all right, and R-rinkey's old man sanctions it. We don't tell any harmful lies; it's all in fun, heh-heh-heh!" he added, with a crinkly laugh and arched eyebrows. He always had been afraid of Ed Miller.

"You guys," said Miller, "think you're the brothers Grimm? What d'ye mean, anyhow? Are you nuts? What's the idea? My God! This is a newspaper; we ain't running any *Weird Tales* magazine! Why, if I—"

"W-what's the matter with it?" asked O'Neil. "I think it's remarkable."

"Remarkable?" howled Miller impotently, "you're damn right it's remarkable! Do you want the whole staff fired? Do you expect anybody to believe all this, eh?—this story about the guy jugglin' bottles of nitroglycerine in the back of Buntz's drug-store!—"

"Oh, listen; that reminds me," said Rinkey Donovan with a soothing smile. "Buntz called up about that. He said he had a crowd fifty deep around his store. Said he did more business yesterday than all last year. Fact, Ed! Said he had to put some fellow with little bottles back there juggling 'em so they'd think—"

Miller hurled the edition to the floor. He grew desperate.

"But listen! You can't get away with this stuff! Oil discovered—president passes through incognito; is questioned on tax reduction and says that unquestionably the church is a fine institution which no American should neglect. Holy!—"

"Shh-h! Now, listen—"

---

3 Like the sports editor in "The God of the Gloves," this character is an avatar of O'Neil Kennedy, who did in fact stammer (Greene, p. 60). Kennedy was a mentor and friend to Carr at the Uniontown *Daily News Standard.*

"They'll discredit you! People won't buy the paper, or advertise!"

"Oh, yes, they will," insisted Rinkey with sudden wisdom. "People'll always be kind of afraid there may be some truth in what we say, and they'll go on buying it because they're afraid that if they don't they may miss something. That's anybody's weakness: afraid to miss something."

Ed Miller intimated that the unmentionable idea was of lascivious habits, doubtful parentage, and canine origin. He decided that he had never seen a person so immorally insane; he told them exactly where the gory paper might be thrust with the greatest possible effect, and he thundered out of the city room in a gust of horrid wrath.

Rinkey Donovan sat down on one of the battered chairs. He began to tap idly at a typewriter.

"O'Neil," he said suddenly and oracularly, "a great American has just left this room."

"W-where?" said O'Neil, startled.

"Ed Miller. Ed Miller is a great American because he represents the only traditions we've got. This country," affirmed Rinkey, "has got to be saved from the relentless intellectual."

"S-sure," agreed the city editor, nodding with a solemn look behind his glasses. He was always ready to agree with anybody, and have his own thoughts on the matter.

Rinkey fired up and tousled his hair.

"I mean from the intellectual *per se;* I mean from the sinister force in politics which is—hm. I mean people like Jeffrey Davis. They're trying to oust the old-time politician who kisses the baby and sneaks out behind the barn to take a drink with the old man. The old-time politician is a great memorial; there ought to be a statue to him. He is passing. What," cried Rinkey, "would the English do to a person who pulled down Kenilworth Castle and substituted an efficient gas-station? What would the Germans do if you took the Lorelei off the rocks and substituted Margaret Sanger and Carrie Chapman Catt?"

In silence the thump of the orchestra came through the windows from the theater opposite, and the song came out poutingly:

> *"I ain't the kind of bloke*
> *Who'd tell a risky joke,*
> *I ain't no hound after dirt—*
> *'Cause I am Sir Galahad—"*

Rinkey buried his fist in the typewriter keys, indicating fury. "There!" he said, "there; listen!"

"D—do you remember Moran's saloon?" speculated O'Neil dreamily.

"We can do whatever we please," pursued Rinkey, "but Jeffrey Davis is going to win. It's useless to kid ourselves."

There was a strange note of bitterness in his voice. He was suddenly so deadly serious, sitting there at the typewriter with his hunched shoulders and thin hawkish face, that O'Neil felt uncomfortable, almost as though he had overheard something. The city editor was not accustomed to being serious. He peered around to see whether any of the reportorial staff might be about, and said, "I h-hope you weren't—that is——"

Rinkey looked up with a grin that was rather childishly wistful.

"I was," he confessed. "Oh, well!"

The door to Colaway's little office opened, and a big heavy-shouldered man stood against the light. It was Hoyd, one of the party leaders.

"That's a good 'un!" said Hoyd, laughing and shifting his feet. "God, it's after three! I got to go—"

From beyond him came the sound of a rich argumentative voice upraised:

"Say, listen: and this guy Davis, you know, if he ever got to Wash'nton he wouldn't have sense enough to find the Capitol! And *tight?* Did y'ever notice him, the way he fills up his pipe and catches all the tobacco that falls?—and puts it back in his pocket? Now, I—"

Through the half-opened door Rinkey could see Billy Mugson, candidate for Congress, sitting with his feet on a table. He was expansive, red-faced, and white-whiskered, rather like Santa Claus. He was genial and blundering as a threshing machine, gesturing around him. At his elbow stood a small glass. This was the old-time politician; he took his God for granted, his liquor straight, and however crooked he might be, he never wavered in the belief that his party must be right, because his father had voted the straight ticket before him. About him clung something almost absurdly serene.

While Rinkey watched him heave his feet down off the table, and puff out his white whiskers and blink his eyes and wave jovially at them through the door, upon the drowsy humming air of the afternoon there rose again the song from the theater:

> *"Now if you want 'em hot*
> *Just go to Lan-ce-lot,*
> *'Cause he's a wow of a flirt!*
> *BUT (pling!) I am Sir Galahad, And if I'm ve-ry bad,*
> *Who'll wash my TIN un-der-shirt?"*

***

All Humberville was faintly frantic. The three newspapers were working overtime in frenzied activity; lies, refusals, bangings, blowings-up, wordy duels kept the presses grinding in fusillades of extras. Nobody knew quite what to expect whenever the *Bulletin* was opened, and crowds stormed the newsstands to sweep the dealers off their feet with demands for copies. The *Banner*, first rival sheet and organ of the rival party, was righteously furious, but it mollified itself by carrying in all sincerity first accounts of a new discovery. The faithful public servant, Jeffrey Davis, candidate for Congress, in his capacity as honorary head of the Humberville Babies' Nursing Home, had by long research developed a new product to feed infants. Compounded of malted milk, glycerin, and some other substances, it would do away with all older methods and make the care of children as mechanical as a fireless cooker. The *Banner* carried a huge photograph of Mr. Davis, sallow-faced and judicial, with some of his comments on the triumphant march of science. The *Bulletin* replied in scareheads with a smashing discovery which would even more completely revolutionize the new science of having children. In a story filled with statistics and mathematical formulae, it announced that the tremendous food value of rum or whiskey had long been recognized by chemists; if only the poisonous elements of alcohol could be removed, a single glass would have enough nourishing properties for an entire day. It announced that Doctor Sigmund von Stubbenheim of Gottingen had found a catalytic agent which, put into liquor, would make any form of alcohol the most nourishing food obtainable, besides doing away with the ghastly amount of time wasted in consuming three meals a day. The *Bulletin* enthusiastically proposed this as another modern efficiency method and laid its aid at Mr. Davis's disposal if Dr. von Stubbenheim's find were perfected, under the slogan of "BETTER BEER FOR BIGGER BABIES." But it was not necessary, because under Mr. Davis's advocated compound one of the babies nearly died, and every mother in Humberville was wild.

Already political sentiment was blossoming. Posters and placards were forced into the shop-windows of gesticulating Jews and Greeks; armies of women with wintry toothful smiles and the grim air of stone virgins paraded in to see the candidates for something and demanded subscriptions for something else. They sent out an avalanche of approval; over the bridge table they chatted vaguely of civil government. Their delegations, as the *Banner* interviewer remarked, found Mr. Davis in his Spacious Library, reading Epictetus[4] in the original, demonstrating an uncanny ease at translation. The *Bulletin* intimated that the demonstration was unquestionably uncanny, inasmuch as Mr. Davis had been reading with the pages uncut. This the *Banner* denounced as an infamous lie, and made sundry allusions to reptiles and vipers. Then, since it was known that Mugson had been running a distillery, the *Banner* sarcastically inquired, "Who Forced The City Administration to Store Twenty-one Barrels of Rye Whiskey in the Court House Cellar?" The *Bulletin* suggested detailing the county detective to discover "Who Forced The City Administration To Drink The Twenty-one Barrels of Rye Whiskey in the Court House Cellar?" Next, the women's clubs were addressed by Mr. Jeffrey Davis on the subject of "The Emancipation of the Woman Militant." Mr. Davis, in scientific language, coldly earnest, set forth his plans for a league called "The Daughters of Chastity," which should pledge itself to preserve strict continence between husband and wife except for a definite purpose. As gleefully reported by the *Bulletin*, there was one meeting of the league, but it was stormed by indignant husbands and ended in a riot.

Everything, moreover, had suddenly assumed the aspect of the topsy-turvy. Desperately the *Banner* and the *Clarion* tried to keep pace with the insane *Bulletin,* finding that (inexplicably) everybody was reading it and that their own news columns looked rather flat. Neighboring papers copied the stories; the disease spread with the ravage of fever, and nobody knew just what was true.

But in the midst of the flurry Jeffrey Davis was thin-faced, black-haired, immovable, with his thinly knit body and slow gestures. He smiled his calm aristocratic smile. The interests were behind him; he was deferential to them; he could not lose, and knew it. He was as smug and quiet as a pair of black gloves; sitting in his home, dark eyes expressionless, like raisins, he received the delegations amid a hush such as you find in a stuffy room where there are flowers, and a casket. Occasionally he would take telephone calls, smile a little, or make calculations on a sheet of paper. He despised the herd. So that sometimes, when he thought of the cheerful Mugson, he got a hot stabbing fear, almost a fury, and vented all his wrath on his wife in bitter tirades about the

---

4 Epictetus, a first-century Phrygian (Turkish) philosopher born into slavery, is, like Socrates, known to subsequent generations only through the writings of his followers. A Stoic philosopher (emphasizing self-knowledge and self-control), Epictetus believed that a person's first subject of study should be the individual's own gullibility and ignorance. Carr's invocation of him here is irony at the expense of Mr. Davis and of the *Bulletin's* readers.

steak, the dust on the piano, the missing vest-buttons. Then he went out to conferences, quietly.

Summer trailed into red-brown fall and winds filled with flying cinders, so that the coke-fires at night, the fires of the ovens with which Humberville was ringed, flared in running streams. Hot and dry, hot and dry and grimy, like the pressure of the newspaper office. The thing was beginning to drum inside Rinkey Donovan's head; hilarity seemed rather grotesquely to have gone. He had lost weight, and the lean face was drawn around the eyes, which had grown feverish. He spoke jerkily, fumbling in his reddish hair. The strain of being constantly ingenious ran *clackety-clack* like a typewriter all around him; incessant jingling of 'phones and voices, clump of feet, never-ending roll of the presses. Sometimes he would sit down and press his hands against his eyes, peer up with a rather bleary stare, and attack the work again. There was always Mugson at his elbow, cheerful, blowing his whiskers like a whale. Mugson waddled into every district and made speeches.

And though all the while Mugson knew that his chances of election were negligible, he remained his assured self, speaking always with the confidential air of one imparting a secret.

"Plenty of chance," he would say to Rinkey, leaning over the desk and lowering his voice, "plenty of chance! You never can tell about these things, especially with the work you got started. Gotta speech for this afternoon; this highbrow stuff of Jeff's don't go at all, not at all!— 'specially outside. Now, I wouldn't buy anybody's vote; you know that. I got ideals, same as anybody else—sure I have! But if we get cars we can line the wenches up at the polls. The thing to do is get 'em there, see?"

The false benevolence, the back-slapping and open-handedness that was almost grotesquely apparent, began to turn Rinkey sick. This mountain, always blowing smoke at his side, irritated him with its gusts of laughter. Rinkey was not quite so wise as he had been a few months before. He wished the man wouldn't be a damned hypocrite. He wished... It swept over him again, relentless. Votes, money, votes, money! County office, city office, state office, every position opposite the little squares on the ballot: blowing storm center, with typewriters going like ticktacks on a windowpane. Rinkey had to fight the whole staff now. They were rebellious, they made fun of a younger man who showed himself easy-going. Colaway, the former manager, had gone over to the *Banner*, which snapped him up. Adams, the local man, was cutting his work; the court reporter's stories were weak; there was always jovial horseplay in the office while Rinkey whipped desperately at the news columns. Incessant turmoil, beginning with the first 'phone call in the morning and not ceasing until the last form had been locked. Advice here, work there; mistake, trouble, with the business office chiming in. One day would rattle on, while Rinkey racked his brains for the stories that had swelled the *Bulletin*'s circulation; one day in a hectic whirl of activity would rattle on, end—and begin again.

The rush, pressing on as fall went by, merged into a blurry turmoil. Mugson was growing cocky, for support was pouring in; hand-shak-ings and back-slappings on the street made him throw out his chest. In Rinkey there were some wild nebulous hopes. In spite of his difficulty he realized that the *Bulletin* was becoming a power. He would not have minded it if he had not been lonely, stark lonely. All his friends were away—at college. What was there in the town for him? Where would he go at night, to whom would he talk? It was a strange ache like an emptiness. He was alone.

No fun in the game, not a bit! He was smoking too much; he was nervous, and headaches struck him dully, coming on in the afternoons when he sat over his typewriter, concocting new spectacular phrases. A wild shouting dusk would whip past the windows. Under the light of a green-shaded lamp he would sit, a single illuminated spot in a high darkness, echoing, as though with the clatter of the day. Tottering ide-als were in Rinkey's mind; Mugson might sweep the district. Fiercely Rinkey wanted the credit. He had always had a weakness for that quo-tation, *"Press where you see my white plume shine, amid the ranks of war."*[5] He used to murmur it shamefacedly to himself. "Press—" *Rattle, rattle—ring!* went the typewriter.

One afternoon he was there. And heavy feet came up the stairway, clumping loudly. Rinkey looked up from bending over his typewriter under the spot of light; he lighted another cigarette, though they were nauseating in his mouth now, and his head ached dully. There was his father. The glasses were low on the elder Donovan's nose. In that wavering light he was an almost stupid figure. More weariness closed on Rinkey like sleep. His father said nothing for a moment; he leaned against the old radiator in half-dusk and listened to the wind.

"Rinkey," he said finally, "we're licked."

(Headache and the roaring wind; sickening inhalation of the smoke.)

---

5 This is a line from Macaulay's poem, "Ivry," celebrating Henry of Navarre's 1590 victory, in which he led royalist and English forces against Catholic League forces of France and Spain. Ironically, Henry would not ascend to the French throne until 1594, following his conversion to Catholicism to appease the French people, who would not accept a Protestant king. For more concerning Macaulay's influence on Carr, see the introduction.

"Oh, what do you mean—licked?" Rinkey asked with heavy petulance.

"It's Mugson. He was grinning about it, but he's scared. He got a girl in trouble some time back. She was afraid, and told on him. The *Banner* has the story. They're going to publish it."

"Mugson—that fellow? His age?"

"Yes."

Rinkey sat a long time with his fingers on the typewriter. Down they came, all his hopes, revoltingly, in utter despair. The headache pounded harder; it made him sick. He threw his cigarette on the linoleum. He put his head down on his arm on the table, and said sobbingly,"Go on home, dad...I don't give a damn whether he wins or not...I don't care...I'm through."

He felt the splintery table against his face, the whirling sensation of dizziness, the sickness. Wind swooped past outside in a roar. *"Press where you see my white plume shine—"*

"I don't care," Rinkey muttered, "go on home..."

"Now, look here," his father said, with a sudden burst of awkward tenderness, "you're going to stop this! You're killing yourself, and—"

Rinkey raised his head. He spoke very quietly, because he was ashamed of being blinded with tears.

"Don't you see," he said haltingly, "that I was in this—because I did think there was some good in it, because I did believe—the party was right, because you always said it was, Dad! I kidded along, and I had hopes in this, and I didn't let anybody know, but I thought if I could help us win...oh, you see, don't you? I just wanted us to win, that's all..." He made a futile gesture. "Go on home, Dad; please."

"Now, listen!—"

"Go home!" said Rinkey fiercely.

His father made a shrugging gesture; he turned round and went to the stairs. The footsteps died out. *"Press where you see my white plume shine—"*

Rinkey lay for a long time with his head on the table, crying a little. Finally he raised his head, and glared, and wiped his eyes, peering around shamefacedly and wondering if anybody had seen him. He got up, shook himself, and started to pace about...

A crazy determination shot through him, pacing up and down and beating his hands together. Exultation! He bit his fingernails, his lips moving to sudden words; he smiled, and swore triumphantly. Almost stumbling, he yanked out the chair again and sat down at the typewriter with trembling fingers. Snap! The carriage began to rattle and ring, and as the whole thing unfolded, as the words began to flow smoothly, powerfully, the exultation caught him in every nerve—eyes shining, with the black smudges still around them. Finally he ripped out the sheet of copy-paper, stood up, smote the table; and through the dusky building his voice went ringing in song:

> *"We'll hang Jeff Davis*
> *On a sour apple tree,*
> *We'll hang Jeff Davis*
> *On a sour apple tree—"*

***

All day long they had polled the vote for the Congressional district. Files, slouching or exuberant, trickled into the little curtained booths; papers rustled, the election boards sat glumly in a babble of voices and the light of dusty electric bulbs. There was a reek of garlic and overheated air; blown by gusts from banging doors, gusts that swept in from a gray day of rain. Outside, horns tooted interminably and cars splattered past in a spurt of mud. From his position in the sixth ward, over to headquarters, around to the *Bulletin* office Mugson waddled frantically with the blue vein quivering at his temple. Hand-wavings pursued him; cries of "Attaboy, Bill!" "Solid for y'; he ain't got a chance!" Horns shrieking, lights making a lopsided pattern on wet streets. A man wielding a huge megaphone was cruising through the streets in a car, shouting, "Let 'em lie about Mugson; what d'we care?" Of everyone he met, Mugson would demand, "D'you think I've got it? D'you think I've got it?" stare into their faces, and hurry on with flying umbrella. He pushed through crowds in the *Bulletin* office, all gesticulating; he went upstairs, where a cataract of faces poured round him. Then he pulled Rinkey Donovan into a side office; Rinkey looked pale and harassed, with a pencil stuck behind his ear.

"It's coming in!" Mugson babbled excitedly, "my God, I think I'm going to *get* it! Nobody believed that story about me. I told you," he added with some nervousness, "I could buy that girl off. She took five thousand and went to New York, and the *Banner* ain't got a bit of proof! After you wrote that stuff about our lying bein' harmless and not intended to 'stab a man in the back like the *Banner*'—ain't that what you said?— I tell you it did it! They thought the *Banner* was lyin' about me, and it made 'em wild! It was the best thing I could 'a' done, playin' with that girl in the first place, because they all just went nuts and said, 'If this is the way Davis plays politics, with dirty work and runnin' a man down and defaming his character, I'm for Mugson!'"—for *me,* see? You done it! They're for me! Listen, every precinct...D'you think I'm goin' to get it?"

The day brought fresh news with every ring of the telephones. Party ticket running high, it reported, with Mugson away in advance. City and county offices were in doubt, because the outlying vote was sluggish. There were conclaves, much jubilation, and the party leaders were holding forth at great length. The elder Donovan was celebrating at the Elks Club. Jeffrey Davis, pursued in his headquarters by the odious song that bellowed through the streets about hanging Jeff Davis on a sour apple tree, was still fairly quiet, but showing his temper. He had removed his coat. He sat by his desk, and his hair was rumpled, and he swore under his breath.

Everywhere the new scandal was debated. If any lying had been done in this town before, they proclaimed, it was at least harmless, and not intended to blacken the fair name of a good citizen. Women's clubs were angry and virtuous. They volleyed sarcastic calls at the bewildered *Banner* office; they used their automobiles and piloted dazed Italian women into booths, uttering kindly words.

Wilder rain with the night only swelled the jostling crowds. There was a brave shouting parade; a hired band played, "Hang Jeff Davis"; copies of the *Bulletin* with the famous philippic of Rinkey Donovan against the defaming of Mugson's character by crooked liars were brandished like war spears. Davis was sitting darkly by a table at his headquarters, and snapping at everybody who came near.

On into the night crowds hung before the *Bulletin* office, in the midst of rain and banging bands. The results were incredible. Old party men were splitting their tickets for Mugson, and people who had followed or bought the straight ballot for twenty years had swung to him. The tellers did not dare tamper with split ballots; it was the one thing which an investigation would make fatal. It was Mugson, Mugson the sinned-against!—a great cry that swelled up into a paean and boomed over into "Hang Jeff Davis!"

The district had never seen such a one-man avalanche. It thundered down and lifted Mugson to a dizzy summit. In the newspaper office, when O'Neil snapped up the receiver and said, "Blair County gone solid!" they throned Mugson in state. The candidate, still redder of face and benignly drunk, sat among his disciples with his feet on a table, toasting them all.

"They know crooked work when they see it!" he announced, "and this party that's been makin' all the elections go crooked'll know that the people of the United States will not stand for dirty—"

Very sleepy, very baffled, Rinkey Donovan watched it, unobtrusive at the edge. His high hope had been fulfilled, and it disgusted him. That, in a vague way, he recognized as something futile. There was nothing else to do. He looked down at the copy of the *Bulletin* he held, and the sham ringing first sentence of his dynamite-story that had made of Mugson a slandered knight, a white-plumed...

He hurled down the paper and went toward the stairs. He did not understand. Over in a corner he saw Ed Miller screwing up his face and pulling thoughtfully at his pipe. In the midst of a hand-shaking circle beamed Mugson, flourishing a glass. O'Neil was patting him on the back. Outside crashed the bands...

Rinkey thought, "I must find Dad; Dad will understand..." As he went stupidly down the stairs, wondering whether he was going back to college, wondering whether he was going to be an incurable romanticist all his days, he heard the thumping and banging on tables as the group burst into song:

"We'll hang Jeff Davis
On a sour apple tree—"

Notes for the Curious: "The Deficiency Expert"

Jack Carr, of Haverford College, planned for "The Deficiency Expert" to be his collegiate literary swan song. Carr had already failed out of school and knew that he was heading home to face his father and an uncertain future. Although it may not seem so chronologically, the story is Jack Carr's amateur swan song. While not his final college publication, "The Deficiency Expert" is the last one during Carr's apprenticeship that is not in the style and subject matter of John Dickson Carr, the professional novelist who would be under contract with Harper & Brothers less than two years later.

Yes, Carr would publish "Héloïse" anonymously the month following, a parting gift to *The Haverfordian*'s new editor, John Roedelheim—but that vignette's cavalier fiction anticipates Carr's historical novels, which would first see issue seven years later with the pseudonymous novel *Devil Kinsmere*. Further, Carr had probably written "Héloïse" several months earlier than "The Deficiency Expert."

Similarly, Carr would, beginning the next year, send back to *The Haverfordian* from off campus his last Bencolin short story, "The Murder in Number Four," and his final amateur effort, the Bencolin novella *Grand Guignol*, published by that literary journal in April 1929. While both were written after "The Deficiency Expert," Bencolin stepped forward with Carr into his professional career, and as Douglas Greene notes (p.50), "the early cases of Henri Bencolin, prefect of police of Paris, would be worthy of many writers past the journeyman stage and aspiring to become masters." These two tales are amateur works only because Carr chose sentimentally to send them to Haverford, where Bencolin's chronicles began. Carr might as easily have sold them as his first professional publications. In any event, the French *juge d'instruction* features in Carr's first four novels (and in five overall). *Grand Guignol* grew up into the first of those novels, *It Walks By Night*, the creative act by which Jack Carr matured into John Dickson Carr.

All this clarifies how "The Deficiency Expert" is Carr's final amateur experiment. Appropriately to the time and context of its conception, the story's premise is heavily autobiographical. While it looks forward from the moment in Carr's own life when he is assessing what to do after his premature departure from college, in its details it looks backward, relying upon Jack Carr's apprenticeship during his high-school years at the Uniontown *Daily News Standard* for its setting and just enough concrete detail to seem believable...more or less.

The twenty-first-century reader, living in what is commonly called the information age, will doubtless find not just humor, but relevance, in Rinkey's deformation of the *Bulletin* from a sedate chronicler of current events to a purveyor of spectacular, deliberate misinformation. In the digital age a century after Carr's story, the comic tale's tension between news and politics may seem startlingly pertinent—and it is, because while twenty-first-century methods and instruments for manipulating facts and perceptions, such as editing (or fabricating!) photos and video, and the viral speed with which untruths traverse social media, color opinions, and deceive their audiences have no antecedent—the danger of mass deception is an inheritance descending across eras and generations. Only its methods change. And so "The Deficiency Expert" leaves readers a century and more after its composition laughing in uneasy recognition.

The story's continued relevance noted, "The Deficiency Expert" begs to be understood biographically, at least by readers interested in better understanding Carr. One of its key autobiographical elements is the disguised appearance, once again, of William O'Neil Kennedy. Carr had already paid tribute to Kennedy in "The God of the Gloves." As mentioned in the footnotes to that story, the sports editor O'Neill is a modestly modified version of the real-life gentleman; Kennedy even had a neatly waxed, spiked mustache. He also commonly went by his middle name, not his first. As noted in the footnotes to this story, Kennedy's stand-in in "The Deficiency Expert" takes for his last name Kennedy's first, as well as reproducing the stammer O'Neil suffered in real life—but gently, not mockingly. The sports editor at the Uniontown *Daily News Standard* during Carr's internship, O'Neil Kennedy was also his mentor and closest friend at the paper. The young author could hardly craft this story dreaming of his professional future and drawing upon his journalism background without embracing Kennedy within it. At the Uniontown newspaper, Jack received from Kennedy both his earliest journalistic assignments and compelling advice and encouragement to become a novelist.

In fact, O'Neil changed Carr's life, and not merely by his encouragement: in 1929, Kennedy wrote a letter of introduction to an associate at Harper & Brothers, which resulted directly in Carr's winning a contract with the publisher. While Carr's first professional publication was dedicated to his parents (understandably, given their two years of support helping John to realize his ambition), Carr inscribed the first presentation copy of *It Walks By Night* to O'Neil Kennedy.

By the time Carr's first novel was published, O'Neil had become general editor of the *Daily News Standard*. Utilizing the power of his position, Kennedy continued promoting Carr with front-page book reviews, admittedly con amore, of Carr's first several novels. The two friends remained close, so close, in fact, that while it was not generally known until 1978 (courtesy of Greene) that Carr was the pseudonymous author of *Devil Kinsmere*, Kennedy, with his personal knowledge of Carr's plans, began to report in the *Daily News Standard* as early as March 1931 that Carr was at work on "a full-fledged historical romance of the glamourous times of Charles II,"[1] for which in May, he reported the working title of *Fop's Folly*,[2] noting that Carr had provisionally completed it. There is no surviving record explaining why, but Carr's romance still needed work. Kennedy reported on January 15, 1932 that Carr set it aside to complete another novel, which was almost certainly *Poison In Jest*, published September 28—and equally almost certainly because Harper had little confidence in the sales prospects for a historical romance and must have insisted on having a detective-fiction novel from him instead to fulfill Carr's contract. The publisher continued to have such reservations about Carr's Stuart-era romance that in December 1933, Carr sent the now-ready novel to Hamish Hamilton, his London publisher. Hamilton published it in 1934 under the pseudonym Roger Fairbairn, in order not to compete with Carr's other two books that year released under his own name. Harper followed suit and published *Devil Kinsmere,* but still had little enough confidence in the marketability of a historical romance by an "unknown" author that for its first printing, Harper used sheets printed by Hamish Hamilton with only a different copyright page. (When the book went into a second printing in the U.S., Harper issued that printing itself.)

Carr's publisher was not alone in doubting whether the author would appeal even to his loyal readers with such a different book. For the first time ever, the lending libraries in Carr's hometown of Uniontown, Pennsylvania, declined to purchase any copies of a John Dickson Carr novel for circulation or even for sale. Kennedy and the *Daily News Standard* briefly editorialized this, on page 1, no less:[3]

> Local circulating libraries are missing a bet by not stocking
> John Dickson Carr's new historical romance. It's published

---

1 Uniontown *Daily News Standard*, March 4, 1931, p. 4.

2 Uniontown *Daily News Standard*, May 15, 1931, p. 1.

3 The reader should recall that *Devil Kinsmere* is the first historical detective novel in the Anglo-American tradition. Only Melville Davisson Post's sequence of "Uncle Abner" antebellum short mysteries preceded it in the genre at all.

by Harper's, titled "Devil Kinsmere," and was written under
a pen name of Roger Fairbairn. And mighty thrilling.[4]

Although non-Uniontown residents waited until October 1978 to learn from Greene that *Devil Kinsmere* was Carr's work, Kennedy had long since pierced Carr's pseudonymity, revealing his authorship of the historical romance to all Carr's friends and neighbors in a full review of the novel on February 15, 1935. The *Daily News Standard*, whenever cataloging Carr's career, continued to list *Devil Kinsmere* openly among Carr's works as late as 1939.

While Carr never aspired to a career in journalism, because the governing theme of "The Deficiency Expert" is the transition from amateur writer to professional, Carr's journalistic background serves the purpose—in its way must, in fact, serve it, because Carr had yet to become a professional novelist. He had no close acquaintance with that area of commercial publishing. "The Deficiency Expert" is a metaphorical act of authorial self-creation, and in that respect, Carr very much desires it to seem believable. Carr's internship at the Uniontown *Daily News Standard* exposed him to the professional activities of journalism he needed to set a story convincingly enough within a publishing office. As to the story's action, Carr swells the modest journalistic responsibilities he had in Uniontown (much of Carr's apprenticeship was coverage of sports and criminal cases)[5] into Humberville's ridiculous drama, and into the outsized consequences of Rinkey's editorship.

Consider too the biographical transformation that has taken place before the story's opening, which springboards "The Deficiency Expert": Rinkey's departure from college. Being dismissed from college for low grades, as Jack was, is ordinary and dull; but being expelled from college for a series of entertaining, antisocial pranks that disrupts the campus, as Rinkey was, is spectacular. Rinkey's strategy as editor of the *Bulletin* is an exponential extension of his campus mischief, and its momentous consequences amount to wish fulfillment by the aspirant Jack Carr. That is to say, the story insists that writing matters and that the writer matters: Rinkey acquires real influence and changes the world around him. Carr of course hoped to matter as a professional novelist—not progressively to change the world for the better, but rather to gain wide recognition in it and to be successful, even influential, within his chosen genre.

Another correlation between Carr's college life and the story is the

---

4 Uniontown *Daily News Standard*, February 25, 1935.

5 According to a brief notice in the Uniontown *Daily News Standard*, May 12, 1922 edition (p. 5), Carr's tongue-in-cheek "official" title was, "Second assistant sporting editor."

Bulletin's news fabrications. These smack familiarly of Carr's hijinks at *The Haverfordian*...not only of the prankish pseudonyms Carr instituted as editor, attributing stories he wrote to others (even once, possibly, to the paper's faculty advisor), but in further elaborating on them with backstories and fictive controversies played out through false letters to the editor and responses.

The definitive instance of this is the "life history" of Eric Hirth. Hirth was a character in Carr's second-ever high-school publication, "The House of Terror." Several years later, Hirth "joined" the writer's stable of *The Haverfordian*. It wasn't only Carr who wrote using Hirth's name: other staff writers published both poetry and prose, clearly not by Carr, using the pseudonym. This tomfoolery climaxed in the March 1928 "Apologia" column of *The Haverfordian*, in which the prankster editorial team repaid Carr in kind by inventing for Hirth a background as a resident of Long Island. In this same column, they contrived a mock dispute over January's authorship of "The Dark Banner" (not by, but attributed to Carr) and "The God of the Gloves" (by him, but attributed to schoolmate George P. Rogers). So given the shenanigans Carr himself set afoot as editor of *The Haverfordian*, he needed only an imaginative step or two to spin the controlled chaos of his college literary journal up into the spiraling controversies Rinkey instigates at the Humberville Bulletin.

"The Deficiency Expert" shares some modest crossover with Carr's later work, mostly in Carr's continuing to employ journalists as featured characters in some of the novels, most prominently, *The Man Who Could Not Shudder* (1940), *A Graveyard to Let*, *Dark of the Moon*, *The Ghosts' High Noon*, and *The Hungry Goblin*. But unlike many of Carr's other early stories, which have explicit callbacks in his professional novels ("The House of Terror," "The Will-o'-the-Wisp," "The Marked Bullet," "The Blindfold Quest," "The Cloak of D'Artagnan," "The Harp of Tairlaine aka "The Inn of the Seven Swords," "The Gordon Djinn," "The Devil-Gun," and "The Shadow of the Goat" all do), this story does not. The closest "The Deficiency Expert" comes to having a second life in Carr's professional fiction is Rinkey's surname being in common with the young perspective character and romantic lead of *The Eight of Swords*, Hugh Donovan. Hugh, however, is unlike Rinkey: he is a happy-go-lucky, middleweight amateur boxer, and like his author, spent a year abroad (Donovan, in New York City, not Paris) avoiding his studies and the career his father planned for him. Hugh is a different sort of surrogate for Carr, although both Donovans reflect that familiar strain of wish fulfillment in Carr's fiction.

To the degree "The Deficiency Expert" is in conversation with any of Carr's other works, it engages with those he had written during the prior four years. Of interest, there is a correspondence between "The Deficiency Expert" and Carr's 1924 poem, "Election Night." This pairing is the last in the pattern of dialog between Carr's apprenticeship fiction and his preceding non-fiction; the earlier two instances (discussed in the commentaries for those stories) were the reliance of "The Harp of Tairlaine" on both the poem "The Voice and the Harp" and the essay "The Land of Lost Causes," and that of "Candlelight: A Ghost Story of Christmas" upon Carr's essay "Christmas Spirit." "Election Night," unlike most of Carr's poems, is not a ballad; it is, rather, a set of four imagistic stanzas, each describing election night from one of the differing perspectives of varied constituencies, such as the opening stanza's "Black mobs swaying in the crowded, misty squares" and the second's "Blear-eyed men in shirt sleeves toiling at the dim-lit poll." The first three stanzas all conclude with the refrain, "election night in town," and then the final stanza signals the poem's end by changing the refrain as dawn creeps over the horizon: "election day in town." It is the third stanza that Carr reserves for the Press, drawing upon his experience at the Uniontown *Daily News Standard* and offering imagery that is consistent with, perhaps even evocative of, "The Deficiency Expert":

> Typewriters rattling in the smoky dens of Press,
> Office-seekers trembling with the dazzle of success;
> White lights whirling, sputtering; carbon arcs and burns,
> Flashing on a building's side the precinct's first returns—
> Men a-caper, shouting-dervishes and hired clown
> Roaring triumph in the streets—election night in town.[6]

Given that "The Deficiency Expert" is Carr's amateur swan song in fiction, it is only natural that the story looks backward to those that preceded it. In its meditation on journalism and in its preposterousness, "The Deficiency Expert" is the comedy variation on the theme for which "The Kindling Spark" is the tragedy. In that earlier story, the newly professional journalist "Jimmy had few illusions. One of them was that editorial writers could mold public opinion; that was a secret sense of power in which he exulted." Jimmy learns that this is not true—in fact, Jimmy, a failure as an editorialist, recognizes that life repudiates all the young ideals he held at school, whether regarding the efficacy of jour-

---

6 *A Book of Hill School Verse*, pp. 126-127.

nalism, or through a global war's dragging his generation to vain deaths in muddy trenches, or in the ugly realization that appetites and messy passions, not gallantry, drive romantic coupling.

Between "The Deficiency Expert" and "The God of the Gloves," beyond the biographical connection by which both stories honor Carr's journalistic mentor Kennedy, there are additional affinities. Superficially, both participate in the trend of Carr's featuring journalists as important characters. ("The Gordon Djinn" does likewise; Kenwood Blake, its main character, is a newspaperman.) More importantly, though, in both "The God of the Gloves" and "The Deficiency Expert," unlike in "The Kindling Spark," journalism makes a difference. "The Deficiency Expert" cynically invites the reader to consider whether the difference is a good one, but in "The God of the Gloves," it certainly is. O'Neill, the sporting editor declares, "Yes, I'll make Michaels take notice of him [Dinny McFarlane] by yelling so loud—you know what a newspaper can do." O'Neill does so, even banding together with the sports editors at other regional papers to generate enough pressure on Streak Martin to prompt his acceptance of Dinny's otherwise unjustified challenge. Without O'Neill, McFarlane's life would never have moved past the debilitation of losing his father.

Readers of *The Kindling Spark* will further recognize the re-use in "The Deficiency Expert" of the narrator's complaint, in "The New Canterbury Tales," in defense of Romanticism. It appears in the closing section ("L'Envoi") of that story cycle:

> Realists are the people who look in a mirror and get disgusted. They are the ones who will explode all your fine ideas. They would pull down Kenilworth Castle and substitute an efficient gas-station; they would take the Lorelei off the rocks and substitute Margaret Sangers and Carrie Chapman Catts. Your realistic author has begun to notice a protuberant stomach and weakening eyes, so he goes right merrily to work and writes a novel exposing something as sordid.

Rinkey, of course, makes the same complaint almost verbatim. "The Deficiency Expert" was published only two months after "The New Canterbury Tales," in May 1927.

While Jack's avatar Rinkey maneuvered his father into appointing him editor of the local newspaper, John Dickson Carr's bargain with Wooda Nicholas Carr was more modest, although equally shrewd: the pater agreed to finance the son for a year of study abroad, with an implicit understanding it was in preparation for a law career. The younger Carr turned that time, beginning in June 1927, into a year of excess, with little to no study to prepare him for the career at the legal bar Wooda intended. In Paris, generally at a different bar, John perfected his French and continued writing fiction. When he returned home, Carr parlayed his time abroad into one additional year, at his father's indulgence, to prove that he could become a professional writer. Shuttling back and forth between his parents' home and his uncle's, as well as spending some of his writing hours locked away alone in the offices of the Uniontown *Daily News Standard*, Jack produced both aforementioned adventures of Bencolin, then *It Walks By Night*, and in doing so, graduated into becoming John Dickson Carr.

Tales of Mystery
and Imagination

The Gordon Djinn (1925)

I

Virginia was going to marry a spiritualist, and that was why I got drunk. People have a great many excuses for getting drunk; they do it both to accentuate joy and drown sorrow—to celebrate or forget. They get drunk on the Fourth of July to glorify independence, and again on the birthday of the Eighteenth Amendment to bewail servitude. But in my own case, I might only have been moderately drunk had not Virginia intended to marry a spiritualist.

Bannerman was not exactly a spiritualist; it would have been cheap and vulgar to have called him a medium. He was psychic, and sat like a fat, milk-white ghost himself with his eyes closed and his mouth open while spirits talked through him. Undoubtedly he was charming, too; anything exotic usually is. When he talked you had an impression of pale draperies with roses woven against them like bloodstains, and incense curling its fingers from the laps of dull, flat-nosed idols. His soul breathed the artistic—that intensified artistry that substitutes the senses for the heart, and drugs for romance. The fascination was there, in his long, languid eyes and soft hands and beautiful voice. I knew Bannerman as the apostle of immorality who was never immoral, and as a poet who had got so far into the future that nobody knew where he was. To him life was a puzzle, and whenever the pieces made some design he jumbled them up again. He had a tremendous following and a tremendous reputation for wit, both of which he used frequently at his teas. Very often he would invite me to one of the teas and point out my literary heresy as a writer of detective stories, but I knew he disliked me ever since I said in my column in the *Democrat* that his new volume, *Orange Seeds and Cannonades*, sounded like somebody playing a stove lid on a phonograph. A man like that should never marry a girl named Virginia.

I ran over the whole final interview as I drove home that afternoon, with the hot dusk smothering the city like a blanket. Washington was sticky with its own heat, but it was with annoyance that I fumed. There he was—Bannerman, watching his lazy cigarette in the long, cool room, and Virginia as brilliantly alive as a flame and as softly alluring as a kiss. Her eyes were clear hazel, and they searched Bannerman's face.

"I may as well tell you this afternoon, Ken," she had said, looking at Bannerman and talking to me; "I may as well tell you before you—say

279

anything. Yes, I'm going to marry him. I think I love him. And I shall be aiding him in his work—"

Bannerman, I remembered, interrupted with a wave of his cigarette.

"Genius," he murmured, "like all gorgeous fairy buildings, can never stand alone. It must be buttressed. I am grateful to you, Virginia."

I had a sudden desire to throw something in his face, like the wild impulse one gets to swear aloud in church. Yet he was so perfect and aloof that to touch him seemed almost sacrilege. He impressed you that way. So I turned my back to him and walked over to Virginia. In the wan light I could not be sure, but I thought I saw her lips trembling.

"You know this hits me pretty hard," I said; it must have sounded awkward, even though I spoke low...My disappointment was almost like a physical nausea, but I didn't want Bannerman to see it. "I knew your mother favored—spiritism, and I know she hates me now. I never knew your own attitude until this moment. And it's kind of tough."

She was so close to me that I felt furious to know that I might not take her up and kiss those warm lips whose yielding pressure I had known only once before. Dusk drifted in the room, blurring her...

"My dear fellow," said Bannerman dreamily, "I know exactly how you feel; so why take it calmly? No heroics, please. You may just as well rage, for then your foolish—shall I say puppy-love? will have gone. A fleeting disappointment is nothing; besides, what does anything matter? Life is simply a noisy little alarm-clock ticking in eternity. Nothing is really important except what is unimportant."

I came slowly across the room and picked up my hat. In the gloom the red tip of his cigarette was motionless, placid.

"Someday," I told him, "someday you're going to turn one of those verbal somersaults and meet yourself coming the other way. I hope both of yourselves break your necks...Good afternoon, everybody."

And as I opened the door Virginia leaped up, and said an astounding thing. "Damn you!" she exclaimed. "Oh, damn you!" and made an impotent gesture as I stalked out...

Almost every detail of that conversation had burned itself into my head; I mumbled it all over again as I rode homeward through the far-flung blaze of pale lights that is Washington by night. I was so morose that I remembered nothing of the drive or of anything else when I kicked open the door of the apartment I shared in the Westmoreland Heights with Lamoreux. You see, Lamoreux and I had formed a curious partnership in college—curious because he was wealthy and I was a newspaperman. We had both been addicted to hell-raising, and had decided to keep it up. Somebody had said that sometimes he looked like

Satan, and sometimes like a lunatic—for he had a long, lean, diabolical face which made his actions all the more ridiculous. He had always been a brilliant loafer whose tragedy was that no one would take him seriously. All his life, therefore, he had played the fool, but so far as I knew he had only two weaknesses: he made abominable puns, and he collected Chinese antiques.

Yes, he had another one. I realized it as I went into our living-room, which was gloriously untidy and gloriously comfortable. He sat at a table under the drop-light examining something dull and gleaming. I knew he was preoccupied; he was in evening dress, but he had absent-mindedly put on a green tie. That meant a new piece for his collection.

"Where," I said abruptly, and slammed the door, "is the gin?"

He fumbled in his hair until it stood upright. When he turned to me his face was quite Satanic.

"Do you know about it?" he demanded.

"Do I know about it?" I repeated, pushing a pile of books out of an easy chair to sit down. "Say, look here..."

"Where did you hear about it, then?"

"Holmes Lamoreux," I said in a deadly tone, "will you tell me where that gin is?"

"Why, in China, I expect."

I jumped out of my chair and announced with extraordinary intensity:

"You're drunk. You're drunk already, and I'll be with you as soon as I can find out where the stuff is! We'll throw a party—"

"Oh! I see now!" He ruffled his hair still more and stared at me. "I understand; you mean the gin!"

I was so desperate and out of tune with everything that I broke down and sobbed.

"No, no! I want the gin! The gin; not the kind that goes to China—the gin! She threw me over, that's why; she's going to marry that white hippopotamus—that—"

"Certainly she is," said Lamoreux consolingly. "Let's have a drink."

"Why? Why 'certainly'? If you think she cares—"

"You'll find the oranges in the coal scuttle," suggested Lamoreux. "You put them there last night; I don't know why, but you assured me it was an idea of unusual merit at the time...Look here, Ken." He put his hands on my shoulders, and I saw for once he was momentarily serious. "Honestly, you hadn't a chance. Her mother was playing against you for that poet Bannerman. If you ask my personal opinion, I think the girl herself cares a lot about you. But the meanest mamas aren't the young ones, and it's mama this time…Besides, what's the difference? The female of the species is more dead wood than the male. I'll get the gin."

II

At nine-thirty I was sitting on one of the bookcases eating crackers and looking wistfully at the empty glass. Lamoreux, a grotesque figure in the wreck of the room, leaned on the table. His hair stood up like a goblin's; his eyes were owlish.

"Consider," he said sternly, pointing to the dull brassy thing he had been examining earlier. "Lamp!"

I took a careful survey of it and agreed.

"'S Chinese lamp. 'S Aladdin's lamp, Ken. You know Aladdin."

"Sure!" I was disdainful. "Aladdin 'n the forty thieves. Sure."

"No. Aladdin 'n the djinn."

"Oh!" said I, reflecting. "I know. Bootlegger."

"No! Chinese. Chinese guy with pigtail."

"Laundryman. I know now. Where's the gin?"

"Not the gin you drink," Lamoreux explained. "This is a genie. Magic lamp, Ken—you rub the lamp, and the genie appears. Slick!"

"Work it," I requested interestedly. "Let's see 'im."

He picked up the lamp and considered it with a scowl.

"Mightn't work. Might have to use sandpaper. Trouble with you is, you always want to go too fast, and you spoil everything. But—"

Somewhere close at hand there was the thin, sweet note of a silver gong. The shaded lamps changed color, and took on a soft pale hue that was like moonlight. A thin raveling of incense trickled toward the ceiling. And:

"The great lord commands," said a voice.

I dropped my glass, shattering it on the floor. There was nothing of visible presence in the room, but I could feel somebody standing in its center. The presence spread out and rolled along the ceiling like smoke; it was overwhelming, like hashish—as vibrant as the clutch of hands. I knew somebody was there. And suddenly I felt a little less drunk.

That deathly moonlight gleamed on marble in that room, where there had been no marble before. There was a murmur as of silver rain on leaves. And Lamoreux, with his grotesque green tie and his lopsided appearance, stood under the towering presence, looking stupidly at the lamp.

"The master commands," repeated the voice, which was like a voice heard through the mists of sleep at midnight, "and I obey. I come from the land where the drowsy sea woos white blossoms, and the cypress trees are black as sorrowing ghosts, and the great golden moon lures the tides from a silver sky. There the nightingale sings the music of his own name, which is a wordless tapestry for the hall of the heart—"

"Well, I'll be damned!" said Lamoreux, and sat down suddenly.

"Ah!" I remarked, fixing my wits on the subject with an effort. "This is unusual. This is most unusual. The properties of this particular djinn are astounding. One might say—in fact, one could say—that he is the whole distillery. Extraordinary!"

"No!" protested my friend. "Saw a purple turkey once. It had a straw hat."

"This," said I, "gives me a very distinct idea. Bannerman!"

"Sure. What about 'im?"

"Fix 'im. Will this gentleman do anything we tell him?"

"It is not for me to question the inscrutable ways," rumbled the voice of the invisible presence. "My lords command, and I obey. The fire-winged stars move in their courses; from them I pluck wisdom or riches for him who holds the lamp. O, fair-skinned idolaters, ask for the red gold of China, that is fiery as the sun upon battlefields; ask for diamonds from a sultan's robe, or pearls from the green water; and they shall be given you. Ask—"

"He's drunk," observed Lamoreux.

"He's providential." I slid down from the bookcase, which seemed oddly changed to a slender column with crimson draperies and fighting dragons in gold. "Take us," I said, "to Bannerman!"

The room trembled in silver spray, making Lamoreux's face writhe and twist like a reflection in water. From moonlight it was dusk. The golden dragons on the walls fought savagely in the gloom. On the walls too tawny fruit was blossoming, yellow and deadly as a panther's eyes. Down distant vistas where the tear-flowers droop white, there was a ghost dance of water in fountains. Night opened its dusky petals slowly, and dripped with dew that was like honey… Now I saw only the whiteness of Lamoreux's hands as he held the lamp, which burned with wondrous smiling flame.

III

"Spiritism," affirmed Bannerman, "is the most practical thing in the world. It is much more practical than mathematics, which is always wrong, because none of its axioms are true. The whole is always more than the sum of its parts, else we humans would be sorry things indeed. Human nature makes circles of straight lines; in fact, all life moves in a circle, with conceit for a circumference. Thus nothing is bound to happen except what is impossible. And—"

He paused, opening his long, dreamy eyes and hanging one grace-ful arm motionless in the air as Virginia got up with a start.

"Ken!" she exclaimed; "and Holmes!"

"Thanking you for your kind attention," I said, closing the door of the library. We were at Virginia's home, without a doubt; there sat her mother, a Matterhorn in white lace, looking down stonily over the icy slopes of herself. Even her face was frozen, and it did not thaw now. She was sitting beside Professor Kittings, who was small, with white hair and pink eyes like a rabbit. Yes, they were all there in the gloomy library, full of cases with gilded books and furniture that was prim as Mrs. Bower herself. The lights were like frozen candle-flames. They gleamed in Mrs. Bower's green glaciers of eyes.

"—and," continued Bannerman imperturbably, as though there had been no interruption, "that is why I am especially anxious to demon-strate to you, Professor. Against me you put God and science, which is foolish, because in themselves they are opposed to each other. In God we rust. The great wheels are stopped by faith. On the other hand, science is hunting for something; it is willing to accept whatever it finds, and call the most logical lie true. It must fail, because of this, and because it is so akin to mathematics, which is silly and futile because it never demonstrates anything that nobody knew before. Mathematics is the refuge of the half-witted curious. Thus—"

"Ken," cut in Virginia, "won't you and Holmes sit down? We weren't expecting you, but you are just in time—"

"Indeed," the Matterhorn interposed with a kind of dangerous sweet-ness, "you come most opportunely, Mr. Blake...You gentlemen have hats? No? At any rate, I am delighted that you remembered about my never desiring visitors to knock."

"Ah," murmured Lamoreux, and smiled broadly and benignantly: "are you in the habit of going into house at night without knocking? Naughty!"

The little professor mumbled "Really!" and shifted uneasily. Mrs. Bower set her lips so tightly that they were invisible.

"Evidently that is the attitude you take..."

"Ah!" said Lamoreux again. "But I have a perfect right to entertain male visitors at night! It shocks me to learn that you—"

"I think," snapped Matterhorn, and towered to her feet with her glacier eyes blazing, "that this has gone quite far enough. You are plainly in no condition to be about, or I should have Mr. Bannerman throw you out..." Lamoreux began to laugh immoderately, and she rushed on: "May I request you to go? I do not recall inviting you here."

I glanced at Virginia. Her eyes were shouting an appeal at me. I suddenly remembered that 'damn' earlier in the afternoon; for the first time I wondered...

"Mrs. Bower!" I began to speak abruptly and with clarity, I think. "Mrs. Bower, Madam. You are wedding your daughter to spiritism."

The matter-of-fact statement made her blink. I went on loftily: "You are intrigued by a lot of ghosts and a most useless person who does sleight-of-hand tricks with words. Now you see it; now you don't, and you wonder what it was, after all. Mrs. Bower," I said deprecatingly, "I realize what a blue-nosed virago you are. I realize that you have unduly exercised on Virginia's choice, and so on. Mrs. Bower, you are entitled to this pursuit of sappiness if you like. But Madam," I announced fiercely, and struck the table, "this won't go down! It won't go down, I insist! If spiritualists are in demand, I offer myself. I am preferred stock. My name is Aladdin. The greatest spiritist of the ages, let me remark—"

"My dear fellow," interposed Bannerman, trying to awe me by looking inexpressibly bored, "don't bluff as well as insult. You must be sober enough to be your usual drunken self. You act very badly."

I took one look at the gloomy room, and the four figures standing still as people in the tensest moment of a play. Then:

"Bannerman, do you see that cuckoo clock?" I asked.

"No. I haven't the slightest desire to—"

"Oh, but you will, Bannerman," I said. "Indeed you will. Hey!"

There was a whirring of weights. Far in the back of the room the clock's tiny door flew open and the cuckoo popped out.

"What the hell do you want?" shrilled the cuckoo querulously. "Take it!" snarled the cuckoo, and slammed his door.

A shower of trombones rained from the ceiling, clattering over the table. One of them hit Bannerman on the shoulder as he got to his feet with an extraordinary contortion, and he tumbled back in his chair, cigarette splashing fire down his chin. The Matterhorn's eyes were like melting ice.

"Ho!" cried a bronze figure of Apollo, striding in at the door with clanking steps.

"What ho!" Lamoreux shouted, and hurled a book at the chandelier. In mid-air it exploded into a burst of roses that drenched the room with color. Three mice, with flag, drum, and fife, marched across the table as the spirit of '76. Bannerman screamed and seized a chair to defend himself as the books began to open and emit tiny armies of words, which swarmed across the floor toward him like deadly ants. Deafening the uproar swelled; a banjo had caught fire, and it was spinning around the room in a burst of ribald song...

"You will observe, ladies and gentlemen," I continued, linking arms with the bronze Apollo and offering him a cigarette, "that Aladdin keeps his word. A little less noise would do no harm; if that victrola will kindly stop breaking records over Professor Kittings' head, 1 shall be greatly obligated. Thank you—"

Mrs. Bower, with her green eyes dull and horrible as a vulture's, leaned over the table with her face like a dead woman's. Her white hands against the mahogany looked as though they had been severed.

"You devil," she said calmly; there were ugly lines of moisture about her mouth. "Blake, you devil—"

"I beg your pardon," I deprecated, "but I think your daughter has fainted," and caught Virginia as she swayed. Her hair brushed my cheek, and I felt a curious faintness, like one recovering from the effect of a drug. Through a kind of mist Mrs. Bower's face was a monstrosity of green eyes, and the room a wreck wherein Bannerman lay horribly sprawled with the black words picking at him like ants.

"I am taking your daughter," I resumed jauntily, and blinked hard to steady myself, "Because I ought to. Bannerman was right. Science doesn't go far enough. The only thing it can't explain is love, and that's what it's afraid of: love. Science always gets beaten. Sometimes it's human nature," I said, fighting my dizziness; "this time—it's the djinn!"

And both the bronze Apollo and I bowed, while the Matterhorn crumbled to the floor and lay with arms flung forward as though in supplication.

IV

It was the telephone bell; I was absolutely sure of that. The furniture in the room danced and bobbed like kegs in the water as I opened my eyes, and my head boomed and rang in barrages of fire. Then through the jumpy air I saw Lamoreux's face. It was drawn and white, and there was a glass in his hand.

"No more liquor," I protested, stirring in bed.

"Shut up!" he growled; "shut up, you damned fool, and take this stuff. You had a close call, I want to tell you! You ape! The idea of trying to commit suicide just because a fool girl—"

"The air in here," I mumbled feebly, "is abominable. Open a window, can't you?—and gimme that 'phone!"

He stared down at me grimly.

"You're better. And no wonder the air's bad! If I hadn't smelled gas— Say, when did you get in here, anyhow?"

"Dry up! I don't know..." I sat up in bed, sniffing the air cautiously and pawing at my fiery throat. The room was taking on a semblance of clarity now; I remembered coming in here at some time or other after leaving Virginia's, and deciding to make the thing melodramatic. "Well, pardon me if I swear," I grunted. "I dreamed it. I'll bet I dreamed the whole thing, lamp and all!"

Lamoreux hurled the glass to the floor.

"So this is the thanks I get! All right— asphyxiate yourself again, then!...And if it wasn't sentiment, what did you mean by freezing tight to that tin Chinese lamp of mine, eh? I came in late and found you..."

"First," I told him with dignity, "I am going to answer the 'phone—"

It jangled again as I reached for it at the head of my bed. My head ached horribly, but the sense of unreality was passing off in a glorious sense of gladness that there was really a morning sun, and that I could see it through the window...

"Ken!" said a voice over the wire, and I nearly dropped the receiver. Virginia! "Oh, Ken!"—she was excited; no doubt about it, "come up here, please! The most dreadful things...Ken, Floyd Bannerman got a whole case of gin or something sent him by an admirer, and last night he drank a horrible lot of it, and oh, he was so drunk! He came up here, and mother was furious...! She took back all she'd said about you, and called Floyd a four-flusher[1]...And Floyd walked around insisting that he was Aladdin and that mother was a—something dreadful; but he said he'd marry me anyway, because he was Aladdin, and he had a lamp that could fix anything...I never saw Mother so angry. I think if you come up here now, Ken...You know how I feel, but I was scared of her—"

I banged the receiver on the hook and leaped out of bed with sudden agility. Dizziness spun me a little, but the transport of that minute was exquisite. I saw Lamoreux's startled face in the sunlit room; I saw, too, the bronze figure of Apollo which had somehow strayed into my sleeping apartment, and I went over solemnly and linked arms with that figure.

"Holmes," I said, "witness a triumph. I remember now. I was a trifle drunk when I came here last night; that was why I tried the gas—but Bannerman—"

"For heaven's sake, sit down!" Lamoreux exclaimed. "Look here, you'll kill yourself that way! This gas...What about Bannerman, anyway?"

"He said he was Aladdin! What do you think? He went up to Mrs. Bower and called her what she is; she—"

"Bannerman! Floyd Bannerman! What on earth made him do that?"

I bowed and tipped the figure with me.

"Prophetic soul!" I said rapturously. "It was—*the gin*!"

---

[1] A four-flusher is one who makes empty bluffs or false promises. The term is derived from Poker: five cards of the same suit is a flush, but four cards of the same suit is nothing.

Notes for the Curious: "The Gordon Djinn"

There is no character named Gordon in John Dickson Carr's satire on the story of Aladdin. The abominable puns that Ken Blake, the narrator, attributes to his roommate Lamoreaux begin with the tale's title. Gordon is the manufacturer of one of the world's oldest brands of gin, produced in London, and seemingly, the student Jack Carr's favorite brand.

While the title might suggest that this story is the fiction-writing equivalent of a schoolboy drinking game—and the editor will not debate the reader who chooses to receive it as such—regular readers of Carr will know that bibulousness is featured frequently in his works, all throughout Carr's career. Given that Prohibition began when Carr was thirteen years old and was not repealed until after he had emigrated to England in 1933, Carr never consumed a legal drink in his native country until visiting the United States during the summer of 1934. So his preoccupation with alcohol, especially during his school years, is somewhat understandable.

With respect to how Carr leveraged alcohol in his fiction, the plots of "The Kindling Spark" and "The Gordon Djinn" both turn on drunkenness; in Dr. Fell's debut novel, *Hag's Nook* (1933), the doctor, an odd sort of lexicographer indeed, is preparing his "great work, *The Drinking Customs of England from the Earliest Days*" (p. 31); Dr. Fell's next case, *The Mad Hatter Mystery*, begins "like most of Dr. Fell's adventures, in a bar" (p. 1); John Gaunt, the detective hero of *The Bowstring Murders*, is continuously inebriated; and despite the murders committed in them, the summaries of *The Eight of Swords*, *The Blind Barber*, *Fatal Descent* (1939), and *The Case of the Constant Suicides* might be (as Greene, p. 144, wryly noted of *The Eight of Swords*), "Let's have a drink." It may also be the theme of "The Gordon Djinn"; it is, verbatim, Lamoreaux's first suggestion.

The examples above are hardly the entire catalog, either; drink serves, to nobody's surprise, as a point of humor in a number of the pseudonymous Carter Dickson's H.M. novels and it provides a full set piece as late as *Panic in Box C*, when too many rounds of drinks and competing college fight songs nearly result in a bar fight.

"The Gordon Djinn" binges, like a drinker itself, on a peculiar form of humor, the "abominable puns" that begin with the story's title and come from the mouths of several characters (contrary to what Blake contends, not only from Lamoreaux), e.g., "In God we rust," "pursuit of sappiness," etc. Whether uttered deliberately or otherwise, there is an appropriateness to the use of these puns in this narrative, because the accidental substitution of one word for another is a common symptom of inebriation. Carr signals Ken's own drunkenness with such imprecise utterings: "I shall be greatly obligated" and "'I beg your pardon,' I deprecated." (The literary-technical term for this specific sort of wordplay, in which a similar-sounding word replaces the proper one and results in humor or multiple valences, is paronomasia. Be certain to impress friends with that bit of trivia over drinks.)

So one interesting undertone of "The Gordon Djinn" is that in its key rhetorical trope, it unites sharp-wittedness with drunkenness: both states of mind produce similar witticisms. In fairness, not all the puns perpetrated in "The Gordon Djinn" are accidental or unthoughtful. Note that Lamoreaux's jape, "The female of the species is more dead wood than the male," is a play upon the line that concludes nearly half the stanzas in Rudyard Kipling's 1911 poem, "The Female of the Species." Kipling, of course, was a favorite author of Carr's.

Considering the troubled history of writers and alcohol—in which long history, unfortunately, Carr has his own chapter—Carr's use of paronomasia in "The Gordon Djinn" comparably to depict both wit and inebriation carries an interesting implication. Greene, writing of Carr in the early 1940s notes:

> It is difficult to believe that Carr could write such brilliant radio plays at a time when his drinking was getting out of control, but that was the situation...he had persuaded himself that he could write while he was drinking, and as far as the quality of his writing indicates, he was correct. (pp. 253–254)

While at the moment in Carr's life when he wrote "The Gordon Djinn" Carr had little access to alcohol and no reputation among his classmates for drinking, as Greene notes, even in Carr's early stories, "drinking is presented as something men do at important moments. He clearly saw it as a sign of being an adult" (p. 36). And because Carr had a genetically predisposed (addictive) personality, as he grew older, unfortunately, his drinking increased: in the 1930s, Carr was a controlled drinker, but inclined to celebratory drinking sprees; by the 1940s, he was writing drunk or working longer when sober to catch up after long binges; by the 1950s, Carr was fully an alcoholic, requiring intervention; and in the early 1960s, drink represented such a danger to Carr's health that his physician, Dr. Barrett, warned him that drinking might bring on a stroke. It did.

At the moment in which Carr writes "The Gordon Djinn," though, the story's preoccupation with alcohol is not an indication of under-aged drinking. Such drinking humor was common, even expected, in

1925. Greene (p. 145) attests to "the belief, which is part of the cinema and the stage of the time, that drunkenness is automatically hilarious." As to the tale's puns, drunken or sober, mercifully, Carr seems to have expectorated in this story most of those he was tempted to perpetrate for most of his career. Carr uses paronomasia much more sparingly in subsequent works.

Carr's wordplay in "The Gordon Djinn" is also reminiscent of another, non-alcoholic, influence upon him: Groucho Marx, that master of comic wordplay. Years later, Carr complimented another writer, Nelson Bond, by writing of his new story collection, *The Thirty-First of February*, "I share your fondness for outrageous puns, which you explode as relentlessly as the Marx Brothers in their heyday."[1]

Carr may have discovered the Marx Brothers as early as their vaudeville tours. Of note, their show *I'll Say She Is* premiered at Philadelphia's Walnut Street Theatre on June 4, 1923. Carr was not far away then, attending The Hill School in Pottstown. Although it opened too late to be an influence on "The Gordon Djinn," Carr may also have seen the Brothers' 1925 Broadway comedy *The Cocoanuts*. *The Cocoanuts* concerns a jewel heist in which the romantic lead is framed for the crime, certainly an appealing premise to Carr! *The Cocoanuts* even performs a little bit of writerly wish fulfillment, which Carr doubtless appreciated. In it (the editor here draws upon the 1929 film version), Bob Adams has been spinning a romantic vision of their future together to Polly, the ingenue, and he sings Irving Berlin's "When My Dreams Come True" to her. His woo-pitching is interrupted when the lovers are approached by two other characters, Penelope Martin and Harvey Yates. Polly decides to retreat:

> *Polly*: It was a lovely story, Mr. Adams. I'd like to hear the rest
> of it sometime. Goodbye.
> *Penelope*: I wonder if I could hear it sometime.
> *Bob*: With pleasure. How about you, Yates?
> *Harvey*: No thanks. You know what happens to bad little
> boys who tell stories.
> *Bob*: Certainly. They marry the beautiful princess.

There is no documentary evidence that Carr saw any Marx Brothers stage performances (this is entirely the editor's speculation), but we know from Greene's biography (pp. 10–11) that Carr attended live the-

---

[1] Letter to Nelson Bond, March 8, 1967.

ater from a young age: "He escorted neighboring girls to see touring theatrical productions that played in Uniontown."

We also know that Carr remained engaged with theater and continued attending stage performances, possibly even as far away as New York City, during his time at both The Hill School and Haverford College. For instance, on vacation from The Hill in 1922, Carr attended the local theater and contributed a guest review for the *Daily News Standard*'s "At the Theatres" column.[2] Not much later, he traveled to Pittsburgh, on January 3, 1923, to see the touring production of Walter Hackett's *Captain Applejack*, which had played on Broadway between December 1920 and June 1922. Then Carr returned to The Hill School for his second term.[3] At the end of 1923, Carr spent several days of his Christmas vacation as his uncle's houseguest in Pittsburgh, during which time he saw "a number of shows, among them being the New York theater [sic] Guild's repertoire starring Basil Sidney, and Eddie Cantor's show, 'Kid Boots'."[4]

Carr collaborated with another student, Sheldon Dick, in 1924 or 1925 on a (now lost) play, *Arms and the God*, which was performed at The Hill School's Dell Theatre. At Haverford, Jack's *The Stewed Prince of Haverburg*, performed during the Fall term of 1926, was a satire of *The Student Prince*, an operetta that opened at Broadway's Jolson's 59th Street Theatre on December 2, 1924. It became the longest-running Broadway show of the 1920s, closing after 608 performances on May 22, 1926. Surely Carr saw *The Student Prince* in person before satirizing it.

As well, as readers have already seen with "The Kindling Spark" (June 1923) Carr borrows its theme from Don Marquis' play, *The Old Soak*, which had opened August 22, 1922, and played at Broadway's Plymouth Theatre for about a year. So "The Kindling Spark" likewise documents that Carr was paying attention to the stage, and during a period when he had the relatively easy opportunity to see the Marx Brothers in person.

Whether or not he saw them onstage, the Marx Brothers became favorites of Carr's at the cinema, and while the humor in his professional fiction stays away from Groucho-style repartee, relying instead upon broad comedy (in particular, slapstick, improbable disguise, and absurd posturing), in this, Carr, while often compared to P.G. Wode-

---

2 "'The Bat' Pleases Two Big Audiences," Uniontown *Daily News Standard*, December 29, 1922, p. 8.

3 Uniontown *Daily News Standard*, January 23,1923, p. 6.

4 Uniontown *Daily News Standard*, December 31, 1923, p. 5.

house, also remains evocative of the Brothers. There is no question that their humor influenced his; the only question is from how early a time.

Carr revisits intense wordplay, particularly paronomasia, as well as Marx Brothers-style stichomythia (the rapid-fire exchange between characters of short lines of dialog), in his comedic Sherlock Holmes playlets. The reader will find this fully in effect—and it is much funnier than "The Gordon Djinn" is—in *The Adventure of the Last Bustard*, Carr's final Holmes sendup for the stage, published later in this collection for the first time anywhere.

Just as the odd bit of humor here or there in "The Gordon Djinn" is allusive, as is typical for Carr, the story more broadly connects with both Carr's literary influences and to some of his own earlier efforts. The most overt relationship is the declared one, with the folktale from the *Thousand Nights and a Night*: "Alaeddin; Or, the Wonderful Lamp."[5] As is Carr's habit, he borrows only a few generalized plot elements from that story and refashions them to his purposes. The most significant resemblance between the two is that Ken Blake, like Alaeddin, invokes the genie to sunder the engagement between his love interest and another, favored suitor. In *The Thousand Nights and a Night*, on three consecutive evenings beginning with the newlyweds' marriage night, Alaeddin orders the genie to remove their wedding bed from the bridal chamber and more so, most uncordially, to remove the groom, the Wazir's son, from that bed:

> "Carry yonder gallows-bird hence and lay him at full length in the privy." His bidding was done straightaway; but, before leaving him, the Slave [the genie] blew upon the bridegroom a blast so cold that it shrivelled him and the plight of the Wazir's son became piteous.[6]

After three days of attempting to consummate his marriage but instead, spending the night petrified with his head immersed in effluvia, the Wazir's son begs his father, and his father in turn begs the Sultan, for an annulment. This clears the way for Alaeddin's marriage to the princess.

---

5   This is how the translator, Richard Burton, translated the character's name and the story's title. Burton's was the only direct and complete English translation, as well as the most popular one, during Carr's lifetime. (We may safely assume that the sixteen-year-old did not read Arabic, so it is likely that he read Burton.)

6   *The Book of the Thousand Nights and a Night* (trans. Richard Burton), The Burton Club (1888), Volume 13 of 17 (*Supplemental Nights*, Volume III), p. 115.

Another key borrowing by "The Gordon Djinn" is that the bride's mother is disposed against the protagonist suitor. In neither story is this a well-developed subplot—actually, it is more important in Carr's version—but Mrs. Bower also happens to revisit one of Carr's earlier tales, "The Cloak of D'Artagnan." In that story appearing a year earlier (June 1924), it is the suitor's own mother, Mrs. Upton-O'Riordan, who is nearly as frigid as Virginia's mother, and who, prior to Mrs. Bower, bears the unflattering sobriquet "the Matterhorn in white lace."

Mrs. Bower is one of several characters in common with Carr's other works. Readers of 2022's *The Kindling Spark* already know that the author relished reusing characters and names—often clearly the same characters, sometimes not—early and often throughout his career. "The Gordon Djinn" is a little gold mine in this respect.

Most significantly, a Ken Blake appears as a recurring character in Carr's professional novels, the first few times as the first-person narrator, in the adventures of Sir Henry Merrivale. Ken figures in in *The Plague Court Murders*, *The Unicorn Murders*, *The Punch and Judy Murders*, *The Judas Window*, and *And So To Murder*. That he is the same character carried forward into Carr's novels, as some others were, is uncertain: while the Ken Blake in the apprentice story is a newspaperman and a detective-story writer, his novelistic namesake is a veteran of the Great War and an intelligence agent—although who can be certain? Perhaps Ken had, like his author, an internship as a journalist...and as the narrator of three H.M. novels and the Watson-style acknowledged "author" of *The Plague Court Murders*, Ken might indeed be considered a writer of detective stories.

Holmes Lamoreaux, with his remark concerning the coal scuttle's contents, is an obvious wink at detective Sherlock, who kept his cigars and pipes, sometimes his tobacco in the coal scuttle. In *Ministry of Miracles*, Carr's novella first published in 1956 and H.M.'s last adventure, Carr gives Holmes Lamoreaux a literary descendent, as it were: Steve. Like the Ken Blake of Carr's novels, Steve Lamoreaux, a wiry thirty-something Canadian, is a cloak-and-dagger man.

"The Gordon Djinn" includes other recurring elements of Carr's fiction. As "The Cloak of D'Artagnan" did, the story transpires in Carr's childhood home between the ages of six and eight, which remained vividly in his mind throughout his life: Washington D.C. Carr occasionally mentions D.C. in the novels, even setting some of his novels' action in that city. Explaining the historical context of *The Ghosts' High Noon*, which begins in the nation's capital, Carr assures the reader in his "Notes for the Curious" afterward that:

> The Congressional Apartments did very much exist, as described and on the site assigned. Among the tenants were Representative W. N. Carr of Pennsylvania, his wife, and their small but noisy son. (p. 254)

Additionally, in "The Gordon Djinn" we perceive Carr's aversion to mathematics, his academic anathema, which Carr would lightheartedly mock over the decades, as well as the theme of the lover aroused to jealousy at the prospective marriage of the woman he loves to another, sometimes through her deliberate provocation (as is the case in "The Gordon Djinn"). This is an inheritance from the tradition of the literary romance and a theme of somewhat more significance in Carr's fiction, complicating the plots of multiple Carr novels including *The Problem of the Wire Cage, Death Turns the Tables, The Emperor's Snuff-Box* (1942), *The Nine Wrong Answers, In Spite of Thunder* (1960), and *Dark of the Moon.*

Finally among its commonalities with other works of Carr, it is noteworthy that "The Gordon Djinn" leverages dramatic ambiguity, which Carr rarely did. Earlier, he had utilized it in "The Will-o'-the-Wisp" and "The Kindling Spark." Later, Carr would employ dramatic ambiguity most famously in *The Burning Court* (1936), but it became a central element in his three late, time-traveling historical romances, too: did the characters in those novels actually travel into the past or were their journeys hallucinations? The stakes of dramatic ambiguity in "The Gordon Djinn" are lower than in any of these others, but appropriately so, given that "The Gordon Djinn" is comedy, and low comedy at that.

Carr makes it readily apparent, beginning with the hint of the title, that probably, nothing supernatural occurs in this tale at all. To a point of certainty, only drunkenness does, and the rest may be fortunate circumstances: Ken sits home, imagining in his inebriation that he fights for Virginia with the aid of a mythical genie. Bannerman's intoxicated outburst is more consequential than Blake's—but with the curious overlap in subject matter between their hallucinations, Carr genially invites the reader who prefers it to believe in the genie...in the djinn, rather than the gin.

In fact, the title goes so far as to fuse the two contending explanations with an unspoken pun: after all, are not a bottle of gin (being distilled alcohol) and the djinn of a lamp both spirits?

In the end, while "The Gordon Djinn" is deliberately thin stuff, superficially unlike most of Carr's other work, it is, as much of the work in Carr's apprenticeship period is, nonetheless connected characteristically to much of his other work in ways that invite insights into how Carr writes.

The Haunting of Tarnboys (1927)

In olden time, there was an earthquake at Tarnboys once in every seven years. It was a very strange thing that the center of it was always the village church, and that the church itself never fell down or suffered the least scathe, while all the other houses had a woundy[1] bad shaking, and there was not a one but had some sort of crack or hole in it. This was a very sad thing, for the people of Tarnboys were poor folk, who could ill afford to have their houses knocked to pieces once in every seven years.

But this is not the whole of the marvel that befell on the seventh year. For it would seem that the graves of such as were not resting sweetly did throw forth the bodies, and the dead did become quick and did walk abroad; and the ground crawled with the foul vermin of Hell, and the air was reeking and nauseous, and filled with filthy daemons, warlocks and hobgoblins, that did shut out the sun or the stars and make a grievous din with howling and screeching and the whir of their great black wings.

All the people crowded into the church, to pray to Saint Anthony, their patron.[2] There they witnessed the greatest of these wonders, for albeit the prayers were somewhat incoherent because that the vehement movement of the building did set the good folk rolling one against the other, and their jaws rattling about so loosely with fear that they made but a sorry jangle of the words, yet nevertheless the good Saint Anthony heard their petition and came in person to aid them. Every man could see him as plainly as the shaking would permit, stumping up and down among the poor mortals on the pavement, as steady as any ship-master, with his staff in his hand and the little bell tinkling merrily at the end of it, and with his great fat pig snorting along behind him;[3] and

---

1 This means very, extremely, or excessively. This word was in use between the seventeenth and nineteenth centuries, so while it "sounds" medieval, it actually is not.

2 Note that the Saint Anthony in Carr's story is Saint Anthony the Abbot (St. Anthony the Great), not St. Anthony of Padua. Saint Anthony the Great is a patron of the poor and oppressed. The son of wealthy and pious parents, Anthony sold off his inheritance and, heeding Christ's call in Matthew 19:21, distributed the proceeds to the needy.

3 The association of a pig with St. Anthony has several possible explanations, among the likelier of which is that in the artistic tradition, a pig accompanying him represented the demonic forces that St. Athanasius reported attacked the hermit. Swine are most notably

old Gaffer Poney hath still the hole in his face where the very reverend hog of Saint Anthony did trample him when he was a lad. All the while that Saint Anthony stalked up and down among the poor souls that were tumbling about on the floor of his church, he did direct the labors of a great number of right fair and luminous angels, the which were busily holding together every stick and stone of the house. In this wise the people of Tarnboys were preserved from death and the altar of God from desecration.

The earthquake continued for three days. When it was over, you may be very sure that the folk were exceeding glad to stand on their legs and breathe regularly as aforetime; but this pleasure was short-lived, for every man's house had been most ruinously battered and rended, and moreover, the devils and hobgoblins had wrought more havoc within than if the place had been sacked by a band of fierce soldiers.

Everyone supposed, naturally enough, that the town lay under a curse of one sort or another, for that the legions of Hell should choose to make their abode there for three days in every seven years; but what puzzled them was that there should be such a mighty quaking of the earth with the holy church right in the thick of it. Some said that this was the Witches' Sabbath, held every seven years there at Tarnboys, in the land of England, but others said nay, that one unshriven, unhallowed, and accurst lay beneath the church, and they pointed to the tomb of Roger de Gunder, a Baron of Tarnboys in old time and a very murtherous, wicked wight. This sepulchre was covered by a fair slab of brass, whereon was wrought the effigy of the old lord, lying in full armor, with his name, degree, and prowess writ out in the Latin tongue; there also was the brazen effigy of his good dame, lying by his side. No one would have suspected this place of aught ill, had it not been situated in the exact center of the nave, and had there not been strange noises and rumblings which could be heard at any time, if one but laid one's ear against the brass.

Now the word of this thing spread far and wide, so that travelers and even holy pilgrims would come to the barony of Tarnboys, in the land of England, to stand in the village church and see Saint Anthony and the angels holding it together; but they went away with loose joints and sore bones, such was the jolting they received, albeit they did intone

---

associated with demons in Luke 8:32-33, when Jesus expels into a herd of pigs the demons possessing a man he heals. The swine then rush into a lake and are drowned. As well, the order named for St. Anthony (the Hospitallers of St. Anthony) supported itself by raising pigs and receiving them as donations. Given this, pork is the traditional meal on the Feast of St. Anthony.

loud praises unto God and to the worthy patron of the village, and did give alms with a free hand unto the poor people thereof.

Now it finally befell that when the appointed time for the earthquake was drawing nigh, that two mighty men came unto Tarnboys with the other travelers, each having in mind to put an end to the disturbances that beset this place, that he might make a display of power before the world. The first to come was Count Rudolph of the Hunderwald, a warrior of mighty strength and valor, who was deemed to be of the progeny of the giants of old, so great was the size of his body; he rode into the village which a company of stout soldiers at his back, for it was his design to subdue the evil sprites by force of arms. This man was a great braggart, of a murtherous and blasphemous humor, who did break bones as regularly as other folk break bread or go to Mass.

The second great man to come to Tarnboys was Bishop Arnold of Quentville, and a beautiful sight he made, as he rode into the village followed by a great number of lords and retainers, lay and ecclesiastical, with many fine banners and crosses among them. It was his design to remedy the evil by prayers, processions, and other churchly devices, to which purpose he had brought his gallant retinue, with singing boys and musicians and jeweled coffers filled with the relics of many holy saints.

Now there came also a third great man into the village, and that in a manner strange unto the greatest wonderment. For he rode thither all the way from the city of Amida[4] upon the back of a great fiery comet and when he came overhead, slid down from the sky upon a streak of forked lightning. Zagoraldus was the name of this third great man, and as ancient as the moon was he, and as learned as the sun. The purpose of his coming was little more than idle curiosity, as he himself affirmed to me when last I was at Amida. And although he was but slight of limb, yet was he so ferocious of aspect and the manner of his coming so marvelous, that the people gave him without complaint a whole house to himself. Thither he brought a great peck of small vials and little black boxes and the stuffed skins of strange reptiles, hanging in the air, and living creatures, very hideous to see, which he kept imprisoned in glass jars. But few paid any attention to these matters, because everyone was taking sides in the great rivalry that had arisen between Count Rudolph of the Hunderwald and Bishop Arnold of Quentville.

Every day there was stabbing and cracking of skulls in the contention as to whether the devils of Tarnboys should be driven away by the

---

4 Amida was an ancient Mesopotamian city that was located where Diyarbakir (in Turkey) is today.

soldiers or exorcised by the priests. The Bishop and his company must needs bolt themselves fast in their inn, nor ever durst to budge therefrom for fear of Count Rudolph and his men; and the Count would surely have burst the doors and entered, had not the angels Gabriel and Raphael stood above the house with flaming swords in their hands, to protect it; so he tramped up and down before it in great dudgeon, slapping his armor with his fist, waving his great battle-axe in air, and shouting out loud threats and boastful words, all the while that his men were going about the town hanging and killing such as took the part of Holy Church.

As the time for the earthquakings and the devils drew nearer, the strife became worse rather than better. For this reason it seemed to many that the town of Tarnboys would have to wait for redemption from its woe, since the lords ecclesiastical were held by force in their tavern and the soldiers could hardly hope to prevail against the daemons of Hell, being excommunicate and under heavy ban and anathema by the solemn action of the Bishop of Quentville himself. But God did not intend that the efforts of these two worthy men towards the relief of Tarnboys should be wasted on one another, as you shall see.

One fine day, Count Rudolph rode out and called loudly upon the Lord Bishop. The Bishop poked his head from the window, making a wry, inamicable expression upon his face. Then Count Rudolph did him grace right courteously.

"My Lord," quoth he, "a weighty proposal hath been conceived within me."

"Tut, tut," said the Bishop, "Be not concerned thereat."

"Suppose," said Count Rudolph, "that I cease from hostilities against you and your folk, and that you in return remove the bans which have been placed upon me and mine. Then suppose that when these troubles do begin, that you take refuge in the church, where you will have the advantage of conferring with the blessed Saint Anthony in person; if I have not cleared these vermin from the streets by the end of the first day, then you shall begin in whatever manner best pleaseth you, on the second."

"Very well," said the Bishop, "et Justus superabit.[5] The third day shall be one of praise and thanksgiving."

"We shall see," said the Count, and thus they parted, each thinking to see the other put to shame.

On the night before the troubles were to begin, Count Rudolph

---

5 This is Latin for "and the Righteous will overcome."

drank his fill and went to bed as if nothing were afoot, telling his men to be ready at crack of dawn, for that he did not intend to give battle to the daemons till they had lost the advantage of darkness. All the other people jammed themselves into the church as tight as they might squeeze.

At midnight, the village of Tarnboys began to quiver a little, this way and that, and there were rumblings in the earth and the sky. The air became fetid and murky, and strange shapes began to appear in increasing numbers and ever the weird din that they made grew louder and louder.

Count Rudolph of the Hunderwald had ordered that every crack and cranny in his inn should be stopped, expecting to issue trium-phantly therefrom at daybreak. Nevertheless, he was betimes awakened by a warm, soft body of exceeding weight that lay upon his abdomen and held him firmly in his bed; it had eyes. Bye and bye, it began to crawl nearer to his face, working its great, flabby body along on stumpy legs. Count Rudolph bawled out for his esquire, very nearly choked by the weight on his chest and by the foul breath of the monster. When the incubus was close enough, it gave him a gash in the cheek with its tongue, and anon its fat, glutinous lips were feeling stupidly over his face for the wound. He raised his arm and dealt the creature a mighty blow, so that his fist sank into the hot carcass as far as it would reach; thereat the beast vanished through the wall with a terrible shriek, leav-ing a black pool of maggot-filled devil-gore on the bed.

The young esquire, gray-faced and wild-eyed, staggered in, carrying a torch that burned green and sparkled strangely. There he found his master standing naked, wiping the blood from his body with the bed clothes, bawling out loud curses, and swearing that he would clear the house of devils if Master Satanas himself were in it.

"The house is given over to Belial,"[6] said the young donzel,[7] ter-ror-stricken, holding to the door, for the place shook as if it rested on jelly, "the men can scarce do on their armor for that they be attacked by ghosts and goblins and ghouls and witches and warlocks and incubi

---

6 Traditionally (not canonically), Belial is the angel of lawlessness; the name Belial literally means, "worthlessness." There is one Biblical mention of Belial, in 2 Corinthians 6:15, in which passage the name personifies wickedness and unbelief. Because of a false cognate in Germanic languages (this includes English), "Belial"'s resemblance to "belie," Belial is also understood to be the Lord of Lies, the Deceiver.

7 A young squire or page.

and succubi and lemures[8] and lamiae[9] and iblees[10] and jinns and afreets[11] and the souls of the infidel damned, and by vampires and basilisks and harpies and furies and all manner of beasts and fiends, and there be a fire-breathing dragon in the kitchen and a two-headed amphisbaena hath been smashing the tuns in the wine cellar, and if it cometh out again in liquor, God help us." But Count Rudolph heard him not, because of the uproar around them.

"Mum wum, yam wam, quotha!"[12] he yelled in a very terrible rage, "Leave off this coward's talk and bring me mine armor! Buckler and sword! Mace! Gisarme! Axe! My poisoned poignard, you dog! We shall clear this place of vermin!"

When he was dressed cap-a-pie[13] in his armor-proof, My Lord strode down the stairs to his men, dealing great blows to right and left at the devils, as if he had spent all his life warring with imps in the murk and stench of brimstone fumes, with the ground rocking beneath him.

When he had mustered his soldiers, he set about driving the assailants from the inn. Never, I ween, was there such fighting since the rebellion of Lucifer. Right valiantly did the mortals wage war upon the fiends, but the more they slew, the more did crowd into the tavern, for devils have a great love of combat and strife. Fiercely their swords drove through the darkness, aimed at the bright eyes of the fiends, while the arrows of the enemy rained upon them and the dead and wounded lay deep about their legs. But the timbers of the house were cracking and rending overhead, and therefore Count Rudolph set fire to the place by cutting off the head of the flame-breathing dragon that had gorged itself in the kitchen, and led the remnant of his company into the street, while the devils stayed to revel in the roaring yellow flames.

Now Rudolph of the Hunderwald was a captain that knew defeat when it came upon him. Therefore he and his men set about fighting

---

8 Carr refers here not to the small mammals, but rather to mythological harpies or bugbears.

9 A lamia is a monster having the body of a woman that sucks the blood of children.

10 This is a variety of genie, a corruptor.

11 In the Islamic tradition, these are demons.

12 "Quotha," a portmanteau (from "quoth he") interjection expresses contemptuous, ironic, or sarcastic intent after repeating another's words. It was, however infrequently, in peak usage between 1780-1920. Carr may well have heard it in actual use, despite its being antiquated. A contemporary rendering of Count Rudolph's rejoinder might be, "Blah blah blah blah, he said!"

13 This means "head to foot."

their way to the church, there to seek refuge. But not one succeeded; for some were struck down by the arrows and poisoned tails of the daemons, and some were swallowed into the cracks that opened in the earth. Only Count Rudolph was left alive. And the farther he went, the more difficult the passage became, for the church was the very center of everything. He found it at last, rolling about like a ship at sea, with the tall steeple waving this way and that in the whirling, roaring darkness above, and he could hear the sounds of the people within. Up he stepped to the door, leaping over the gaps in the earth, with his shield above his face and his sword waving around his head. Crack! Crack! The whole church rolled over against him of a sudden, and so smote him that he was thrown, rattling and gurgling, head over heels, down into a great chasm in the road which probably had no bottom. Before he had gone very far, he was pluckt forth again by an angel, and haled away to the house of Zagoraldus the magician. This place was as steady and stolid as the city of London, despite the hubbub around it. The angel took off his helmet and dried his face with a sweet-scented cloth.

"I am Zagoraldus of Amida," said the magician, "I believe you came to Tarnboys for to fight with sin; to that purpose I had one of my angels drag you from the pit into which you fell."

"Thankye," said the Count, as an angel brought him a steaming goblet. "Yea, good master magician, an it be fighting, I stand at your service, and in any combat whatsoever I pledge mine honor to acquit me right valorously. You and I shall be partners in this business, for know that I am Count Rudolph of the Hunderwald, of whose mighty deeds you have undoubtedly heard bruit,[14] and me thinketh that you be a greater captain of angels than My Lord Saint Anthony."

"Anthony seeketh purely for holiness, and hath not the scientific mind. He hath borrowed the sprites that serve him from the host of Heaven. My angels," said the old man haughtily, "are brought by mine own puissance from the planets and the stars!"

I shall tell you of what was happening in the meantime at the church of Tarnboys. There, indeed, was Saint Anthony, too busy to think of anything but the preservation of his sanctuary; and there was the Bishop of Quentville, sitting on the floor of the chancel, very doleful and in the dumps for that all his retinue, and especially the little singing boys, had fallen sick at their stomachs from the motion of the church: things were in a terrible way, and there was no hope of even gathering enough people to carry the banners and candles and images and the relics in a

---

14 To bruit is to report widely.

procession. The Bishop hoped sincerely that My Lord of the Hunder-wald was being rent into little pieces outside. Anon, as the saint came jostling by, the Bishop arose and caught his arm and begged a word.

"Look you," said he, "this thing must be stopped at the root. Can you not lend me enough angels to make a procession with the holy relics—the sacred nail parings, milk of the Virgin, all the rest, you know— Quentville—"

"Good Heavens, no!" cried Saint Anthony, very impatiently, "Don't you see that I haven't a one to spare? Look out up there, Yzron[15]—there's a loose brick coming out right by your left hand! No! There! That's right! Holy thorns!" The old man was beginning to weep, out of pure worry and excitement. "Why do I have to be plagued by devils all my life? When I get into Heaven, then they come to defile my holy places." He was blubbering hysterically on the Bishop's shoulder.

"There, there," said Arnold soothingly, trying to disentangle the sacred hog from his cassock. This failing, the two sat down abruptly on the floor.

"Now, there is one way in which you might perchance employ your office ecclesiastical to advantage," remarked the good saint after a short space. "I suspect that the tomb of Roger de Gunder, over yonder, hath some connection with this mischief. Suppose that ye open it and make sure that there be nought but holiness within, as befitteth such a place."

"It shall be done," said the Bishop, "and you and I shall be partners in ridding the village of Tarnboys of this pest, for that we have the forces of Heaven on our side; justos deducet Dominus!"[16]

Then the sexton brought his tools and Bishop Arnold set men to work, prying at the corners of the brazen effigy, whence came strange scratchings and weird voices raised in Hellish din. Holy water was made ready, and the sacred relics of Quentville. Such of the priests as were able, chanted Magnificat[17] and Domine quasurnus.[18]

All the while that the men in the church were struggling to raise the great slab of brass, Zagoraldus and Count Rudolph were making good use of their time.

---

15 This is not a typo; perhaps the Bishop's first name is Hezron, which the Saint pronounces in a variant manner (of Carr's invention). The biblical Hezron was the grandson of Judah and a direct ancestor of David. Hezron was also an eponymous plain south of Judah (Joshua 15:3). The Book of Joshua details Israel's possession of the Holy Land according to God's holy covenant. The name "Hezron" is a reminder of the necessity to keep faith with God.

16 Latin for, "the Lord will lead the just!"

17 This is from the canticle of Mary (Luke 1:46-55), "(My soul) magnifies (the Lord)."

18 In Latin, "We beseech you, O Lord."

"You may have observed," remarked the sorcerer, "that the center and source of all this disturbance is the tomb of a certain Lord and Lady of Tarnboys in the church of Saint Anthony."

"No, I didn't," said the Count; "I wish I had."

"The soul of the Baroness of Tarnboys is now among the blest," said the other, "but her husband is not to be found in Heaven, Purgatory, nor in Hell, where he was most to be expected. Therefore it would appear that this Sir Roger de Gunder hath escaped the Pit, his proper home, and sleepeth still in his own tomb, snoring very comfortably indeed, for many people have heard the sound, though they reckt not what it was; and in every seventh year, some great daemon, with a legion of attendant devils, cometh ripping through the earth to pass a riotous three days with him. Now I will drive away the daemons by mine art if you will but go down into the tomb and bring me the head of Roger de Gunder, for it is well that a mortal man should do this thing."

This pleased Count Rudolph well enough, and they shook hands upon it. Then they went into a little square room all hung with black, and lighted by one silver lamp that hung from the ceiling. On the floor there was a circle drawn in blood and around it writing, to wit: "ADO-NAI JAH SABAOTH EL ELOHIM ELOHE ZEBAOTH ELION ESCRREHIE,"[19] and other mighty words in the Hebrew characters.

When the two had entered the circle, Zagoraldus drew from under his robe a little golden seal, curiously graven, and spoke the conjuration to the ministering angels of the Powers:

"I, Zagoraldus of Amida, a servant of God, call upon thee, desire and conjure thee, spirit Scheol, through the most holy appearance in the flesh of Jesus Christ, by his most holy birth and circumcision, by his sweating of blood in the garden, by the lashes he bore, by his bitter sufferings and death, by his resurrection, ascension, and the sending of the holy spirit as a comforter, and by the most dreadful words: Dai, Deorum, Ellas, genio Sophiel, Zophiel, Canoel, Elmiach, Richol, Hoamiach, Jerazol, Vohal, Daniel, Hasios, Tomaiach, Sannul, Damamiach, Sanul, Damabiath, and by those words through which thou canst be conquered, that thou appear before me in a beautiful human form, and fulfill what I desire. Fiat. Fiat. Fiat."[20] And when the fair angel appeared, he commanded that he bring spirits to assist the company of Saint Anthony in holding the church together, and to comfort the poor folk within.

---

19 This is a variation on the seven names of God, which legend says once written cannot be erased; praying or writing them was a way to entreat holy strength for the petitioner.

20 This is Latin: "Make it so, make it so, make it so."

"My Lord, it shall be done," quoth the angel, and vanished.

Then Zagoraldus drew forth the seals of the spirits of the planet Mars, and spoke as follows:

"I, Zagoraldus of Amida, cite thee, spirit Emol, by Deus Sachnaton, Luil, by Acumea, Luiji, by Ambriel, Tijlaij, by Ehos, by Jeha, by Zora, Ageh, by Awoth, that you appear before me in a beautiful human form, and accomplish my desire, thus truly in and through the anepobeijaron, which Aaron heard and which was prepared for him. Fiat. Fiat. Fiat." And when the kingly angel did appear before them, he commanded that all the lesser devils be driven away, and that the damage that had been wrought in Tarnboys be repaired, and that all that had been lost be restored, and that the town be protected from evil for all time to come by the spirits of the Planet Mars.

"My Lord, it shall be done," quoth the angel, and vanished.

Then Zagoraldus drew forth a third golden seal, all sparkling with little jewels; this he laid upon the ground, and raised his arms above it, as he spoke the conjuration to Schemhamphoras.

"I, Zagoraldus of Amida," he cried in a loud, clear voice, "cite and conjure thee, Spirit of Schemhamphoras, by all the seventy-two holy names of God, that Thou appear before me and fulfil my desire, as truly in and through the name Emmanuel, which the three youths Sadrach, Mijsach and Abed-nego sung in the fiery furnace from which they were released![21] Fiat! Fiat! Fiat!"

Thereat the room grew strangely warm and brilliant, waves of light followed one another over the black curtains and the letters of blood upon the floor, albeit no shape was visible.

"Schemhamphoras," said the magician, full courteously, "let the evil spirit in the tomb of Roger de Gunder, Baron de Tarnboys, be driven thence."

"Master," replied a very sweet voice, "she hath already come out of the tomb." And so saying, the lights faded and were gone.

So these two set out for the church, hot foot, to learn what was happening there; and a queer sight they made: the little old man in his long black gown, and the great giant in his battered armor, all besmeared with devil blood of many colors. The sun had risen long before, but the darkness was not yet fully dispelled by the bright angels who flashed hither and yon; scarcely a daemon was to be seen, save here and there

---

21 See the Book of Daniel 3:8-30.

a barguest[22] or empusa,[23] whose hideous ugliness is not repelled by the light of Heaven, as with most devils. Phantoms and specters were hurrying about in loud distress, and the uneasy dead, with their bare bones or with rotten flesh hanging to them like soft pudding, were scurrying off to the burying ground, trailing their ragged shrouds behind them.

"Lilis![24] By the breastplate of Moses!" shrieked the old man when they entered the church.

Sure enough, there was the goodwife of Satan herself, so foul and lecherous a hag that the blood grew cold to look upon her, and she was flying about the nave of the church, screaming, gnashing her teeth, vomiting vermin and blood, while her eyes flashed sickness and woe upon the folk beneath. There too was the open tomb of Roger de Gunder, and Saint Anthony, and the Bishop of Quentville, with banners trampled, the relics upset and everything in wild disorder; the earthquake, at least, had ceased. The people rushed in mad panic towards the door, and Zagoraldus raised himself and his companion a few yards in the air to allow them to pass underneath.

Very soon the church was empty of all save the Count and the magician, Saint Anthony and the Bishop, who were standing tight clasped in each other's arms, and the very reverend hog, that lay panting on the floor. I, too, was there, but no man wotted thereof, for I had wrapt me in the great gonfalon[25] of Quentville and laid me away in a dark corner. Then did Lilis swoop down from aloft and knock the Bishop's miter from his head with a triumphant screech; in so doing, however, she burnt her fingers upon Anthony's halo, and retired behind the rood screen, gibbering mournfully.

"We must have the angels take her away," said Saint Anthony tremulously.

"Pooh!" said the magician, "as if the angels could manage Lilis."

"I'll call the saints of Heaven, I'll call on the Trinity!" screamed the other.

------

22 This is a goblin in the shape of a large dog having various horrible characteristics and portending imminent death or misfortune.

23 This is a female demon or evil spirit associated with the goddess Hecate, which devours humans and can take different forms. More generally, the term refers to an evil spirit, a hobgoblin, or phantom.

24 Carr is using a variation on the name of the Talmudic Lilith, Adam's first wife and the mother of his demonic offspring. Sometimes Lilith is depicted as the bride of Satan himself, as she is here.

25 This is a banner or ensign.

"The situation," quoth Zagoraldus very coolly, "demandeth one who can call on the Arch-fiend. Lilis, if you don't behave and that right shortly, your husband shall get wit of these doings." Whereat Lilis flew to the window, bellowing hideously; there she met her handmaid, Ogere, who had not the temerity to venture on holy ground, and the two vanished away in the distance, although one could still hear their ugly yelling for a long while after.

Now it fortuned that when Count Rudolph had made himself ready for battle, and leapt down into the open tomb, that he found the body of Roger de Gunder with the soul fled from it; nevertheless, he hewed the carcass to pieces ere he clomb forth again.

"Lauda anima!"[26] cried Bishop Arnold, as he peered down into the hole. "Lo, the wicked soul hath been driven away to its appointed home by virtue of the holy relics of Quentville!"

"What's that?" said the knight, and he began to swear and blaspheme most vilely, much an angered by this saying; and there might have been harsh words and violence between them, there in the house of God, had it not been that each was in great haste to be home among his own people, to boast and brag of having driven Lilis and her brood from the village of Tarnboys, in the land of England. Thus, each blazed forth his own fame as loud as he was able; but you and I know the truth of the matter.

"Well, master magician," sighed Saint Anthony when the two had gone, "I am going back unto the eternal bliss of God's celestial Paradise. I am sorry that you cannot accompany me."

"Not a jot of thanks, I suppose," said the doctor, and thereat he blew a volley of sparks from his nose, that fell a-coursing down his beard and lay winking on the floor.

"Well, that idea of calling on the Devil was rather clever," and this was the most that Saint Anthony would allow him.

"What say you of all the angels that I sent—all these Powers that came in the nick of time?" Zagoraldus spake hotly, in an injured tone. "I brought them especially from Heaven to save your feelings; I might have brought nine times as many from the stars, and I got me more of them than you could gather in seven years."

"But after all, you are only a devil-monger," for Saint Anthony would grant him no credit in the matter, and not without cause, methinketh, since he himself had striven so long and so honestly to remedy this evil.

---

26 In Latin, this means "praise the soul!"

"There was dirt in the business somewhere. They may have been devils in disguise for all that I know." He was beginning to disappear.

"I doubt me whether you could tell the difference between agthodaemons and cacodaemons!"[27] screamed the old sorcerer in a rage, and with the red flames dancing up behind his eyeballs. "You are an insipid, faith-healing funda—" But Saint Anthony had vanished.

The old man sighed deeply, his little gray eyes gazing afar into the dim future, and then, awakening, shot through the roof and away to the tall tower in Amida, there to resume his age-old search for the root and source of knowledge.

---

27 In the event the reader likewise cannot tell the difference, an agthodaemon is a good spirit, and a cacodaemon, an evil one.

Notes for the Curious: "The Haunting of Tarnboys"

The reader is warned: While this commentary does not reveal any solutions, it discusses some key aspects and plot details of Carr's novels *The Burning Court*, *The Crooked Hinge*, *The Sleeping Sphinx*, and *Below Suspicion*. If you have not read those novels yet, you may prefer to do so before reading the following commentary.

—

"The Haunting of Tarnboys" is an outlier among Carr's fiction, in several respects. First, it is a supernatural fantasy. Carr wrote only two stories in this genre: "Tarnboys" and "The Gordon Djinn." "The Haunting of Tarnboys" differs from "The Gordon Djinn" in that, in "Tarnboys," there is no doubt of the existence of the infernal and magical. This is not to say "Tarnboys" is Carr's only tale in which the supernatural is genuine; Carr experimented with otherworldly explanations a few times during his apprenticeship period, not only in this story. Other early stories that turn on unearthly influences include "The Riddle of the Laughing Lord," "The Legend of the Cane in the Dark," and "The Legend of the Hand of Ippolita." None of these offers a rational alternative to its magical phenomena. The third distinctive characteristic of "Tarnboys" is its narrative voice, one unlike any most readers of Carr's other works will have encountered elsewhere.

"The Haunting of Tarnboys" shares its unusual narrative tone with only one other tale, "The Legend of the Neckband of Carnelians," which appears in the 1927 story cycle "The New Canterbury Tales," published two months after "Tarnboys." Both are more wry than frightening, so despite this tale's being filled with cataclysmic occurrences and gory details, the apocalyptic perils of "Tarnboys" feel more amusing than threatening. The narrative voice of "Carnelians" has a similar, ironic remove, despite a climactic murder. The voice of these two stories was likely inspired by James Branch Cabell's *Chivalry*, a lifelong favorite of Carr's, which is a book-length story cycle of ten medieval romances narrated in an amusing, faux-archaic dialect. Here is a representative excerpt (pp. 155–156):

> Holland was the surname he assumed, the name of his half-brothers; and to detail his Asian wanderings were both tedious and unprofitable. But at the end of each four months would come to him a certain messenger from Glyndwyr, whom Richard supposed to be the devil Bembo, who notoriously

ran every day around the world upon the Welshman's business. It was in the Isle of Taprobane, where the pismires are as great as hounds, and mine and store the gold the inhabitants afterward rob them of through a very cunning device, that this emissary brought the letter which read simply, "Now is England fit pasture for the White Hart." Presently was Richard Holland in Wales, and then he rode to Sycharth.

While the mature Carr accurately explored any number of dialects associated with specific places and times, he left behind, after a few months' experimentation with it, the pseudo-medieval diction and sardonic narrative tone so distinctive in "Tarnboys."

Carr did not leave behind the supernatural, of course; where that is concerned, readers of Carr's best-known and most popular titles, with a single possible exception—*The Burning Court*—have the accustomed expectation, whenever seemingly otherworldly impossibilities threaten the ordinary world, that Carr's detective-hero will restore the sense of an orderly universe by exposing the human evil behind any apparent impossibilities and explaining those comfortingly away. Lawbreakers are punished, and the sun rises the next morning.

What most sharply recommends interest in "The Haunting of Tarnboys," though, and separates it from Carr's other early paranormal tales, is an aspect that ties "Tarnboys" more closely to several of Carr's mature novels: it is grounded in authentic occult lore. As Greene has observed, "Throughout his life, John Dickson Carr was fascinated by tales of witchcraft, demonism, and ghosts."[1] Carr's interest in the occult, which manifests itself for the first time in this story, was lifelong; his appetite for it was as edacious as for conventional history. Carr drolly confesses this in *The Crooked Hinge* (p. 9) by making John Farnleigh's boyhood a mildly fictionalized version of his own, mixed (of course) with some wish fulfillment:

> "...There was no real harm in him; it was merely that he didn't fit and wanted to be treated as a grown-up before he had grown up. In nineteen-twelve, when he was fifteen, he had a fully-grown-up-affair with a barmaid in Maidstone—"
> Page whistled. He glanced out of the window, as though he expected to see Farnleigh himself.
> "At fifteen?" page said. "Here, he must have been a lad!"

<hr>

1 *The Door to Doom*, p. 213.

"He was."

Page hesitated. "And yet, you know, I'd always thought from what I've seen of him that Farnleigh was—"

"A bit of a Puritan?" supplied Burrows. "Yes. Anyhow, we're talking about a boy aged fifteen. His studying occult matters, including witchcraft and Satanism, was bad enough. His being expelled from Eton was worse."

Perhaps Carr's earliest real-life exposure to the literature of dark magic was Bram Stoker's *Dracula*, for which Carr nostalgically hungered near the other end of his life:

> Some fifty-odd years ago a publisher whose name escapes me issued a set of books called the International Adventure Library, Three Owls Edition, featuring *Dracula* and continuing with mystery or adventure novels of fair to dubious quality... And I want it.[2]

Of course, if *Dracula* was a starting point and its reacquisition near the endpoint of Carr's career-long intrigue with the occult, as with all topics of interest to him, Carr consumed a great deal in between, engaging in extended research and reading concerning vampires, werewolves, witches, the undead, black magic, and so forth. Carr digested diverse materials: fiction of the occult, naturally, but as well, primary materials (reports from centuries past concerning witchcraft, witchcraft trials, etc.), quasi-religious mysticism, supernatural charlatanism—that rich source of material for any novelist of the unlikely!—and even anthropology.

Greene recounts in the biography that Carr, admitting what readers expected of him—the restoration of the rational when confronted by menacing impossibilities—wrote in response to the mystery author and critic Anthony Boucher that were Carr to write a novel in which the supernatural were the unambiguous explanation (as Boucher had encouraged him to do in his letter), Carr "feared that the faithful customers would murder me" (p. 172). He enjoyed terrifying his readers with the prospect of the unearthly—as Carr's readers enjoyed its suggestive chills—but for him, ultimately the terror within ourselves is a more unsettling, more pertinent and interesting motif than the imagined hosts of the abyss. Greene (p. 352) comments:

____

2 Letter to Oscar Baron, April 18, 1972.

> Carr made a psychological point...In many of his novels, Carr
> had controlled his fear that the universe may indeed be cha-
> otic by providing human, material, and rational explanations
> for seemingly impossible events. In some books, however...
> human rationality was not enough, and chaos threatened to
> burst through...we see that the chaos, the irrationality, may not
> only be part of the universe but also be within us as humans.

In his work featuring the diabolic, Carr sometimes reveals to readers a given narrative's underlying sources and inspirations, whether fictional or factual. How he does so varies; in some cases, Carr simply footnotes these as he might a conventional historical or a true-crime reference establishing that the work has its basis in the possible and the actual. In other cases, Carr has characters explore legends of witchcraft or the demonic within the narrative, uncovering the book's true-life bases more organically, and at suspenseful moments. Either way, when Carr reveals sources and inspirations, he does so not to draw back the curtain on his craft, but rather, to encourage the reader's credulousness. Carr's argument to the reader in these instances is that, however improbable and sensational his plot, "It not only could have happened before; it did happen before."

The most notorious work in which Carr divulges its occult underpinnings is *The Burning Court*. In its day, *The Burning Court* was controversial both because, surprisingly to its audience, the novel violates the detective-fiction genre (on which Carr's popularity and reputation were based) and because the book explores abortion and sexual deviancy bordering on necrophilia, barriers not commonly crossed in popular detective fiction of the 1930s. These challenging aspects are intertwined narratively and suggestively with the novel's theme of witchcraft: the supernatural serves in *The Burning Court* as both metaphor and plot device. Is black magic the explanation for seemingly impossible circumstances, or is it a symptom of psychological derangement? Struggling with this question, one character, Edith Despard, reads aloud to her companions a long passage from a fictive history of witchcraft. With characteristic Carr cleverness, the attributed author of Edith's history is Professor Grimaud, from Carr's *The Three Coffins*. Carr's footnotes confess the true sources of this history to be Montague Summers' *History of Witchcraft* and some sixteenth-century primary materials (pamphlets, trial proceedings, letters, and journals). As Greene documents in the biography, Carr also relies in *The Burning Court* upon Margaret Murray's *The Witch-Cult in Western Europe* and Summers' *The Geography of Witchcraft*, though Carr does not quote these volumes or acknowledge them. It is Summers' *The Geography of Witchcraft*, for instance, that describes the witch's ladder, a knotted string hinting at devilry in *The Burning Court*:

> An apron was found to be tied up by a string which had nine curious knots fastened in it. This was a baleful charm, the witches' ladder, *la ghirlanda delle strege*.[1]

Summers also documents in *The Geography of Witchcraft* witches' special affinity for wood, whether in the form of staves, statuettes and idols, or other wicked appurtenances. In *The Burning Court*, Uncle Miles emphatically demands to be buried in a wooden coffin (p. 52). In providing this detail, Carr probably has in mind Summers' account in the *Geography* (p. 77) of the deathbed conversion of the witch of Berkley:

> She had been wealthy, but on her death-bed she confessed that her riches were derived from a compact with the Devil. Accordingly she bids them sew her body in the hide of a stag and place her in a stone coffin, binding it with heavy chains of iron. Fifty psalms are to be sung each night, and fifty masses to be said each morning, and if her body can be thus kept safe for three nights, upon the fourth day they may bury it deep in the churchyard, the Devil will have sought and not have found.

Summers was of lifelong interest to Carr; Carr kept at least one of the anthropologist's other studies, *The Werewolf*, in his personal library until his death.

Regarding the burial receptacles of Uncle Miles (and as compared to the witch of Berkley), Carr may also have in mind a West Highlands fairy tale, recorded in book form by John Francis Campbell in 1860, "The Red Book of Appin." Carr borrows this title later, in *The Crooked Hinge*, recasting the folk tale as a mysterious, unpublished manuscript. (More on that below.) The original "Red Book" concerns a young man's encounter with the devil. The red book the devil carries records the signatures of the corrupt and the unwitting whose souls he has snared,

---

1 *The Geography of Witchcraft*, Alfred A. Knopf (1927), p. 97. All subsequent excerpts are drawn from the same edition. Of note, Summers in turn traces the witch's ladder back to an 1892 source, Charles Godfrey Leland's *Etruscan Roman Remains in Popular Tradition*.

whether through trickery or seduction. The young man's encounter affirmatively answers a question discussed between the tale's teller and listener as to whether there is "any virtue in iron against witchcraft or fairy spells": "you must know that iron was the principal safeguard against evil spirits."[2] If he is buried in a simple wooden coffin—not stone, not iron—Uncle Miles believes that he can walk again, through the power of witchcraft, as a member of the non-dead, immortal worshippers of the devil.

Details such as these quietly underlying Carr's occult coloring, once recognized, can be illuminating. "The Haunting of Tarnboys" is the earliest instance in which Carr silently borrows from authentic sources. Disguised as so much contrived teenaged nonsense, underneath the story's narrative is a real-world origin for Zagoraldus's incantations; the young author's awareness and exploitation of such an obscure text demonstrates how surprisingly well read this twenty-year-old already was. Carr in "Tarnboys" borrows the sorcerer's spells verbatim from an eighteenth- (perhaps early nineteenth-) century apocryphal work, *The Sixth and Seventh Books of Moses*, translated in 1880 by Johann Scheibel from German into English. The Sixth Book describes seven magical seals (seven of course being a mystical number); the Seventh Book enumerates twelve tables, presumably evocative of the twelve tribes of Israel. Eleven of the twelve are named not for tribes, though, but for elemental spirits (e.g., fire, air) and heavenly bodies (e.g., Mars, Venus, the Sun), while the final table's designation is for Schemhamforasch, according to the occult tradition the sacred Biblical name of God. It invokes all the spirits of white and black magic. So when Zagoraldus cries out...

> "I, Zagoraldus of Amida, cite thee, spirit Emol, by Deus Sachnaton, Luil, by Acumea, Luiji, by Ambriel, Tijlaij, by Ehos, by Jeha, by Zora, Ageh, by Awoth"

...he is quoting the Seventh Table, of the Spirits of Mars, which: "brings good fortune in case of quarrels the Spirits of Mars will help you."[3] This makes perfect sense within the context of "The Haunting of Tarnboys."

When the sorcerer, drawing forth his third golden seal, subsequently conjures...

---

2 *Popular Tales of the West Highlands, Orally Collected with a Translation*, Edmonston and Douglas (1860), Volume II, p. 87.

3 *The Sixth and Seventh Books of Moses*, Laurence, Scott & Co. (1910), p. 20. All subsequent excerpts are drawn from the same edition.

> Schemhamphoras, by all the seventy-two holy names of God, that Thou appear before me and fulfil my desire, as truly in and through the name Emmanuel, which the three youths Sadrach, Mijsach and Abed-nego sung in the fiery furnace from which they were released!

...his utterance comes directly from the Twelfth Table, the most powerful of the incantations in the apocryphal tome. According to the book's writer, "This Twelfth Table, laid upon the Table or Seal of the Spirits, will compel them to appear immediately, and to serve in all things."[4] In Carr's story, they do.

Additional inspirations upon which Carr draws—fiction of the occult, primary materials, anthropological studies, even singular affairs and stage illusions—lend color and depth to several of his works involving suspicions of witchcraft. In addition to the novels *The Crooked Hinge*, *The Reader is Warned* (1939), *The Sleeping Sphinx*, Below Suspicion, and *Papa Là-Bas*, Carr's 1943 radio drama, *The Devil's Saint*, explores the ancient practices of:

> The Old Religion...The witch-cult...There were many to worship unashamed at the Grand Sabbat; to receive all favors from Satan, their master; and to dance forever, joyously, in the red quadrilles of the nether world![5]

The Devil's Saint also features two other favorite Carr motifs, a masquerade ball and a room that kills, but its occult backstory is drawn directly from Carr's standbys, Murray and Summers.

Below Suspicion follows the investigation into a practicing coven, and likewise concerns the "Old Religion." To Murray (citing an additional volume, her *The God of the Witches*, p. 161) and Summers, Carr adds, in a helpful bibliography enumerated by Dr. Fell (p. 204) studies by Reginald Scot, Joseph Glanvil, Wallace Notestein, C. L'Estrange Ewen, and C.W. Olliver. Of these, Carr makes little close use in his narrative, but we may safely infer that these titles were taken from the shelf of Carr's own library. He also mentions Arthur Machen's *Witchcraft*, from which Dr. Fell quotes, and the French writer J.K. Huysmans' 1891 novel *Là-bas*. (The novel's title translates to "down there in Hell," or, "the Damned.") Dr. Fell, mouthing his author's opinion of that last's

---

4 Ibid, p. 24.

5 *The Devil's Saint* is collected in *The Dead Sleep Lightly*. The excerpt is from pp. 45-46.

depiction of the Black Mass, declares, "No fiction writer has portrayed it with accuracy, except Huysmans in *Là-bas*" (p. 156). Huysmans' lurid narrative is set in nineteenth-century Paris. The main character, Durtal, is a writer researching a fifteenth-century child murderer. Durtal retreats from what he views as the tawdry modern world into the shelter of a bell tower, immersing himself there in medievalism—but he is seduced into diabolism, practiced by the simple bell ringer, a doctor knowledgeable about the occult, and Durtal's lover, a dark seductress.

Carr employs Huysmans and the anthropological sources for *Below Suspicion* in mostly straightforward manners: good research and allusions to real-life studies of witchcraft, mixed in with authentic details he has culled from these such as seven-branched candelabra, reversed crosses of Satan, the notorious cult the Hellfire Club, and the history of poisonings perpetrated by covens make his novel more convincing. With some of these symbols of witchcraft, Carr implies the duality of human nature, e.g., a regular cruciform image is pious, but reversed, is indicative of evil. Perhaps the most interesting instance of this duality is Dr. Fell's explanation connecting the founding of the Order of the Garter to witchcraft:

> "The story goes that during the reign of Edward the Third, in the fourteenth century, a certain Lady (most versions identify her as the Countess of Salisbury) danced at a court-ball given by the king. While dancing, she dropped her garter and was overcome with confusion. King Edward instantly picked up the garter, fastened it on his own leg with the words '*Honi soit qui mal y pense*' and on this incident founded the Order of the Garter, the highest of knightly Orders in all Europe."
>
> Dr. Fell puffed out his lips under the bandit's moustache, making a wry and satiric noise.
>
> "Now the interest of that little tale lies not in whether it is true or partly legendary. But centuries of repetition have made it lose its point."
>
> Here Dr. Fell made a still more satiric face.
>
> "It took very much more than a dropped garter, believe me, to shock a lady of the fourteenth century. In fact, the incident would have caused only mild embarrassment under Queen Victoria. Any child today can translate '*Honi soit qui mal y pense*' as 'Evil to him who evil thinks.' Where on earth could there have been any suggestion of evil?

"But King Edward knew. He knew what overcame Lady Salisbury and terrified the guests. His quick thinking, as Miss Murray has pointed out, probably saved her life. For the garter, then used as cord or string or lace....was the mark of the witch-woman. It designated the creature, skilled in lechery and murder, who stood out against the lurid sky of the Middle Ages. And the red garter, above all, meant the head of a group, or coven; high in unholy councils, closest of all to the person, usually a man, who towered over them in the role of Satan." (pp. 161–162)

There is also a minor dramatic echo of Huysmans' *Là-bas* in *Below Suspicion*, but to reveal more would be to spoil reading one or both!

With respect to the underlying sources for *The Crooked Hinge* and *The Sleeping Sphinx*, and how Carr utilizes them, these are, being more sophisticated, worth peculiar attention.

The Crooked Hinge is very much in the idiom of *The Burning Court*, but it goes further. To lend the novel authenticity—and to make it more unnerving—Carr relies in it, as he does in *The Burning Court*, upon seventeenth-century accounts of witchcraft, upon anthropological research, and even upon medical analysis. For instance, Carr carefully, faithfully observes the ingredients in an ointment witches smeared on their bodies before attending black sabbaths, which included deadly nightshade and aconite. Then, to satisfy his reader as to the pharmacological effects of the ointment (p. 215)—which is important to the plot—Carr cites documentary sources, including those same studies by Murray and Summers on which he relied for *The Burning Court* and J.W. Wickwar's *Witchcraft and the Black Arts*.

Carr more openly incorporates primary sources into the narrative (not merely the footnotes, as is sometimes the case in *Below Suspicion*) of *The Crooked Hinge* than he does in *The Burning Court*, early and repeatedly: on page 5, Brian Page, a dilatory writer and the perspective character, sits reading a scarce seventeenth-century pamphlet, *A Tryal of Witches, at the Assizes Held at Bury St. Edmonds for the County of Suffolk; on the Tenth day of March, 1664, Before Sir Matthew Hale Kt. Lord Chief Baron of His Majesties Court of Exchequer.* This is a real historical pamphlet. Carr does not explain Page's interest in the dark arts. He does not explain how Page acquired a surviving copy of a nearly three-hundred-year-old rarity. Carr simply lets the suggestion of witchcraft linger, which becomes stronger and more frightening as the novel builds.

Carr places the next true-life volume of the occult (the 1613 translation of the inquisitor Sébastien Michaëlis's *Admirable History of Possession and Conversion of a Penitent Woman: Seduced by a Magician that Made Her to Become a Witch*) at the bedside of a murdered woman. Dr. Fell summarizes the book as "the confession of Madeleine de la Palud, at Aix in 1611, for her participation in ceremonies of witchcraft and the worship of Satan" (p. 142).

Sir John Farnleigh, the steward of Farnleigh Close, confirms that this work and others, a compendium of wickedness, are "books of darkness which my father, and his father before him, kept locked in the little room in the attic" (p. 142). Are the murders that Scotland Yard has come to the village of Mallingford to investigate the acts of a Kentish coven? Carr's incorporation of the witchcraft tomes strongly suggests this.

Although the prospect of Satanic masses darkens the novel's atmosphere, the most uncanny nonhuman presence in *The Crooked Hinge* is a centuries-old automaton called the Golden Hag. Carr first teases it to the reader with the title of Part II of the novel, "The Life of an Automaton." He readies the reader to dread the hag with an epigram (p. 75) taken from Ambrose Bierce's 1899 short story, "Moxon's Master." In Bierce's story, a chess-playing automaton comes inexplicably, murderously to life:

> Then all was silent, and presently Moxon reappeared and said, with a rather sorry smile:
> "Pardon me for leaving you so abruptly. I have a machine in there that lost its temper and cut up rough."
> Fixing my eyes steadily upon his left cheek, which was traversed by four parallel excoriations showing blood, I said:
> "How would it do to trim its nails?"

This second section of *The Crooked Hinge* quickly stirs grisly imaginings for the reader. Part I, titled "The Death of a Man," has been climactically fulfilled, revealing a corpse "with marks on his throat... like the marks of fangs or claws" (p. 130)—or perhaps, scratches from the skeletal, steel fingers of a rotting automaton. A witness saw "something looking at me through one of the glass panels of the door, one of the panels down nearest the ground....I received the impression it was dead" (pp. 137–138)...."a crawling, legless something" (p. 139). Could the hag, a neglected and decaying mechanism secreted away in an attic for decades, have come to life, escaped its locked chamber, and committed murder?

As do the novel's accounts of the history and traditions of witchcraft, the hag has real-life antecedents. One of the characters, Madeline Dane, inexplicably preoccupied with the hag, reveals them (p. 113), asking Dr. Fell and Inspector Elliot: "Did you ever hear of Kempelen's and Maelzel's mechanical chess-player, or Maskelyne's 'Zoe' or 'Psycho,' the whist-playing figure?" In a number of his novels for which Carr requires impossibilities that can be explained rationally, he borrows stage illusions. His usual source is the "Maskelyne Mysteries," as it is in *The Crooked Hinge*. (Carr also relied, notably, upon Harry Houdini's 1924 skeptical survey of spiritualism, *A Magician Among the Spirits*.) Neither the borrowed secret of how the hag operates—which in the novel is allegedly recorded in Carr's reimagined *Red Book of Appin*—nor Madeline's history of automatons is superfluous, either: they offer clues as to how the murder was committed and to the murderer's identity. Carr is telling the reader, once again, "It not only could have happened before; it did happen before."

Because this is a John Dickson Carr novel, not everything mysterious merely imitates life. Carr is no mechanical borrower of others' cleverness. Carr's Golden Hag can do what John Nevil Maskelyne's automatons could not: it seemingly vanishes of its own will and reappears elsewhere, terrifying the unsuspecting...almost as if by witchcraft.

Carr borrows Maskelyne's Psycho once more in 1944's *He Wouldn't Kill Patience* (written as Carter Dickson). In that comic novel, the animatronic dummy, Fatima, is not sinister at all—it confines itself, as Psycho did, to playing whist. Nevertheless, as in *The Crooked Hinge*, the secret to Fatima's animation matters: it provides a clue to the solution of an impossible murder.

In addition to Ambrose Bierce's short tale of horror and "The Red Book of Appin," there are several other dark literary inspirations behind *The Crooked Hinge*. The epigram to Part III (p. 173), "The Rise of a Witch," comes from *Là-bas*. Carr reproduces his selected passage in the original French:

> Car, au fond, c'est cela la Satanisme, se disait-il; la question agitée depuis que le monde existe, des visions extérieures, est subsidiare, quand on y songe; le Démon n'a pas besoin d'exhiber sou des traits humains ou bestiaux afin d'attester sa presence; il suffit, pour qu'il s'affirme, qu'il élise domicile en des âmes qu'il exulcère et incite à d'inexplicables crimes.[6]

---

6 "Because, in the end, this is Satanism, he said to himself; that vexing question since

The evocation of *Là-bas* intensifies *The Crooked Hinge*'s disturbing mood and encourages speculation about what sinister agents might be at work. Are unholy masses being celebrated in the nearby wood? Are the novel's two mysterious deaths ritualistic killings? Who might be a witch? And while the practice of witchcraft in *Là-bas* is genuine, the excerpt Carr chooses from it for the epigram, shrewdly and characteristically for Carr, leaves available the inference that demonic evil may emanate from within ourselves, not from external, supernatural corruptors. As Count Kohary puts it in *The Devil's Saint*, "The devil's agent may be flesh and blood, surely?"[7]

The Crooked Hinge also draws, with reasonable subtlety, on both Bulwer Lytton's *The Haunters and the Haunted* and Robert Southey's poem "The Battle of Blenheim"—the latter not named outright, but conjured through an allusion. The reader need not be familiar with either of these—nothing is lost—but for the reader who does know either or both, Carr quietly delivers some extra, shivering delight through their resonance with his novel.

That barely any of its occult ancestry is disguised makes *The Crooked Hinge* kin to *The Burning Court*; indeed, readers of both novels, keeping in mind the novels' similar reliance on the question of witchcraft and their double-surprise endings, each with a change of narrative voice in its final chapter disclosing the final twist, might reasonably interpret *The Crooked Hinge*, in part, as Carr's "penance" for the shock and controversy of *The Burning Court*. It is as if, at one level, Carr desired to remake *The Burning Court*—not with the same plot, but with similar premises and tensions—and then put these safely back into the box of convention, the box bounded by his readers' expectations of the detective fiction genre. To be clear, there is no record of any sort suggesting this was Carr's conscious intention—but it is a tempting reading.

The Sleeping Sphinx resembles the "The Haunting of Tarnboys" most pointedly because, as in the early story, Carr leaves unacknowledged the novel's most striking inspiration: a treatise on the occult. While an apparent ghostly procession after midnight through the great hall of an ancestral manse does figure among the conundrums of *The Sleeping*

---

the world has existed, of external appearances is secondary, when one thinks about it; the Demon has no need to manifest human or bestial features to reveal his presence; it is enough, to assert himself, for him to take residence in souls he agitates and incites to inexplicable crimes."

7 Published in the collection *The Dead Sleep Lightly*, Doubleday & Company, p. 49.

Sphinx, the supernatural is not a looming menace in the book's plot. Instead, the novel's urgent puzzle is the mysterious death of a woman, Margot Devereux Marsh—and whether the cause was natural, suicide, or murder, no one suggests it was otherworldly.

Because *The Sleeping Sphinx* is a novel of human agency, Carr builds upon its hidden mystical underpinning in a different way than in *The Burning Court* and *The Crooked Hinge*: he fashion's the novel's title, also its most striking image, from occult lore. Within the narrative, the title *The Sleeping Sphinx* derives from a gnomic description of a signet ring that belonged to Prince Metternich of Austria. Before Carr reveals this connection, Margot's sister, Celia Devereux (p. 52), half summons it, muttering as if spellbound while a bit of sand pours between her fingers: "The sand, the lock, and the sleeping sphinx!"

Later, the reader and Sir Donald Holden, her lover and the novel's perspective character, learn what Celia meant. Dr. Fell happened absent-mindedly to have the ring with him when Margot Marsh was entombed; the doctor opportunistically used it to emboss the plasticine seal of her locked crypt. He explains:

> "The ring, Inspector, was cut for Prince Metternich of Aus-
> tria. You may take my word for it, or Professor Westbury's,
> that there isn't another like it in existence....It was designed,
> during the days of Metternich's Black Cabinet, so that the
> impression of the seal couldn't be copied or forged or replaced
> once it had been stamped on a soft surface." (p. 141)

In the novel's central impossibility, inside that sealed vault, the heavy coffins have been lifted and flung about, and a bottle of poison that may have killed Margot left inside the tomb—all without leaving a single footprint in the sand scattered across the floor at the time the crypt was sealed.

Carr describes the signet in full detail, as recorded on a bronze plaque that Donald Holden discovers at a crime scene:

> Here is a sleeping sphinx. She is dreaming of the *Parabrahm*,
> of the universe and the destiny of man. She is part human,
> as representing the higher principle, and part beast, as rep-
> resenting the lower. She also symbolizes the two selves: the
> outer self which all the world may see, and the inner self
> which may be known to few. (p. 206)

In cold editorial daylight, Carr's sudden incorporation of Hinduism is incongruent. *The Sleeping Sphinx* does not otherwise reflect or discuss that faith; no character in the novel practices Hinduism; nor is there any connection between the crime scene and Professor Westbury, the collector and authority from whom Dr. Fell accidentally borrows Metternich's signet.

According to his earned reputation, John Dickson Carr is an author on whom readers rely to leave no unanswered puzzles, no loose threads. So what is happening here? It is this: Carr found one of his readings, which describes a system of mysticism, so compelling, and its central image so engaging, that he determined to borrow its core concept for one of his own novels. The reader is simply witnessing the same adolescent enthusiasm, two decades later, as that which provided Zagoraldus his spells in "The Haunting of Tarnboys."

For Dr. Fell's adventure, the inspirational source is Franz Hartmann's 1904 occult volume *Magic, Black and White*. The book bears a frontispiece, reproduced below, and a description explaining it on the facing page.

DESCRIPTION OF THE FRONTISPIECE.

AT the foot of the picture is a sleeping Sphinx, whose upper part (representing the higher principles) is human; while the lower parts (symbolizing the lower principles) are of an animal nature. She is dreaming of the solution of the great problem of the construction of the Universe and of the

nature and destiny of Man, and her dream takes the shape
of the figure above her, representing the Macrocosm and the
Microcosm and their mutual interaction.[8]

It is interesting that Carr chooses to disguise his literary source, rather
than (as in his witchcraft novels) inventing an excuse to incorporate it.
Instead of using mysticism and Hinduism as elements in the novel, Carr
invents a signet for Prince Metternich of Austria—who is also otherwise unrelated to the novel's action and circumstances (in contrast, say,
to the historical figures closely incorporated into background and plot
of *The Burning Court*). Had Prince Metternich possessed a signet, convention suggests it would have been in the form of the Prince's coat of
arms, reproduced below...

...but Carr's invented signet does not. What this demonstrates to
us is that Carr's fascination with Hartmann's frontispiece and its mystic
implications was so strong that he desired to borrow it, almost without
modification, as the governing metaphor and titular inspiration for his
own novel. (Carr's addition of the outer and inner, hidden, selves, is
generic, but nonetheless appropriate to *The Sleeping Sphinx* and to mystery novels generally.)

Carr's impulses in *The Sleeping Sphinx* do not lack context. As noted,

---

8 *Magic, Black and White*, Theosophical Society (1904), p. 4.

it begins in 1927 with "The Haunting of Tarnboys," but even as a professional novelist, Carr had relatively recently—and successfully—invented an artifact that once belonged to a famous figure, Napoleon, and which figured eponymously in a contemporary detective novel: *The Emperor's Snuff-Box*. Nor is Carr's transformation of his source for *The Sleeping Sphinx*, Hartmann, either surprising or "dishonest": this sort of appropriation is the regular work of fiction, after all, and it is a defining characteristic of Carr in particular, one he evidences across different media. For his radio dramas, Carr notably borrows (and during this same period) the titles and plot elements of some of his well-known predecessors and literary models: Poe, Robert Louis Stevenson, Melville Davisson Post, Conan Doyle, G.K. Chesterton, and (as in *The Crooked Hinge*) Ambrose Bierce. So while *The Sleeping Sphinx* in its own peculiar way fascinates with its appropriation, it is, despite its unusual and obscure occult inspiration, consistent with Carr's usual approach.

The reader can even recognize in Carr's synthesis of mysticism and fiction the literary epistemology he inherited from James Branch Cabell and mainstream Romanticism generally. In Cabell's key literary-critical work, *Beyond Life,* which had great influence upon Carr, Cabell summarizes the intensity of the intersection between faith, mysticism, and literature:

> And it is this will that stirs in us to have the creatures of earth and the affairs of earth, not as they are, but "as they ought to be," which we call romance. But when we note how visibly it sways all life we perceive that we are talking about God.[9]

---

9 *Beyond Life*, Robert M. McBride and Company, 1924, p. 358.

The Ruby of
Rameses (1921)

I

The mysterious voice of the night wind wailed its melancholy dirge through the dark, somber aisles of the woodland. The gaunt, nude oaks of the manor park scintillated coldly in their winter raiment; while, rising above the outlying fringe of trees like a rugged gray wall of the world, the bleak, snow-shrouded ramparts of Dartmoor loomed somber and still in the pallid moonlight. Outlined in silhouette against the slate-hued sky, a high, narrow tower reared its arrogant head above the distant trees. Scattered lights winked mockingly down from its small, slit-like windows, as though derisive of the few snowflakes which had already begun to swirl lazily earthward in the van of the approaching storm.

Truly it was as entrancing a nocturne as might well be found—but to this I was oblivious. With benumbed fingers I drew the heavy lap-robe closer about me and strove vainly to shield my face from the merciless blast. Its sharp, biting gusts cut through robe and great-coat like the thrusts of a knife; the very wagonette itself creaked plaintively as it wound slowly up the wooded ascent to Pollard Hall. My guide, his bent, angular figure perched on the driver's seat like that of some gaunt scarecrow, alone refused to bow to the fury of the gale. The moon had already disappeared; the wind shrieked its shrill complaint through the cowering trees until the very forest resounded with its wild halloo; and the careening snowflakes swirled and eddied about our light four-wheeler like sentient creatures of the storm; but still that attenuated form remained immobile. Taciturn, lantern-jawed, flint-visaged, his entire attention was devoted to the road before us; ostensibly he minded neither the lash of the wind nor the whip-like sting of the relentless tempest. Not thus I. Buffeted into submission by the relentless tempest, I abstractedly watched the towering oaks flit past in panorama until Pollard Hall, its vague outline dimly discernible through the snow's white sheen, loomed in sight. Without a word my uncommunicative guide reined in the horses, sprang down from his seat, and assisted me to alight. Relievedly stretching my cramped muscles, I descended from the wagonette and followed him over the antiquated causeway before which the convey-ance had been drawn up.

Below us the frozen moat glistened beneath its light coating of snow; while on either side of the causeway the cheerless gray walls of the ancient manor-house towered menacingly above our heads, as though resenting our intrusion into precincts so sacred. Elaborate in their very simplicity, venerable even in the lifeless solitude of the surrounding park, those hoary walls, on which the dread scythe of time had left its ineffaceable scar, impressed me with an indefinable sense of awe. In their presence I found it difficult to believe that, as the hand of man had wrought that mighty pile, so might the hand of man destroy it.

Now was no time, however, for idle speculation. In response to my guide's knock the ponderous jaws of the massive bronze double-doors confronting us swung slowly inward, revealing in the aperture the wizened, time-seasoned countenance of a woman whose gnarled figure and deep-set, beady eyes, as curiously fascinating as those of a rattler, reminded me, singularly enough, of one of the witches in *Macbeth*. The disfiguring seam of a contracted scar, extending from brow to chin like a devil's brand on her evil yet finely molded visage, completed the likeness. I half expected her severely plain gown of black silk to resolve itself into a hooded cloak; her candle into a crummock;[1] and the hallway behind her into a wild, desolate heath.

"You, Alloway?" she queried in a dry, rasping voice that was again reminiscent of the weird sisters. "And Mr. Radbourne? Ah, yes. Come in."

Doing as I was bid, I found myself in a long, dimly illuminated corridor, luxuriously, even sumptuously, furnished in the fashion of a bygone day.

"The master's awaiting you, sir," continued the woman in her irritating voice. "If you'll step this way...?"

I nodded my assent, and turning, she hobbled laboriously off. My erstwhile guide having silently effaced himself, I followed her down the hallway, rich in its moldering tapestries but funereal in its huge, grotesquely carven chairs, ranged with mathematical precision against the walls, and ascended the square-cut, heavily-balustraded staircase at its farther end. Flight after flight she plodded slowly up, and I myself was beginning to tire when she at length turned into a high, vaulted passage on what I judged was the topmost floor. With the end of my wearisome journey apparently in sight, I breathed a fervent prayer of relief—but no! there was yet another stage to the ordeal. Throwing open a heavy, bolt-studded door at the farther end of the hall, she bade me enter. For a moment I hesitated on the threshold; then, as the feeble light of her candle penetrated the Stygian gloom beyond, I saw that before me a flight of roughly hewn stone steps wound upward into darkness.

---

1   A crummock is any small, crooked item.

"This way," she repeated patiently. "Come."

Without further ado she seized my arm and drew me after her into the enclosed stairwell. Reluctantly I permitted myself to be led up the precariously rough steps. The affair, I told myself, was beginning to verge on the bizarre; and when a stray gust of wind blew the door to below us with a hollow bang that echoed and reechoed eerily through the silent house, I could not repress an involuntary start. The murmur of the tempest had increased to an angry roar— the blank walls which flanked the staircase were evidently those of a tower—yet higher, ever higher, we ascended.

At length, however, the stairs terminated in a landing on which opened several doors. To the largest of these my conductor vigorously applied her bony knuckles, across which, I noticed, ran another inflamed scar, and, in response to her knock, there issued from within the soft rustle of slippered footsteps and the short, sharp click of a drawn bolt. With a querulous creak the door swung open, revealing to my startled gaze the face of a man who seemed at best no more than some fantastic figure from the dream of an opium-addict. His countenance was not unlike a grotesque mask; withered, yellow, furrow-fretted, his shrunken flesh reminded me of fine parchment drawn skin-tight over the features of a Laocoon.[2] From between their slanting, wrinkled lids his eyes, green and glittering as the emerald, peered out like twin jewels; that unknown something which had bent his bony shoulders and wasted him away to a mere pitiful parody of a man had alone failed to quench the smoldering fire of those terrible eyes. Brandon Pollard—for in him I recognized my one-time Oxford classmate—was clad in a dressing gown of faded blue silk, and clamped between his slender, drug-yellowed fingers a cigarette emitted a feverish glow. As I advanced into the room his thin lips writhed in a grimace no doubt intended for a smile of welcome.

"You, Rad?" he queried.

Aghast at the apparition thus disclosed, I stood for a moment like one stunned. Then with a muttered expletive I sprang forward, and, seizing him by the shoulders, swung him about to the light.

"Pollard!" I cried, my words tumbling over themselves in my amazement. "Brandon Pollard! It's not—it can't be—you!"

Wearily he nodded.

---

2 Laocoon was a Trojan priest who tried to convince the city's residents to burn the Trojan horse. In response, Athena blinded him; then giant serpents the goddess sent following his continued protestations strangled Laocoon and his sons. (In other versions of his story, the serpents were sent by Poseidon or Apollo for transgressions against them.)

"The years have used me sorely, Rad," he replied, that twisted smile again contorting his lips. "But you, old friend—you've changed little since I saw you last."

"Five years since," I reminded him. "Five long years—and never a line from you until today. Why—where—"

"Sit down, Rad," he interposed quietly; "sit down, and let me tell you a story."

Wonderingly I obeyed. With a gesture of dismissal to the woman, Pollard threw himself into a chair opposite my own and sat for a moment staring meditatively into the cheery blaze which roared and crackled in the broad-throated fireplace. Stifling as best I might the thousand queries which leaped of their own accord to my lips, I watched him in fascinated silence.

"Mine is a strange, wild story, Rad," he began, "and I had best commence with the origin of it all.

"Three thousand years ago, a Pharoah of Egypt—Rameses I, I believe—possessed, among other precious stones, a ruby which even yet stands unparalleled in magnificence among jewels of its kind. The gem grew to be a veritable monomania with him; he fairly worshipped its lustrous beauty and on state occasions wore it set in a golden circlet about his head. But even kings, in spite of their 'divine right,' are not immortal, and in time Rameses I was laid to rest in the great pyramid which he had built as his sepulcher. With his last breath he requested that his cherished ruby might accompany him to the tomb, and, in accordance with his wish, the circlet containing the gem was put with him into the sarcophagus. Thus the stone which had once graced the brow of a pharaoh was relegated to the dark recesses of its owner's crypt, and ere long the 'Fire Ruby of Rameses,' ceased to exist in the memory of man.

"Several thousand years later there arose in Egypt a religious fanatic who, by his own statement, had come to teach his fellow-men the gospel of the 'true God.' Despite the radical unsoundness of his ideas his adherents were many, and for centuries after his death the cult which he had instituted flourished. To further devotional zeal the sarcophagus of Rameses I—who, incidentally, was the object of the organization's worship—was taken from its niche and removed to a hidden temple which Ahrida—the present 'high priest'—had caused to be made in the Ramesian pyramid itself. It was, therefore, only through accident that some five years since one of a party of archaeologists touring the pyramid who, having strayed away from his companions, had lost himself in the labyrinth of passages which honeycomb such edifices, stumbled on the temple's well concealed entrance. Being of mercenary nature, he did not hesitate to despoil the altar of its costly ornaments, and, on removing the cloths which swathed the mummified body of Egypt's former ruler, came upon the long-lost Fire Ruby. Not knowing how best to dispose of his find, he communicated with his colleagues, who, dazzled by the sum which a sale of the gem would undoubtedly net them, colluded to smuggle it into England. This they accomplished without a great deal of difficulty, but no sooner had their vessel docked at Liverpool than they knew that in the meantime the high priest of Rameses had not been idle. Several attempts were made to purloin the stone, but, possessing as a whole that rarest of traits, honor among thieves, they contrived to retain their find.[3]

"At this time I was a third-form Oxford man—your roommate, you'll remember—and, incidentally, in debt to the amount of five hundred pounds. Heaven knows how it came about, but somehow this devil incarnate of a high priest got wind of my predicament and approached me with a proposition. A thousand pounds cash, he said, would be paid me if I secured him the jewel. Ahrida was no fancifully-garbed Egyptian such as novelists are fond of depicting, but a suave, polished gentleman, whose personal attire was always immaculate and who, but for the peculiar formation of his features, might have been mistaken for a dark-skinned Englishman. He was, however, known to the archaeologists; in view of which fact any attempt on his part to regain the ruby through strategic means would prove worse than useless. Hence his proposal. That I should yield to his persuasion was inevitable; it was the one way out of my difficulties, and I seized it with avidity.

"I needn't go into detail regarding the manner in which I secured the stone; an intimate acquaintance with the archaeologist to whose care it had been entrusted; a plan of his house; a venture in the dark; and all was over. And now I come to that part of my narrative in which fate, the fabled Imp of the Perverse, or the Fire Ruby itself took a hand. When, in the seclusion of my own room, I brought out that flashing bauble to examine it, a strange, compelling madness seized my soul. To possess the Fire Ruby suddenly became the one passion of my life. I was enthralled—captivated by its sinister beauty—even as Rameses must have been—and at last—at last"—slowly Pollard's shoulders had drooped, and, the climax of his extraordinary recital reached, a sob tore

---

3 Carr is characteristically borrowing a plot device, but here more overtly than he would later. The young author is imitating the premise of Wilkie Collins' *The Moonstone* (1868), one of the earliest English detective-fiction novels.

its way from his throat and with a shudder he buried his face in his hands— "God forgive me. I fled to America with the accursed stone!"

For a moment after this startling disclosure had been made, absolute silence reigned in the room. The crackle of the flames seemed hushed; the very gale without the tower stilled. Then with a dogged air Pollard raised his head.

"Since then," he resumed, "I have lived the life of a hunted animal. Ahrida, I knew, would hound me to the ends of the earth to regain his diabolic ruby; but this time it would be no mere case of theft. His twisted brain was bent on vengeance—a vengeance that would not be satiated until I lay dead at his feet. I'll not dwell on the mental hell I endured throughout four long, bitter years—the black dread that shriveled my very soul—the tortures worse, a thousand times worse, than those of the fanatic Inquisition, I underwent beneath the white-hot irons of fear. My life became a constant source of dread; and little by little I wasted away to the pitiful wreck I am now. Several times I all but gave up and sought solace in the Hudson's dark oblivion, but somehow I—I couldn't make up my mind to part with life in such a cowardly manner. Like a ghoul I prowled the streets of New York when decent, law-abiding citizens were abed; by day I sought my miserable retreat and there remained until the merciful curtain of dark had fallen once more. But everywhere I saw HIS hated face, and several times his steel all but found my heart. When at last I plucked up sufficient courage—and funds—to return to England, HE followed me. That's why I summoned you here. Perhaps between us we can stave him off until—until the Fire Ruby claims its own at last."

"You still have the jewel?"

"Look!" With a lightning-like movement Pollard whipped out a folded handkerchief and as swiftly unrolled it. In the palm of his hand glittered a single huge, blood-red ruby whose brilliance fairly dazzled my eyes. Yet above all I was conscious of its evil charm, and with a shudder I motioned him to put it up.

"And now, Rad," he concluded, returning handkerchief and gem to his pocket, "you've heard enough for one night. I'll have Alloway show you to your room."

"But, Pollard," I protested, "I—"

"No 'buts,' please," he interrupted firmly; "I really must insist."

Despite my protests Alloway was summoned and ere long the door of the tower room closed behind me; I heard the rattling click of its bolt; and the next instant I was alone on the landing with my inscrutable guide. Full of my own thoughts—not least among them the problematical cause of my friend's abrupt change from garrulousness to taciturnity—

I tramped slowly down the steps behind him. We had reached the first turn of the staircase when, of a sudden, the silence of the night was split by that which caused me to bring myself sharply erect with a sibilant intake of my breath—the short, staccato bark of a pistol.

For a moment I stood as though turned to stone. Then, as I saw Alloway spin round and dash up the stairs ahead of me, I too was galvanized into life. With a bound I was after him, and together we gained the landing, the same thought, I dare say, uppermost in our minds.

"Break down the door!" I ordered tersely; "break it down, in heaven's name!"

Obediently he drew back a few feet, flexed his muscles for a spring, and hurtled forward like the human juggernaut he was. With a splintering crash the door yielded to his onslaught, precipitating him into the room on its top. One glance into the spacious, vaulted apartment sufficed to tell that my worst fears had been realized. Slumped forward on the floor beside his chair was the still figure of Brandon Pollard, his muscles curiously lax, his eyes wide open in a fixed, unseeing stare. Shaking off the momentary dizziness which assailed me, I sprang across the room, thrust an arm beneath the recumbent figure, and seized one already clammy wrist. Well I knew, however, what I should find. Beneath the dim stain on the shoulder of that time worn dressing-gown there was a new, fresh one. The heart that lay beneath it was at peace.

II

Long and deeply I gazed into the glowing embers of the dying fire on the hearth. The cold, gray dawn was stealing in at the windows, yet still I lingered before the fire, a thousand unanswerable questions befogging my brain. The crashing suddenness of the tragedy had left me well-nigh stunned; but above the turmoil of my thoughts one query rang through my mind with a dull, throbbing insistence. When Alloway and I had broken into the room, I recalled, the door had been bolted on the inside. Our subsequent search of the great, bare apartment had yielded us but one discovery—the paradoxical fact that the room's lone window had likewise been locked—on the inside. Both the servant and I would be prepared to swear that no one had passed us on the staircase, and to gain entrance through the locked door was, moreover, manifestly impossible. The same rule could be applied to the window—a narrow, arched affair, possessing a single thick, leaded pane whose two catches we found on inspection to be intact. There was, moreover, absolutely no secret means of ingress or egress, as an exhaustive search of the walls, the floor, and even the ceiling had convinced me. How, then, had the assassin been able to enter and leave a locked room? That was the question which racked my soul.

But even that was merely one query among many. My benumbed senses still failed to grasp the significance of the weird tale which had been unfolded to me by lips forever stilled. That a man in this enlightened twentieth century of ours could be menaced by such deadly, never-ceasing danger I found difficult to believe. Yet—there was proof. Suicide I refused to consider as a possible solution of the enigma; even if Pollard were minded to take his own life the mere fact that no weapon could be found near the scene of the crime in itself precluded the theory of self-destruction. Yet in opposition to the murder hypothesis stood the incontrovertible evidence of the locked room—a room whose very chimney flue was less than two inches wide, and whose walls possessed not even so much as the smallest crack through which the assassin might have fired. It was all a puzzle; the most intricate, baffling puzzle I had ever encountered. As I thus soliloquized, there came from behind me:

"Mr. Radbourne?"

Low, dulcet, imperious, the words rang out like the soft, clear notes of a bell, and, turning I beheld that which caused me to give vent to a gasp of astonishment. Framed in the doorway, her slim, petite figure muffled in a dark cloak, stood a girl whose like I have never seen, before or since. Her glossy hair, hung free about her shoulders like that of some wild creature of the forest, framed like a sable cloud the white, alabaster oval of her face. Her dark eyes blazed like illuminated jade; her lips were set in a firm crimson slit, from between which her words hissed sibilantly; and there was about her a vague, exotic perfume, hauntingly reminiscent of the bazaars and shops of Cairo. With a blank, uncomprehending stare I regarded her as she slowly advanced into the room. At length, however, I aroused myself sufficiently to reply to her query in the affirmative.

"Ah," she commented with a faint yet perceptible foreign accent; "that is well. I've come to give you—this."

With a quick, snake-like movement she drew from the pocket of her cloak a glittering something which flashed fire in the candlelight, and, hurling it at my feet, swung round and sped for the door. It needed no second glance to tell me that the Fire Ruby itself lay before me; and with a hot rush of anger and chagrin I realized that I had entirely overlooked the possibility that the jewel might have been stolen. Awaking to the exigencies of the situation, I was after her like a shot; and, as I sped down the tower stairs in the wake of her flying figure, I saw her turn; caught the gleam of metal in her hand; heard the venomous crack of a revolver; and felt the sting of innumerable powder-grains as a bullet sang past my cheek and buried itself harmlessly in the wall behind. Pausing no more lest I overtake her, she sped on, and presently I saw her fling open the lowest door, flash into the corridor, and skim down its length like a hare that has heard the whine of the hunter's bullet. Throwing open a door on the staircase landing, she dove within; I heard the protesting screech of a bolt and the next instant found myself alone in the long dimly illuminated hallway.

"Open this door!" I enjoined sharply, vigorously applying my knuckles to it. "Quick, now before I break it down!"

Receiving no answer, I resolutely backed away a few feet and with a sudden rush carried the door from its hinges. The great, bare room thus revealed was almost entirely devoid of furniture; a rush-light burned dimly in the empty fireplace, and in its wan illumination I saw that, despite the fact that there was no closet of any kind in which the fugitive might have taken refuge, the chamber was empty. The mystery girl had entirely disappeared!

III

"What say you, Lamar?" Coroner McAllister turned to the last-named individual, a tall, dark young man whose delicate, sensitive face bore the scars of a skillfully healed wound. Obviously in his twenties, he held himself with an erect military air, the Croix-de-Guerre on his lapel attesting the gallantry that had cost him his sight. And now, at the question, he bowed slightly, smiled, and turned his soft, blind brown eyes instinctively in the direction of the speaker.

"A very pretty little problem, monsieur," he responded in his grave, courtly voice, "but not in the least a difficult one."

"You think not?" My sarcasm was but thinly veiled. "Perhaps, then, you can explain how the murderer was able to make his exit from a locked room?"

"I can, monsieur," was his calm reply.

"Indeed! Quite an unusual achievement for a bli—" Abruptly I paused, a trifle ashamed of my own bluntness.

"Perhaps so," he acknowledged quietly; "but we blind men have eyes in our ears—our noses—our fingertips. In my profession, monsieur, sight is a handicap."

"Your profession?"

"But yes, monsieur; I am a detective."

His calm, matter-of-fact statement not only startled me, but aroused my ire as well.

"Then suppose you give us your explanation," I suggested—a trifle roughly, I fear.

"If you desire it—yes." Lieutenant Rene Lamar, late of the French air service, bowed slightly. "Will you please to send for one of the policemen who wait downstairs?"

Taking my assenting nod, the wondering Alloway left in search of the official in question, to return presently to the room of tragic memories with a 'Bobbie' in tow, the latter closely followed by the curious-minded woman servant, Marie.

"In the first place," began Lamar, "there is in our midst one of the most notorious woman crooks in England. She came here in quest of the Fire Ruby, and—and—Take it off, Jeanne Darin, take it off!" shot out abruptly. With a bound he had reached the door, seized the woman Marie in his powerful grip, and dragged her into the room. With a quick movement he passed a hand across her face, and there came off to his touch—A MASK OF PAINTED WAX! Before us stood revealed the mystery girl herself, gazing defiantly about the dumfounded group.

"She did not know that Pollard was subject to a disease known in medical annals as Insanitas Diaboli," continued Lamar inexorably—an ailment which manifests itself in a disorder of the mind as well as of the body. She did not know that he was, therefore, insane—that the whole story of the Egyptian fanatic was a myth, and the ruby itself—paste! However, when she stole the jewel after he had been shot, she learned the truth, and in a spirit of bravado returned it. She had nothing to do with the matter of the murder, but the assassin himself is here—in this room!" Slowly, inexorably, he raised a denouncing finger. "You needn't attempt to deny it; the brand of Cain is on you—Alloway!"

Harshly Alloway laughed, as though he had sensed the coming accusation all along. "If I killed him," he returned equably, "how did I get into the room?"

"Easily. The shot you and Mr. Radbourne heard was a plant! When that shot was fired Pollard was alive; but, in the instant you fell into the room on the top of the door which you had broken down, you fired through your pocket, using a Maxim silencer to still the report of the pistol. You had but one second in which to accomplish your design, but that second was enough. Pollard was instantly killed."

"But how," I put in quickly, "did you know?"

"That I will explain. The scar across Jeanne Darin's knuckles gives her away; my finger-tip eyes saw it when she led me to this room and I knew her for what she was. Obviously she was masked for a purpose—which could be no other than that of securing the ruby. After all her labor, however, she returned it. Consequently there must have been something wrong with the stone—something that made it worthless. When I learned from the coroner that Pollard's eyes were an unusual shade of beryl, I knew the fact for a symptom of Insanitas Diaboli, and an explanation forthwith presented itself. As regards the real murderer, the wound made by the bullet slanted obliquely upward. Pollard could not have been shot from the floor; and there were no indications of a struggle; inference: that he had been killed by someone who fired while falling, either purposely or unintentionally. Alloway was the only person whom we knew to fall; and, since no one else could have committed the crime, he was guilty. No doubt he, too, sought to gain the ruby for himself. In connection with the girl's escape from the room, I imagine that instead of entering the apartment itself, she went into a secret passage opening into the corridor side by side with the door. Hoping to deceive you, she slammed the latter shut, and its slanting bolt, disturbed by the jar, slid into place. She—here! What are you doing?" Swiftly he turned on Alloway, who up to this time had stood without a sign of life. The servant had suddenly jerked his hand free of Lamar's restraining grip; I saw him convey a small, grayish pellet to his mouth, and the next instant he sank exhausted into a chair, his thin lips contriving to articulate:

"I did—what I did. It's too late for an antidote now!"

Notes for the Curious: "The Ruby of Rameses"

"The Ruby of Rameses" is included in this collection for practical reasons: not only is it John Dickson Carr's first-ever short story, written in the waning month before his fifteenth birthday, but with the publication of this collection, by including both it and "E'en Though It Be a Cross" (in the chapbook accompanying the limited edition), the editor completes, after nearly half a century, the project begun with Douglas Greene's posthumous Carr collection *The Door to Doom*. All surviving works from Carr's apprenticeship period have finally reached professional print, readily available to lovers of Carr—none of whom, understandably, would forgive the editor (whose two volumes have focused on Carr's juvenilia) for omitting—of all things—Carr's fledgling effort, and a detective tale at that.

While Carr's first story is by definition his most immature effort, admittedly demonstrating many of the weaknesses expected of any teen-aged author, the story nonetheless presents some features of interest, including characteristic Carrian themes and techniques, which the mature Carr employs so skillfully to the gratification of five generations of readers.

Before noting them, let us first confess and forgive the tale's short-comings: as it remains in Carr's second story ("The House of Terror"), the language of "The Ruby of Rameses," is somewhat overwrought, notably and a little clumsily imitative of Edgar Allan Poe—as is the story's premise. Surely, the opening of "The Ruby of Rameses" calls to the reader's mind Poe's "The Fall of the House of Usher." In any event, our tyro's language delivers almost no noun without an adjective, if not two, and no verb without an adverb.

While his effort is conscious and vigorous, the young Carr, in "The Ruby of Rameses," is anything but the reliable practitioner of the pathetic fallacy he would become within five years, and a master within ten.[4]

---

4 "Pathetic fallacy" is a term coined by John Ruskin in the third volume of his study *Modern Painters*, published in 1856. In Chapter XII, Ruskin defines pathetic fallacy as the boundary "between the ordinary, proper, and true appearances of things to us; and the extraordinary, or false appearances, when we are under the influence of emotion, or contemplative fancy....[a] state of mind which attributes to it [nature] these characters of a living creature." Ruskin uses some lines by Alton Lock as an example: "They rowed her in across the rolling foam—/The cruel, crawling foam," and avers that the foam is neither cruel nor crawling. He initially intends the term to be pejorative, but Ruskin acknowledges that when this type of personification is both beautiful and emotionally true, it is the work of a poet of the first order. "Now so long as we see that the feeling is

Much of the success of Carr's gothic and supernatural atmospherics in his later works depends upon, successfully, the echoes of fright and menace between the minds of their characters and the dark settings in which they find themselves. In "The Ruby of Rameses," we see that Carr has already learned the importance of this, even if his execution of it here is not fully successful. Later, of course, Carr would potently collapse the boundaries between the ordinary appearances of things and how they seem under the influence of emotion, whether or not he fully endowed nature in any given instance with the qualities of a living thing. In *The Unicorn Murders*, for instance, Carr regularly and with sufficient subtlety echoes in the landscape, particularly the sky, the dispositions of the characters, whether it is the opportune flickering of lightning underlying the tensions of the moment or the relative light and color of the sky, seemingly a projection of that moment's dominant mood.

Carr's most celebrated use of the pathetic fallacy appears in *The Problem of the Wire Cage*. which in its opening immediately establishes parallels between the weather and those underneath it: "Possibly because the day was sultry, emotions were growing sultry too" (p. 1). The sky grows darker (p. 32) as persons' expressions do, and the air stirs with faint lightning, but no thunder clap (p. 34) as confrontation threatens to flash out, as well. Then, "Nerves and heat had been strung to too high a pitch on the earth. A balance tilted; a decision was made" (p. 39). Shortly thereafter, "the sky burst across and the storm tore down" as "the first deluge struck"—both meteorological and interpersonal.

Carr's most notorious use of the sympathy between landscape and psychological tone is the opening of *Till Death Do Us Part*. As does *The Problem of the Wire Cage*, it begins with an overt connection between the storminess of the sky and among the denizens of the village of Six Ashes. The first sentence links them:

> Thinking the matter over afterwards, Dick Markham might
> have seen omens or portents in the summer thunderstorm, in
> the fortuneteller's tent, in the shooting range, in half a dozen
> other things at that bazaar. (p. 1)

---

true, we pardon, or are even pleased by, the confessed fallacy of sight which it induces." Literary readers have preserved Ruskin's phrase because it is useful, but without the presumption of defect: as with other literary devices, the pathetic fallacy can be used either well or badly.

The menacing suggestions of weather continue to grow, as effectively written as in *The Problem of the Wire Cage*, until:

> It was partly the brief glare of lightning, illuminating the whole grounds with a deathly pallor, and followed by a shock of thunder striking close. Lightning picked out every detail as though in the flash of a photograph. (p. 16)

"The Ruby of Rameses" is more than a precursor, though, of Carrian imagery (generally better done) to follow in his later fiction. The story also suggests the inevitability of Henri Bencolin, Carr's first series detective, conceived five years after Lieutenant Rene Lamar. Bencolin is a fitter detective for Carr to develop and explore than Lamar. As multiple readers have noted, Lamar is too obviously inspired by Max Carrados, Ernest Bramah's blind detective, whose adventures were published between 1914–1935, and by Thornley Colton, Clinton H. Stagg's blind detective. Colton, who solves impossible crimes, appeared a year earlier than Carrados. Unfortunately, that detective's career, and his author's, were cut short when Stagg, only 27, perished in a 1916 automobile accident. It is of course possible, as Greene notes (p. 24) that Lamar, by being French, also follows in the tradition of the very first fictional detective, Poe's Auguste Dupin.

With Bencolin, in many ways a second and more successful draft upon Lamar, Carr discards the detective's blindness (a difficult device for a young writer to manage, after all) but retains from his two earliest detective tales the atmosphere of the macabre, the seemingly impossible circumstances, and the detective's opposing ratiocination. This formula becomes the basis of Carr's success not only with Bencolin, but in stand-alone novels and the early adventures of Dr. Fell and H.M., throughout the late 1930s—which Carr still uses from time to time afterward.

Although Carr would also move on from Bencolin, fussing, "I can't do anything with the damned detective! He's unreal, he's lifeless, he's a dummy,"[5] Carr was not finished with French detectives. *The Unicorn Murders* features a showdown between Chief Inspector Gasquet of the Sûreté, France's greatest detective, and Flamande, its greatest criminal. Both are masters of disguise. The winner? Sir Henry Merrivale, Carr's recently invented series detective, who outwits both. Some readers (including the editor) take Gasquet to be a stand-in for Bencolin, signifying a changing of the guard between Carr's first series detective and his newest.

The premise of *The Unicorn Murders* is borrowed from G.K. Ches-

---

5 Quoted by Greene (no source specified), p. 149.

terton's first Father Brown story, "The Blue Cross," in which the little priest bests Flambeau, a super criminal pursued by the head of the Paris Police, Aristide Valentin. Flambeau, always incognito, is famed for never having been identified...but little Father Brown sees through him. As to Aristide Valentin, when one considers Chesterton's description of him, one readily perceives points in which he served as an inspiration for Carr's Bencolin:

> Ruthless in the pursuit of criminals, he was very mild about their punishment. Since he had been supreme over French—and largely over European—political methods, his great influence had been honourably used for the mitigation of sentences and the purification of prisons. He was one of the great humanitarian French freethinkers; and the only thing wrong with them is that they make mercy even colder than justice.[6]

The early Bencolin shows more of Valentin's ruthlessness and coldness, but in his 1937 curtain call, *The Four False Weapons*, Bencolin exhibits a side akin to his predecessor's humanitarianism.

Carr gives us another French police detective, the Prefect of the Police in La Bandelette, a certain Monsieur Goron. In 1939's short story "The Silver Curtain," he goes by the Christian name Jean, but three years later, in *The Emperor's Snuff-Box*, he is called Aristide—his middle name, perhaps? More likely, his name in the novel is a tribute to Chesterton's detective. By 1944, when Carr retells "The Silver Curtain" as the radio drama *Death Has Four Faces*, Goron is once again named Jean.

Four years later, Goron has an eccentric radio successor, "Papa" Bo, *juge d'instruction* in Marseilles, who repeatedly bangs his fly swatter like a gavel despite a complete absence of flies. Monsieur Bo investigates two murders in *The Nine Black Reasons*. Like Bencolin, Bo is called a "French Mephistopheles" because of his diabolical entrapment of a murderer.

A second French radio detective nicknamed Papa, Henri "Papa" Duchene of the Sûreté, comes to England without Scotland Yard's permission to arrest a serial killer in 1954's *White Tiger Passage*. Duchene enjoys reciting dirty limericks, loudly, in public places, and scrawling them where shocked patrons will discover them later.

---

6 G.K. Chesterton, "The Secret Garden," *The Complete Father Brown Stories*, Penguin Classics (2012), p. 19.

It seems that with every successive French detective Carr invents, he deprives each of a little more dignity.

As Greene notes (p. 24), Sax Rohmer's *Tales of Sacred Egypt* (1919) was probably a subject-matter influence on "The Ruby of Rameses," providing inspiration for its backstory. Likewise, Lamar's summation of the case as "a very pretty little problem" is clearly language Carr, again too tempted by his heroes, borrows from Arthur Conan Doyle and the detective, Sherlock Holmes. (See for instance "A Scandal in Bohemia" and "The Musgrave Ritual.")

That Carr in his earliest fiction is having trouble stretching it to express his individual brilliance is evident in the repetitive similarities between "The Ruby of Rameses" and his detective stories shortly following it. There is of course Carr's overuse of, and too much faith in it as the perfect murder weapon, the Maxim silencer, which reappears in "The Masked Bullet"—and which it is also clear the young author borrowed, strongly impressed by the device, from Arthur B. Reeves' "The Silent Bullet." (Greene is likely the first to publish this observation, on p. 17 of the biography.) Also peculiarly in common with "The Masked Bullet," there is the twinning of their endings, nearly word for word:

> I saw him convey a small, grayish pellet to his mouth,
> and the next instant he sank exhausted into a chair, his thin
> lips contriving to articulate:
> "I did—what I did. It's too late for an antidote now!"

Even with all this relative unoriginality and re-use of gimmicks and elements, the John Dickson Carr who would become one of the all-time great mystery writers, is already glimmering recognizably in "The Ruby of Rameses." Note, for instance, that Carr's fascination with masks and, and the uncanny terror they can induce—a motif throughout his career (see the introduction)—is already present. There is both Jeanne Darin's literal mask, of painted wax, which could in reality not possibly be either practical or sufficiently deceptive, and Pollard's metaphorical one: his countenance "not unlike a grotesque mask; withered, yellow, furrow-fretted, his shrunken flesh...drawn skin-tight."

In the centrality of masks' importance to the narrative, Carr here is perceptibly under the influence of Thomas and Mary Hanshew, in whose adventures of Cleek, "the Man of the Forty Faces" could assume the appearance of any other person at will. (See the introduction for additional comments on the Hanshews and Cleek.) Nonetheless, Carr's use of masks in "The Ruby of Rameses," if inspired by the Hanshews, is also thoroughly unlike them. In this we note another of Carr's writerly characteristics emerging promptly: his gift for borrowing a plot element, a technique, or a premise, but making it his own, and in his own style.

Likewise evident is Carr's ambitiousness: although "The Ruby of Rameses" is his first detective story—his first story at all—Carr gravitates immediately to challenging the reader with not merely one impossible circumstance, but two. The reader in this context can consider Carr's interview for the article "Two Authors in the Attic," published by *The New Yorker* in 1951. In the interview, Carr, a successful and bestselling mystery author for more than two decades, asserts, "The majority of detective writers usually rest on the one big surprise...but I prefer the double. It's more ingenious."[1] Even if the most unsympathetic of readers feels Carr completely fails to dazzle with his two impossibilities in "The Ruby of Rameses" (which would be perhaps too unkind an estimate), what a glorious first failure, all the same!

Also worth the reader's attention are the circumstances of Pollard's recruitment. Readers familiar with "The Legend of the Softest Lips," one of the tales in Carr's 1927 story cycle "The New Canterbury Tales," will spot the resemblance to how that story's protagonist, O'Riordan, stumbles into his own intrigue. With "The Ruby of Rameses," the reader first witnesses the importance of "fate, the fabled Imp of the Perverse" in Carr's narratives. Coincidence is an important recurring element in Carr, perhaps most memorably (and entertainingly) summarized, resentfully, by H.M. in *The Unicorn Murders* as "the blinkin' awful cussedness of things in general" (p. 167). While Carr had already come to appreciate the power of coincidence as a dramatic element through one of his favorite authors, Dickens, in Carr's works, consistently, it is the unlikely or coincidental event that singularly spurs on a crime, or confounds its appearance, making the crime seem impossible. (The editor offers no specific examples so as not to spoil the surprises or solutions of any of Carr's novels.)

Perhaps one cannot assess "The Ruby of Rameses" without complaining with some justice about its explanation, which relies upon the fictive malady, Insanitas Diaboli. Since this disease does not actually exist, Carr's reader can hardly anticipate it. The solution's exposition in this story is condensed, to say the least, and without being prepared with fair-play clues, is not especially satisfactory.

In 1936, fifteen years after writing this first detective story, and in one of the early great moments of his career, Carr would place his hand

---

1 Robert Lewis Taylor, "Two Authors in an Attic" (Part I), *The New Yorker*, September 8, 1951, p. 39.

upon "Eric the Skull" as the first American initiate (of only two ever!) into England's fabled Detection Club. He would take an oath that his detectives would "well and truly detect the crimes presented to them" and not to rely upon "Jiggery-Pokery" (among other specifically named cheats). Carr would make good on that vow, as he had already been doing for the better part of a decade.

It is easy to forgive the young Carr's first outing if it seems all in all a little unsatisfying to readers who cherish him for the consistent fairness and brilliance of his detective fiction, since there is enough indication in "The Ruby of Rameses" of the writer Carr would become. In this, the reader might also be reminded of the author's own look back at his younger self, in Carr's 1952 introduction to *Maiden Murders*, a collection of first-ever mystery tales by professional writers. In that essay, Carr describes every eager initiate's first foray into crime fiction:

> A new window had opened. A fiery new idea hummed in our heads. On the beach, say, lay a fine fresh corpse, strangled, with only its own footprints leading out across the damp waste of sand. We might not yet be able skillfully to maneuver with that corpse: no, not yet. But one fine day we would. One fine day, by thunder, we would succeed![2]

---

2 *Maiden Murders*, Harper & Brothers, 1952, p. xii.

The Other Hangman
(1935)

"Why do they electrocute 'em instead of hanging 'em in Pennsylvania? What" (said my old friend, Judge Murchison, dexterously hooking the spittoon closer with his foot) "do they teach you youngsters in these new-fangled law schools, anyway? That, son, was a murder case. It turned the Supreme Court's whiskers gray to find a final ruling, and for thirty years it's been argued about by lawyers in the back room of every saloon from here to the Pacific coast. It happened right here in this county—when they hanged Fred Joliffe for the murder of Randall Fraser.

"It was in '92 or '93; anyway, it was the year they put the first telephone in the courthouse, and you could talk as far as Pittsburg except when the wires blew down. Considering it was the county seat, we were mighty proud of our town (population 3,500). The hustlers were always bragging about how thriving and growing our town was, and we had just got to the point of enthusiasm where every ten years we were certain the census-taker must have forgotten half our population. Old Mark Sturgis, who owned the *Bugle Gazette* then, carried on something awful in an editorial when they printed in the almanac that we had a population of only 3,265. We were all pretty riled about it, naturally.

"We were proud of plenty of other things, too. We had good reason to brag about the McClellan House, which was the finest hotel in the county; and I mind when you could get room and board, with apple pie for breakfast every morning, for two dollars a week. We were proud of our old county families, that came over the mountains when Braddock's army was scalped by the Indians in seventeen fifty-five[1] and settled down in log huts to dry their wounds. But most of all we were proud of our legal batteries.

"Son, it was a grand assembly! Mind, I won't say that all of 'em were long on knowledge of the Statute Books; but they knew their Blackstone

---

[1] Early in the French and Indian War, British general Edward Braddock attempted to capture Fort Duquesne, near what is today Pittsburgh. Braddock's column was repulsed at the Battle of the Monongahela by a combined force of approximately 800 French and 600 native Americans. Along with more than 500 of his soldiers, Braddock himself was slain in the battle, possibly by friendly fire. Among the British side's survivors were a 23-year-old Lieutenant Colonel, George Washington, and a certain Carolinian militia teamster and blacksmith named Daniel Boone.

and their Greenleaf on Evidence, and they were powerful speakers. And there were some—the top-notchers—full of graces and book-knowledge and dignity, who were hell on the exact letter of the law. Scotch-Irish Presbyterians, all of us, who loved a good debate and a bottle o' whisky. There was Charley Connell, a Harvard graduate and the district attorney, who had fine white hands, and wore a fine high collar, and made such pathetic addresses to the jury that people flocked for miles around to hear him; though he generally lost his cases. There was Judge Hunt, who prided himself on his resemblance to Abe Lincoln, and in consequence always wore a frock coat and an elegant plug hat. Why, there was your own grandfather, who had over two hundred books in his library, and people used to go up nights to borrow volumes of the encyclopedia.

"You know the big stone courthouse at the top of the street, with the flowers round it, and the jail adjoining? People went there as they'd go to a picture-show nowadays; it was a lot better, too. Well, from there it was only two minutes' walk across the meadow to Jim Riley's saloon. All the cronies gathered there—in the back room, of course, where Jim had an elegant brass spittoon and a picture of George Washington on the wall to make it dignified. You could see the footpath worn across the grass until they built over that meadow. Besides the usual crowd, there was Bob Moran, the sheriff, a fine, strapping big fellow, but very nervous about doing his duty strictly. And there was poor old Nabors, a big, quiet, reddish-eyed fellow, who'd been a doctor before he took to drink. He was always broke, and he had two daughters—one of 'em consumptive—and Jim Riley pitied him so much that he gave him all he wanted to drink for nothing. Those were fine, happy days, with a power of eloquence and theorizing and solving the problems of the nation in that back room, until our wives came to fetch us home.

"Then Randall Fraser was murdered, and there was hell to pay.

"Now if it had been anybody else but Fred Joliffe who killed him, naturally we wouldn't have convicted. You can't do it, son, not in a little community. It's all very well to talk about the power and grandeur of justice, and sounds fine in a speech. But here's somebody you've seen walking the streets about his business every day for years; and you know when his kids were born, and saw him crying when one of 'em died; and you remember how he loaned you ten dollars when you needed it...Well, you can't take that person out in the cold light of day and string him up by the neck until he's dead. You'd always be seeing the look on his face afterwards. And you'd find excuses for him no matter what he did.

"But with Fred Joliffe it was different. Fred Joliffe was the worst and nastiest customer we ever had, with the possible exception of Randall Fraser himself. Ever seen a copperhead curled up on a flat stone? And a copperhead's worse than a rattlesnake—that won't strike unless you step on it, and gives warning before it does. Fred Joliffe had the same brownish color and sliding movements. You always remembered his pale little eye and his nasty grin. When he drove his cart through town—he had some sort of rag-and-bone business,[2] you understand—you'd see him sitting up there, a skinny little man in a brown coat, peeping round the side of his nose to find something for gossip. And grinning.

"It wasn't merely the things he said about people behind their backs. Or to their faces, for that matter, because he relied on the fact that he was too small to be thrashed. He was a slick customer. It was believed that he wrote those anonymous letters that caused...but never mind that. Anyhow, I can tell you his little smirk did drive Will Farmer crazy one time, and Will did beat him within an inch of his life. Will's livery stable was burnt down one night about a month later, with eleven horses inside, but nothing could ever be proved. He was too smart for us.

"That brings me to Fred Joliffe's only companion—I don't mean friend. Randall Fraser had a harness-and-saddle store in Market Street, a dusty place with a big dummy horse in the window. I reckon the only thing in the world Randall liked was that dummy horse, which was a dappled mare with vicious-looking glass eyes. He used to keep its mane combed. Randall was a big man with a fine moustache, a horseshoe pin in his tie, and sporty checked clothes. He was buttery polite, and mean as sin. He thought a dirty trick or a swindle was the funniest joke he ever heard. But the women liked him—a lot of them, it's no denying, sneaked in at the back door of that harness store. Randall itched to tell it at the barber shop, to show what fools they were and how virile he was; but he had to be careful. He and Fred Joliffe did a lot of drinking together.

"Then the news came. It was in October, I think, and I heard it in the morning, when I was putting on my hat to go down to the office. Old Withers was the town constable then. He got up early in the morning, although there was no need for it; and, when he was going down Market Street in the mist about five o'clock, he saw the gas still burning in the back room of Randall's store. The front door was wide open. Withers went in and found Randall lying on a pile of harness in his shirt-sleeves, and his forehead and face bashed in with a wedging-mal-

---

2 A rag-and-bone man was a small-time scavenger living on the edge of poverty who wandered the streets during the 19th and 20th centuries calling out, "Rag 'n bone! Or any old iron!" This junk collector would also sometimes ring a bell to attract attention. Residents would toss into the ragman's cart whatever trinkets, scraps, or other disjecta they had on hand. The ragman would use or resell whatever he could.

let. There wasn't much left of the face, but you could recognize him by his moustache and his horseshoe pin.

"I was in my office when somebody yelled up from the street that they had found Fred Joliffe drunk and asleep in the flour-mill, with blood on his hands and an empty bottle of Randall Fraser's whisky in his pocket. He was still in bad shape, and couldn't walk or understand what was going on, when the sheriff—that was Bob Moran I told you about—came to take him to the lock-up. Bob had to drive him in his own rag-and-bone cart. I saw them drive up Market Street in the rain, Fred lying in the back of the cart all white with flour, and rolling and cursing. People were very quiet. They were pleased, but they couldn't show it.

"That is, all except Will Farmer, who had owned the livery stable that was burnt down.

"'Now they'll hang him' says Will. 'Now, by God they'll hang him.'

"It's a funny thing, son: I didn't realize the force of that until I heard Judge Hunt pronounce sentence after the trial. They appointed me to defend him, because I was a young man without any particular prac-tice, and somebody had to do it. The evidence was all over town before I got a chance to speak with Fred. You could see he was done for. A scissors-grinder who lived across the street (I forget his name now) had seen Fred go into Randall's place about eleven o'clock. An old couple who lived up over the store had heard 'em drinking and yelling down-stairs; at near on midnight they'd heard a noise like a fight and a fall; but they knew better than to interfere. Finally, a couple of farmers driving home from town at midnight had seen Fred stumble out of the front door, slapping his clothes and wiping his hands on his coat like a man with delirium tremens.

"I went to see Fred at the jail. He was sober, although he jerked a good deal. Those pale watery eyes of his were as poisonous as ever. I can still see him sitting on the bunk in his cell, sucking a brown-paper cigarette, wriggling his neck, and jeering at me. He wouldn't tell me anything, because he said I would go and tell the judge if he did.

"'Hang me?' he says, and wrinkled his nose and jeered again. 'Hang me? Don't you worry about that, mister. Them so-and-so's will never hang me. They're too much afraid of me, them so-and-so's are. Eh, mister?'

"And the fool couldn't get it through his head right up until the sen-tence. He strutted away in court; making smart remarks, and threatening to tell what he knew about people, and calling the judge by his first name. He wore a new dickey shirt-front he bought to look spruce in.

"I was surprised how quietly everybody took it. The people who came to the trial didn't whisper or shove; they just sat still as death, and looked at him. All you could hear was a kind of breathing. It's funny about a courtroom, son: it has its own particular smell, which won't bother you unless you get to thinking about what it means, but you notice worn places and cracks in the walls more than you would anywhere else. You would hear Charley Connell's voice for the prosecution, a little thin sound in a big room, and Charley's footsteps creaking. You would hear a cough in the audience, or a woman's dress rustle, or the gas-jets whistling. It was dark in the rainy season, so they lit the gas-jets by two o'clock in the afternoon.

"The only defense I could make was that Fred had been too drunk to be responsible, and remembered nothing of that night (which he admitted was true). But, in addition to being no defense in law, it was a terrible frost[3] besides. My own voice sounded wrong. I remember that six of the jury had whiskers, and six hadn't; and Judge Hunt, up on the bench with the flag draped on the wall behind his head, looked more like Abe Lincoln than ever. Even Fred Joliffe began to notice. He kept twitching round to look at people, a little uneasy-like. Once he stuck out his neck at the jury and screeched: 'Say something, can'tcha? Do something, can'tcha?'

"They did.

"When the foreman of the jury said: 'Guilty of murder in the first degree,' there was just a little noise from those people. Not a cheer, or anything like that. It hissed out all together, only once, like breath released, but it was terrible to hear. It didn't hit Fred until Judge Hunt was halfway through pronouncing sentence. Fred stood looking round with a wild, half-witted expression until he heard Judge Hunt say: 'And may God have mercy on your soul.' Then he burst out, kind of pleading and kidding as though this was carrying the joke too far. He said: 'Listen, now, you don't mean that, do you? You can't fool me. You're only Jerry Hunt; I know who you are. You can't do that to me.' All of a sudden he began pounding the table and screaming: 'You ain't really agoing to hang me, are you?'

---

3 This is not merely an eye-catching word choice by Carr, unexpected to a twenty-first-century reader, but a clever one: he is simultaneously employing two different meanings for frost, each of which carries its own implication. The first meaning is to cover over or obscure, as does frost. It is equivalent to the contemporary expression "gloss over," which is to disguise something unfavorable by mentioning it misleadingly or briefly. The second meaning, a humorous slang usage since the late nineteenth century, meant to annoy, anger, or irritate. It was often expressed in coarse phrasing, such as "frost his balls" or "frost my ass." So the narrator is confessing to having irritated the jury, judge, and even Joliffe himself by offering this conspicuously weak defense.

"But we were.

"The date of execution was fixed for the twelfth of November. The order was all signed. '…within the precincts of the said county jail, between the hours of eight and nine a.m., the said Frederick Joliffe shall be hanged by the neck until he is dead; an executioner to be commissioned by the sheriff for this purpose, and the sentence to be carried out in the presence of a qualified medical practitioner; the body to be interred…' And the rest of it. Everybody was nervous. There hadn't been a hanging since any of that crowd had been in office, and nobody knew how to go about it exactly. Old Doc Macdonald, the coroner, was to be there; and of course they got hold of Reverend Phelps the preacher; and Bob Moran's wife was going to cook pancakes and sausage for the last breakfast. Maybe you think that's fool talk. But think for a minute of taking somebody you've known all your life, and binding his arms one cold morning, and walking him out in your own backyard to crack his neck on a rope—all religious and legal, with not a soul to interfere. Then you begin to get scared of the powers of life and death, and the thin partition between.

"Bob Moran was scared white for fear things wouldn't go off properly. He had appointed big, slow-moving, tipsy Ed Nabors as hangman. This was partly because Ed Nabors needed the fifty dollars that was the fee, and partly because Bob had a vague idea that an ex-medical man would be better able to manage an execution. Ed had sworn to keep sober; Bob Moran said he wouldn't get a dime unless he was sober; but you couldn't always tell.

"Nabors seemed in earnest. He had studied up the matter of scientific hanging in an old book he borrowed from your grandfather, and he and the carpenter had knocked together a big, shaky-looking contraption in the jail yard. It worked all right in practice, with sacks of meal; the trap went down with a boom that brought your heart up in your throat. But once they allowed for too much spring in the rope, and it tore a sack apart. Then old Doc Macdonald chipped in about that fellow John Lee, in England[4]—and it nearly finished Bob Moran.

"'hat was late on the night before the execution. We were sitting round the lamp in Bob's office, trying to play stud poker. There were

---

4 John Babbacombe Lee is one of only two men known to have survived three attempts to hang him. All three tries took place successively on February 13, 1885. After the failure to execute him, the Home Secretary, Sir William Harcourt, commuted Lee's sentence to life in prison. A subsequent petition campaign to the Home Secretary (at this time, Herbert Gladstone) between 1905-1907 resulted in his outright release. At some point after 1916, Lee emigrated to the U.S., where he died in 1945.

tops and skipping-ropes, all kinds of toys, all over that office. Bob let his kids play in there—which he shouldn't have done, because the door out of it led to a corridor of cells with Fred Joliffe in the last one. Of course the few other prisoners, disorderlies and chicken-thieves and the like, had been moved upstairs. Somebody had told Bob that the scent of an execution affects 'em like a cage of wild animals. Whoever it was he was right. We could hear 'em shifting and stamping over our heads, and one old n——[5] singing hymns all night long.

"Well it was raining hard on the tin roof; maybe that was what put Doc Macdonald in mind of it. Doc was a cynical old devil. When he saw that Bob couldn't sit still, and would throw in his hand without even looking at the buried card, Doc says:

"'Yes, I hope it'll go off all right. But you want to be careful about that rain. Did you read about that fellow they tried to hang in England?—and the rain had swelled the boards so's the trap wouldn't fall? They stuck him on it three times, but still it wouldn't work...[6]

"Ed Nabors slammed his hand down on the table. I reckon he felt bad enough as it was, because one of his daughters had run away and left him, and the other was dying of consumption. But he was twitchy and reddish about the eyes; he hadn't had a drink for two days, although there was a bottle on the table. He says:

"'You shut up or I'll kill you. Damn you, Macdonald,' he says, and grabs the edge of the table. 'I tell you nothing can go wrong. I'll go out and test the thing again, if you'll let me put the rope round your neck.'

"And Bob Moran says: 'What do you want to talk like that for, anyway, Doc? Ain't it bad enough as it is?' he says. 'Now you've got me

---

[5] Carr wrote the entire ethnic term here, which the editor has elided. Carr, trying to write with fidelity to time and place, puts this word into the mouth of a nineteenth-century character; further, even at the later time Carr wrote this story, the term's use was still common and acceptable. While there is no reason to infer racism on Carr's part, the term's use a century later is in any event unacceptable. Of interest in terms of acceptable language, note that Carr, characteristically of himself and of the times generally, substitutes the phrase "so-and-so's" for a profane reference the reader is expected to recognize and silently provide (probably "sons of bitches" or "fu—ers," which the editor hesitates to print in full). So in terms of etiquette, we note that in the early twentieth century, certain profane phrases were considered improper for print, but this racist term was considered perfectly acceptable.

[6] According to the Home Office, its investigation concerning Lee's execution determined that because the gallows had been recently relocated, the draw bar was misaligned, which caused the hinges on the trap door to bind and prevented the trap door from dropping cleanly through its opening.

worrying about something else,' he says. 'I went down there a while ago to look at him, and he said the funniest thing I ever heard Fred Joliffe say. He's crazy. He giggled and said God wouldn't let them so-and-so's hang him. It was terrible, hearing Fred Joliffe talk like that. What time is it, somebody?'

"I was cold that night. I dozed off in a chair, hearing the rain, and that animal-cage snuffling upstairs. The n— was singing that part of the hymn about while the nearer waters roll, while the tempest still is high.[7]

"'They woke me about half-past eight to say that Judge Hunt and all the witnesses were out in the jail yard, and they were ready to start the march. Then I realized that they were really going to hang him after all. I had to join behind the procession as I was sworn, but I didn't see Fred Joliffe's face and I didn't want to see it. They had given him a good wash, and a clean flannel shirt that they tucked under at the neck. He stumbled coming out of the cell, and started to go in the wrong direction; but Bob Moran and the constable each had him by one arm. It was a cold, dark, windy morning. His hands were tied behind.

"'he preacher was saying something I couldn't catch; everything went off smoothly enough until they got halfway across the jail yard. It's a pretty big yard. I didn't look at the contraption in the middle, but at the witnesses standing over against the wall with their hats off; and I smelled the clean air after the rain, and looked up at the mountains where the sky was getting pink. But Fred Joliffe did look at it, and went down flat on his knees. They hauled him up again. I heard them keep on walking, and go up the steps, which were creaky.

"I didn't look at the contraption until I heard a thumping sound, and we all knew something was wrong.

"Fred Joliffe was not standing on the trap, nor was the bag pulled over his head, although his legs were strapped. He stood with his eyes closed and his face towards the pink sky. Ed Nabors was clinging with both hands to the rope, twirling round a little and stamping on the trap. It didn't budge. Just as I heard Ed crying something about the rain having swelled the boards, Judge Hunt ran past me to the foot of the contraption.

"Bob Moran started cursing pretty obscenely. 'Put him on and try it, anyway,' he says, and grabs Fred's arm. 'Stick that bag over his head and give the thing a chance.'

---

7 The hymn is *Jesus, Lover of My Soul*, written as a poem in 1738 by Charles Wesley, who at that time was only a convert to Christianity for a few months. It was adapted into a hymn in 1797 through the addition of music by Simeon Butler Marsh.

"'In His name,' says the preacher pretty steadily, 'you'll not do it if I can help it.'

"Bob ran over like a crazy man and jumped on the trap with both feet. It was stuck fast. Then Bob turned round and pulled an Ivor-Johnson .45 out of his hip-pocket. Judge Hunt got in front of Fred, whose lips were moving a little.

"'He'll have the law, and nothing but the law,' says Judge Hunt. 'Put that gun away, you lunatic, and take him back to the cell until you can make the thing work. Easy with him, now.'

"To this day I don't think Fred Joliffe had realized what happened. I believe he only had his belief confirmed that they never meant to hang him after all. When he found himself going down the steps again, he opened his eyes. His face looked shrunken and dazed-like, but all of a sudden it came to him in a blaze.

"'I knew them so-and-so's would never hang me,' says he. His throat was so dry he couldn't spit at Judge Hunt, as he tried to do; but he marched straight and giggling across the yard. 'I knew them so-and-so's would never hang me,' he says.

"We all had to sit down a minute, and we had to give Ed Nabors a drink. Bob made him hurry up, although we didn't say much, and he was leaving to fix the trap again when the courthouse janitor came bustling into Bob's office.

"'Call,' says he, 'on the new machine over there. Telephone.'

"'Lemme out of here!' yells Bob. 'I can't listen to no telephone calls now. Come out and give us a hand.'

"'But it's from Harrisburg,' says the janitor. 'It's from the Governor's office. You got to go.'

"'Stay here, Bob,' says Judge Hunt. He beckons to me. 'Stay here, and I'll answer it,' he says. We looked at each other in a queer way when we went across the Bridge of Sighs. The courthouse clock was striking nine, and I could look down into the yard and see people hammering at the trap. After Judge Hunt had listened to that telephone call he had a hard time putting the receiver back on the hook.

"'I always believed in Providence, in a way,' says he, 'but I never thought it was so personal-like. Fred Joliffe is innocent. We're to call off this business,' says he, 'and wait for a messenger from the Governor. He's got the evidence of a woman...Anyway, we'll hear it later.'

"Now, I'm not much of a hand at describing mental states, so I can't tell you exactly what we felt then. Most of all was a fever and horror for fear they had already whisked Fred out and strung him up. But when we looked down into the yard from the Bridge of Sighs we saw Ed Nabors and the carpenter arguing over a cross-cut saw on the trap itself; and the blessed morning light coming up in a glory to show us we could knock the ugly contraption to pieces and burn it.

"'The corridor downstairs was deserted. Judge Hunt had got his wind back, and, being one of those stern elocutionists who like to make complimentary remarks about God, he was going on something powerful. He sobered up when he saw that the door to Fred Joliffe's cell was open.

"'Even Joliffe,' says the judge, 'deserves to get this news first.'

"But Fred never did get that news, unless his ghost was listening. I told you he was very small and light. His heels were a good eighteen inches off the floor as he hung by the neck from an iron peg in the wall of the cell. He was hanging from a noose made in a child's skipping-rope; black-faced, dead already, with the whites of his eyes showing in slits, and his heels swinging over a kicked-away stool.

"No, son, we didn't think it was suicide for long. For a little while we were stunned, half crazy, naturally. It was like thinking about your troubles at three o'clock in the morning.

"But, you see, Fred's hands were still tied behind him. There was a bump on the back of his head, from a hammer that lay beside the stool. Somebody had walked in there with the hammer concealed behind his back, had stunned Fred when he wasn't looking, had run a slip-knot in that skipping-rope, and jerked him up a-flapping to strangle there. It was the creepiest part of the business, when we'd got that through our heads, and we began loudly to tell each other where we'd been during the confusion. Nobody had noticed much. I was scared green.

"When we gathered round the table in Bob's office, Judge Hunt took hold of his nerve with both hands. He looked at Bob Moran, at Ed Nabors, at Doc Macdonald, and at me. One of us was the other hangman.

"'This is a bad business, gentlemen,' says he, clearing his throat a couple of times like a nervous orator before he starts. 'What I want to know is, who under sanity would strangle a man when he thought we intended to do it anyway, on a gallows?'

"Then Doc Macdonald turned nasty. 'Well,' says he, 'if it comes to that, you might inquire where that skipping-rope came from, to begin with.'

"'I don't get you,' says Bob Moran, bewildered-like.

"'Oh, don't you?' says Doc, and sticks out his whiskers. 'Well, then, who was so dead set on this execution going through as scheduled that he wanted to use a gun when the trap wouldn't drop?'

"Bob made a noise as though he'd been hit in the stomach. He stood looking at Doc for a minute, with his hands hanging down—and then he went for him. He had Doc back across the table, banging his head on the edge, when people began to crowd into the room at the yells. Funny, too; the first one in was the jail carpenter, who was pretty sore at not being told that the hanging had been called off.

"'What do you want to start fighting for?' he says, fretful-like. He was bigger than Bob, and had him off Doc with a couple of heaves. 'Why didn't you tell me what was going on? They say there ain't going to be any hanging. Is that right?'

"Judge Hunt nodded, and the carpenter—Barney Hicks, that's who it was; I remember now—Barney Hicks looked pretty peevish, and says:

"'All right, all right, but you hadn't ought to fight all over the joint like that.' Then he looks at Ed Nabors. 'What I want is my hammer. Where's my hammer, Ed? I been looking all over the place for it. What did you do with it?'

"Ed Nabors sits up, pours himself four fingers of rye, and swallows it.

"'Beg pardon, Barney,' says he in the coolest voice I ever heard. 'I must have left it in the cell,' he says, 'when I killed Fred Joliffe.'

"Talk about silences! It was like one of those silences when the magician at the Opera House fires a gun and six doves fly out of an empty box. I couldn't believe it. But I remember Ed Nabors sitting big in the corner by the barred window, in his shiny black coat and string tie. His hands were on his knees, and he was looking from one to the other of us, smiling a little. He looked as old as the prophets then; and he'd got enough liquor to keep the nerve from twitching beside his eye. So he just sat there, very quietly, shifting the plug of tobacco around in his cheek, and smiling.

"'Judge,' he says in a reflective way, 'you got a call from the Governor at Harrisburg, didn't you? Uh-huh. I knew what it would be. A woman had come forward, hadn't she, to confess Fred Joliffe was innocent and she had killed Randall Fraser? Uh-huh. The woman was my daughter. Jessie couldn't face telling it here, you see. That was why she ran away from me and went to the Governor. She'd have kept quiet if you hadn't convicted Fred.'

"'But why...' shouts the judge. 'Why...'

"'It was like this,' Ed goes on in that slow way of his. 'She'd been on pretty intimate terms with Randall Fraser, Jessie had. And both Randall and Fred were having a whooping lot of fun threatening to tell the whole town about it. She was pretty near crazy, I think. And, you see, on the night of the murder Fred Joliffe was too drunk to remember anything that happened. He thought he had killed Randall, I suppose, when he woke up and found Randall dead and blood on his hands.

"'It's all got to come out now, I suppose,' says he, nodding. 'What did happen was that the three of 'em were in that back room, which Fred didn't remember. He and Randall had a fight while they were baiting Jessie; Fred whacked him hard enough with that mallet to lay him out, but all the blood he got was from a big splash over Randall's eye. Jessie...Well, Jessie finished the job when Fred ran away, that's all.'

"'But, you damned fool,' cries Bob Moran, and begins to pound the table, 'why did you have to go and kill Fred when Jessie had confessed?'

"'You fellows wouldn't have convicted Jessie, would you?' says Ed, blinking round at us. 'No. But, if Fred had lived after her confession, you'd have had to, boys. That was how I figured it out. Once Fred learned what did happen, that he wasn't guilty and she was, he'd never have let up until he'd carried that case to the Superior Court out of your hands. He'd have screamed all over the State until they either had to hang her or send her up for life. I couldn't stand that. As I say, that was how I figured it out, although my brain's not so clear these days. So,' says he, nodding and leaning over to take aim at the cuspidor, 'when I heard about that telephone call, I went into Fred's cell and finished my job.'

"'But don't you understand,' says Judge Hunt, in the way you'd reason with a lunatic, 'that Bob Moran will have to arrest you for murder, and—'

"It was the peacefulness of Ed's expression that scared us then. He got up from his chair, and dusted his shiny black coat, and smiled at us.

"'Oh, no,' says he very clearly. 'That's what you don't understand. You can't do a single damned thing to me. You can't even arrest me.'

"'He's bughouse,' says Bob Moran.

"'Am I?' says Ed affably. 'Listen to me. I've committed what you might call a perfect murder, because I've done it legally...Judge, what time did you talk to the Governor's office, and get the order for the execution to be called off? Be careful now.'

"And I said, with the whole idea of the business suddenly hitting me:

"'It was maybe five minutes past nine, wasn't it, Judge? I remember the courthouse clock striking when we were going over the Bridge of Sighs.'

"'I remember it too,' says Ed Nabors. 'And Doc Macdonald will tell you that Fred Joliffe was dead before ever that clock struck nine. I have in my pocket,' says he, unbuttoning his coat, 'a court order which authorizes me to kill Fred Joliffe, by means of hanging by the neck—which I did—between the hours of eight and nine in the morning—which

I also did. And I did it in full legal style before the order was countermanded. Well?'

"Judge Hunt took off his stovepipe hat and wiped his face with a bandana. We all looked at him.

"'You can't get away with this,' says the judge, and grabs the sheriff's orders off the table. 'You can't trifle with the law in that way. And you can't execute sentence alone. Look here! "In the presence of a qualified medical practitioner." What do you say to that?'

"'Well, I can produce my medical diploma,' says Ed, nodding again. 'I may be a booze-hister,[8] and mighty unreliable, but they haven't struck me off the register yet…You lawyers are hell on the wording of the law,' says he admiringly, 'and it's the wording that's done for you this time. Until you get the law altered with some fancy words, there's nothing in that document to say that the doctor and the hangman can't be the same person.'

"After a while Bob Moran turned round to the judge with a funny expression on his face. It might have been a grin.

"'This ain't according to morals,' says he. 'A fine citizen like Fred shouldn't get murdered like that. It's awful. Something's got to be done about it. As you said yourself this morning, Judge, he ought to have the law and nothing but the law. Is Ed right, Judge?'

"'Frankly, I don't know,' says Judge Hunt, wiping his face again. 'But, so far as I know, he is. What are you doing, Robert?'

"'I'm writing him out a cheque for fifty dollars,' says Bob Moran, surprised-like. 'We got to have it all nice and legal, haven't we?'"

---

8 "Booze-hister" is the less common form of the slang, "booze-hoister," or drunkard.

Notes for the Curious: "The Other Hangman"

The reader is warned: This commentary freely discusses Carr's first historical mystery story, "The Will-o'-the-Wisp," which was published in 2022's *The Kindling Spark.* If you have not read that story yet, you may wish to enjoy it before reading the following commentary.

—

"The Other Hangman" is Carr's first professionally published short historical mystery, and only his fourth short story after becoming a professional novelist. It first appeared in a 1935 anthology, *A Century of Detective Stories.* As Greene reports in the biography (p. 219), "Since the introduction was to be written by Carr's literary idol, G.K. Chesterton, he [Carr] 'shot in one of my best plots which I should have been sensible enough to reserve for a novel.'"

The story has been popular in the decades since its first appearance, being reprinted multiple times: next after *A Century of Detective Stories,* it appeared in Carr's collection *The Department of Queer Complaints* (1940, cited as one of the 125 most important crime fiction books ever in Ellery Queen's *Queen's Quorum*). Then "The Other Hangman" was reprinted in: *Avon Detective Mysteries* (issue #2, 1947); *MacKill's Mystery Magazine,* April (UK) and May (US) 1953; *Ellery Queen's Mystery Magazine,* January 1965; the anthology *Alfred Hitchcock Presents: Stories Not for the Nervous* (1965); *Ellery Queen's Anthology* (#21, Spring/Summer 1971); and in Greene's *Fell and Foul Play* (1991). Possibly, the editor has overlooked some reprintings. The story appears in this collection not, as do the other selections, for any rarity, but rather for its resonance with them.

The principal action of "The Other Hangman" takes place in Uniontown (as does 1922's "The Will-o'-the-Wisp"), where Carr was born; Judge Murchison's invocation of familial heritage and tradition of place has underneath it the author's own genuinely felt pride. In 1900, John Dickson Carr, the author's grandfather, relocated his family to from Fayette City to Uniontown. That Carr was elected mayor in 1918 and died in 1919. The younger John Dickson, born six years after this relocation, personally knew and was doubtless proud of his distinguished namesake.

In the framing narrative, the unidentified listener Judge Murchison addresses may "secretly" be a fictionalized, young John Dickson Carr—perhaps the one his father Wooda intended for a career in law. While there is no explicit mention (indeed, Carr does not circle back to the framing narrative at the conclusion), it is certainly the sort of grand joke Carr, who enjoyed populating his fiction with reflections of himself, would perpetrate. The invocation of "your own grandfather, who had over two hundred books in his library" is clearly suggestive of Carr's father, if not of Carr's grandfather. Wooda had "probably the best-selected if not the largest private library in the state,"[1] and he "was always willing to lend volumes even to neighborhood children" (Greene, p. 6). While nothing in "The Other Hangman" relies upon this being true, it seems likely that Wooda inherited some of his books from his father's library, as John did from Wooda's. Either way, the selection of Uniontown as its setting and the familial history underneath the narrative are personal touches by the author.

In comparison with its earliest predecessor "The Will-o'-the-Wisp," "The Other Hangman" reminds readers what a strong writer the still young, now-professional Carr had become, and with what varied strengths. His novels between 1930 and 1935 are chiefly in the Grand Guignol style: dark, menacing, and gruesome; their credo, words Dr. Fell famously intones in the locked-room lecture of *The Three Coffins*, is, effectively, "I like my murders to be frequent, gory, and grotesque" (p. 221). This story, by contrast, is in another tone altogether, as accomplished in its presentation of everyday, regional voices as Carr's novels at the time are in their invocation of Gothic dread. One strength here is the story's fidelitous reproduction of a place, time, and its voices, unsurprising to any reader of Carr's historical romances, amateur or professional.

Readers of *The Kindling Spark* will recall that "The Will-o'-the-Wisp," although only the fifteen-year-old aspirant's third-ever story, demonstrates a quickening maturity of technique, particularly by its exchange of stock language that Carr had borrowed from Edgar Allan Poe in his first two tales for more original language of his own. "The Will-o'-the-Wisp" also incorporates images better and more usefully resonant than its two predecessors: instead of tread-worn and non-contextual similes, those Carr employs in his first historical tale are thoughtful, fresh, and pertinent. It is promising work by an inexperienced author. "The Other Hangman" likewise delivers some fine, fruitful imagery. Note how the judge's description of Fred Joliffe elegantly strengthens the character sketch, as well as further inclining the reader to believe Joliffe is Fraser's murderer:

> Ever seen a copperhead curled up on a flat stone? And a copperhead's worse than a rattlesnake—that won't strike unless

---

1 John W. Jordan and James Hadden, *Genealogical and Personal History of Fayette County Pennsylvania*, Lewis Historical Publishing Company (1915), Volume I, p. 36.

> you step on it, and gives warning before it does. Fred Joliffe
> had the same brownish color and sliding movements. You
> always remembered his pale little eye and his nasty grin.

And if that is not enough, Judge Murchison almost explains that, additionally, Joliffe was believed to be a poison-pen writer. Carr does not actually offer a poison-pen mystery until fifteen years later, in H.M.'s twentieth outing, *Night at the Mocking Widow*.

Neither short tale is, in its technical form, a detective story, but both are fairly clued such that each's climactic revelation of its criminal feels fully justified. "The Will-o'-the-Wisp" first foreshadows the story's course with its description of Marcia Gallivan's face; it hints at the Wisp's identity through a matching pattern on the duelists' rapiers. In "The Other Hangman," Carr warns the reader in a deceptively matter-of-fact tone about Fraser's philandering, about Nabors' runaway daughter, and plainly recounts Nabors' medical background. The reader, Watson-like, might comment to Carr, "It is simple enough as you explain it,"[2] but "The Other Hangman" proves one of Carr's own axioms: "Your craftsman knows…that it is not necessary to mislead the reader. Merely state your evidence, and the reader will mislead himself."[3]

Both stories even engage in modest duality: in "The Will-o'-the-Wisp," the narrator and Alvez are each drawn toward Marcia Gallivan, "a girl dangerous in the nth degree." The narrator escapes the attendant danger by perceiving it, while Alvez's easily manipulated libido ruins him. In "The Other Hangman," Fred Joliffe and Ed Nabors each believes the law cannot touch him, but as in the earlier story, one escapes conviction through his knowledgeable caution, while the other's passion proves ineffective in avoiding the worst outcome, even contributing to it.

Douglas Greene and Anthony Boucher have both noted the influence of Melville Davisson Post on this story.[4] Post's twenty-two "Uncle Abner" stories, published between 1911–1928 and set in antebellum Virginia, created the Anglo-American genre of historical detective fiction.

Post's influence is surely present in "The Other Hangman," but in its matter-of-fact, almost understated presentation of the sensational,

---

2 Arthur Conan Doyle, *A Study in Scarlet*, reprinted in *The Complete Sherlock Holmes*, Doubleday and Company (1930), p. 24.

3 *The Grandest Game in the World*, p. 10.

4 Greene cites on p. 219 correspondence between Carr and Anthony Boucher in which the latter expressed confidence that this story "brought gleams of rejoicing" to the deceased Post's "spirit eye."

and its subtle, confidently humorous presentation of high coincidence and outright impossibility, "The Other Hangman" as strongly demonstrates the influence of O. Henry upon Carr. (Greene also compliments, on p. 291, its "fine O. Henry twist ending.") Consider as an example O. Henry's tale, "A Municipal Report," in which the narrator tantalizes the reader by explaining:

> The mark of the beast is not indelible upon a man until he goes about with a stubble. I think that if he had not used his razor that day I would have repulsed his advances, and the criminal calendar of the world would have been spared the addition of one murder."[5]

The narrator of that story and his individual voice might have found a home in "The Other Hangman." Note the narrator's self-description:

> I desire to interpolate here that I am a Southerner. But I am not one by profession or trade. I eschew the string tie, the slouch hat, the Prince Albert, the number of bales of cotton destroyed by Sherman, and plug chewing. When the orchestra plays Dixie I do not cheer. I slide a little lower on the leather-cornered seat and, well, order another Würzburger[6] and wish that Longstreet had—but what's the use? (p. 153)

Once more, we perceive the lessons Carr learned from Henry about imbuing an otherwise flat central character with an idiosyncratic and enticing voice.

In general, too, the reader easily understands how "The Other Hangman" is a successor not only to "The Will-o'-the-Wisp," but to Carr's amateur tales of the past, written with the same adept conjuration of another place and time and having the same deft, interesting mixture of period and suspense.

As noted earlier, Carr knowingly honored Chesterton with "The Other Hangman" by selecting "one of my best plots which I should have been sensible enough to reserve for a novel." Interestingly, Carr

---

5 "A Municipal Report" was originally published in *Hampton's Magazine*, November 1909, and collected the next year in Henry's collection *Strictly Business*. The quoted line appears on p. 153 of this same previously cited edition.

6 A Bavarian wine known both for its quality and the unusual flattened, round shape of its bottles.

almost certainly *unknowingly* honored his hero by pioneering the historical mystery genre in his short fiction and, especially, with his novels. In "The Historical Detective Story," an essay unpublished until after both writers' deaths (rediscovered and published for the first time in 2024), Chesterton argues that detective fiction could and should freshen its appeal by transporting readers into times past:

> ...the police romance tends of its own nature to fossilisation in certain conventional forms; especially in this matter of the murder of a millionaire, and also in the incurable habit of the millionaire of getting himself murdered at his little place in the country....I suggest that we try to do a little more with what may be called the historical detective story. The play of masks and faces in the mysterious heart of man would be just the same, but we could use a hundred variations, and some emancipations, touching the externals of the action...It would be much easier to imagine a struggle of men familiar and even careless with sword or dagger, ending in a killing that was not really premeditated or culpable.[1]

Chesterton's essay was not written for commercial print; rather, it was an exhortation to fellow members of the Detection Club, for which Chesterton served as president, and to which, in 1936, Carr himself would be inducted. The essay was intended as a feature article in a Detection Club magazine that never materialized. In it, Chesterton further coincidentally advocated for a detective novel based upon a famous, real-life unsolved murder:

> Suppose we selected the curious affair of the death of Sir Edmund Godfrey at the beginning of the business of the Popish Plot. That is exactly like a detective story, for there are three plausible theories of murder and one of suicide....I put that random case, rather as an example or experiment, to my brethren of the Detection Club. Shall we publish a book or a series, with seven different explanations of the end of Sir Edmund Berry Godfrey?[2]

Carr himself, unaware of Chesterton's unpublished sentiments, brought

---

1 "The Historical Detective Story," *Strand Magazine*, September 2024, p. 6.

2 Ibid, p. 7.

forth that exact novel in 1936, less than six months after Chesterton's death. (Carr had been working on it since 1934.) *The Murder of Sir Edmund Godfrey*, in fact, given Carr's assiduous thoroughness, considers a dozen different explanations.

It is passingly possible that Carr did take his cue from Chesterton, but only if (while still at school in the U.S.) Carr read Chesterton's January 1927 contribution to The Strand, "The Case of Sir Edmund Godfrey," in which Chesterton sized up the real-life mystery as potential detective fiction:

> I think my favorite murder in real life is the murder (if it was a murder, for even that is doubtful) of Sir Edmund Berry Godfrey, which produced the final frenzy about the Popish Plot... [T]he personal problem itself was picturesque in the same sense as a really good detective story. Two details especially have precisely the character that makes such a story: the presence of clues that are not clues, that can baffle and mislead more than they enlighten. The poor magistrate's body was found in a ditch transfixed with his own sword; but it was also evident that he had been strangled. Any properly constituted person will feel tempted to make a mystery story out of that. There is something of the true dance of death in the suggestion of somebody being hanged and then run through the body with a sword; or perhaps killed with a sword and then hanged for some reason on a tree. And as the romancer could easily introduce characters like Titus Oates and Shaftesbury and Charles the Second and Pepys, he could have a high old time.[3]

Either way, *The Murder of Sir Edmund Godfrey* became a cornerstone of both historical mystery fiction and true-crime novels. Carr's is the first true-crime detective novel in the Anglo-American tradition, and it inspired multiple mystery writers, after Carr blazed it, to follow this path Chesterton yearned to explore.

---

3 *The Strand*, January 1927, p. 93.

The Adventure of the Last Bustard (1950)

<table>
<tr><td>NARRATOR</td><td>The Adventure of the Last Bustard!

(Changes to tone of Watson.)</td></tr>
<tr><td>NARRATOR:</td><td>As I turn over the pages of my notebook, I am struck by the fact that I have made no mention of one remarkable adventure of my friend Mr. Sherlock Holmes during the early spring of 1891. March 2nd, of that year, found us far from our lodgings in Baker Street. We were driving in a trap across the bleak Yorkshire Moors, towards Bursted Old Hall, country seat of His Grace the Duke of Bursted. As we saw the towers loom up ahead in mist, I observed a light in a ground-floor room of the north tower. In that room, even as we approached...

(Curtain up, revealing main hall of the manor. Table with lamp in center. In the middle of the table, alone and distinguished a sort of case without glass in it: it is actually a toy aquarium, but might have contained a bird about the size of a turkey. A little distance away, what looks like bottle of Scotch whisky with siphon and glass.)

(H.G.[1] the Duke of Bursted, elderly but vigorous, stately but far from bright, sits on one side of the table in an attitude of utter dejection. On the other side sits his niece, Lady Emily Paterson, a pretty Victorian picture, at needlework.)</td></tr>
</table>

---

1 "His Grace."

DUKE: (looking up, tragically) The bustard! The poor, poor bustard!

EMILY: (tragic but soothing) So foul a deed was never done before.—Yet I pray, dear uncle: let it not prey too much on your mind.

DUKE: Easy words, Emily! (Rises and moves towards whisky.) When I think of what has happened...

(She throws aside the knitting, and rushes to put her hands over the whisky bottle before he reaches it.)

EMILY: No, dear uncle! This devil's brew has been the ruin of our family for generations. You are the fourteenth Duke of Bursted. Live up to it!

DUKE: (turning away) So be it. Yet the bustard... stolen! Our family jewels...stolen! My estates mortgaged to the neck. And, at the same time, there is in the house a Barstead!

EMILY: (his name) Oh, treacherous Barstead!

DUKE: (determined) No! I cannot believe that Sir John Barstead, the son of my oldest friend, would stoop to such villainy!

EMILY: Yet Scotland Yard itself is baffled!

DUKE: (straightened up, quoting) "There is no clue," said Lestrade.

EMILY: (quoting) "None whatever," said Gregson.

DUKE: Emily, we are lost; I have written to the only man who could help us; and, it appears, in vain. The only man who could save us is...

(Enter Barrymore, the butler—conventional except that he has a large black beard like Barrymore, the butler, in *The Hound of the Baskervilles*.)

BARRYMORE: Mr. Sherlock Holmes!

(Enter Holmes, in cape and deerstalker hat. He takes a brief survey of the characters.)

BARRYMORE: Dr. John Hamish Watson!

(Enter Watson, cloak and top-hat over frock-coat, very dignified.)

HOLMES: I believe I have the honour of addressing His Grace the Duke of Bursted?

DUKE: A poor honour; but you have it. (To Watson, bowing) Your servant, Dr. Watson.

WATSON: (bowing) Yours to command, sir.

(During this coats and hats have been removed by Barrymore, who goes out.)

DUKE: This, gentlemen, is my niece the Lady Emily. She is related to the Bursteds of Yorkshire, of Sussex, and of Paterson, New Jersey.

HOLMES: (thoughtfully) New Jersey, eh? (thoughtfully) New Jersey, eh?

WATSON: A part of the American Riviera, I think.

HOLMES: Pray let us proceed to business. I have some notes on my cuff here. (Examines cuff.) The problem, Your Grace...

DUKE: (grief) The problem, Mr. Holmes, is a bustard!

WATSON: (stately) My friend has solved many such. (Double-take) But surely. In the presence of ladies...!

HOLMES: Come, Watson! The bustard is a bird!

WATSON: A bird?

HOLMES: Exactly. A middle-sized bird, now extinct. The last bustard in England was shot in 1871, and acquired by the Duke there. I believe there is some family connection!

EMILY: It figures in our coat-of-arms. Unhappily, there are also three drinking- flagons in chief on a field argent.

DUKE: Take pride it in it, girl! There was a Bursted under the table at the signing of Magna Charta!

HOLMES: (cutting in brusquely) Quite, quite, but to our problem!—The Bursted Bustard, stripped of its feathers, was covered from head to foot in jewels to the value of five hundred thousand pounds. It was placed in this handsome case, I deduce, and soldered up on all sides with glass.

WATSON: Holmes, this is amazing!

HOLMES: Obvious, Watson, obvious!—Your Grace! Can you tell me what happened on the night of the theft?

DUKE: I am not a young man, sir. My memory...

EMILY: (running to him on the other side of the table) Dear uncle remembers nothing!

DUKE: Stop! I recall being roused, upstairs, by a crash of glass. When next I remember, I was standing here in my night-attire. A hammer lay on the floor—there. But the case was smashed; the bustard gone!

HOLMES: Sir John Barstead, I apprehend, was here at the time?

(Off, several peals of heh-heh laughter. Enter Barstead, lounging. He is not aesthetic; he is of the shootin', huntin', fishin' heavy-villain type. He wears large curled black moustaches, which he constantly twists. He is either in evening-dress or riding-clothes. Emily runs to other side, right.)

BARSTEAD: Jack Barstead, eh? Rather thought I heard my name called, b'gad! Always like to be there when that happens, damme!

Chuckles and moustache-twistings to director's taste.)

DUKE: May I present...?

BARSTEAD: Oh, I know! Here's the great detective, up from London. (Offensively) I say, Holmes!

HOLMES: (not liking it) At your service, Sir John.

BARSTEAD: They think I stole the Bursted jewels. No, no! The only jewel I want... (pointing to Emily)... is that proud beauty there, who will soon be m'wife and a Barstead too.

EMILY: Never, sir! Always shall 1 remain Bursted!

WATSON: Magnificent!

(Barrymore, the butler, rushes in and stops short.)

DUKE: (testily) Yes, yes, Barrymore? What is it?

BARRYMORE: Forgive me, your Grace. But there's an urgent special-delivery letter for Sir John. The boy won't give it up unless Sir John signs himself.

BARSTEAD: Aha! (Looking at Emily) Now, m'proud beauty, we shall see what happens. Lead on, Barrymore!

(Both Barrymore and Barstead hurry out, right. Emily has again gone to her uncle. While they seem to be whispering, Holmes and Watson at the other end of stage engage in a very loud confidential talk.)

HOLMES: Quick, Watson! Follow them and discover the contents of the letter!

WATSON: (fussed) But how can I?

HOLMES: You know my methods; employ them!

WATSON: That's just the trouble. I won't discover 'em in thirty years.

HOLMES: Under favour, Watson : what's your theory? Who stole the bustard?

WATSON: (Impressive and mysteriously) It was Barrymore, the butler!

HOLMES: (Surprised) Barrymore!

WATSON: Such a beaver, my dear fellow, could have hidden the jewels in his beard. And don't you remember Barrymore, the butler, at Bast—. Baskerville Hall?

HOLMES (dubiously) A long shot, Watson; a very long shot!—Shall I provide you with a clue?

WATSON: If you can.

HOLMES: Not one of the stolen jewels has been offered
               for sale to any fence in London. Now be off;
               and find that letter!

               (Exit Watson, right. Holmes swings round to
               Duke and Emily.)

EMILY: Mr. Holmes, do you give us any hope?

HOLMES: Yes, my lady. If you tell me what blackmailing
               secret this Barstead holds over you.

DUKE: Blackmail?!

EMILY: There is none, Mr. Holmes. None at all!

HOLMES: You swear it?

EMILY: I swear it!

HOLMES: Then I fear I must act alone.

               (He goes to table, behind it, and examines case
               with magnifying glass. Then looks slowly round
               walls, and up at ceiling. Backs to backdrop,
               comes forward again.)

HOLMES: This is the Main Hall, I think. It is very old?

DUKE: Older than the Norman, Mr. Holmes. Observe
               the groined roof and many beams.

HOLMES: I have already done so. (Changing tone) This
               problem, your Grace, has presented some small
               features of interest. But it is already solved.

DUKE:
EMILY: }   Solved!

HOLMES: Hark! Who approaches now on such leaden feet?

(We have heard briefly, off right, a sound like a man marching heavily with a load of misery. Enter Barstead, stamping slowly and heavily; hair disarranged. He sits down and looks glassily at audience.)

BARSTEAD: BUSTED, BY GAD!

EMILY: And serve you right, o villain that you are! How pray, were you busted?

BARSTEAD: Bisterd! Yes!—(Fumbling at pockets) All m'work in vain! Had a letter here...somewhere... in my pocket...

(Watson has entered, unobtrusively, just behind Barstead. Holmes and Watson seem to be conferring, right, over a letter in Watson's hand. Holmes turns round.)

BARSTEAD: Yes, curse you!

HOLMES: The Duke's estates, I think, were heavily mortgaged. It was Sir John Barstead, acting through a third party named Bisterd, who took up these mortgages. If he threatened to foreclose, he might win the fair Emily of Bursted Hall. (Holds up letter) But the mortgage money has been paid back. You acknowledge the letter, Sir John?

BARSTEAD: (grinding his teeth) O bungling Bisterd!

HOLMES:	And now, Watson, do what I bade you a moment ago!
	(Watson goes to back-drop, back turned, and seems to be turning a small wheel just above his head.)
DUKE:	What wizard's work is this?
HOLMES:	Behold the bustard!
	(From the ceiling descends what appears to be a large dummy turkey, ready for the oven. After a moment for audience reaction, these speeches cover its descent squarely into the case. It does not matter whether the speeches overlap the landing of the bustard or not.)
EMILY:	Dear uncle, you are saved!
DUKE:	(ecstatic) *Nil nisi bustardum!*[2]
BARSTEAD:	But where are the cursed jewels?
HOLMES:	Surely the inference is obvious. Someone, filled with family pride, arranged this mechanism of invisible threads to hide the bird in the roof-beams. Someone sold the jewels to legitimate jewelers and paid back the mortgages.
DUKE	"Family pride"? Surely you do not imply that I...

---

2 Carr is punning on the well-known Latin aphorism, "De mortuis nil nisi bonum dicendum est" ("Of the dead let nothing but good be spoken"), commonly abbreviated to "nil nisi bonum." Carr's pun, translated, means, "Nothing but the bustard!" The Duke is chagrined, because the bustard has been plucked of all its jewels. Note that this kind of humorous verbal play on words with similar sounds but different meanings, paronomasia, was a favorite technique of O. Henry's. Given the very different sorts of fiction they wrote, Carr did not often have the opportunity to imitate Henry in this. His first experiment with paronomasia was "The Gordon Djinn."

HOLMES: No, Your Grace! (Takes Emily's hand) But let me present you to Miss Irene Adler, wife of Godfrey Norton, whom I once toasted as *the woman*. I knew her at once when I received a hint that she was born in New Jersey.

EMILY: (rapt) I am a Bursted, sir. I would have done in New Jersey what I did here, were there any Bursteds there.

WATSON: (shocked) Then, deuce take it, Holmes, no crime has been committed!

HOLMES: None whatever, Watson. Because one man would not permit it.

WATSON: One man? Which of us?

HOLMES: A man, Watson, who would never permit a woman's honour to be tarnished. A man who would never allow a woman to be involved in vice or crime... (Starting, looking towards right)...Indeed, we have a visit from him now!

(Enter Barrymore, well back. Enter, after him, a very large, very thickset figure with greyish moustache, pipe, and cloth cap. He passes Barrymore and beams round.)

BARRYMORE (shouting) Sir Arthur Conan Doyle!

(Curtain.)

Notes for the Curious: "The Adventure of the Last Bustard"

Note: the editor is gratefully indebted to Elliot Han (韩东), a fellow Carr collector, researcher, enthusiast, and friend, for his collaborative research, which helped to narrow the date when Carr wrote this playlet.

The reader is warned: While this commentary does not reveal the solution to either novel, it mentions some plot elements and suspects' motives from Carr's novels *The Problem of the Wire Cage* and *The Nine Wrong Answers*. If you have not read either of these, you may wish to do so before reading the following commentary.

—

Between 1948 and 1952, the Mystery Writers of America (MWA) produced a series of comedy skits for its annual Edgar awards ceremonies, written by attendee members and performed by them and their guests. The series was dubbed, "The March of Crime." At the 1948 banquet, for which Carr served as a presenter, his Holmesian parody *The Adventure of the Conk-Singleton Papers* was performed; at the 1949 celebration (Carr that year served as president of the MWA, and again, as an awards presenter), another Carr-penned Holmes farce followed, *The Adventure of the Paradol Chamber.*

In the subsequent issue of *The Unicorn Mystery Book Club News* each year, Hans Santesson (the editor) memorialized one of the ceremony's comedy sketches. Both Carr's satires were so preserved, and each (with slight changes) was afterward published in *Ellery Queen's Mystery Magazine*. (*Paradol* was further reprinted in The *Baker Street Journal* and two other Ellery Queen collections.) The two farces finally took book form together in Douglas Greene's 1980 Carr collection, *The Door to Doom.*

In the "Booked for Murder" column of *The Unicorn Mystery Book Club News*, March 1950, Clayton Rawson enticed readers with the promise of a third installment, to be performed at the April MWA ceremony: "The great Holmes and the inimitable Watson once again face the footlights in a hitherto unrecorded case, *The Adventure of the Last Bustard*, from the pen of John Dickson Carr."[1]

Unfortunately, Rawson's promise went unkept. While Carr had already written *Bustard*, he was in early 1950 not the model of eucrasy: he was suffering from eye trouble and a fistula that would persist for

---

[1] *The Unicorn Mystery Book Club News*, March 1950, p. 2.

several years, finally developing into an abscess in 1953. Photographs from the 1948 and 1949 banquets depict Carr and his wife Clarice hamming it up happily in the "March of Crime" skits. Unable to relish doing so again in 1950, Carr canceled the performance of *Bustard* (although Clarice, her health fine, performed in Rawson's sketch *The Unsuspecting*). Carr, in keeping with prior practices, would almost certainly have played the villainous Sir John Barstead.

By March 1951 (*Bustard* might perhaps otherwise have been performed that April), Carr had decided to resume London residence; he made no plans for participation in that year's Edgars ceremony. After a delay to attend their daughter Julia's wedding in July, the Carrs departed the U.S. They remained abroad until 1953, effectively concluding Carr's participation in the MWA's "March of Crime."

Before resurfacing in 2023, Carr's hand-corrected typescript languished for nearly seventy-five years among the effects of an MWA officer who had provisionally received it in 1950 in preparation for the Edgars ceremony.

As do the earlier parodies, *Bustard* frames itself in silly, but knowledgeable, relation to the canon and to the BSI's engagement with it. As Greene notes in *The Door to Doom*:

> Carr disliked the idolatry with which some Baker Street Irregulars approached "the sacred writings"...Carr found nothing sacrosanct in Holmes's adventures, and the two plays exhibit what Robert E. Briney calls Carr's "irreverent and rowdy sense of humor." Holmesian experts will immediately recognize several sly and not-so-sly references to the canon. (pp. 275–276)

The same is true of Carr's third playlet. Some sibling examples from Carr's third Holmes parody include...

...*Bustard*, set in March 1891, precedes Holmes's tumble over the Reichenbach Falls, and apparent death, by only a month. The playlet does not foreshadow that milestone, coyly framing itself instead with respect to *The Hound of the Baskervilles* (Holmes's first adventure published following his death, set back in 1889 to avoid resurrecting him). Nonetheless, by walking right up to the edge of Reichenbach, as it were, Carr is inviting his audience to consider *Bustard* Holmes's penultimate adventure. In Carr's comical canon, Holmes, on New Year's Eve of 1887, apprehends Moriarty in *The Adventure of the Conk-Singleton Papers*. That play ends with Moriarty's menacing assurance, "One day, Mr. Holmes, you will try my patience too far!" Moriarty is in mind again in *The Adventure of the Paradol Chamber*, which takes place later in the same year of 1887, but that time, it is Moriarty's henchman, Colonel Sebastian Moran, who serves as Holmes's antagonist.

...The filching of the butler Barrymore from *The Hound of the Basker-villes*, beard and all, is of course an openly declared theft by Carr.

...Almost as much so is Holmes's erroneous "unmasking" of Emily Bursted as the woman, the late Irene Adler, of dubious and questionable memory—the woman whose wit beat the best plans of Sherlock Holmes himself. How could Emily be Irene Adler? She never fools the detective.

...The jewel-encrusted bustard, the center of intrigue, is a plot device evocative of the Christmas goose in Doyle's "The Adventure of the Blue Carbuncle."

...Barrymore's announcement of Watson as, "Dr. John Hamish Watson," is a jape at the expense of Conan Doyle idolators. Responding to the odd discontinuity of his own wife Mary calling Watson "James" in "The Adventure of the Man with the Crooked Lip," some of the Conan Doyle faithful concluded that Dr. John H. Watson's middle name must be "Hamish," the Scottish form of James. Carr is humorously skeptical. He can afford to be: it was in his own *The Life of Sir Arthur Conan Doyle* that the world learned Holmes's faithful sidekick is a tribute to a real-life friend of Doyle's, Dr. James Watson.

In any event, Carr is always one who will play the game for the game's own sake: while later praising Chesterton as a superior plotter to Conan Doyle, Carr acknowledged that Holmes's "pride of place" atop detective fiction was in part because, "we never know Father Brown and Flambeau as we know Sherlock Holmes and John Hamish Watson.... never have two characters so captured our affections." 2 Although this reference to Watson's middle name is free of all wryness, Carr contains himself only momentarily, adding, "(let's face it) Holmesian scholarship has grown tiresome." Then, summarizing his appreciation for the pair, Carr smirkingly rolls the doctor's alleged middle name once more off his pen, confessing, "But we are inclined to make game of John Hamish Watson more than he really deserves."

...The exchange between Holmes and Watson ("You know my meth-ods; employ them!" "That's just the trouble. I won't discover 'em in thirty years.") is not only a good belly laugh, but may well reflect Carr's acquaintance with Doyle's own Holmes parody, "How Watson Learned the Trick." The action of the little satire revolves around the good doc-tor's attempt to turn the tables on Holmes and startle him through the

---

2   "Hail Holmes!" in *The New York Times Book Review*, February 14, 1965, p. 4. All subsequent excerpts are drawn from the same article and page.

exercise of subtle powers of deduction. Doyle wrote the vignette in 1924 (nearly 30 years before Carr composed *Bustard*, arguably a hinting reference by Carr) to be published, of all things, in a tiny book on a tiny shelf in the tiny library[3] of a toy dollhouse created beginning in 1922, as Princess Marie Louise explained in correspondence soliciting Doyle's participation, by "a number of artists, authors, craftsmen and others [who] have conspired to present"[4] it to Queen Mary. The dolls' house was exhibited to the public at Wembley for seven months. Afterward, all the newly written library texts, including Doyle's, were collected into *The Book of the Queen's Dolls' House Library* (the second of a two-volume set commemorating the exhibition), issued by Methuen in a limited edition of 1,500 copies. From time to time subsequently, Doyle's parody appeared in other publications.

The story being compact, Doyle quickly sets the premise:

> '...I was thinking how superficial are these tricks of yours, and how wonderful it is that the public should continue to show interest in them.'
>
> 'I quite agree,' said Holmes, 'In fact, I have a recollection that I have myself made a similar remark.'
>
> 'Your methods,' said Watson severely, 'are really easily acquired.'

From there, a predictably, comically wrong series of deductions by the good doctor ensues.

Can we be certain Carr had read Doyle's self-satire? Not entirely—there is no written record of Carr alluding to it—but it was published as part of a feature article about the dolls' house in *The New York Times* on August 24, 1924. Carr would have been very likely to read it then. Given, too, that Carr was Conan Doyle's official biographer and had access to all the family's resources (including Doyle's papers, among which was the 1922 correspondence with Princess Marie Louise, which Carr cites in the *Life* among his biographical sources, on p. 294), and Carr's

---

3 How tiny was the library? According to Stephen Gaselee C.B.E., who wrote the chapter describing it in The Book of the Queen's Dolls' House (Methuen, London, 1924), "it is...45 inches long, 21 inches broad, and 15 ¼ inches high. The panelling and bookcases are of Italian walnut" (p. 69).

4 The Queen's cousin, in a letter to Arthur Conan Doyle soliciting his own participation, dated August 29, 1922.

otherwise having exhaustively researched his subject, it seems very likely Carr would at some point have read "How Watson Learned the Trick."

Either way, all three of Carr's Holmes pastiches delight in word play, in manic dialog, puns, Holmesian allusions, and in the joyously comic potential of alliteration projected loudly and boldly to a perhaps half-inebriated audience in which were collected the day's best mystery writers, many among them Carr's friends.

Because this little farce is by Carr, *Bustard* shares common motifs with his serious fiction, too, not just with Conan Doyle's canon. The most notable of these is Barstead's plot to force himself, by blackmail, in marriage upon Emily. Readers had encountered this device more than a decade before, in *The Problem of the Wire Cage*, wherein the middle-aged Dr. Nicholas Young lives up to his nickname, "Old Nick." Outwardly, Young supports the engagement of his ward, Brenda White, to Frank Dorrance, a brutal cad. Only by marrying Frank can Brenda receive her inheritance. But as Dr. Fell explains, Old Nick actually has his own designs upon the nubile heiress:

> "You understand," pursued Dr. Fell, "he hoped to marry you...
> We mustn't underestimate this gentleman's vanity. He is stuffed
> with vanity. That's why he won't grow old. That's why he
> smashes racing cars and challenges people to running-matches.
> He looked in the mirror and saw no reason he shouldn't be
> the husband of a rich and grateful wife..." (p. 272)

After *The Adventure of the Last Bustard*, Carr soon returned, and more closely, to this motif of the old black ram[5] and a marriage proposal in the form of financial blackmail. Uncle Gaylord Hurst, the scheming antagonist of *The Nine Wrong Answers*, lusts after Marjorie Blair, protagonist Bill Dawson's romantic interest. Bill considers Gaylord "an exhausted old satyr who longed to be thought a young satyr" (p. 136), and so at first, Bill looks only with unthreatened disgust on the older man's nympholepsy.

Gaylord, though, is a formidable and subtle manipulator. Marjorie, as does Emily Bursted, fears a great debt[6] her father owes to Gaylord will

---

5 Iago, inciting Desdemona's father Brabantio against Othello, taunts him, "Even now, now, very now, an old black ram is tupping your white ewe" (Othello, I.i.97-98).

6 The amount, £3,250, is nearly £140,000 in 2025 value, or more than USD $175,000.

result in a marriage of obligation to an uninspiring suitor, Eric Cheever. Cheever has offered to pay Mr. Blair's obligation. Marjorie explains to Bill how Gaylord drew her unsuspecting father, an architect and builder, into a ruinous building contract. Without the materials secured and project being initiated, or in the alternative, the builder repaying the advance funds to Uncle Gaylord, the result will be Mr. Blair's prosecution for fraud:

> "My father, either too happy or full of liqueur-brandies, missed that part of the clause. It's legal-proof and water-proof; we've tried. He can't get those materials, Bill; he can't. But unless he pays that enormous great sum by next Monday, we're ruined. I don't mean just being hard up with a few debts; I mean wiped out. And he can't pay; that's that." (p. 243)

Of Cheever, she insists (which puts him in pointed contrast with Barstead):

> "Bill, he is nice. He may be a bit dull and boast too much, but....There's absolutely nothing of the 'Heh-he' or the mustache-twisting nonsense about it. If we take the money and say thank you, he'll not mention another word. He is a gentleman." (p. 244)

And yet, Marjorie confesses shockingly how she really feels: "Every woman who marries without being in love...is a slut" (p. 244). She does not desire this marriage.

Despite having perceived the lecherousness in Gaylord's gaze, neither does Marjorie recognize the far-reaching perversity of his plans. Mr. Blair is not Gaylord's target, and Uncle Gay's intended marriage of Marjorie is not to Eric Cheever; he plans to extort and seduce her for himself. Gaylord divulges this to Bill, taunting him: "'I must warn you,' the murmur grew even softer. 'I mean to take her away from you. You smile? But it will happen'" (p. 183).

At the same MWA ceremony for which performance of *The Adventure of the Last Bustard* was canceled, Carr received a special Edgar award for his 1949 biography, *The Life of Sir Arthur Conan Doyle*. (Biography and criticism did not become a regular Edgar category until 1977.) It seems likely that Carr would have savored his comic conjuration of Doyle at the playlet's end as a kind of celebratory and raucous counterpoint to the staid, if happy, solemnity of winning his first Edgar for his definitive study of Doyle. (Carr would go on to receive two more Edgar awards.) In any event, Carr's readers are fortunate that a single copy of this little, lost gem survived obscure decades, enabling us to enjoy it alongside the rest of Carr's works.

THE UNEXPECTED INSTINCT

The Unexpected Instinct is printed on 60-pound paper, and is designed by Jeffrey Marks using InDesign. The type is Adobe Garamond Pro, a digital interpretation of Claude Garamond's original roman font. The cover is by Gail Cross. The first edition was published in two forms: trade softcover, perfect bound; and two hundred fifty copies sewn in cloth, numbered and signed by the author. Each of the clothbound copies includes a separate pamphlet, "E'en Thought it be a Cross," a short story by John Dickson. *The Unexpected Instinct* was printed and bound by Imprint Press. The book was published in March 2026 by Crippen & Landru Publishers, Inc., Cincinnati, OH.

Crippen & Landru, Publishers
P. O. Box 532057
Cincinnati, OH 45253

Web: www.Crippenlandru.com
E-mail: orders@crippenlandru.com

Since 1994, Crippen & Landru has published more than 100 first editions of short-story collections by important detective and mystery writers.

This is the best edited, most attractively packaged line of mystery books introduced in this decade. The books are equally valuable to collectors and readers. [Mystery Scene Magazine]

The specialty publisher with the most star-studded list is Crippen & Landru, which has produced short story collections by some of the biggest names in contemporary crime fiction. [Ellery Queen's Mystery Magazine]

God bless Crippen & Landru. [The Strand Magazine]

A monument in the making is appearing year by year from Crippen & Landru, a small press devoted exclusively to publishing the criminous short story. [Alfred Hitchcock's Mystery Magazine]

Previous Crippen & Landru Publications

Challenge the Impossible: The Impossible Files of Dr. Sam Hawthorne by Edward D. Hoch. Full cloth in dust jacket, signed and numbered by Josh Pachter, $45.00. Trade softcover, $19.00.

Nothing Is Impossible: Further Problems of Dr. Sam Hawthorne by Edward D. Hoch. Full cloth in dust jacket, signed and numbered by the publisher, $45.00. Trade softcover, $19.00.

Swords, Sandals And Sirens by Marilyn Todd.
Murder, conmen, elephants. Who knew ancient times could be such fun? Many of the stories feature Claudia Seferius, the super-bitch heroine of Marilyn Todd's critically acclaimed mystery series set in ancient Rome. Full cloth in dust jacket, signed and numbered by the author, $45.00. Trade softcover, $19.00.

All But Impossible: The Impossible Files of Dr. Sam Hawthorne by Edward D. Hoch. Full cloth in dust jacket, signed and numbered by the publisher, $45.00. Trade softcover, $19.00.

Sequel to Murder by Anthony Gilbert, edited by John Cooper. Full cloth in dust jacket, $29.00. Trade softcover, $19.00.

Hildegarde Withers: Final Riddles? by Stuart Palmer with an introduction by Steven Saylor. Full cloth in dust jacket, $29.00. Trade softcover, $19.00

Shooting Script by William Link and Richard Levinson, edited by Joseph Goodrich. Full cloth in dust jacket, signed and numbered by the families, $47.00. Trade softcover, $22.00.

The Man Who Solved Mysteries by William Brittain with an introduction by Josh Pachter. Full cloth in dust jacket, $29.00. Trade softcover, $19.00

Constant Hearses and Other Revolutionary Mysteries by Edward D. Hoch. Full cloth in dust jacket, signed and numbered by Brian Skupin, $45.00. Trade softcover, $19.00.

Subscriptions

Subscribers agree to purchase each forthcoming publication, either the Regular Series or the Lost Classics or (preferably) both. Collectors can thereby guarantee receiving limited editions, and readers won't miss any favorite stories.

Subscribers receive a discount of 20% off the list price (and the same discount on our backlist) and a specially commissioned short story by a major writer in a deluxe edition as a gift at the end of the year.

The point for us is that, since customers don't pick and choose which books they want, we have a guaranteed sale even before the book is published, and that allows us to be more imaginative in choosing short story collections to issue.

That's worth the 20% discount for us. Sign up now and start saving. Email us at orders@crippenlandru.com or visit our website at www.crippenlandru.com on our subscription page.